RELENTLESS

HARROW CREEK HAWKS
BOOK 2

TRACY LORRAINE

Development Editing by Pinpoint Editing

Content Editing by Rebecca at Fairest Reviews Editing Services

Proofreading by Sisters Get Lit.erary

Photography - Wander Aguiar Photography

Model - Bernardo F

AUTHOR NOTE

Dear reader,

Relentless is the second book in the Harrow Creek Hawks series. It is a dark captive why choose romance. This means our lucky lady gets to enjoy three guys and doesn't have to choose.

If you're not okay with that, or any of the warnings below, you might want to pass this one by!

Dub con, non con, rape and coerced sex (not on page, but implied from past), bullying, violence, child sexual abuse (in flashbacks), child abuse (in flashbacks), talk of self harm, captivity, knife play, breath play, sociopathy, physical abuse, confinement, nightmares, PTSD, detainment, obsession, narcissism, verbal abuse, torture, blackmail, slut shaming, scars, sibling loss, infertility, loss of the ability to conceive via trauma.

If, like me, you're now internally screaming *give it to me*, after reading that, then let's go.

Enjoy the ride!

T xo

1

ALANA

Distant, deep rumbling voices float to my ears as the darkness that has held me in its clutches finally begins to release me.

My body is heavy, my limbs aching like I've run a marathon, but they've got nothing on my pounding head.

Everything is fuzzy, like someone has replaced my brain with cotton.

Shifting slightly, I slide my hand along the bed beneath me, immediately noticing that it's soft.

It takes every bit of energy I possess, but when I push down, it's spongy.

I've no idea where I am, but I do know that I'm not lying on the hard cot in my cell.

What happened? Where am I?

I'd have thought if they'd killed me and sent me to hell, where I no doubt belong, they wouldn't have memory foam mattresses.

Stretching my legs out, the soft sheets slide over my bare skin and I moan in appreciation.

Forcing my eyes open, darkness greets me.

I blink, willing my eyes to adjust.

Slowly, really freaking slowly, a dark gray room reveals itself. The bed I'm lying in is huge. Beyond huge. It's as if it's been designed to sleep about six people. I bet I look like a child lying in the middle of it.

With my hands planted on the mattress, I try to push myself up, but my arms tremble, barely holding my weight. My head swims in a way that only comes from heavy medication. My brows pinch as I try to remember what I might have had, and more importantly, why.

Giving up, I flop back onto the pillow and close my eyes again.

Exhaustion seeps through my muscles, making me sink into the incredible softness beneath me. Closing my eyes, the relief comes for me. The voices in the distance continuing to float through the air.

I might not know who they belong to, but just hearing them, knowing that I'm not alone, is all I need to drift back off.

"Ow, you fucking bitch," the man above me bellows as three bright red scratches appear across his cheek. *"Pin her down,"* he demands.

My arms flail, desperate to escape despite knowing it's futile.

What these men want, they get.

I can fight, punch, kick, scream, bite. None of it matters. They always overpower me and take what they think they're owed.

I don't know why I still bother trying. I guess it's not in my DNA to just lie back and take it. I do have Hawks blood running through my veins, after all. And they never stand down in the face of adversity. Something which I'm sure my father wishes I didn't inherit sometimes.

All I can do is pray that Kristie did too because I can only protect her for so long. One day soon, Dad is going to decide that she needs to pay her way and something tells me that he's not going to send her out to do our neighborhood paper route.

"Fuck's sake," he complains when I manage to strike him again. This time, he takes matters into his own hands—literally—and wraps his fingers around my throat.

His dark, soulless eyes stare down into mine.

But still, I will not back down.

Blood from my first hit trickles down his cheek, giving me a sense of achievement. It's a small win in the grand scheme of things, knowing that it'll probably scar, but I'll take whatever I can get.

Finally, the man standing at my head captures my wrists and restrains them against the coffee table they've pinned me on.

"Your father promised a feisty one. I think we might have underestimated you, princess."

His expression turns feral when I spit in his face.

I shouldn't do it. I shouldn't rise to it. The pain that follows will only be worse, but I can't help myself. I'll do anything I can to let every single one of these disgusting men know that I'm not a willing participant in this. Even if my fight gets them hotter.

I will not back down and let them think I'm okay with this.

His angry roar fills the room before he rips my shirt right down the middle, exposing my bare breasts to him and the creep standing next to my head.

"Now those surely make up for it," he murmurs, studying me closely. Jealousy darkens his eyes, his lips thinning, as the bleeder reaches for me.

Bile rushes up my throat as his cold, rough calloused fingers dig into my skin.

"We're going to have so much fun with you, princess." He groans.

"Fuck you," I gasp before his fingers cut my air off completely.

Their dark laughter bounces around the room as black spots dance in my vision.

My eyes narrow on the bleeder while he continues to laugh at me.

"Yeah, princess. That's the fucking idea. I'm glad you're on board."

The darkness takes me and the next thing I know, Mav's there.

The relief is like nothing I've ever known. I focus on him, letting the other men in the room disappear as if they never existed.

But Mav never comes closer, he just stands in the doorway watching. His top lip begins to peel back, disgust filling his features as if he can't believe what he's seeing.

"Mav, please," I cry, desperate to reach for him, but my arms are still pinned back. I buck and fight, but their hold on me never loosens.

And then my worst nightmare happens. He starts backing away.

"Please, Mav," I beg. "Help me. They're holding me captive. MAVERICK."

I wake with a start, my skin covered in a sheen of sweat and my heart pounding an unsteady beat in my chest.

Ripping my eyes open, I blink against the bright sunlight streaming in from the slightly open curtains.

"Please," I whimper, still seeing Mav walking away from me as clear as day, "come back."

Footsteps race up the stairs, making them creak loudly and I scramble up the bed, clutching the sheets to my chest.

I want to hide. Drop down and cower behind the huge mattress.

But I don't because that's not who I am.

I'm Alana Murray.

I was born to fight, raised to endure whatever was thrown at me.

My body trembles as the footsteps get closer. My head still swimming in my dream, alone and fuzzy as shit.

Where am I?

The second the door is pushed open and someone steps in, reality begins to crash around me.

"This is your room," I state, feeling stupid that I didn't figure it out earlier.

He stands there in a white t-shirt that is sprayed with more than a little blood. It should be terrifying, but after the life I've lived, I barely give it a second glance. Honestly, it's more shocking if the people I spend time with aren't covered in the stuff.

"How are you feeling?" he asks in a deep, raspy voice as he walks farther into the room. His movements are almost hesitant and it makes my brows pinch.

"W-what am I doing up here? I shouldn't be in your bed," I say confidently.

He smirks. "No, you really shouldn't, but I guess it's a bit late for that now, huh?"

"I-I don't remember..."

"Seafood allergy?" he questions, his brow quirking up.

"Uh... yeah. Cooked seafood and me don't mix."

"There were prawns in the curry," he says, reaching up and rubbing the back of his neck as he looks away from me.

Is he... is that... guilt?

"Are you okay?" I ask, immediately regretting the question.

It's just... he's distant. Hesitant in a way I've never experienced before. And I'm not sure I like it.

More footsteps move this way before the door behind him opens wider and a man I vaguely recognize joins us.

"Nice to see you awake, Mrs. Murray. How are you feeling?"

"Uh..."

"Doc," he says with a soft smile. "We've met before. Was a good few years ago now though."

He holds my eyes and I gasp as I manage to dredge up a long-lost memory I've tried so hard to wipe from my mind. Pulling the sheets higher, I try to hide.

"H-hi," I stutter, unable to keep eye contact with the man who knows intimate details about one of my deepest and darkest moments.

"Could you give us a minute," he says, barely sparing our spectator a glance.

"Of course. Coffee? Would you like coffee?"

"Two sugars and a generous amount of cream," Doc says.

"I meant Alana, but sure. Coming right up."

The door clicks closed behind him, leaving me and the doctor alone.

"You sure gave them a fright tonight, ma'am."

I stare at him in confusion as he grabs his stethoscope and blood pressure monitor.

"I'm sure it takes more than a mild allergic reaction to a cooked prawn to cause a reaction from the men of this house." As I say the words, I know I'm underplaying what happened.

The exhaustion tugging at my muscles and the

pounding of my head tell me it was anything but mild.

"Prior to tonight, I'd have said the same thing. But I've seen a different side to them."

I stare at him blankly, unsure as to whether I should believe him or not.

I remain silent as he checks me over, nodding and murmuring that everything is as it should be.

"You're anemic and your vitamin D levels are very low," he informs me as if it'll be a shock.

"I guess that's what happens when you're locked in a basement for days on end."

I'm expecting a reaction. But I get nothing.

"Doc?" I ask when his lips don't so much as twitch. "Can you get me out of here? I need to find my husband."

"Sweet girl," he muses. "You know I can't do that. Seems to me that you've made your bed. Now you have to lie in it."

"At least this one is more comfortable," I muse.

"You're probably going to be lethargic for a few days. You were lucky I was close when they called. Much longer and we wouldn't be having this conversation now. May I suggest that if you find yourself locked up again that you inform your captors of your allergy?"

"I'll keep that in mind," I mutter, unsure if I'm amused or irritated by his brand of humor.

He begins packing his supplies away and I replay his words over in my head.

"If I get locked up again?" I question. "You mean I'm no longer a prisoner?"

He glances up. "In case you hadn't noticed, you're no longer in the basement. And that door," he says, jerking his chin in the direction of the exit. "It isn't locked."

"You're saying I could run."

He chuckles. "I wouldn't advise it. Now, if you'll excuse me, I have another visit to make before I leave."

I watch with a frown as he bids me farewell and saunters toward the door. But he pauses before he disappears from my sight.

"Running five years ago was the right thing to do. But if you were to try again now, I can say with full confidence that you'd regret it. Get some rest, Mrs. Murray. Something tells me that you're going to need it."

With those ominous words hanging in the air, he slips out of the room, leaving me alone.

I glance around the room, but there isn't much to really look at.

A massive fuck knows how many inches TV is mounted to the opposite wall. The image of him sitting on this very bed watching me down in my cell appears in my mind. He saw it all. My tears, my fear, my nightmares. He watched every moment of mine and JD's time together.

It's a reminder I don't need right now that all of this is a game. We're nothing but a game and Reid Harris is controlling all our pieces.

"Twisted fuck," I mutter before scanning the rest of the room. But other than a speaker, a cell charger and an alarm clock, there is nothing to give me any clues about the man who sleeps in this room.

The only thing I learn is that he likes sleeping in a big bed. I wonder if he's a fidgeter or likes to sleep like a starfish. Or if he prefers plenty of company.

Resting my head on the pillow, I stare at the ajar door that I assume leads to a bathroom. Curiosity burns through me, but my exhausted body doesn't allow me to go and explore because before I even think about moving my legs, my eyelids lower and sleep claims me once more.

2

ALANA

"Everything okay?" a familiar voice rumbles.

"Oh, fucking peachy." Another grunts, each word a little louder as if he's getting closer.

There's a shuffle before a loud sigh.

"Don't give me that fucking look. None of this is my fault." This time the owner of the voice registers in my brain. The sheets tighten around me as a weight presses down on them and I slide my hand out to reach for him.

But I come up empty.

Disappointment consumes me, but I don't keep searching for someone clearly so out of reach. And I'm glad I don't when he speaks again.

"She's going to kill you for this, you do know that, right?" JD teases.

"Yes," Reid spits. "Do you need to keep mentioning it?"

JD laughs. "You fucked up. Of course I'm going to keep mentioning it."

"Asshole." Reid hisses.

"She's going to be okay though, yeah?" The concern in JD's voice is evident, and it makes my heart rate increase.

He cares.

I know in the grand scheme of things, I don't matter, not really. His concern for my well-being doesn't change anything.

Even being in a room without a locked door doesn't mean anything. I have no power here. No control. I'm nothing but their puppet.

Doc was right.

I could try running, but I wouldn't get very far.

"How many times?" Reid sighs. "Doc says after a few days' rest, she'll be good as new."

"Thank fuck."

"Her pussy can't be that good," Reid mutters under his breath.

JD doesn't say anything for a few seconds, but I swear I can hear the smirk on his face.

"That's for me to know, bro. And for you to sulk over."

"I'm not sulking." He scoffs.

"Oh, you so fucking are. Admit it, dude. You lost."

His words make my brows knit together and the flicker of happiness I felt earlier having them here ebbs away.

"You lost."

What game were they playing?

The answer is obvious.

Me. I'm the game.

The pawn.

A pained, disappointed sigh slips from my lips. There's a beat of silence where I pray they haven't heard me. But I know they have. The air is charged, crackling around us like a live current. And then the bed shifts and JD's stare makes the side of my face burn red hot.

"Dove?" he whispers, his hand finding mine on top of the sheet, where I was searching for him not so long ago.

Warmth surges up my arm, making me yearn for more of his touch.

But then I remember his words.

"You lost."

I tug my hand free. Or at least, I try to. JD's grip is too firm.

"Dove?" he repeats firmly. "Open your eyes, baby."

I don't want to. I want to defy him. But my ingrained need to do as I'm told, to be a good and compliant little girl means my body takes on a life of its own and my eyes pop open.

The second our gazes connect, the most incredible smile spreads across JD's face, his eyes lighting up with relief.

"You're okay," he breathes, almost as if he's reassuring himself more than anything.

I search his face, hunting for the truth of what I just overheard. But all I find is concern.

I've no idea how long I've been out of it, but JD's eyes are ringed with dark circles, as if he hasn't slept in days.

Tearing my eyes from his, I glance at Reid. He doesn't look much better.

"What's wrong?"

I glance down at myself, assuming that I'll be covered in blood like the two of them.

Did I slice myself on something as I went down? Bang my head so hard I split it open?

But there is nothing. Just a blank Hawks tank.

I tug my arm again, this time able to slip my fingers free of JD's grip.

"Get out," I whisper, although from the way JD startles, you'd think I screamed it.

"W-what?" he breathes, staring at me as if I've suddenly sprouted an extra head.

Holding his eyes firm, I let those two words he said not so long ago repeat over and over in my mind.

My heart races and I've no choice but to grip the sheets tightly in my fists as I force out the words he so clearly doesn't want to hear.

"I don't want you here. I want you to leave."

"Dove, you're sick. You need—"

"Go."

"But we brought you—"

"Leave."

Thankfully, Reid is a little less shocked and surprisingly not as stubborn as his best friend because he pushes from the chair. He wraps his hand around JD's upper arm and none too gently drags him from his seat on the edge of the bed.

"No, we can't. She needs—"

"Space." Reid growls. His understanding of the situation and his willingness to give me what I need make my forehead wrinkle.

"She's going to kill you for this, you do know that, right?"

I stare at both of them as I focus on those words, trying to drag up a memory of how I got here.

My vision blurs as I fight with my subconscious, but it's not until JD calls for me when Reid has him almost out the door that something slams into me.

"Come for me, Dove. I want you squeezing down on my fingers while you stare into his eyes. Show him exactly what he's missing."

Suddenly, I'm in the hallway. My back pressed against the solid, cold wall that led down to the basement I've called home for the past... I don't know how long. The heat of JD's huge, hard body burns mine as his fingers work inside me. But while he might be the one bringing me to ruin, my eyes aren't locked on his electric blue ones, but a dark even more dangerous pair just a few feet away.

Looking up, my gaze collides with JD's dark ones. The despair and concern that stares back at me wraps around my chest like a band forcing all the air rushes from my lungs.

"Alana, please," he begs. His voice is so quiet, I wonder if he actually said it or if I imagined it. My subconscious's way of stopping me from following through with sending him away and ending up alone again. Locked up in a room that isn't mine, with even more questions swirling around in my head.

But I don't respond. I can't. The lump of emotion is so thick in my throat I can barely breathe, let alone speak.

I'm so confused. So lost.

"Let's go," Reid barks, finally shoving his stubborn friend through the door and with one last loaded look, he closes me inside.

Slamming my hand over my mouth, I catch the loud sob that wants to erupt. The last thing I need is for them to hear me falling apart.

They've already seen way too much over the past few days. I've given them too much. More than I ever intended to. But I guess I shouldn't be surprised. It's Reid Harris. He gets whatever he sets his mind to. And if he wants me on my knees begging for mercy, then I should be prepared for that to happen.

Their footsteps move away before their deep booming voices float through the air.

"She shouldn't be alone right now," JD barks. "She nearly fucking died. You nearly fucking killed her."

Killed me?

I squeeze my eyes closed, desperately trying to remember what happened after JD got me off in the hallway while they continue bickering beyond the door.

If the situation wasn't so fucking dire, I might laugh at the way the big bad gangsters are squabbling like children.

Over a girl too.

No. Not a girl.

Me.

Eventually, the hallway falls silent and after a few more seconds, I figure that Reid won the argument because JD doesn't come storming through my door, ignoring my demand for them to leave.

You were nothing more than a bet.

I don't know why it hurts so much. It shouldn't. All of this has been a game for far longer than I care to admit.

From the very moment Victor approached me and told me with absolute certainty that I was going to be working for him going forward, all of this has been a game.

Angrily, I wipe the wetness that's spilling from my eyes before throwing the covers back.

Swinging my legs off the side of the bed, I groan in delight when my bare feet sink into thick, luxurious carpet.

Wiggling my toes, I slowly push to stand. The room spins around me, my entire body weak from my anaphylactic shock.

Reaching out, I use the wall for balance as I make my way toward the door that I hope hides the bathroom.

"Wow," I breathe when I step inside.

Firstly, much like the bed, the space is colossal. I shouldn't be surprised; this entire building is fucking massive. You could fit Mav's cabin into less than a quarter of it. It's bigger than any home I've ever seen in real life. It's the kind of thing you usually see the wealthy living in on TV. It's certainly not something anyone would expect in Harrow Creek.

But I guess a king does need a castle.

Makes me wonder why Victor never claimed it as his own as my feet touch the warm tiles that cover the bathroom floor.

This is a million miles from the cold, dank basement I've become accustomed to.

Much like the downstairs bathroom, the suite is black. The tiles are the darkest of grays. The only light accents are the chrome fittings. It's stunning. It's... Reid.

With my eyes locked on the massive shower, I move toward the toilet, trying to imagine what he looks like standing behind the glass screen, naked with water running over his body.

I do my business before moving to the sink. A single toothbrush sits there, taunting me with the promise of a fresh mouth.

There's a cupboard beneath it but despite my best—okay, maybe not my best—efforts, I fail to figure out a way to open it.

"Fuck it," I mutter. That jerk owes me.

Reaching out, I pluck his toothbrush from the holder and squirt a generous amount of toothpaste onto it.

Feeling a little more alive, I splash my face with cold water and walk back to the bedroom with slightly more strength in my limbs.

It's been a long time since I had an allergic reaction. So long, I hardly think about it.

I cooked all our meals at home, and Mav was more than aware of my allergy and ensured that if we went out, everything was safe. He always protected me.

I've no doubt that if it weren't for him, I'd be in hell right now. It wouldn't matter if I were dead or alive; I'd have ended up there regardless after everything I've done in my life.

If he didn't find me that night, then someone would have. Even if I escaped town, they'd have come for me. And when they did... a violent shiver rips down my spine, and I stumble forward, barely catching myself on the windowsill.

Squeezing my eyes closed for a beat, I remind myself I'm safe.

Yes, I'm currently living—okay, surviving—with two of the most dangerous men in town. But if they wanted me dead, they'd have done it by now. And if JD's performance just now tells me anything, it's that he cares. Whatever I was feeling for him down in my cell wasn't just one-sided. Maybe I wasn't just an easy fuck for him.

Maybe it was more.

Or maybe you're just so desperate for a connection, for the high of being wanted that you'll latch onto anything you can get your hands on.

Stuffing that little voice back in its box, I open my eyes and look out at the view.

My breath catches at the sight. But while it might be stunning and cast the hellhole that is Harrow Creek in a whole new light with the sun shining down on it, that's not what catches me off guard. It's the memory of looking at this very view from Reid's kitchen last night with the scent of homemade curry filling my nose and my stomach growling as if it hadn't been fed for a month.

The image of the dinner table fills my head. Reid sitting at the head—obviously. And JD, beside a pulled-out empty chair, waiting for me with a twinkle in his eye and a bulge in his sweats.

The plates were black, the cutlery the same. There was wine. My wine.

And the curry.

Fuck. It was so good.

I remember shoveling it into my mouth without a care in the world.

He's made chicken curry. I hear the words as if JD just whispered them in my ear.

Why would I question the ingredients in a chicken curry?

After a week or so of captivity with barely any food, I wasn't likely to question anything unless he provided me with a seafood platter.

But then there is nothing. No other memories of the night's events.

Nothing until I woke up here with Reid watching me with a concerned and guilty expression on his face. If I hadn't seen that look, I might have been tempted to say that poisoning me was intentional.

Allowing me upstairs, luring me into a false sense of security by allowing me a taste of freedom, only to knock me even lower than he already has.

But that wasn't it. This was an accident.

Everything else hasn't been, though.

Spinning around, I rest my ass on the windowsill and scan the room again.

There is nothing. No personal possessions, no photographs. Nothing to tell me more about the enigma that is Reid Harris.

There has to be more to him than the evil torturing machine he's labeled as.

But as curious as I might be, I don't have the time or energy to try and figure it out.

Right now, there is only one thing I need to focus on.

Getting the hell out of here.

I need a plan. A really fucking good one.

That, or a miracle. But I seem to be shit out of luck with those.

3

___

JD

"What the fuck are you doing?" I bark the second Reid turns to my room instead of the stairs, where I was expecting him to go.

"I need a shower."

"Then use your own," I hiss, throwing my arm out in the direction of his bedroom that I was just dragged out of.

Without a word, or even a glance back, he reaches behind his head and drags his bloodstained shirt from his body.

"Don't go back in there," he warns darkly before kicking my door closed.

I fall onto the end of my bed as the shower begins running and drop my head into my hands.

When he suggested bringing Alana up for dinner, I thought he had some twisted plan to get her talking. I fucking wish he did because this has been a fucking shitshow.

I want to say that we should have left her down there, but if we did and she had that reaction when she was alone...

I swallow roughly and squeeze my eyes tighter.

No. I can't even think about what the outcome of that could have been.

Dropping my hands, I stare at them as they tremble violently.

Clenching my fists, I will the fear to abate. But it does nothing.

Shifting my gaze, I track each of the blood splatters that stain my arms, my stomach knotting as the true horror of the night plays out again in my mind.

I'm not scared of blood, or ever fazed by the things we do. But tonight hits differently.

And I know exactly why.

It's her.

My defiant, feisty little dove.

"FUCK," I roar, combing my fingers through my hair and pulling until it hurts. But it's not enough.

We fucked up tonight.

I fucked up tonight.

I deserve the pain. I should be the one hurting.

Do it. Make it hurt.

Hanging my head, I fight to push the voice away.

My short nails dig into my palms as I focus on my breathing.

Fight it, Julian.

She needs you.

Do not give in.

Fight.

I startle when the bathroom door is suddenly ripped open.

Reid takes two steps into my room before he pauses.

"You okay, man?" he asks, his brows pinching together, leaving a deep crevice between them. The demanding tone in his voice from before is gone, in its place a softer one I despise. I've only ever heard him use it on me, and it takes me back to a time I never want to remember.

Pushing to my feet, I follow his lead and drag my tank off, throwing it in the direction of the laundry basket.

I march toward the bathroom more than ready to be alone, or at least I try to.

Just before I get to the door, Reid's hand darts out and clamps around my shoulder.

"JD?" he says, giving me little choice but to look at him.

His eyes narrow at whatever he sees swirling in the depths of mine.

"She's okay," he assures me. "Doc said—"

"I fucking know what Doc said. I'm not fucking deaf," I snap, twisting from his hold.

"I know but—"

"I'm fine," I lie, continuing toward the safety of the bathroom.

Truth is, my fucking skin is itching like a million ants are racing over it. My need to relieve it is stronger than it's been in years.

"Fuck," I hiss, as I kick the door closed and flip the lock.

It won't stop him if he suspects I'm losing the very thin grasp I have on my sanity, but it makes me feel better about it.

Shoving my sweats down, I step into the already wet shower and turn it on.

I'm immediately hit with warm water, but I don't need warm. That's too nice. That won't kill the ants.

Twisting the dial, I turn it up as high as it'll go, letting the scorching water rain down on my head and shoulders.

My skin burns, slowing down the ants and my need to scratch my own skin from my body.

Resting my palms on the tiled wall, I hang my head and close my eyes. Instantly, the image of Alana's limp body hanging from Reid's arms fills my head.

I've been scared a time or two in my life, but it's been a long time since I felt it as keenly as last night. And it wasn't just because she could barely breathe. It was the realization of just how deep she's wormed her way into my heart.

She was meant to be a bit of fun. A playmate to help pass the time. She sure was funner than any of the other motherfuckers downstairs.

But I wasn't meant to care.

Watching her fighting for her life wasn't meant to rip my own heart out in the process. And that's only the beginning of what happened down in the kitchen. The events after that and the level of hate she's going to feel toward us because of it is enough to send me spiraling down into a bottomless pit I never want to visit again.

I stand there fighting with my old lingering demons until the water runs cold. And the second the burning stops, I turn the shower off and step out.

With a towel around my waist, I step up to the vanity and reach out, wiping the steam from the mirror.

A hazy version of myself stares back and I instantly understand why Reid looked so concerned.

My usually bright blue eyes are dark and stormy. There's something dangerous swirling within their depths. Something none of us need.

Opening the cupboard before me, my eyes linger on two things.

A bottle of pills.

A razor.

One good. One bad. Only right now, I've no idea which is which.

One banishes the itch for a few invigorating minutes, the other dulls everything for a long ass time.

I can't remember the last time I took them. They're probably out of date. Since my last relapse, I've done everything I can to stay on the right side of the line.

My therapy comes in the form of exercise, sex and routine. The former of those is more reliable with the lives we live. But fuck, I wouldn't give it up for the world.

The blades hiding within that razor, though. They hold a promise that makes my mouth water and my grip on the sink tightens until my nails are trying to carve into the porcelain.

My heart beats faster for it. For the relief, the moment of pure freedom that will come from it.

But then I think of her and hang my head.

Don't do this, Julian.

She needs you.

With a renewed sense of purpose, I reach into the cupboard, ignoring the most tempting item in favor of my toothbrush.

The ants are still there. The need for relief is just as strong, but I've fought it before. Many, many times before. And I can do it again.

For her.

"You've lost your fucking mind to a girl," I mutter to myself as I stalk through my bedroom to find a clean pair of sweats once I've dragged myself away from temptation.

You should have seen it fucking coming.

You should have been stronger.

Shaking my head, I banish my stupid thoughts and drag my pants up my still-damp legs.

With water running down my back from my hair, I

wrench my bedroom door open, my eyes immediately darting to Reid's.

It's shut. Just like I knew it would be.

She kicked you out because she doesn't want you.

She doesn't need you, Julian.

Clenching my fists, I turn away and head for the stairs.

I've no idea what time it is, but the scent of grilled cheese floods my nose and my stomach growls obnoxiously. And it only gets louder as I get closer to the kitchen.

Despite being focused on what he's doing and having his back turned, he still knows the second I walk into the room.

Fucking know-it-all.

He glances over his shoulder and stares me dead in the eyes.

I'd be naïve to think he couldn't see me struggling up there. Honestly, I'm surprised he left me alone. There have been times in the past when that hasn't happened for fear of what I might do once I was by myself.

Maybe he could tell I wasn't that far gone, that I'd be able to drag myself out of it. Deal with the itch still burning my skin and the need for relief.

"You good?" he asks calmly.

One of my shoulders bounces up in a half-assed shrug as I pull a stool out and sit down. Keeping the dining table and the sofa where everything went down last night behind me.

If I look then I'll see her lying there unable to breathe and it'll all return.

What I need right now is her. I need to crawl into Reid's fucking massive bed and wrap myself around her. Feel her warmth, listen to her breathing. Let her body remind me that she's here and that she's okay.

You've fallen too hard.

Fuck my actual life.

She belongs to someone else.

Dropping my head into my hands, I fist my hair and squeeze my eyes closed.

This isn't news to me. I knew she belonged to another the first time I teased her, touched her, and made her moan my name.

But knowing it and seeing the wrecked look on his face as he stares at her are two entirely different things.

It's easy to forget the outside world exists when we're living so far away from it up here.

But looking it in the eye. Fuck me, that was a reality check I was not fucking ready for.

"J?" Reid asks. The concern in his voice makes my stomach knot up and guilt trickles through my veins.

Releasing the breath I'm holding, I loosen my grip on my hair and finally look up at my best friend.

"Yeah, man. I'm good," I lie.

His eyes narrow, a deep frown forming between his brows again.

Everything he wants to say swirls darkly in the depths of his orbs, but his lips remain closed.

And I'm fucking glad. There is nothing he could say right now that will make any of this better.

I want things I can't have.

Story of my fucking life.

As soon as I find something and get settled somewhere, it gets ripped away right from under my feet.

The only regular thing in my life is him.

Reid Harris.

The man everyone sees as the devil. But little do they know. He's the best fucking man on the planet.

They all think he's heartless, careless, and nothing but a monster. But I know the truth.

Yes, he might be all those things. But he's so much more as well.

If it weren't for him. I've no doubt that I wouldn't be here right now. There's no two fucking ways about it.

He's saved me time and time again. And in return, I'll do whatever I can to return the favor. I'll fight as hard as I fucking can, all the while hoping that it's enough.

His lips part, but whatever he was going to say dies on his tongue.

"You hungry?" he asks instead.

"Fuck, yeah."

"Good. Eat this. Then you can go and do your job," he says, attempting to keep me focused on what I need to do.

"What about Al—"

"She's fine, J."

"But—"

"Just give her time," he says softly. Too fucking softly when it comes to our favorite inmate.

Is she even our prisoner anymore? She's lying upstairs in a place no other woman has ever been before.

Does that change things? Or, once she's recovered, will Reid march her straight back downstairs to continue punishing her for crimes she had no choice but to commit?

A plate slides under my nose and I reach out on instinct and lift the grilled cheese sandwich to my lips.

"What happens next?" I ask once I've demolished the entire thing like I haven't eaten for a week.

"Honestly?" Reid says, resting his ass back against the counter, his eyes focused out the windows. "I'm not sure." He swallows before his dark eyes turn to me again. "But one thing is for certain," he warns, "the time for change is coming."

"You ready?" I ask hesitantly. I know just how hard he's worked to get all his ducks in a row, so he's in the strongest position he can be to make a move for his father's control over this town. But as far as I'm aware, he's not quite there yet.

A smirk pulls at his lips, his chin lifting arrogantly. "I'm Reid fucking Harris. I'm always ready."

"Fucking love you, man." I laugh, making his smile widen and his eyes sparkle in a way most never see.

"Someone's got to. Now fuck off downstairs and feed the rats."

"And what about—"

"Do what you've got to do. We need him alive."

"There's something I never thought you'd say. You going soft in our old age, man?"

"Fuck you, bro." He laughs. "Fuck you."

I'm still laughing as I descend the stairs to the basement.

Fuck me, that woman upstairs has more fucking power than she could ever understand.

One day she'll discover it, and fuck, that's going to be even more dangerous than the three men she's managed to wrap around her little fucking finger.

4

———

ALANA

I wake with a start and the fear lingering from my nightmare only increases when the wall of heat at my back and the weight crushing my ribs makes itself known.

My heart races faster as my fight-or-flight instinct kicks in.

Throwing my free arm back, my elbow makes contact with something and the vise grip on my body loosens as a deep grunt of pain fills the air.

Scrambling from the bed, I back toward the window with my hands up ready to strike.

But the second my eyes focus and I find JD staring back at me with one eye—he has his hand covering the other, letting me know what my elbow collided with—everything in me relaxes.

"What the hell are you doing?" I shriek, wrapping my arms around myself as if they'll help me keep my shit together.

He shifts until he's sitting, resting against the incredibly uncomfortable headboard, exposing the bare, sculpted artwork of his chest and abs to me.

But I don't cave to it. I stay strong and force my eyes to stay on his narrowed one.

"I was sleeping," he mutters, finally releasing his face to comb his hair back.

I wince a little at the redness around his eye, but I quickly shove the reaction aside.

A black eye is the least of what he deserves.

"I told you to leave," I point out, my hands finding my hips now that I'm feeling a little less vulnerable.

"I know but—"

"But nothing. I wasn't joking, Julian." His nostrils flare as I hiss his first name. "I guess it's a drastic change from moaning it. "Go sleep in your own bed," I say flippantly, marching across the room and pulling the door open, gesturing for him to walk through it.

But the stubborn fuck doesn't so much as flinch.

"JD," I hiss, quickly losing my patience.

"It was an accident, Dove. We had no idea you were allergic—"

"I know that," I snap. "If he wanted me dead, I've no doubt he'd want to cause more pain and spill more blood than allow me to suffocate because of a fucking prawn."

"Can't argue there." He smirks.

Irritation rolls through me.

"Don't," I warn.

"Don't what?" he asks innocently.

"Try and worm your way out of this by being cute. It won't work."

His eyes twinkle with amusement before he shoves the sheets lower, shamelessly exposing himself as if he thinks it'll help his cause.

"Aw, come on, Dove," he says, his voice all deep and growly.

My thighs clench as he gives me his best seductive look. His cocky smirk tells me that he's aware of just how it hits me.

Sliding his hand over the bed, his eyes drop down my body.

"Come and get back in bed, little dove. You're tired, come rest."

The temptation is strong. It would be so easy to crawl back into the warmth and let him wrap me up in his protective arms while I sleep off the lingering exhaustion that's come with my reaction.

You lost.

Those two words deep in my subconscious are enough to bring me back to Earth.

"Leave, JD. I don't want or need you here," I state, pulling the door wider.

His face drops in a way I didn't think possible and shadows darken his usually bright blue eyes as he stares at me.

I think he's waiting for me to tell him that I'm joking. But I'm not.

I refuse to get swept back up into the bubble of JD and his magic dick.

I'm not locked in the basement anymore. He isn't my only source of entertainment now. The only thing to keep my mind active.

I have bigger things to think about. Like how best to get out of here.

As much as I think it might be easy to wait for them both to fall asleep and then walk out the front door, I know better than that.

Reid might have given me the space I requested. But I'm under no illusion that it's because anything has changed.

It's guilt.

He poisoned me. Almost killed me. I'm not sure a man like Reid Harris ever almost kills anyone. If he wants the job done, then he does it properly. No half-assed accidents.

JD hesitates, still not believing that I'm serious. I hold his eyes firm, silently telling him that I am.

"I need to know you're okay," he says, his voice cracked with emotion. "I need—"

"I don't really care what you need right now. You're not the one who's been held against their will and tortured in the basement of a monster's house. You're also not the one who's been the butt of their fun and games."

Finally, he swings his legs off the bed and pushes to his full height, filling my vision with nothing but toned muscle, intricate ink, and his impressive semi.

Asshole.

I'm not sure what I just said, but his sadness seems to have been replaced with his signature smirk once more.

He prowls closer, not giving a shit about his nakedness. And he doesn't stop until the heat of his body is warming mine.

Pressing his hands to the door on either side of my head, he leans down, letting his breath rush down my neck before his lips brush my ear.

"I think you like our games, little dove."

Gritting my teeth, I attempt to move back, to put some space between us, but there is nowhere to go.

There's a heavy door at my back and a wall of muscle at my front.

"I know as much as you do that your idea of fun is the same as mine."

My fists curl, my nails digging into my palms as I fight to keep my agreement off my face.

Yes, we had fun.

But it's done now. It's over.

I left the basement, and soon, I'm going to be leaving his life as well.

My heart twists painfully at that thought alone. But he's already shown his true colors and proven to me that I'm wrong.

He doesn't care. He just wanted to get one up on Reid.

Well, he achieved it. I can't imagine that the man of this house loses very often. It must be paining him to come second to his best friend.

"We're done, JD. The basement was fun and all, but it's over."

He chuckles, refusing to believe my words.

"Nothing's changed, Dove. You might have made it up here into a comfortable bed, but you still belong to us."

"You're wrong." The image of my husband's smiling face fills my mind, making the pain in my chest even more potent. "There is only one man I belong to, and I'll do whatever it takes to find my way back to him. I don't care who I have to fight through. It will happen."

He pulls back, staring deeply into my eyes, as if he can see all the secrets I'm still keeping playing out in my mind like a movie.

I startle, my gasp of shock sucking the air out of the room when his knuckles gently graze my jaw. The move is so tender that I can't help but lean into it.

His eyes flash with accomplishment and instantly remind me of all the reasons I'm holding firm.

My fingers ache as I uncurl my clenched fist before pressing my palm to the center of his chest and forcing him back.

We're both aware that he could easily overpower me, but for some reason, he complies and allows me to put some space between us.

"Dove?" he whispers, that vulnerable lilt back in his voice again.

I never heard it, never saw this side of him downstairs. It makes me wonder what's changed. But other than me having a little freedom, I've no memory of anything else.

"I don't want you, Julian." His expression drops and I refuse to acknowledge how that makes me feel as I deliver my next blow. "You were fun. A good lay. Perfect way to waste some time down there. But it's done. I'm leaving here soon and returning to a man who'd never use me as a pawn in his games."

"Dove," he warns.

I push from the door, and he's so lost, so desperate to hear what I've got to say, that I manage to back him out of the room.

"You're welcome, though," I say, forcing a saccharine smile onto my lips. "I can't imagine you win a bet over Reid Harris very often. I suggest you go bask in that success instead of trying to convince me that you're a decent human being with actual real-life feelings."

His jaw drops, and I just catch the wrecked expression on his face before I swing the door closed, cutting off any comeback he might have had.

Long before the echo of the slam drifts away, I've fallen to my ass, my back against the door as some kind of human doorstop. It wouldn't be enough if he decided he wanted back in, but as I wrap my arms around my legs and drop my head to my knees, I realize that he's not going to even try. And it's that realization that forces the first sob from my throat.

Clapping my hand over my mouth, I catch the sound before it can be heard on the other side of the door.

I've no idea if he's still there, but the last thing I need is for him to know that everything that's happened between us has affected me.

I shouldn't care. He was Reid's accomplice, keeping me down there. His form of torture might have come in a different form than the Devil's, but he still played me. He saw my weakness and used every skill at his disposal to get my secrets out of me.

And if I'm honest with myself, the fallout of all this is hurting way more than anything Reid could have done to me with any instrument he has in his closet of tools.

By the time my tears fade, my limbs are heavy and my swollen eyes barely open. I don't want to succumb to them, to this, but it's all I can do to crawl back to bed.

It's not until I sink under the covers and nestle my head into the soft pillow that I realize my mistake. This bed was always laced with Reid's scent. But now I have JD's to battle with as well.

Without warning, the tears come again, and they don't stop until sleep claims me.

Maybe the next time I wake, I'll be stronger.

Stronger and have a plan.

"Mav," I cry as he steps into the doorway.

This time, I'm laid out on the couch. I'm not alone. They are here. Their disgusting stares burn into my skin, making my stomach churn with acid.

But their presence fades into the background as my eyes

lock on those of my husband. The man who's single-handedly saved me from these monsters. For whatever reason I've never been able to figure out, he took me away. He rescued me and gave me a life I could only dream of.

And he's here now. It's as if all my prayers have been answered and someone sent him for me.

But he doesn't say anything. He just stands in the doorway and stares at me.

"Mav? What's wrong? It's me. Please."

The dark figures move closer, lingering right in my periphery. Close yet far enough away not to be able to make out their features. Not that it matters, the men my dad brings here for me can look as sweet as pie. Often, they're the worst ones. You always need to be the most wary of the innocent ones. The ones who make you laugh, the ones who lure you into a false sense of security.

"Take me home with you, please," I beg when Mav remains motionless in the doorway.

The shadows move closer again and recognition flickers in my subconscious.

Mav watches them, his top lip curling in disgust.

"She's ours now," a deep voice states, making Mav stumble back.

"We treat her right. Give her what she needs," the other confirms.

My heart pounds and my head spins.

"No, don't leave me. I need you. Please, Mav. Don't leave—"

A scream rips from my throat as a loud bang bounces around the room. I squeeze my eyes closed, trying to deal with the noise, and when I open them again, I find the reason for it.

My husband is lying on the floor in a puddle of his own blood.

"NOOOOO," I scream.

I wake up sitting in the middle of Reid's massive bed, my trembling body slick with sweat.

It was just a dream. Just a dream.

5

REID

I lie in the guest room, staring up at the ceiling.

I should have passed out hours ago. But I can't.

My mind is spinning with too many things I don't want to be thinking about.

JD is my biggest concern. That haunted look in his eyes after Alana kicked us out is something I never want to see again in my life.

It takes me back to a time I would happily forget.

I thought I was going to lose him. I really did. I don't think I've ever been more terrified than I was then. Every morning, the first thing I would do was message him, praying that he'd reply. I'm pretty sure I didn't breathe until I saw that my message had been read and then the dots were bouncing to show he was replying. Looking back, those were the worst minutes of that time. I tried to convince him to stay with me as much as I could, but more often than not, he wanted his own space. And while I understood that, the fear of what he might do with that space was terrifying.

He made it through, and while he's had his moments

over the past few years, he's found ways to deal with his issues and I've only ever seen hints of the darkness that lingers right beneath the surface.

But yesterday, it was darker, more dangerous.

I knew he was getting attached to her. But I assumed that was more to her pussy than anything else.

But that look in his eyes, it hinted toward his feelings for her being stronger than I anticipated.

And that is a really fucking bad thing.

She can't be his.

She already belongs to someone else. And as fun as it might have been playing with her, at some point, we're either going to have to kill her or give her back. And something tells me that the former isn't going to be an option.

With a pained sigh, I throw the covers off and get to my feet.

I can't lie here lost in my own head when our world is on the verge of imploding.

Her location has been compromised.

Who else knows?

I've had my boys scan the property's perimeter, but none of them came up with anything suspicious, and there haven't been any more security alerts.

That would suggest he was working alone. Hell knows he's acted desperate enough to be that stupid over the past week or so. But would he?

Would he really risk his life by breaking onto my property? And what was he expecting? To find his wife and walk hand in hand out the fucking front door.

Fucking idiot.

I always knew there was something fucking wrong with him. Now I have proof.

Without turning a light on, I open the bedroom door and march down the hallway toward the soft glow that filters up from below.

I turn the corner and almost fall over a lump of a man dressed only in a pair of boxers passed out on the carpet right outside my bedroom door.

"The fuck?" I hiss, catching myself on the wall before I go down on top of him.

He groans, shifting into what I can only assume is an equally uncomfortable position before his snore fills the hallway. The move reveals the almost empty bottle of whiskey behind him and my stomach knots as I reach down for it.

"Fucking hell," I mutter, combing my fingers through my hair.

The temptation to wake him is strong, but I don't. If I do then he might not get any more sleep. And right now, he needs it.

Stepping over his sprawled-out legs, I continue down the stairs not bothering to miss the creaky steps, they won't wake him.

I need him with me one hundred percent, and I'll do anything I can to ensure that happens.

Caving to temptation, I twist the top of the bottle and lift it to my lips.

Just one shot. Something to settle the unease and dread that's knotting up my stomach.

There might be some light down here, but it's not enough to see everything. Just a sidelight in the hallway and soft decorative ones in the kitchen, illuminating what I need.

My coffee machine.

The rich scent of beans already permeates the air. It's

standard in this house and something I wouldn't change for the world.

With my sights set on the liquid gold, I set about making myself a cup before turning toward the sofa. But I barely take a step when reality hits me.

"How long have you been there?" I bark, my heart pounding as I chastise myself for not being more aware of my surroundings.

If you got some sleep, you might have a fucking clue what's happening around you, asshole.

"Long enough," she says, sipping her own coffee as her eyes drop down my body. "Being up here sure has its benefits," she muses.

"Why is JD sleeping outside my bedroom door like a hobo?"

She shrugs one shoulder dismissively.

"Seems like your boy doesn't do so well with being told no."

"What did he ask for?" It's a stupid question, but it comes out anyway.

"Me."

I shake my head, an unamused laugh punching from my chest.

"Then maybe you shouldn't have given yourself to him in the first place," I suggest, dropping onto the couch opposite her, where she's sitting cross-legged, still wearing my tank.

"Me?" she asks incredulously. "You're blaming me for him acting like a toddler who's had his stuffie taken away?" She shakes her head in disbelief. "Do you not realize how not my fault all of this is?"

I stare at her.

"When did you figure that out? Before or after you claimed to be pregnant with Kane's child?"

She laughs, but it's not the amused, happy kind. It's full of pain and a lifetime of disappointment.

"You really don't have a clue, do you? Living up here in your corrupt manor, looking down on all the little people like some fucked-up king. You don't know what it's like down there for the locals. For the young girls. The kids. The women who have everything ripped away from them because men like you think they're God's gift to the planet and are owed everything their sick and twisted hearts desire.

"You're all disgusting, corrupt, sick bastards."

"All?" I ask, lifting a brow.

Her lips snap closed as she hears my unspoken words.

"Fine. Not all."

"Talk to me about him, Pet," I encourage softly.

She was so close to giving me more before those prawns put an end to our evening, and I'm more than ready to revisit it.

"What do you want to hear? That's he's ten times the man you are? That he actually has a heart, and some morals, and some common decency? That despite having initiated into one of the most corrupt and despicable gangs in this country, he's still a nice person."

"Wow, say it as it is. Don't hold back," I mutter, amused by her word vomit.

"After everything we've been through, hardly." She scoffs.

"I'm sure you've figured it out by now, Pet. But I'm not my father."

"Thank fuck," she mutters. "Just because you're different, it doesn't mean you're any better, does it?"

"I'd like to fucking think so." I scoff before sipping my coffee.

"Having experienced you at your worst, I'd say not."

My eyes widen as the steaming hot liquid gold coats my tongue, settling just a little of the unease inside me.

"My worst? Oh, Pet. You most certainly haven't seen that. Yet," I add for fun. She doesn't look shocked by my words.

She's taunting me.

I've given her freedom and now she's the one trying to play me.

Spreading my legs wider, I sit back into the couch, getting comfortable.

Her assessing eyes roam over my body.

"See something you like, Pet?" Her eyes dart to mine at my taunt.

"No. You're a little bit too bitter and toxic for my taste," she seethes.

"It would serve you well not to lie to me," I warn.

"Why? What are you going to do? Lock me up in your torture chamber again? Starve me? Make me freeze to death."

"You think I'd let you take an easy way out like that? I thought you had me all figured out. Maybe it's all an act."

She smirks, holding my eyes, proving to me, once again, that she's not scared of me in any way.

"Maybe it is. I guess you'll never know."

My own smirk grows to match hers.

"I think we both know that I will. Now, shall we continue where we left off the other night?"

"Where we left off? You mean before you tried to kill me?"

"There was no attempt on your life. Not yet at least."

"Yeah, I told JD that I knew it was an accident. Death by prawn isn't really your style."

"You should have told us."

"Or maybe you should have given me a heads up about the ingredients of the curry."

I glare at her.

"Would have saved a lot of drama, don't you think?"

"Yeah, like having JD sleeping outside my bedroom door." My words sound innocent enough, but inside, I'm like a coiled spring, worried over his state of mind.

"Not my fault he can't accept the fallout of his actions."

"What did he do?" I ask, assuming I've missed something.

She laughs and shakes her head. "Don't play the innocent. You're just as guilty as him. And I thought playground games would be beneath you."

"I guess it all depends on the prize, don't you think?" I taunt.

"I suppose. But it doesn't really matter in this case, seeing as you lost. Not that it was ever going to go another way, you were betting on who'd fuck me first."

I can't help but laugh.

"What?" she balks.

"I hate to break it to you, Pet. But I never would have won that bet."

"O-oh," she sings, looking at me through her lashes. "I guess that explains your closeness and why you were so against him touching me. Silly me."

My brows pinch.

"How long have you been in love with your best friend for exactly?"

"What?" I blurt, successfully spraying my chest and legs with coffee.

"It's okay, Big Man. Your secret is safe with me."

"I don't fucking want JD. Jesus, Pet."

"Shame. With all that time alone I had down there, I'd come up with some pretty epic fantasies," she muses, sipping her coffee.

"Glad to know you were productive with your time."

"I had to keep myself entertained somehow. But you'd know that, wouldn't you? You were watching."

I don't respond or react.

"You watched him win too, didn't you? Even after you told him not to touch me. That must have stung. Your right-hand man defying your orders. That's not how the mighty Reid Harris should be running his empire."

"Oh, so you're agreeing that it's my empire now?"

"Nope, just stroking your ego, Big Man."

"You're a pain in the ass."

"Then let me go and I can leave you to your lonely, pathetic little life."

My brow lifts.

"You wouldn't want me to do that," I state confidently.

"I beg to differ." When I don't respond she continues with, "Enlighten me."

"It would be too easy if I just let you walk out the door. You'd feel like you'd failed."

"No, I'm pretty sure I'd be delighted to be going home."

"To start with, yeah. But then you'd realize that you crave the fight, the challenge. And you'd always know that you never gave everything up and didn't get whatever it was you wanted that got you locked up here in the first place."

"Or maybe I did," she counters.

"JD might have a rep, but becoming our prisoner is a drastic way to get a taste of him."

"I dunno," she says, her eyes getting this far-off glazed look. "He was pretty spectacular."

"That's because aside from Kane, you've been forced to fuck old, beat-up gangsters whose dicks barely get hard."

"You seem to know a lot about it. You one of them, Big Man?"

"Hardly." I scoff. She's felt just as well as I have that I have no issues getting hard. Hell, I'm battling a semi just sitting here sparring with her.

That's something that's never happened before. But there's something about her mouth, her wit, her lack of fear that speaks to something within me that most women don't get anywhere near.

Her eyes drop to my crotch as if she's hoping to find the evidence for herself and I force myself to think of Hannah and Dad fucking.

Thankfully, it does the trick and my semi sinks faster than I thought possible under her stare.

"Honestly, a few could use a couple of lessons from JD. There's this thing he does with his tongue that—"

"Your husband for one, right?"

"I can't comment on his skills, but something tells me that he knows what he's doing."

"Sure. There are plenty of whores at the club who could probably confirm that. He wasn't always the celibate prick he is now."

"If you want anything from me, insulting my husband isn't the way to go about it," she warns.

"Help me understand then," I urge. I'm way more curious about their relationship than I should be.

It's wrong, but since she's been here, all our lives have become so intertwined that I can't help wanting to know everything.

I've already uncovered enough to know that there is a lot more going on than anyone knows. But this is so much bigger than Mav not being able to get it up or Alana not wanting it.

But as curious as I am, I'm also terrified because it's bad. Worse than what I already know.

But I need it. Every dark and dirty secret that she's hiding. She's the catalyst. The one that is going to finally blow the top off everything I've been planning.

I've been waiting for the right trigger to knock my first domino over and watch as everything falls into place.

And she's right in front of me.

I had no idea when Kane brought her to me that night that she'd play perfectly into my plans. She has no idea, and she still doesn't. And until she uncovers everything, it'll stay that way. Until I know I can trust her. Trust them. I'm going to keep them exactly where I want them—at an arm's length.

6

ALANA

I might put on a good show but being under the intense glare of Reid Harris while he's sitting in only a pair of tight-fitted black boxer briefs is unnerving as fuck.

My heart pounds and my grip on my now-empty mug gets tighter and tighter with every passing second.

But while it might be slightly terrifying, I can't deny that the adrenaline of sparring with him gives me one hell of a buzz.

You'd think that after all my years being forced to submit to powerful and dominant men, I'd hate this situation. But honestly. I thrive on it. The thrill of trying to bring him down a peg or two is addictive.

I might not be able to get him on his knees for me physically, but there are other ways of claiming the power in this exchange.

"Why did you marry him?" he blurts out, dragging me from my thoughts and forcing a memory of him asking the same question over the dinner table to the forefront of my mind. "You love him, sure. I can believe that. And as much as I hate to think about him or what he does, I'm pretty sure the feeling is mutual."

Emotion crawls up my throat as he lays out our situation so simply. But there is nothing simple about what's between Mav and me. I wish there fucking was.

"But there's more to it, and I can't quite figure it all out."

Straightening my spine, I roll my shoulders back. I haven't backed down from his attempts to get the truth out of me yet, but I must be honest, it's easier with us on a similar footing for once. He's lost his armor, leaving him with nothing but his underwear and ink.

"I'm pretty sure there is more to every marriage than meets the eye. It's not really for us to judge, though, is it?" I counter.

"Not judging, Pet."

I tilt my head to the side, my brows shooting up in disbelief.

"Talk to me about Jonno," he demands, sending a rush of ice-cold fear shooting through my veins.

"W-what?"

"Oh, come on," he taunts. "You can't tell me you don't remember him. You killed him after all."

I swallow down the bile that wants to escape my body.

"Nothing to tell," I whisper, the roughness of my voice instantly giving me away.

"So you always take the opportunity to drive a knife into a man's chest, do you?"

My teeth grind as I remember exactly how it felt as I broke through his skin with the point of that blade, how warm his blood was as it sprayed over me.

The relief. A lifetime's worth of it rushed through my system. It was so powerful; it brought me to my knees.

And he picked me up.

This monster of a man, who tortures people in ways I can only imagine, was the one to scoop me off the floor while I was a sobbing, bloody mess and cradled me in his arms as if I mattered. As if he couldn't cope watching me fall apart.

And then he dropped me. Walked away as if he couldn't stand the sight of me after discovering the truth. It wrecked me. For just a moment, I thought he cared, or at least felt some kind of empathy toward me. But no. He's exactly like all the others. Cold and uncaring.

"Knowing everything about my life isn't going to make a difference to yours, I can assure you of that," I tell him firmly, finally getting a grasp on my emotions.

"See, that's where I think you're wrong. I think whatever you're hiding, and what I'm planning are very closely interlinked," he says, giving more away than he has since this whole ordeal started.

"How so?" I ask, leaning forward and resting my elbows on my knees when my curiosity gets the better of me.

One side of his mouth twitches into a smirk and I prepare myself to be shot down. He's not exactly been forthcoming this far, so really, I'm not expecting any kind of useful answer.

"I think..." he starts, making my heart rate pick up, but he stops before he says anything good.

I stare into his eyes, urging him to continue. If he gives me something useful then maybe I can do the same back.

Maybe.

"I think that maybe we're searching for the same end goal here," he finally confesses.

"Oh yeah? How so?"

"Give me names, Alana," he demands, his voice cold and dark. "Prove to me that you're with me, not against me, and I'll do everything I can to make your dreams come true."

"You're going to buy me a house on the beach so my husband and I can grow old together?" I taunt.

His jaw ticks in irritation.

"Don't play games with me, Pet," he warns, his deep, raspy voice sending a shiver racing down my spine.

"I don't know what you want me to say."

"I want the truth," he roars, his patience with me finally running out.

"So you believe we're not after you now? What did I do to convince you that you've never been anything significant enough in my life to waste time on?"

His teeth grind with irritation, but he doesn't respond.

"Must hurt to know that someone in this town doesn't worship you like a god. Your poor ego, how will it ever cope."

"Enough," he snaps, surging forward.

I brace myself for what's to come. But I don't flinch or cower. Years of being at the wrong end of a man's anger means I continue to sit there, ready to take it like the strong, unbreakable woman I am.

But he doesn't get close or even attempt to reach for me.

"How about," I say, uncurling my legs and pushing to stand. I abandon my mug on the coffee table and stalk closer to him.

He leans back against the couch as I close in, keeping his eyes on mine.

"How about you tell me your plan and then I'll decide if you need my secrets," I offer.

"That's not how this works, Pet," he warns through gritted teeth.

"You're wrong," I state, stepping confidently between his spread thighs. "That's how you think it works. You might be used to your little foot soldiers stepping into line the second you open your mouth, but I'm not one of them."

"Don't I know it," he mutters under his breath.

Leaning forward, I press my hands onto the back of the couch on either side of his head.

If I thought his almost naked presence was unignorable before then add his manly, rich scent to the mix and it becomes almost overwhelming.

A surge of power coils and explodes inside me. I can't imagine there have been many people over the years who've had the mighty Reid Harris beneath them like this.

My heart pounds so hard it makes my head spin as he allows me to continue staring down at him.

"I don't care who you are, how dangerous you are, how many men you've killed, you don't deserve my secrets."

He smirks, totally unfazed by our position. "And what if I already know them," he taunts.

The image of my notebook left abandoned in my cell flashes behind my eyes and my stomach knots.

He wouldn't...

Who the fuck am I kidding, of course he fucking would.

Our eyes hold in a silent battle of wills, me desperate for him to confirm that he hasn't dove into my deepest, darkest thoughts without permission and him urging me to just spill, to finally release all my best kept secrets.

"Start with the names. I'll make sure they burn in hell just like Jonno. I don't care who they are. No one under my watch treats girls like that."

All the air rushes from my lungs, feathering over his face.

His lids lower ever so slightly, but I'm so close, I've no choice but to notice his reaction to me.

Butterflies take off in my stomach as hope blooms.

Does he really mean that?

If I tell him everything, will he help me make a change?

Will he... will he help me search for the truth about my sister? Will he try and give all those other families with missing girls answers, closure? Hope?

It takes a couple of seconds, but I manage to gather myself enough to respond.

"Just one problem there, Big Man. None of this is on your watch. What exactly do you think you can do about any of it?"

I'm so lost in his dark eyes and the hope his previous words gave me that I don't see his arm dart out. I sure fucking know about it when his fingers wrap around my throat and I'm forced back until I'm lying out on the couch I was on not so long ago with him looming ominously over me.

His chest heaves, forcing his breath past his lips. The warmth rushes over my face and makes my skin erupt in goose bumps.

He is one of—if not—the most dangerous men in this town and here I am getting turned on being completely at his mercy.

I always knew I was fucked in the head. Nothing but a product of my abusive upbringing. But it's never been as obvious as it has been since Reid locked me up here.

Fear and lust are just different sides of the same coin, so tightly intertwined that I can't even begin to separate them.

I gaze up at him with wide eyes as he glares at me. The air around us crackles as the silence stretches on. My skin prickles and my body aches with the need to feel his hands on more than just my throat.

His grip on me is just short of being perfect, his fingers dig into those two magical spots on either side of my throat that promise the perfect oblivion.

"Please." The whimpered plea slips from my lips without instruction from my brain. My face burns with shame that one touch from him reduces me to this level of pathetic.

I don't want him.

I hate him.

My husband hates him.

But my body doesn't care. The broken little girl who, despite everything, craves the touch, the pain, and the feeling of being at the mercy of a dangerous man screams the opposite.

His lips curl into a snarl.

"You really are nothing but a dirty whore," he sneers. "If only your husband knew the truth. I doubt he'd be as desperate to rescue you."

"Shut the fuck up," I bark, anger licking at my insides at his mention of Mav. "Mav is a better man than you'll ever be."

"I guess that depends on your definition of better. He's weak and allowed himself to be wrapped around your little finger. All the while you're running around town whoring yourself out like it's your favorite hobby.

"He won't want you when he learns the truth. Or maybe he already knows and it's why he refuses to stick his dick inside you."

My hand moves before the decision is made. It's a knee-jerk reaction in my need to protect my husband.

Crack.

Reid's eyes flare with fury as my palm collides with his cheek.

His grip on my throat tightens, cutting off my air.

"You survived your near-death experience the last time you were on this couch." He growls, his voice so deep I can barely make out the words. "You might not be so lucky a second time."

My fingers curl into a fist as my palm burns from the collision. The bright red print on his cheek makes the pain so worth it, though.

My lungs burn with the need for more air. But he doesn't allow it.

Time is suspended with us locked in our stare-off, my head beginning to swim. Only inches separate our noses, his breath heating my face, the heat of our barely covered bodies burning between us.

Nothing else matters. Nothing but the promise of what could come.

My thighs rub and my back arches in the hope of finding some friction, but I'm met with nothing but his dark stare.

His fingers twitch around my throat. I've no idea if he's aware of the slight movement, but it tells me everything I need to know. He's holding back just as much as I am.

A smile curls at my lips, making his press into a thin line.

"And you think you're so different from all the others."

Reaching between us, I wrap my fingers around his hard dick.

His nostrils flare as he sucks in a sharp breath.

"But really, you're all the same. Horny little boys who'll do anything for good pussy," I taunt.

"You're wrong," he spits.

I stroke him, amazed he's letting this continue, and his jaw ticks.

"JD's right. You really do need to get laid," I taunt. "I wonder if you'd even smile after."

He bares his teeth on a growl.

"You know what? I'm feeling charitable." Planting my feet on the couch cushions, I part my thighs, exposing myself to him, not that he can see. "I won't even fight."

"You're fucked up, Pet," he accuses.

I smile, taking his words as a compliment they certainly weren't delivered as. "Takes one to know one, don't you think?"

I squeeze him tighter and he grunts in pleasure.

"You act all high and mighty, but you are just as weak as all the others. Say what you like about Mav, but at least he can make a decision and have the willpower to see it through." Even if it drives me to the brink of insanity.

His grip tightens again, and I smile in accomplishment, but then there's a noise from another room, and he's gone in a flash.

My attention turns toward the doorway, waiting for someone—JD—to emerge, although I don't miss Reid shoving his hand into his boxers beside me to rearrange himself.

Something flickers in my mind, a barely there grasp on a memory. It's not an uncommon feeling for me. There are so many awful memories I've tried to suppress over the years that often get triggered by something.

But this is different.

When nothing else happens and I'm unable to reveal any more of the image that's wanting to break through, I push to my feet, letting Reid's tank fall back into place, covering me up.

"What's that look?" I ask, staring at Reid's profile as he looks across the room as if I'm not here and those last few minutes never happened. "Guilt?"

"Unless you want to return to your cell, I suggest you get out of my fucking sight," he warns.

The temptation to push him is right there. I could, and something tells me that I'd break him eventually. But in the end, I decide against it and walk toward the doorway that was trying to tell me something only seconds ago.

I pause when I get there and look back at the empty couch, trying to imagine how we looked together just now.

What would have happened if JD found us?

My teeth sink into my bottom lip as I conjure more than a few fantasies from that little scenario.

"Alana," Reid snaps, dragging me out of my dirty thoughts.

With one more look at one of the men in question, I spin on my heels and walk toward the stairs.

At the top, I find JD exactly where he was when I left my room in search of different walls to stare at and some coffee.

Dropping to my haunches, I study his face.

Even in slumber, his brow is furrowed and his lips are pressed into a thin line. It's a far cry from the relaxed man I watched sleep in my cell not so long ago.

It's my fault. I know it is.

Maybe I shouldn't have been so hard on him over a stupid bet when he's so clearly struggling with something. Really, it's at the very bottom of the list of awful things they've done to me during my stay, but for some reason, it cuts the deepest.

I can deal with the physical pain. I learned to

compartmentalize that years ago. It's the emotional game-playing that always trips me up.

You'd think my skin would be thick enough to deal with it by now. I thought it was. But it seems that JD and Reid somehow managed to slip under that armor and take a swipe at the vulnerable girl who still hides beneath.

Flopping onto Reid's giant bed, I reach for the TV remote with an accomplished smile on my face.

I got to him downstairs. And now I'm rolling around in his bed.

I bet he's downstairs wishing he followed me.

Just before I hit the power button, heavy footsteps pound up the stairs before a door slams somewhere down the hallway.

A laugh tumbles from my lips as I think about him losing his shit in the guest room.

I'm still giggling to myself when I finally turn the TV on.

The second it comes to life, I swear my entire world grinds to a halt at what I find.

7

JD

Something wakes me, and it takes a couple of seconds to recognize where I am. My back aches, and my hip is burning in pain despite the thickness of the carpet beneath me from my awkward angle. My head swims thanks to the whiskey I drank before curling up here like a pathetic cunt and passing out.

I'd hoped she might take pity on me when—if—she discovered me and let me back into bed with her. But it seems that hasn't happened because I'm still here.

Another scream comes from inside Reid's room and before I know what I'm doing, I'm on my feet and launching myself toward the door.

I assume she's having a nightmare. They seem to be a nightly thing. But when I fly through the door, I don't find her thrashing about in bed, being haunted by night terrors; instead, she's running full speed toward me.

"Whoa." I grunt, catching her upper arms before we collide.

"You fucking asshole," she screams so loudly it makes me wince.

Clenching her fists, she slams them against my upper arms and chest as tears fall from her lashes, splashing onto her cheeks.

"What's wrong?" I ask in a rush. "What's happened?"

"I fucking hate you. Both of you," she wails, her tears falling faster as I finally manage to grab her flailing hands and spin her around, pinning them to her sides as I wrap my arms around her trembling body.

"LET GO OF ME," she screams, her high-pitched voice bouncing off the walls. She fights to suck in the air she needs as her sobs get louder and louder, her hysteria becoming almost uncontrollable.

"It's okay, Dove. I've got you," I say softly, hoping it's enough to bring her down from whatever hell she's lost in.

She roars, thrashing against my hold, trying to break free.

"Motherfucker." I grunt when her heel collides with the top of my foot.

I'm struggling to keep her contained when something on the wall at the end of the bed catches my eye.

I freeze as my vision clears, and I find footage of her old cell clearly displayed.

"Oh fuck," I breathe.

"How could you?" she screams. "H-how c-could you?"

Footsteps sound out behind me before the ominous presence of my best friend fills the room.

"What the fuck is going on?"

At the sound of his voice, Alana rips herself out of my grasp and flies at Reid.

I could have probably stopped her; it wouldn't have been that hard. But what's the fun in that?

"Jesus. What the fuck are you doing?" Reid barks as she rains fury down on his chest just like she did mine not so long ago. "So much for being a delicate fucking bird," he mutters.

It takes a few minutes, but he finally manages to restrain her, much like I did with her back to his chest and her arms pinned to her sides.

"Let him go," she demands, her cheeks slick with tears and her eyes red and swollen.

"We can't do that, Pet."

"Please," she begs. "He doesn't deserve to be down there."

Reid turns her, forcing her to stare at the screen, which shows a high-definition image of her beloved husband lying on the cot that used to be hers.

He's awake, staring up at the ceiling blankly. He has no idea if it's day or night, or how long he's been down there.

All he knows is that he's locked up at our mercy, and we have his wife.

Personally, I don't get that big a kick out of it. I've never really had an issue with him. But after years of stupid childhood rivalry, I know that Reid has got a half-chub over it.

In the space of only a few days, Reid's beaten his ass and locked Mav in his basement. It doesn't get much sweeter than that in the world of Reid Harris.

"But that's where you're wrong, Pet," Reid murmurs, his lips so close to her ears that her skin breaks out in goose bumps, and her nipples pebble against the thin fabric of her shirt. "He more than deserves it."

"No. He hasn't done anything wrong. He's not involved in any of this."

"Maybe not. But that all changed when he broke into my house and pointed his gun at my head."

"No," she cries, her body sagging in his arms. "No, he wouldn't do that."

"Look at his shoulder, little dove," I say, moving closer to them.

Her sobs of despair get louder, her body growing weaker in Reid's arms.

"You shot him," she states, her voice cold and broken before falling still. "I remember," she whispers so quietly that we wouldn't hear it if it weren't the dead of night. "He came for me and you shot him."

"I'd do the same to anyone who was stupid enough to break in, Pet. You should be thanking me really."

"You're insane," she cries, regaining her strength and starting to fight against his hold. "I'll never be thankful to you for anything. All you've done is ruin my life."

"That's a bit harsh, Pet. Right now, you're looking at your husband. I can assure you that if he were anyone else the other night, they'd already be shark bait."

She screams, her shrill voice echoing in the silent house.

In her anger, she missed the unspoken words in Reid's confession.

He *should* be dead. He's not lying when he says that anyone else would be.

Reid spared his life because of Alana.

One day, she'll figure that out. But something tells me that it won't be anytime soon because she's blinded by anger.

She continues fighting, but Reid isn't having any of it. He spins her around, forcing her to tear her eyes away from Mav, and throws her down on the bed before jumping on top of her, pinning her thighs with his own and her arms with his fingers around her wrists.

"Enough." He growls.

It's the closest I think I've ever seen them, and fuck me, if they don't look good together.

"Fuck you," she spits.

Reid chuckles darkly.

"I'm not interested in Victor's trash, Pet."

My stomach knots, knowing that his words are going to hurt her. Not that she'll show it.

"Then throw me out, asshole. If I'm nothing but trash, why the fuck would you want me in your house?"

"Because you're the final piece of my puzzle," he roars, shocking the shit out of me.

Silence follows his booming confession. No one speaks. Hell, I'm pretty sure no one breathes as the words settle around us.

He usually keeps his cards so close to his chest. I've no idea if he's starting to believe that offering up a little bit of honesty with her will get results or if he's just so pissed off with this entire thing that his mouth is running away with him.

No. It can't be that.

Reid never loses sight of his goal. Ever.

It doesn't matter how hot the girl is glaring up at him with nothing but unfiltered hate in her eyes, or how magnificent her pussy is.

He will not let go until he gets what he wants.

"What the fuck is that supposed to mean?"

He sucks in a deep breath, his nostrils flaring and his chest expanding and shoulders widening.

"Tell me everything, Pet. All the dark and ugly secrets that leave you screaming alone in the darkness at night."

I move closer, equally as terrified as I am excited to get something out of her finally.

"What's the point? You already know," she seethes.

"No. I'm guessing. Putting together the few nuggets of information I've already gleaned from you."

"It's enough," she insists.

Her chest heaves as she stares up at him, her eyes swollen from crying and tears glistening on her cheeks.

Fuck me, she looks beautiful.

"Kurt," he spits darkly. Alana physically flinches at the mention of her father.

"I remember you as a kid. I remember coming to your house. You were a pretty little thing. All that long dark hair, a sweet smile and all-seeing eyes. I remember watching you, wondering how easy your life was being born as a female in our world.

"I was being trained to take over for my father from the moment they discovered I was a boy. I'm pretty sure my first real toy was a gun, and for my eighth birthday, he took me to target practice. At ten, I witnessed him kill someone. And at twelve, he decided that I was old enough to be the one to pull the trigger."

Alana gasps at that revelation, but she doesn't interrupt his little trip down memory lane. None of it shocks me, though, I've heard it all before.

The perfect life I thought the Harris brothers had with their seemingly loving father and stepmother was all a cover. The truth about their lives was very, very different.

"You wouldn't have had to deal with all that. Yeah, your mom had left, but kids deal with that shit all the time.

"Your dad cared. I remember watching him watch you as you cleaned up empty beer bottles and returned with new cold ones for him and his friends.

"I remember thinking how lucky you were to escape all the darkness."

She shakes her head, her eyes closing as if the image he's painting for her is physically painful.

"You were so sweet, so happy, so friendly. Although never really toward me. From the first time I saw you and Mav together, it was obvious that you preferred him to me. The way you used to smile at him..." It's his turn to shake his head, his jaw ticking as if he can't believe he's confessing all this.

I move closer still, too intrigued to discover where this little story is leading.

Did big bad Reid Harris have a crush on young, innocent Alana?

The idea of Reid ever having a crush is bizarre. The only interest I've seen him have in girls is to hold power over them and take what he needs. Total fucking alpha male bullshit that all the girls in this town seem to get off on.

"I guess you saw something different in him. Just another reason for me to hate him back then. I used to wonder what it was. The two of us were more alike than I ever wanted to admit back then. We'd had the same childhood, the same expectations put on our shoulders. Things could have been so different if we could stand being in the same room as each other for more than five minutes."

My brows pinch as I wait to discover more to the lifetime rivalry the two of them have, but when he speaks again, he's turned away from it.

"But I think I've figured it out now."

Alana remains silent as we both wait impatiently for him to explain.

"Victor was first, wasn't he?"

Alana gasps, her body visibly trembling beneath him.

"You saw me, and you saw him. I'm assuming that Razor joined the party at some point—those sick cunts like to do everything together after all—but it was too late by then. You'd formed some kind of friendship with his son. You didn't look into his eyes and see a monster like you did when you looked at me.

"But your life was far from perfect, wasn't it? Victor, Kurt, Razor, Jonno? How many others, Alana?" Her eyes fill with tears, her fingers twisting so hard in the sheets, her knuckles turn white.

"How many others what?" I ask, fear of where this is going dripping through my veins.

I'd be lying if I said I didn't suspect something. I'd be an idiot not to after everything I've discovered about my little dove.

She doesn't react to things like most women. She gets turned on by the darkest of things that Reid and I have forced her to endure.

"No," I blurt, refusing to accept what I already know.

The thought of the men who have brought us up, taught us everything we know, destroying something so pure, so innocent, so... perfect.

"No," I repeat, tugging at my hair until I'm only moments away from ripping it clean from my scalp.

Alana looks at me, desperately pleading with me to make him stop, although I can't be anything more than a blur with the number of tears swimming in her eyes.

But I can't do anything. I'm frozen as the horrors of what her past really looks like, the pain she's endured, grips me in a tight hold.

"Tell me, Pet. Give me everything, and I'll take you down there."

Those words break through my trance, turning the fire in my veins to ice.

"You're going to give her back to him?" I ask in disbelief.

8

ALANA

JD's wrecked expression makes my chest fracture straight down the center. I can't help it.

There's something about the loveable idiot that just talks to me even when I'm pissed at him.

"I said I'd take her down, not that I'd hand her over," Reid explains, dragging me back to the here and now.

My teeth grind and my muscles tense.

"I'm telling you nothing," I spit, making him rear back in shock.

"You don't want to see your husband?" he asks incredulously.

I keep my mouth closed as he stares down at me.

But I barely see him. All the things he said about my past and the men who've ruined my life and body are still haunting me.

He knows. And now so does JD. But there is no way I'm giving him any more than that in exchange for seeing Mav.

I don't just want to see Mav. I want him to wrap me in his strong arms and take me home.

I want everything. Not just the scraps that Reid will

allow us to have. Because that's all it'll be—the bare minimum.

All Reid cares about is himself and his beloved gang. He doesn't give a shit about us, our marriage, or our future.

He wants my secrets for his own gain. And why should I allow that when all he's done is hurt me?

Just like the men who have come before him.

His form of torture might be different, but the result is the same. They all want something from me.

My innocence.

My pain.

My fear.

"Not under your terms, no," I finally confess.

"You're just going to leave him down there?" JD asks curiously.

"Opposed to what? I highly doubt you'll leave the door unlocked so we can run as far and as fast as possible."

The answer is clear in his eyes. It doesn't matter what I say, Reid will continue with his mission until he gets exactly what he wants. And then where will that leave us?

Probably still locked up and at his mercy.

Dragging my eyes from JD, I attempt to look around the beast of a man pinning me to the bed in order to see my husband.

The sight of him gives me strength, reminds me why I'm fighting. I force down the devastation and the pain of the memories Reid's dragged up and rediscover my fire.

Once I'm feeling a little stronger, I turn my eyes back on the man above me.

"Twice in the same night," I taunt, remembering all too vividly the way he held me against the couch not so long ago. "Anyone would think you like having me at your mercy."

"Oh, Pet." He growls. "You've no idea."

His eyes bounce between mine before they glance to his best friend.

"I think JD likes it too. He's been missing you," he teases. "I really think you should forgive him and cheer him up a little."

I bite down on my lip to stop from responding.

"She doesn't look like she wants to play, bro."

Finally, he releases my wrists and sits up, giving me a full, close-up view of his inked chest and stomach. He isn't as hard as he was downstairs, but there's definitely some interest going on inside his boxers.

"Can't say the same about you. You claim to be a better man, but really, you're just a younger, prettier version of your father, getting your kicks while making a woman bend to your whim." His eyes flare with anger at being compared to his father. "But I'm not that little girl anymore. I've grown and matured. And in case you weren't aware, I've been trained to fight back."

I know my performance not so long ago didn't exactly show it, I blame the explosion of anger that took over my body the second my eyes landed on my husband's still form on the cot in my cell. Mav has spent the last five years ensuring I have the skills to fight off any man who tries his luck with me. My aim is solid, and I have every confidence that I could have both of these gangsters on the floor in tears, should I want to try hard enough.

I can't help but smile as the image of them rolling around clutching their junk fills my head.

"What's funny?" JD asks, a deep frown between his brows.

I shake my head. "Nothing you'd understand. Can you get off me now?" I ask, smiling sweetly at Reid.

"Unless you're going to make it worth my while, I'm not interested in having you on top of me, or touching me, really."

He sneers before climbing from the bed gingerly, as if I'm about to throw myself at him again.

The fact I've got him second-guessing me makes something bloom in my chest.

He likes control, for everyone to be singing from his hymn sheet, but he's never going to get that from me.

I'm so far from his sheet that I'm in my own book.

He backs toward the door and when his eyes flick toward the TV, I can practically read his thoughts.

"I'll be good," I lie, smiling at him like an obedient child. It's a look I was forced to perfect over the years, and it comes all too easily.

"Shame I don't believe you." He scoffs.

"Fine, lock me up again. Really makes no difference to me."

I push myself back against his headboard and cross my arms beneath my breasts.

"What can she really do?" JD asks, trying to get back on my good side.

Reid glares at his best friend, suspicion dancing in his dark eyes.

"It's not her I'm worried about."

Oh, the power.

I shouldn't be as pleased as I am about causing a rift between these two best friends. But really, I'm smug as fuck.

"What's wrong, Reid? You not trusting your BFF all of a sudden? That's gotta hurt after all these years of bromance."

JD's face twists in frustration, but he doesn't say anything. How can he? We all know he's the weak link here.

If anyone is going to be convinced to let me into the basement to see Mav then it's going to be him.

"If you're going to start arguing, can you please do it elsewhere? I'm not interested in your little domestic drama."

Reid's eyes turn on me. There's a stark warning lingering in them, but I don't take it seriously, despite the fact I probably should. Both my husband and I are now rocking extra holes in our bodies, thanks to him.

I keep my eyes on his, letting him see my indifference to his silent threats. And finally, after a few minutes, he grabs JD by his upper arm and shoves him toward the door.

"Wait, I don't—"

"Go," Reid barks, refusing to listen to any excuse JD might have to stay.

I stay where I am until the door clicks closed behind them, and then I'm on my feet, rushing toward the TV screen.

"Mav," I sob quietly as my tears resurface, flooding my eyes and spilling over my lashes. My fingers lift and I trail them across his skin, wishing I could feel the warmth of it. "I'm so sorry," I whisper.

He's here because of me.

He's been shot because of me.

The guilt over that realization is almost too much to withstand. My knees give out and I crash into the dresser beneath the TV before sinking to the floor where I crumble.

I must cry myself to sleep, because when I crack my sore, swollen eyes open again sometime later, I'm still on the floor where I fell.

Looking up, I find Mav still in the same position as he was earlier, only now, he looks to be sleeping although his body seems tense, his muscles locked up tight. He's shirtless, wearing only a pair of jeans, exposing the ink he has on his chest with one arm resting over his stomach, the other lying on the cot beside him.

I focus on the large white bandage covering his shoulder. A lump of emotion crawls up my throat, it's so huge I struggle to breathe around it.

My hands tremble with my need to go down there, to free him, to tell him to go and get on with his life and forget all about me.

But it's pointless.

He's here for me. He came for me.

Just like he always promised he would.

And look where he's ended up.

Self-hatred like I've never known before poisons my veins, forcing me to curl in on myself in an attempt to hold it together.

This wasn't how it was all supposed to go.

When Victor propositioned me with a job, I didn't fight it. It wasn't just because I knew I didn't have a choice. When Victor Harris tells you to jump, the only thing you can ask, if you want him to spare your life is, how high? It wasn't just because he threatened Mav, which would have been enough to have me agreeing in a heartbeat, because no one goes after my husband and gets away with it. But it gave me a chance to infiltrate his inner circle. And for us to implement some kind of plan to take them all down, we needed intel, badly.

We knew they were all corrupt, drug-dealing murderers. But with Victor having every single cop and influential person in this town under his control, getting anything to stick was going to be a challenge.

We needed something bigger than what we already had. Something so much bigger and has enough evidence that it couldn't be ignored.

It's just a shame I never really found anything of use.

It was coming. I could sense it.

I just never expected the turning point to end up being this.

Reid Harris.

I think about the things he said, the anger he's shown toward his father that no one on the outside ever gets to witness.

As far as the rest of Harrow Creek is concerned, Reid is Victor Harris's little protégé. He toes the line and does the job that Victor expects from him.

But it's not true.

I scoot back and rest against the foot of the bed, my eyes on the screen as my brain spins at a million miles a second.

Reid has called me the missing piece to a puzzle. Clearly, he has an agenda here. He needs me for something. Something important.

With my eyes locked on the screen, hope begins to bloom inside me, the petals uncurling like a rose on a summer morning.

Could we all want the same thing?

The realization hits me with the force of an articulated truck.

My hand trembles as I push my hair back from my face.

All of Reid's words about this town being under his control. His hatred of Victor.

Is he planning to overthrow him?

But how?

Victor has ensured that he's anything but an easy target. He has to or he'd have been dead a long time ago. His allies might be powerful but so are his enemies.

If Reid has a plan, then it has to be something epic. Something well-planned.

A plan he wasn't expecting me to intrude on. But one I could ultimately help with.

Letting my head fall back, I close my eyes for a beat.

Maybe I was right all the way along. I was meant to end up here. But maybe it isn't about punishment for my stupid decisions. Maybe it's to get the one thing I've always wanted.

Justice.

My heart rate picks up and I lift my head, focusing on my husband.

We're going to do it, Mav.

We just need to get Reid on our side. And there is only one way to do that.

I need to tell him the truth.

The thought of saying the words, of letting their names roll off my tongue makes bile swirl in the pit of my stomach.

I'm on my feet before I've realized I can't contain it and I drop heavily to my knees in front of the toilet before I retch, bringing up what little I've eaten today.

Wiping my sweaty brow, I can't help but wonder how I will ever tell them everything they need to know if I can barely even think about it without vomiting.

Focus on the end goal, Alana.

Think of the future, walking around a white sandy beach

73

with Mav's fingers entwined with yours and for the first time in your life a happy, relaxed smile on your face.

I squeeze my eyes closed and try to picture it. But unlike every other time I've done the same thing, the image is hazy.

Our future even more uncertain than ever.

I can't even see it anymore.

A sob threatens, but I force it down. Now isn't the time for that.

Stealing Reid's toothbrush again, I freshen up before marching across the room. I pull the door open and poke my head out. I'm expecting to find a bodyguard loitering to stop me from escaping, but surprisingly, the hall is silent.

As silently as possible, I tiptoe toward the stairs and descend slowly. The interior of this manor might have been completely modernized, but it's the existing structure, which means with every step I take, there is another loud creak. I'm sure in the bright light of day they're barely audible. But right now, they're loud as fuck, and if anyone is waiting for me then they'll be more than aware of my movement.

There's no sign of anyone either behind me or on the ground floor, so with my heart in my throat, I continue.

I'm aware that I'm probably as likely to be able to break into the basement as I am to escape out the front door of this place. But I'm still willing to try.

I glance at the door that would lead me back to the world outside these walls, but the thought of going out there fills me with more apprehension than returning to the basement.

I park that thought, stuffing it down with everything else I don't want to think about as I search for the hidden door that will lead me to my husband.

9

—

JD

The second the first creak fills the air, I'm on my feet, my bottle of whiskey coming with me.

Reid told me to go to bed and sleep, and I made it look like I was following his orders by disappearing into my room. But the second I heard him shut himself in the guest room, I made my escape. The need to return to Alana's room and try and dig myself out of the massive hole I've put myself in was too tempting. Reid is the bad guy now. He's the one who shot her husband and locked him up in the basement. Surely my crimes are looking inconsequential compared to his. Right?

But I refrained. I figured she probably needed some time to get over the shock. That or she needed to believe she wasn't being monitored.

I might still have a lot to learn about Alana Murray, but her love for her husband is more than obvious, despite how much it might hurt.

I want her; I've made no secret of that fact. Looking back, I probably should have caught myself sooner to protect myself. But I was powerless. I've only ever felt like that once in my life. And I know all too well how that ended. I've been suffering the consequences ever since.

I should have been smarter. I should have seen it coming. I should have known that it would only end in pain, just like the last time.

But she wrapped me around her little finger and lured me in like a lamb to slaughter.

I was weak.

Pathetic.

Drawn in by her tempting smile, sinful curves, and addictive pussy.

I shake my head as I reach for my bottle of whiskey and silently move toward the door that leads to where I know she's heading.

When I first came down, the under-cupboard lights in the kitchen and a lamp in the hallway were on. The first thing I did was turn them all off. I needed the darkness. Craved the fucking nothingness of the dead of night, and am I glad I did.

The shadow of her body moves down the final few steps before she slowly makes her way down the hallway. It's instantly apparent she doesn't know the house. Navigating around it in the dark is a challenge long before she collides with a dresser and shrieks in shock as I assume she stubs her toe on the solid walnut.

A smirk pulls at my lips as she frantically looks around, waiting for someone to jump out of the shadows to catch her.

I've no idea where Reid is. I find it hard to believe that he closed the guest bedroom door and forgot all about the blonde bombshell residing in his bedroom, rolling around in his bed, or the reason for the tears he saw cascading down her cheeks not so long ago.

Fuck. I hated seeing that.

There should be only one reason why my little dove has tears in her eyes, and it's not because one of us douchebags has hurt her.

Well... not unless she's begged for it.

I have little choice but to step out into the hallway when she turns the corner in search of the almost invisible door. If you know the door is there, it's easy to find. But if you don't then you'd have no reason to be suspicious that there's a hidden route to the basement beneath our feet. But in the dark, unless you know exactly where it is, then you'd have no chance finding it, or the panel that allows only two of us access when it's locked up tight like I know it is now.

She continues forward, her fingertips trailing over the wall and the beading that is designed to hide the secret door. Every now and then, she gives a little push. I can't help but shake my head. Surely, she has more faith in Reid than that.

She has to know that we'd predict this move the second she discovered our new inmate.

When she thinks she's found it, she fully turns to face the wall and pushes both hands against it.

I smother a laugh as I take a step forward, and then another.

Her magnetic pull is too much for me to ignore. It speaks to the broken, desperate parts of me that I try my best to fight every day. I know caving is going to hurt. But then I guess every junkie knows their next hit might be their last. Doesn't fucking stop them from shooting that shit straight into their veins.

Seems that Alana is just as irresistible. An addiction too fucking strong for me to deny.

She continues fighting with the wall, desperately

searching for the way to get inside, as if there will be something as simple as a fucking door handle to allow her to slip through and descend the stairs.

Who'd have thought she'd be so desperate to go back down there now that she's been granted a little freedom?

I guess she was always a little too comfortable in her cold, almost uninhabitable cell.

My mind cycles back to what Reid said in her bedroom —the accusations he made.

If it weren't for her reaction to hearing the names he said to her, then I might not believe it.

But the fear was too pure, too intense for it to be lies.

Anger unfurls inside me as I think about what they might have done to her.

It's no secret that Victor and his closest men are a bunch of sick scumbags.

But pedophilia.

My fingers curl, my grip on the bottle so tight, I'm amazed it doesn't shatter.

As murderous as the thought of anyone touching her without permission makes me, I know it's the truth. Everything we did to her in the basement, how she unraveled for us, how the most twisted of things turned her on... All of it makes so much fucking sense. And as much as I loved the reaction she had to us, I fucking hate it as well.

My skin continues to itch with self-hatred. But with my sights set on her, thoughts of that razor in my bathroom cabinet or the knives in the kitchen are far from my mind.

Reaching out with my free hand, I wrap my fingers around the doorframe, letting the square edges of the wood bite into my skin as I continue to watch her.

There's something else that will help squash the incessant need to remind myself that all of this is real, that

I'm alive and that there is something worthwhile sticking this shit out for.

Forgetting herself, she lets out a quiet wail of frustration when the wall refuses to allow her entry. Her voice echoes around the ancient building, making the hairs on my neck stand on end. It might help if she'd found the actual door, of course. Maybe if she paid a little more attention when she was backed up against it the other day, instead of being too busy sucking my fingers into her cunt, then she might have more of a clue where to find the entrance.

Taking another swig from my bottle, I wince when the whiskey sloshes, but she's too focused on her task at hand to notice.

With a smirk, I close in on her, my mouth watering the second her scent hits my nose.

Placing my bottle on the dresser that usually houses our keys, I move silently, stepping right up behind her as the first signs of dawn begins to light up the space around us.

It takes her a moment to register the heat of my body, and I make the most of that millisecond to suck in a lungful of her scent.

She stills, and just before she screams, I move. Clamping one hand around her mouth and wrapping the other around her waist, pinning her against my body.

"Looks to me like someone is being a naughty girl." I growl in her ear.

She shudders in my hold as my breath rushes down her neck.

"Looking for something?" I ask.

"Let me go," she snaps the second I release her mouth, collaring her throat instead.

I chuckle, my chest vibrating against her back.

"I don't think I will," I confess, my lips brushing her ear, my cock quickly growing against the fullness of her ass.

"JD," she hisses, trying to fight against me.

"Keep grinding against me like that, little dove. I missed the feel of your body against mine."

"Not interested," she lies.

"Oh no?"

My grip on her throat tightens and a whimper of need rips from it.

"Your words might say one thing, but your body says another."

"Didn't you get the memo upstairs? I'm fucked up, Julian. My body is tainted and wants things it shouldn't have."

"Not the way I see it," I confess.

Yes, I hate what she's been through. That she's had men's hands on her who didn't have the right. But that doesn't stop me from wanting her something fierce.

"Then maybe you're just as fucked up as I am," she suggests, as if it's going to be news to me.

"Oh, I can fucking guarantee it, Dove. You think I'm the nice one? The funny one? The light to Reid's twisted darkness?" I ask, my lips trailing down her neck. "Then you're very, very wrong."

She gasps as I cup her breast, squeezing until I know it hurts, sending a bolt of electricity to her clit. I'm proved right when she arches into me, offering up more of herself while her ass grinds against my dick.

"If you knew what they did to me, you'd never want to touch me," she says, some of the armor she usually has locked tight around her cracking open just a little.

"Then you don't know me as well as I thought you did."

She shudders as I lick a trail up her neck before sucking on the skin beneath her ear.

"I'm serious, Julian," she breathes, unable to fight the desire that's flooding her body.

"So am I. I've never been more serious about anything in my life."

Releasing her waist, I take a step forward, forcing her against the wall.

"Julian." She moans as I rock against her.

A wicked idea fills my mind the second my name falls from her lips as nothing but a desperate plea and I pull my cell from my pocket. I wince as the brightness sears my eyeballs, but I quickly locate the app I need and change the settings before I place it on the dresser, next to the whiskey. I grab it and take a shot, loving the burn as it slides down my throat.

"Open your mouth, little dove," I demand, twisting my fingers in her hair and dragging her head back, giving her little choice but to follow orders.

"JD." She gasps, making me smirk, but it's quickly drowned out when I pour the liquid into her mouth.

She splutters a little, but eventually swallows it down.

Coughing, she cusses me out.

"Good, huh?"

"No," she spits. "I fucking hate whiskey."

"Aw, don't tell Big Man that. It's his favorite. He'll be pissed enough that I'm drinking it."

"I don't give a shit about him or his precious whiskey."

"No, all you care about right now is my cock, isn't that right, little dove?"

"Get fucked," she hisses, but even as she says the words, her ass is shifting against me, letting me know what she really wants.

"Yeah, that's pretty much the idea."

I wrap my hands around the bottom of Reid's tank and drag it up her body.

"Arm's up, little dove. Let me see those incredible tits."

She fights me, or at least she tries to for a few seconds at least. But eventually, she admits defeat and I get the joy of peeling the fabric from her body, leaving her deliciously naked.

"Fuck, I missed this body, Dove. Do you have any idea how many times I've played out our times together in my head? How many times I've jerked off to the memory of your lips wrapped around my cock? To the sensation of your pussy sucking me deep, milking me until I'm fucking dry."

She whimpers like a needy little whore.

"You want it, don't you, Dove? I bet you're already soaking your thighs with your need for my cock."

Pulling her hips from the wall, I slide my hand down her stomach until my fingertips find the smooth skin of her mound and then the slickness of her folds.

A growl rumbles deep in my chest as I circle her clit, coating my digits in her juices.

"Oh God." She gasps as I continue teasing her.

Her head falls back on my shoulder, and I finally let go of some of the tension I've been carrying around since the moment she passed out in Reid's arms.

"Been too long since I tasted you, Dove," I say, smirking when she complains as I remove my fingers from her and push them into my mouth instead. "So fucking sweet," I mutter.

"Please," she begs.

"Oh, little dove. You're such a needy little whore. I love

it. Put your hands on the wall and stick your ass out. Let me see you."

When she doesn't immediately comply, I press my palm between her shoulder blades and shove her forward.

"You don't deserve to fuck me again," she seethes.

I can't help but laugh as I shove my boxers down, freeing my aching dick.

"I never said I deserved anything, Dove. Isn't going to stop me from taking."

"Asshole," she hisses.

"Fight all you like. You know you want it. Your pussy is practically crying for me to fill it up."

"I can give myself what I need."

"Now I know you're lying. For as beautiful as you look doing just that, you can't get yourself off like I can. Now stick that ass out and let me see you."

The second she follows orders, my palm cracks across her flawless skin. It instantly reddens with a handprint so bright, I can clearly see it in the early morning glow. Precum leaks from my slit at the sight.

"So fucking beautiful," I muse before taking myself in my hand and rubbing the head of my dick through her wetness.

But just before I push inside, I change my mind and drop to my knees. I need more of her taste on my tongue before I sink inside her.

"Julian," she screams when I grip her ass cheeks in my hands and lick her clit to asshole.

10

MAVERICK

"Julian."

My wife's needy, desperate cries fill the cell and echo off the bare walls and floors, ensuring I hear them over and over again. As if once wasn't enough to get the message through.

I hear it loud and fucking clear.

"Fucking addicted to this pussy." His words are muffled, and I can only imagine why.

Squeezing my eyes closed, I clench my jaw so hard, I'm amazed one of my back teeth doesn't crack with the force.

My cock aches listening to them, imagining what they're doing.

I've heard Alana getting herself off before. While I might have done my best to keep my desires and needs locked down when I knew she was around, she did the opposite.

I swear she bought the loudest vibrator she could find. Either that or she never actually used it and instead teased me mercilessly by pressing it against the wall that separated our bedrooms while she made all the right noises to try and force my hand.

I wanted it. Fuck me, did I want it.

The thought of marching into her room, ripping that battery-operated toy from between her thighs—assuming she was actually using the thing—and showing her how it's properly done used to make me hard as fucking nails.

My mouth waters as I try to imagine exactly what JD is tasting right now.

I bet she's so fucking sweet. And I've no doubt that he's right. She'll be so addictive too.

I'm obsessed with every inch of that woman. I don't need to wonder about the parts I haven't experienced. I'll fucking love them too.

"ARGH," I bellow as my legs thrash against the bed in frustration.

The last thing I remember from the night I broke in is both mine and Reid's gun going off simultaneously, but while my shock from seeing my wife barely conscious on his couch ensured my aim was off, his wasn't.

His motherfucking bullet ripped straight through my shoulder, sending me careening back against the wall before my knees gave out, and I collapsed to the floor in a heap.

I remember them looming over me, Reid's dark eyes glaring nothing but hate into me. And I remember thinking, this is it. I'm going to be wiped from this Earth, failing to protect my wife like I'd promised I would and at the hands of a man who'll probably piss on my grave. Not that he'd go to the effort of giving me one. Motherfucker probably has an incinerator here somewhere that he feeds bodies to on a daily basis. The only good thing about the whole situation, as far as I could see it, was that Alana hadn't been thrown into it. And while she might not have looked good, something niggled in my brain that they were trying to help. It was all I could hope for.

To my surprise, when I opened my eyes some unknown time later, it turned out I wasn't dead. I was, however, in hell.

The stark gray concrete cell was not the place I'd hoped to be, but there was a sweetness in the air there that made my stomach knot painfully.

She'd been here. Wherever the fuck here is.

Those motherfuckers had been keeping my wife locked in a cell.

And when I found the strength to push myself up, I found even more evidence that this had been where Alana had been for the past week and a half.

The only thing I could do was look on the bright side. If I were in her cell, then she wasn't in it. Maybe she was being looked after by the two sick pricks living in the house I found her in. I couldn't even consider the other option for why this cell was suddenly empty.

But the biggest question of all was why she was here in the first place.

As far as I knew, she had nothing to do with Reid or JD. Sure, she was always polite to them if our paths crossed, just like she was with everyone else. Her ability to smile at the men entwined with everything she went through—even if they only share DNA—always blew me away. I knew it was because underneath it all, she was silently planning their painful and bloody deaths, but it still astounded me.

My girl is so strong. So incredibly fucking strong. I was in awe of her the day I caught her trying to run away, and it's only grown every day since then.

The only thing I've been able to come up with in my

endless, lonely hours here is that she's done something to try and get inside information.

Nothing else makes sense.

"Oh my God, please," she cries, making my dick jerk in my pants.

"Fuuuuck." I groan as the sound of JD lapping up her juices fills my ears.

I've never made a secret of how much Alana means to me. I've never regretted it. Until now.

That motherfucker knows what he's doing. Starving me. Locking me up in a room that is always as bright as a fucking summer's morning. Taunting me with the fact she's been here. None of that even compares to listening to this right now.

There is no escape. No way to block them out. To hide how much I want her. How much I need her.

I'm not stupid. If I can hear them, that means they can hear me, and probably watch me too.

They'll know exactly how this is affecting me. I can try and lock it down as much as possible, but I am only so fucking strong. And after five years of abstinence, I'm always on the fucking edge where my wife is concerned.

If I thought the past few years were hard—pun intended —then every day recently has been torture. Each one harder than the last.

But knowing they have her. Listening to JD take what I've spent years dreaming of, all the while convincing myself I couldn't have, is the worst thing they could do. I'd sooner have them kill me than force me to listen to this.

A loud crack fills the air before Alana screams. My breath catches and my fists curl tighter at the thought of him hurting her.

Anger explodes inside me and before I know I've

moved, I'm on my feet pacing back and forth as her howl of pleasure rocks through the cell.

She likes it.

Of course she fucking does.

Sinking my fingers into my hair, I pull until it burns, punishing myself for enjoying this.

My cock weeps, and my balls ache. I'm desperate for a release, but I refuse to do it.

If I'm right and they're watching...

I shake my head as her cries of pleasure and demands for more continue.

I can picture them so clearly just from the basic description JD gifted me.

Her arms pressed against the wall, her ass sticking out while he's on his knees between her thighs, feasting on what I've denied myself all these years.

I told myself that I was a better man because I abstained. That I was a better man for her because I wasn't like those of her past.

But here she is being the whore Victor accused her of being.

I didn't want to believe it. I don't want to believe it. My sweet little Alana isn't a whore. She can't work for Victor and do his bidding.

But as much as I try to convince myself of that, I know it's true.

Is this a job?

Is she here not because she's finding intel for us but for him?

I continue pacing, realizing that the reason she's here doesn't really matter. It all ends in the same place.

I failed her.

All the promises I made, the future I painted.

I couldn't deliver on any of it.

She's almost back where she started, being used and abused by the cunts that run the streets of this town.

"Oh fuck, Julian," Alana screams. I've no idea where they are, but I do know that she's loud enough to wake the dead.

It leads me to wonder where Reid is.

"Yes. Yes. Yes," she chants.

Squeezing my eyes closed, I try to block everything out as my blood turns to lava.

I swear it burns straight through my veins and explodes out through my skin.

"JULIAN," she cries as he finally pushes her over the edge.

Every single muscle in my body is pulled tight as I have little choice but to listen to her ride out the waves of pleasure he's bestowed upon her.

Jealousy like I've never felt before surges through me. My knees buckle and I crash back to the bed as her release fades to nothing but a memory and a lingering high.

"Fuck, little dove. Your juices are dripping down my chin." JD groans, the smugness in his voice loud and clear.

That cunt knows what he's doing.

"JD," Alana begs, making my head hang.

This isn't over.

Of fucking course this isn't over.

"Such a good girl, Dove. Are you going to take my cock like the dirty little whore you are?"

My teeth grind as I picture him getting to his feet and lining himself up behind her.

Fuck, I miss sex.

I miss it so fucking much. But still, not enough to use her.

The desire to shove my hand into my pants and take the edge off right alongside them is strong.

But I hold back.

This is a game, I'm more than aware of that, and if I give in to my baser instincts then I'm handing myself over as a willing participant in this bullshit.

I try to convince myself that JD doesn't know the past. Doesn't know what she's been through, all the pain she's suffered.

Or maybe he does, and he doesn't care.

Or maybe she begged him for it.

I slam that thought down as soon as it emerges.

Of course JD isn't as strong-willed as I am. Even if he knew, she'd break him down. He's a fucking whore. There probably isn't a club slut he hasn't tapped.

I shake my head, remembering a time when the others probably said the same about me. I saw action in that place every night of the fucking week from the age of fourteen to the day I caught Alana in the woodland trying to escape.

It feels like another life. Like that Maverick was an entirely different person to the one I am now.

But despite getting my cock wet on the regular, I knew, without having to put any thought into it, which version of me is happier.

I was living a lie back then. I knew what was happening around me; I'd put the pieces together and it was poisoning me from the inside out because I didn't know what to do about it.

"Yes, yes. Please," she begs.

"Fuck, yeah. I fucking love it when you're desperate for my cock, little dove."

She cries out as he pushes inside her, his low grunt of pleasure filling the air.

Resting my elbows on my knees, I squeeze my eyes closed and twist my fingers in my hair in the hope the bite of pain is enough to drown them out.

It's not, of course. Nothing fucking is.

The sounds of their mixed pleasure and the unmistakable slap of skin on skin continue to echo around me as I drown in the worst kind of hell.

They should have just killed me.

If all they want is to take my wife from me.

I might as well be dead.

Every cry makes my skin burn hotter; every grunt makes my dick jerk as if he's the one getting the attention.

I feel everything they're doing so keenly, I might as well be right there with them.

It doesn't matter that I can't see them. After all these years of withholding, my imagination is vivid enough.

I rock back and forth, trying to force down the desire that's swirling within me like a hurricane. The power of it only increases with every second and every desperate plea for more hits my ears.

I'm balancing on a knife edge like a pre-teen who has no idea how to control his new desires and urges when a pretty girl walks by.

Shame burns down my neck.

This is wrong. So fucking wrong. But my body reacts nonetheless.

"Fuck, yeah." JD groans. "You're so fucking tight."

"Julian," she squeals as the sounds of their slick skin slapping continue to fill the air.

Make it stop.

For the love of God, make it fucking stop.

"Fucking addicted to this pussy, Dove. Love it. Fucking love it."

"Oh God," she whimpers.

I know that sound. Not only have I heard it recently, but I hear it in my dreams.

Every time I close my eyes, she's there. Taunting me, tempting me. Showing me everything I could have if I put my fears aside.

I'm terrified that I'll take what I need, and then she'll look at me like I'm one of them.

The kind of rough sex I like isn't the kind of thing that she should be forced to endure after everything she's been through.

She deserves someone who'll take their time with her, touch her as if she's something precious, something breakable instead of someone like me who will want to see her broken, her makeup smeared and tears streaming down her cheeks as she chokes on my dick.

"Fuck, fuck," I mutter as that image pushes me that much closer to the release my body craves.

"You're sucking me so deep, Dove. Can you feel me?" JD grunts.

"Yes. Yes. Fuck, I'm gonna—"

"Come all over my dick, Dove. I want your pussy strangling my cock as you scream my name."

Their loud panting breaths fill my ears for a few seconds before she falls.

"JULIAN," she screams just like he demanded she did.

And it's the final straw.

A low groan rumbles in my chest and my head hangs lower as my shame-filled body lets go with them.

"Fuck, Dove. Fuck. Fuck. Motherfucking fuck," JD chants before he comes. "Shit. Can you feel that? You're going to have my cum dripping out of you for hours now."

"MOTHERFUCKER," I bellow, as I learn he's taking her bare like the reckless cunt that he is.

Failure.

You're a failure and an embarrassment, Maverick Murray.

"Fucking look at that, Dove. So fucking pretty with my cum running down your thighs in the early morning sun."

Clapping my hands over my ears, I attempt to muffle his wicked words as desire still thrums through my body and the evidence of how much I enjoyed that little show cools in my boxers.

11

ALANA

My legs tremble as I lean against the wall, but they're only going to be able to hold me up for so long.

Regret surges through me as I rest my brow against my forearm and try to catch my breath.

The cool night air washes over my sweaty, heated skin and in only a few seconds, goose bumps are erupting, and a shiver races down my spine.

Coming down here was a mistake. I knew at least one of them would have been watching me. Hell, maybe even both.

But my need to at least attempt to get to my husband was too strong to ignore, even if I knew there wasn't any chance of it actually happening.

Reid isn't stupid enough to leave the door wide open for me. He isn't going to make anything about this new development easy to navigate.

He wants me desperate. It's how he's going to get his answers.

But what he doesn't seem to realize is that he already has the worst of my secrets. JD does now too.

They know what happened to me. Okay, so they might not have the sordid details, but they both have pretty vivid imaginations, so I'm sure they have a very good idea.

Plus, Reid knows my medical history. There's enough clues there to know how those men treated me over those years wasn't delicate.

My stomach knots and bile burns up my throat. But there's nothing left. I've already purged myself of the poison. Many many times over the years. Not that it seems to help.

Thankfully, movement behind me drags me from my dark thoughts and when I look back, I find JD with a smirk playing on his lips as he takes a photo of my pussy.

"What the fuck are you doing?" I shriek, jumping back and crossing my arms over my exposed breasts.

His eyes start at my feet and his lopsided, satisfied smirk only grows as he climbs up my body.

"Little late to cover your modesty, don't you think?" he taunts.

"Delete that photo," I demand, my heart pounding at the thought of it existing or landing in the wrong hands.

It's a pointless reaction. JD and Reid have been filming me since the first moment they locked me in that cell downstairs. I'm sure there's a hell of a lot worse they could take from that footage than whatever he just took but all that is easy to forget in the moment.

"Nah, I don't think I'll be doing that, little dove. It's going straight in my spank bank for my lonely nights."

I scoff. "Lonely nights? From what I've heard, you don't have many of those."

I might not have spent much time at the clubhouse, but

the few times I have been there at the same time he's been present, he's always had a club whore draped over him like a cheap throw.

"Careful, Dove. You're sounding a little jealous there."

"As if. They're welcome to you. You're nothing but a liar and a player."

If he's offended in the slightest by my words then he doesn't show it. In fact, as his grin grows, I'd be inclined to say he's actually proud of them.

"Oh, Dove. I'm that and so many other things," he confesses, his voice deep and raspy as he closes the space between us. "You're looking dirty, how about we go and get cleaned up?" he suggests, snagging his bottle of whiskey from the dresser and taking another swig.

My eyes drop to his lips as he swallows, and because he knows I'm watching, his tongue pokes out to lick away any excess.

Desire floods my core and my thighs clench as I vividly remember how those lips felt against me not so long ago.

He lowers the bottle and steps right into my body, letting his heat sear my skin.

"You know you want to, little dove. The shower is our place, after all."

Pushing the desire and the wicked promises that sparkle in his eyes aside, I focus on what I should say, not what my body wants.

"No. Take me to the basement to see Mav."

An amused laugh erupts.

"Nice try, Dove. Your pussy is good, but it isn't a ticket to get you everything you want. Not under this roof, anyway."

Irritation bubbles just beneath the surface as I stare into his mirth-filled eyes.

"I hate you, Julian Dempsey. As soon as I get the chance, I'm getting Mav and leaving all of this behind. You're nothing to me. Nothing."

His expression drops a beat before I spin around and run toward the stairs.

With the first orangey rays of dawn flooding the house, I miss the furniture as I make my escape.

My toe still burns from kicking the dresser in my search for the hidden door earlier, but I give it little thought. I'm used to a little pain. And it pales in comparison to the ache in my chest, knowing that Mav is stuck down there.

Does he even know where he is? Was he awake when Doc patched him up and they threw him down there?

Those questions and so many more spin around my head as I run up the stairs, the creaks nowhere near as loud now that I'm no longer trying to be discreet.

I want to say I'm surprised when I find a demon hiding in the shadows as I step into the hallway.

"It's okay," I snap. "I already know you're a creep. You don't need to hide."

With a smirk, Reid steps from the doorway he was loitering in, his eyes dropping to my naked body.

I shake my head as he takes his fill.

Holding my arms out from my sides, I let him indulge.

"You're just as sick as your best friend, you know that?"

He remains silent.

"Go on, if you want something," I offer, stepping closer. "Every other scumbag in this town has taken something from me, why should you be any different. You want to follow in Daddy's footsteps? Then what are you waiting for?" I taunt, the knot in my stomach tightening with every word I spit.

His expression darkens, his lips pressing into a flat line.

"I'm nothing like that cunt," he sneers. "The only thing I want from you is the truth."

"Would rather you steal pleasure from my body than make me confess to those."

His eyes narrow.

"So I've seen. You forgiven JD now, huh?"

"Sex and pleasure don't need to come from someone you like. I thought you of all people would know that. I can't imagine any woman you've been with actually liked you. Bet it didn't stop you either."

"You have a really low opinion of men, don't you?"

"You're surprised?" I gasp. "I have only ever met one who didn't want to use me, abuse me, or steal something from me. And all he's got in return is a gunshot wound and to be locked up in my cell."

"Oh, Pet," he muses, something dark flashing in his eyes. "I think he's got a lot more than that."

"I hate you."

He shrugs one shoulder, not giving a single shit about my opinion of him.

"You could be back in the basement right now. You should be thanking me."

"If you're suggesting that I get down on my knees and—"

"I'm not," he sneers as if the idea alone is the most disgusting thing he's ever heard.

"Right, of course not. I forgot you're disgusted by me."

"Pet, that's not—"

His words are cut off as footsteps begin climbing the stairs behind me.

"Oh, look out, Big Man wants in on the action. It'll be a tight squeeze but I reckon the three of us could just fit into your shower. You can take her pussy, I'm more than ready to slide into her ass." JD's words are a little more slurred compared to what I remember from downstairs.

"You need to sleep that shit off," Reid demands.

"Always such a party pooper," JD mutters as he steps up behind me and wraps his hands around my hips, dragging me against his body. "She's fucking hot, right?"

I fight against him, but his grip is too tight.

Reid's eyes focus on where his best friend is touching me and I swear fire burns bright within them.

"Let her go," he demands, his voice low and deadly.

JD hesitates, but after a second or two, he does as he's told.

"Always been a selfish prick," JD scoffs as the warmth of his body disappears before he steps around me. "Just know that I warmed her up. And if you eat her out, it'll be my cum you're swallowing."

There's a beat of silence following JD's taunt before Reid jumps into action, pinning his best friend against the wall with his forearm against JD's throat.

My eyes go wide as I watch them face off.

Anyone else would probably be intimidated being the object of Reid Harris's wrath, but it's clear that JD doesn't give a shit.

His lips curl into a smirk and he openly laughs at the devil looming over him.

There isn't much difference in their size, but Reid has him on muscle. I've no doubt that if they were to really go at it that Reid would end up the victor.

Something stirs within me as I think about them sweaty and throwing punches. Yeah... that really shouldn't be as hot as I'm imagining.

And fighting over me...

I lock that thought down as soon as it emerges. There is going to be no fighting over me.

JD might be right, the cum currently running down my thighs does belong to him, but he doesn't own me. He never will.

The only person I belong to is somewhere beneath my feet, and the first chance I get to step into his arms, I'm never going to let go.

Fuck revenge. Fuck everything we've been working toward. My time here has taught me that the only thing that matters is him. Him and our future.

"All of this would be easier to take if you just fucked her and got it out of your system. It's not like she hasn't offered. And it's not like you're not interested. I know you were watching us just now. And I also know that coming into your own fist was nowhere near as satisfying as it was to finish in her pussy."

"Enough." Reid growls, pressing harder against JD's throat. His entire body is vibrating with the need to cause JD some pain. But in true Reid Harris fashion, he keeps a lid on his anger.

I didn't think I'd ever meet someone with a similar level of self-restraint to my husband, but it seems that Reid and Mav might have a lot more in common than they'd ever care to know.

I guess it helps me to understand why they've never gotten along. They're too similar and have butted heads at any opportunity that has arisen over the years.

Finally, Reid releases his grip on JD's throat, allowing him to suck in a deep breath, the redness from the lack of air quickly fading from his face.

"Go and shower. You smell like cheap pussy."

"Nah, man. Nothing cheap about this one. She makes you work for it, don't you, Dove?"

"Go and do as you're told, Julian. We're done, remember?"

His eyes find mine over Reid's shoulder before he glances back at his best friend.

Something passes between them. Some kind of silent conversation that only a lifetime of friendship creates.

Jealousy twists up my stomach. I once had that kind of connection with Kristie.

A lump crawls up my throat as I remember our little glances across the room, allowing us to know exactly what the other was thinking.

It feels like another life now.

Without another word, JD caves and backs toward his bedroom door. He pauses on the threshold, giving me one last loaded look.

I might be saying we're done, but he isn't accepting it, that much is obvious.

I'm not expecting to feel anything as he disappears. But the second the click of the latch pierces the air, loss tugs at my chest, making the lump clogging my throat grow until I have no chance of swallowing it down.

My eyes burn with tears and my nose itches with the need to let them free. But I refuse to do that while under Reid's intense stare. With my shoulders low and defeated and my arms protectively wrapped around myself, I turn toward Reid's bedroom, more than ready to wash JD's scent from my body and his quickly drying cum from my thighs.

I've almost escaped when Reid's deep voice gives me pause.

"I need names, and I need everything you were

planning. He's as stubborn as you are, not that I'm surprised. But give me what I need and I'll let you see him."

My chin drops to my chest as I accept his words.

There are so many things I could say. I could just give him everything he wants. According to him, it should be easy enough.

I guess it is easy for anyone to think that who hasn't been through it.

They're just names, right? Memories of the past.

Wrong. Every single one of them still haunts me nightly. Saying their names out loud. Listing them off like some fucked-up roll call... A violent shiver rips down my spine.

And then there are the ones whose names I never knew...

Without responding, I kick the door closed, letting it slam on his face.

Without looking back, or at the TV screen, I march straight through to the bathroom. I turn the shower on and then stand in front of the sink, my reflection taunting me. For the longest time, I don't look up. I just stand there as steam fills the room, making the mirror fog and my vision blur.

You're stronger than this, Alana.

Throw your shoulders back and lift your head high.

Mav is here. He came for you. Now you need to grit your teeth and do what needs to be done to buy your freedom.

Squeezing my eyes closed, I suck in a deep breath and find some inner strength. Although it doesn't last very long. All the air comes rushing from my lungs as I stare at the broken mess I've been reduced to.

My new short hair is nothing but a bird's nest on my

head, my roots growing out fast. My skin is pale and I'm breaking out all over the place, thanks to stress and lack of water. My lips are dry and cracked, the circles around my eyes are dark, showing just how haunted I am with every night that passes here. My collarbone and hips protrude more than they have in years, thanks to the pathetic diet Reid has put me on. I can only imagine how bad it would have been if he never started feeding me, if JD didn't smuggle me in burgers and donuts.

But none of that is really what steals my attention. It's the love bites that litter my skin and the red marks on my throat from JD's harsh grip as he fucked me from behind.

Heat blooms on my cheeks and spreads down onto my chest as I remember him moving inside me.

I should have told him no, fought him off. But it was pointless to even try. We both knew I needed it, and that I'd take whatever he had to offer.

He called me a dirty little whore, and that's exactly what I am.

It's the reason why my husband has never touched me.

He's ashamed of me. Disgusted. And I can't even blame him for feeling that way. Hell knows I feel the same about myself.

With one last look at the bars now adorning my nipples, I turn away from the haunted version of myself and step into the shower.

The water is scalding and it burns every inch of my skin as it washes over me.

Closing my eyes, I tip my face up to the torrent and pray that it'll wash everything away. That when I step out of this massive stall that everything will be over and I'll be back home with Mav, living the life we've carved out for ourselves in this shithole town.

But it doesn't matter how long I stand there, or how red my skin becomes from the scalding water, when I finally reach out and shut the shower off, everything is still the same.

With one of Reid's towels wrapped around my body, I walk out of the bathroom, but one look at the image on the TV screen, and I pause, my world once again being ripped from beneath me.

12

REID

The clunk of the locks disengaging fills the air before I push the heavy door open. But I don't get the rush of sweetness I've become used to when I visit this cell. Instead, it's just like all the others again. Occupied by a male who smells anything but appealing.

Mav is laid out on the cot with his legs crossed at his ankles and his arms over his chest, his eyes locked on the ceiling.

He doesn't bother looking over, but he's more than aware of my presence. The tick in his jaw and the thinning of his lips give him away.

So far, JD has been the one to come down here and make sure he's still alive. I like to tell myself that I've done it for JD. His mental health is always better when he's busy and has a job. The last thing any of us need right now is for him to cave to the darkness that's threatening to drag him under.

I want to hate her for it. She did it to him. But honestly, I can't find it in myself because for a while there, I got to spend time with the boy who became my best friend all those years ago. The sparkle in his eyes was back, one that I didn't even know was still missing until he started to get closer to Alana.

But while I might not have noticed, I knew he was still suffering from the loss that rocked his entire world as a teenager. He's never going to forget, and I'd never expect him to. I just didn't realize how much of him was still lost to the events of that day.

I wish I could do something to make it better permanently. But as much as I might want to tell him that he can keep Alana, that we'll keep her locked up here for the foreseeable future, I know I can't.

What they have—had—will never be the same now that she's no longer the resident of this cell.

Maybe I made a mistake letting her up for dinner on Tuesday night. I was hoping to make her nervous. She was too at home down here and she was doing her best to wrap us both around her little finger. But up there, we were in my territory and fully on my terms.

I just never expected the night to end up with her almost dying of anaphylactic shock and her husband with a bullet wound in his shoulder.

Should have stuck to my first instinct and blown his head off.

Maybe JD would have been able to keep his spark then.

I grit my teeth, refusing to regret anything when there's no way of changing the events of that night or anything that's followed.

All I can do now is make the best of the situation we've been left with. That, and hide all the knives and blades in the hope I don't find JD bleeding out because of his fragile heart.

My grip on the bottle of water in my hand tightens

before I launch it across the room, watching as it lands on Mav's stomach.

He grunts in shock, his body jolting with the impact.

The cereal bar I stole from the kitchen follows, but he sees this one coming and manages to catch it.

"If you're expecting a thank you, you're going to be waiting a long time," he mutters, his voice deep and rough from its lack of use.

"I wasn't. I've got plenty of better things to be doing than waiting for anything from you," I confess, moving toward the chair I dragged in here not so long ago to watch his wife scream in her sleep.

Something tells me that this motherfucker won't be half as exciting to watch.

"If you've got better things to do, why the fuck are you getting comfortable?" He scoffs, watching as I rest my elbows on my knees and study him.

He looks like shit, and I can't help but smile.

"Thought it was time we had a chat?" I say, clenching and unclenching my fists.

His bruises from Fight Night are fading, but the yellow hue that lingers beneath his eyes and around his jaw fills me with a certain satisfaction.

"Hit me if you want. It's not going to get you anywhere."

"Probably not," I agree. "It would feel fucking good though."

Silence spreads between us, the air loaded with unspoken questions and crackling with hate.

I can't even pinpoint the moment things turned sour between us. Although, equally, I don't really remember a time we tolerated each other.

He's older, and my main memory of him from being a kid was him talking down to me like I was beneath him.

I am not, and never have been, beneath him.

The fact I had Harris blood flowing through my veins pissed him off. Yeah, he was powerful as Razor's demon offspring. But he wasn't a Harris and he knew he'd never have the authority I would as we grew up. So while he was older and bigger than me, he made sure I knew that I was the lesser of the two of us for a few years at least.

It was bullshit. A few inches in height doesn't make any cunt on this Earth any better than me. Nor does the number of years you've been alive.

Respect is earned, even if you're born as the prodigal child of Victor Harris.

I never expected anything because of my surname. I have earned every motherfucking bit of respect and fear the residents of this town show me. And I will fucking demand it from him now as well.

Finally, the silence gets too much for him and his need to know about his precious wife becomes too much to ignore.

"Where is Alana? What have you done to her?"

I continue to hold his stare, but eventually, my stone façade cracks and one side of my mouth twitches with a smirk.

His lips purse in anger and his own fists clench at his sides.

So fucking easy to play, Maverick Murray. Who holds all the power now?

"I think we both know that I'm not the one who's done anything to her," I taunt, my smirk growing.

Anger burns through him, making his face turn beet red.

"I'm sure listening to that was fun, but you should have seen them. Fucking porn worthy."

I wish I was lying. But sadly, I'm not.

I knew the second Alana escaped my room, but I also knew that JD hadn't followed orders and gone to bed to sleep off the bottle of whiskey he'd downed either.

The fact they both honestly thought I'd gone to bed and fallen fast asleep after everything just proved how much they underestimate me.

Standing in the shadows watching as JD turned the audio on to Mav's cell and fucked his wife against the wall was fucking epic. Even I can admit that.

"My boy has a lot of good things to say about your wife's pussy. Fucking stellar, apparently."

While he's furious at my words, I don't miss the flash of relief that I'm not talking from personal experience. Almost makes me regret not acting on the opportunities I've had. Almost.

"Bet it was fucking painful, huh? Listening to someone you hate take exactly what you want." Sitting up, I rub my jaw, thinking back. "The way she screamed his name. Fucking beautiful."

"Shut the fuck up." He grunts.

"But then I guess she knows all about putting on a show."

His warning growl rips through the air, bouncing off the bare walls of his cell. But he can do it all he likes; he can fucking come at me if he wants. He's not going to win here.

He is never going to win against me.

"You really had no idea that she was Victor's little whore, did you? How fucking pussy-whipped are you, man?"

His jaw pops with irritation as he glares at me.

"Oh, but you're not, are you? Because what my boy did last night with your wife isn't something you have any experience of. While she's been spreading her legs for Hawks all over town, you've never once gotten between them. Have you ever felt like more of a pussy than knowing everyone else is servicing your wife?"

He's on his feet before his angry roar hits my ears, but seeing as he's been down here with limited food and water, his actions are sluggish and I'm ready for him long before he launches himself at me.

Slamming my palms down on his chest, I shove him backward. He stumbles over his own feet and collides with the wall.

I have my forearm against his throat just like I did JD not so long ago, only I use a hell of a lot more force with this cunt than I did my best friend.

His face brightens again as I cut off his air.

"Watch yourself, Murray. If it were my choice, you'd have died the night I fired my gun."

"Then why the fuck aren't I?" he wheezes. "Going soft in your old age, Harris?"

My eyes narrow at his taunt.

"Fuck knows what your wife sees in you," I sneer, looking him up and down. "Nothing but an ass-licking fucking pussy, if you ask me."

"Good thing no one fucking asked you then, isn't it?"

We stare at each other. The only sounds that can be heard are our heaving breaths.

"You don't know anything about me," he seethes. "You judged me as a kid and you've never bothered to look close enough to see that it's nothing but lies you tell yourself to stoke your ego."

"Bullshit. I remember watching you running around

after my dad like, kissing his ass, hoping to be his favorite little pet. You're so fucking desperate for my position, it's pathetic."

"Is that really what you think? That I want to be you?" Amusement fills his eyes and his lips curl. I'm pretty sure if he could, he'd be laughing at me right now.

"Fuck you, Murray. You couldn't be me. Not in a million fucking years. Our fathers know it too. You're nothing but a weak little bitch who allows a woman to control his life. A woman who's running around town getting her rocks off while you're more than likely at home doing her fucking job. It's a fucking joke that they ever let you initiate."

Most of it is lies. Despite my words, Mav has proved himself as a loyal, doting soldier more than a few times. Something which pisses me off more than I want to admit.

He's been trained almost as well as I have.

While we might have spent our lives battling for supremacy, our fathers aren't any less competitive. They just so happen to be friends as well.

Something I doubt the two of us will ever be.

"It's funny. Everyone out there." He jerks his chin to reference people outside this cell. "They think you're this terrifying, dark, depraved, confident soldier. But really, you're a scared little boy. You're scared that Daddy is going to rip all of this away from you. You're terrified that me, or any of the others, might be better than you. And the only way to stop anyone from figuring all of that out is to ensure they're all petrified of you."

"Shut the fuck up," I snarl.

"Why? Did I touch a sore spot?"

Pulling my free hand back, I plow my fist into his stomach.

All the air rushes from his lungs in a painful grunt. As I step away, he doubles over, clutching his shoulder.

"I want to know everything," I demand, refusing to allow his previous conversation to continue.

This isn't about me or his bullshit opinion about the reason I am the way I am.

This is about him and Alana and everything they've been planning.

"Well, unlucky for you, I don't give a flying fuck about what you want," he grits out, standing to full height again.

A bitter laugh spills from my lips as I watch him battle the pain I've inflicted. It feeds some dark part of me, and I can't deny that the need for more is fucking addictive.

"Where is my wife, Harris?" he demands.

"Probably in JD's bed."

Credit where credit is due, he almost manages to cover his reaction to that statement.

"Why? Why do you have her? What do you want from her? From me?"

I smirk, unwilling to play my hand quite so soon.

13

MAVERICK

"Do you really think you're in any kind of position to be making demands?" Reid taunts. My fists curl with my need to wipe the smug fucking look off his face.

But it's pointless. He's already proved that he can overpower me.

He'd probably take me down even on a good day. But I've been down here for... too fucking long with barely any food or water. And thanks to that prick, I've got a fucking hole in my shoulder.

"She's my fucking wife, Harris. She's been missing for almost two weeks. You fucking abducted her. Why?" Desperation is clear as day in my voice, but I don't care.

He already knows that Alana is my weakness. It's the whole reason I'm here in the first place.

"She fucked up, needed punishing," he states simply, like it's just another day in his fucked-up world.

I guess it is. Fucking psycho.

"She doesn't deserve to be here."

He laughs again. There's no humor in it, just darkness and the need for pain and destruction.

"Do you have any idea of the shit she's been through? The last thing she deserves is to put up with your brand of fucked up."

He rests back against the wall and folds his arms across his chest. The move is way too casual for the suffocating tension of the room. But then that's just Reid for you. Totally unaffected by normal shit like everyone else on the planet.

"Oh, I don't know," he muses. "I think she's very much enjoyed her time with me. I gave her diamonds and everything."

My eyes narrow suspiciously while his dances with mirth.

Fucking asshole.

"What did you do to my wife, Harris?" I seethe.

His smirk grows, but he doesn't respond.

"I need some answers before I give you any," he explains.

"This isn't a fucking game. These are our lives. You've already stolen her from me. Let your yappy little puppy fuck her. What else could you possibly want?"

"Why did she agree to be Victor's whore?"

My teeth grind as I think about the things she's done for that cunt.

"I'd like to know the answer to that as well." Although, really, I know.

She wants revenge. And the best way to get intel for that is from the inside. It's what I should have been doing. But Victor, Dad, and Kurt, unsurprisingly, kept details of their sordid activities hidden. Even when I discreetly started digging, they weren't willing to divulge anything.

For all I know, Reid is fully invested in the whole fucked-up thing. Hell, he might have taken the reins from his father and be the one running the human trafficking ring they've got themselves tangled up with.

"Why does it matter to you what she does?"

"I'm not discussing my business with you. Hawk or not, I don't fucking trust you."

"Lucky for me, your wife has been much more amenable with giving me the information I need."

My stomach knots as I search his eyes for any hint that he might be lying.

Alana wouldn't give him anything unless she was one hundred percent confident that he can be trusted. It took her years to confess the horrors of her past, and I was looking after her. Yes, I might have abducted her, but I can't imagine there is much comparison between the way I treated her to the way he has.

"Where is she?"

"Safe. Looked after. For now," he taunts.

"I swear to God, if you hurt her then I'll—"

"You'll what, Murray? You're locked up in my basement, what do you really think you're going to do to me to save your precious princess."

"She's everything. She deserves so much more than this shitty town and these bullshit lives we're forced to live."

His chin drops in shock from my words. And for a moment, I get a real reaction from him. Maybe there is more to him than being Victor's robot.

He really wasn't expecting me to say that.

"You love this life. All you've ever wanted was to take over from your father, from mine. You want power," he states. His words are spoken so confidently that it gives me pause.

Suddenly, everything is starting to make so much sense.

"Do I? Right now, the only thing I want is my wife, but you seem to have her."

"What are the two of you planning, Mav? Why did she agree to be Victor's whore? Why was she fucking Kane and every other motherfucker Victor pointed at instead of you?"

"What has she told you?" I counter, unwilling to give him anything that would hurt Alana more than she already has been.

"I know they hurt her. I know you took her in and protected her in your fucked-up way. Would have been cute if you didn't fail, I guess."

"Fuck you."

"I know she loves you for some fucking reason." My heart swells with his words. Fuck, I miss her. "And I know she's desperate. Desperate for what you won't give her. I want names, Mav. I want to know who my father is working with."

My eyes narrow.

"You don't know?" I ask, shocked.

"I thought I knew everything," he mutters "But it turns out that hot little blonde upstairs has opened up something I didn't know existed."

"Fuck off," I scoff. "You really expect me to believe you don't have your fingers in every part of your father's business?"

"Do you?" he asks, turning it back on me.

"If I knew who he was dealing with, I promise you, they'd all be dead."

"Big promises for a man who can't protect his wife."

"Will you shut the fuck up?" I bark. I might feel like a massive fucking failure, but I really don't need Reid rubbing it in my face every chance he gets.

r RELENTLESS

I fucked up where Alana is concerned, and I'm unlikely to ever forget that she put herself back into the middle of her own nightmare.

"She did it to protect you," Reid suddenly states. "That leads me to one question... what the fuck did you do that was bad enough to give your wife no choice but to open her legs for any cunt who was interested?"

All the air rushes out of my lungs at his question.

"That's not important."

"I beg to differ. Correct me if I'm wrong, but my father is one of the men that leaves your wife screaming in her sleep on a nightly basis. Whatever you did must be pretty fucking bad to send her back to him, let alone agree to work for him."

"I want to see her. Please," I beg, no longer caring about what he thinks of me.

I'll get on my fucking knees if he lets me see her. Proves to me that his words about her being okay are true. From what I saw before he buried his bullet in my shoulder, she was far from fucking okay.

"You two are just as fucking stubborn as each other, you know that, right?"

I shrug one shoulder, not really giving a shit about his opinion of me.

"Wait," I cry as he moves toward the door.

He pauses with his fingers wrapped around the metal that's about to keep me in this place.

"I love her. I fucking love her more than anything. All I've ever wanted is to protect her. To give her justice. Everything else is just white fucking noise."

"Well, you're not the only one who wants her." My heart sinks as I remember her calling out JD's name as he made her come not so long ago. "And unless you're willing

117

to give me the information I want, you might never get a chance to give her anything."

With those ominous words hanging in the air, he slips out of the cell and locks the door up behind him.

I swear the roar of frustration that ripped from my lips the moment Reid locked the door behind him still echoes off the walls around me hours later.

No one else has been down to visit me. Not that I really expected it after the way our conversation ended, but still, something more than a fucking bottle of water and a cereal bar would be nice.

I sit on the bed with my feet planted on the floor on either side as I stare down at the notebook I found in here.

I know it's hers. I'd recognize the 'Keep out. Do not read.' scrawled on the front cover anywhere. I've no idea why she does it. I've never even lifted a cover of one of her diaries. It's not because I haven't been tempted. In those early days, when she refused to say anything about what she'd endured at the hands of the men who her father deemed worthy of corrupting her, I almost did it.

She was so broken, so terrified of every bang and every shadow. I was desperate to help her, but I had no idea how to do so other than to keep her safe. I wanted to understand. I figured that if I at least knew some of the horrors, then it might give me an idea how she felt and what she might need.

I sat like I am now many, many times. The only difference is that I was always in her room, sitting in the chair in the corner, watching over her, waiting for the first blood-curdling scream to tear from her lips.

I wanted to know who haunted her. Was it Dad? Victor? Kurt? Others? Or all of them?

Now that I know most of it, thinking of them in a room with her turns my stomach.

If it were as simple as pulling a trigger and taking them all down, then I'd have done it the day I discovered the truth.

But it's not that easy. Nothing ever is.

Killing them without proper planning would be a death sentence. With me gone, there would be no one left to show her how life could really be. I wanted to give her that more than anything else in my life.

Reaching out, I tuck my finger beneath the cover, my heart racing at the thought of seeing more of her handwriting, reading her thoughts.

She was the resident of this cell before I was. I don't need Reid's confirmation to know that's true. But what I don't know is how they treated her. Did they hurt her? Has JD been fucking her since she first got here? Has she fought back?

Clearly, she hasn't given Reid the answers he's demanding. Not that I expected her to do so.

He's right. We are both as stubborn as the other. But it also takes one to know one. I'm pretty sure that Reid Harris has us both beat on the most stubborn asshole in Harrow Creek.

He won't stop until he gets every last morsel of information out of us.

Prior to his visit earlier, I'd been adamant that I wouldn't give him shit.

But there was something different about our exchange. Yes, it was full of hatred and anger, like all our previous ones. But listening to him tell me what he really thought of me... the way he spoke about Alana being hurt... what if he didn't know what Victor was doing?

As far as I know, I'm the only one who looked deep enough to learn that the pretty smile Alana used to give everyone covered nothing but pain and fear. It wouldn't be too hard to believe that Reid didn't see it.

But his life is so tightly entwined with his father's. Is it even possible for him not to be involved in all his business deals?

Yes, it's well-known that Reid deals with drugs. He has control of everything from here to Rosewood and Maddison. But he also has his fingers in everything else. Dad might have the weapon trade under his control, but there isn't a week that passes where Reid doesn't let him know that he's watching. But what about Kurt, because he's the ringleader in all this. He's in control of the whores and the strip clubs in this town. Human trafficking is only a skip and a jump from that.

He has to know. Has to.

But what if he doesn't...

I lift the cover, staring down at her neat handwriting with my heart in my throat.

I might see the words, but none of them register. I'm too lost in my own head, remembering all the little notes I've found in different spots of the house over the years. The little reminders that she was safe, that she was with me.

I'm not stupid. I know the reason she agreed to marry me was because, above all else, she wanted revenge. It was never about love. Not for her at least.

All I can do now is hope that once we get the revenge she deserves, she won't turn her back on me and run off into the sunset to find her happily ever after.

I guess that's another reason I never fully committed to making her mine.

She might wear the ring and use my name, but without that final piece, she still has the freedom she deserves. I guess time will only tell whether she uses it or not.

14

ALANA

I wake to the sound of my stomach growling like a wild beast.

Groaning, I curl back up into the warmth of Reid's comfortable bed and will myself to go back to sleep. But as tired as I still am from everything I've endured over the past couple of weeks, my hunger is stronger.

Another angry growl fills the room and I cringe as I throw the covers back.

I'm wearing another one of Reid's t-shirts that I found in his drawers after my shower last night, along with a pair of his boxers that I've rolled at least four times around my waist in the hope of keeping them up.

What I really need are some clothes. Clothes, my own toiletries, and a freaking hairbrush. But I fear that demanding even one of those things will be met with deaf ears.

Unless you give Reid what he wants...

I need to. I know I do.

After my realization last night that we could actually be

all fighting the same enemy here, I vowed to dig up some strength and at least tell him the bare minimum.

If I'm right and he's gunning for Victor, just as much as we are, then hiding the truth could be the worst thing I could do. I should have told him right away.

If this whole thing is because we're on the same side, we could have been almost two weeks into planning a way to take him and his sick and twisted friends down.

But instead, I've been fighting them at every turn. Trying to keep my secrets along with everything Mav and I have been planning.

After cleaning up, I poke my head out of Reid's bedroom and find an empty hallway.

Relief and disappointment war within me as I stare at the spot where JD was sleeping before.

He didn't want to give up on me when I forced him to leave me alone. But he's no longer here. But then that look he gave me before he slipped into his room last night was full of filthy promises and his desire to fight me as long as he could.

The truth is, just like last night, there won't be much fighting necessary.

I can try and do the right thing as much as I want. But the second we're close, the moment he touches me, kisses me, I lose my goddamn head.

My need for him is all-consuming. The way he plays my body gives me exactly what I crave. It's too much to deny.

For so long, the only sex I've had has come in the form of selfish assholes who've only cared about getting off and then passing out. Suddenly having someone who cares, who seems to enjoy getting me off as much as he does himself is addictive.

I shake my head, trying to retain the sensible part of my brain as I descend the stairs.

Just like I suspected, the creaks are nowhere near as loud as they were last night. It's amazing how different everything seems in the bright light of day.

More silence greets me as I hit the ground floor. I was expecting to be accosted by someone by now. Either growled at by Reid or teased by JD. Being here without either of them breathing down my neck is unnerving, to say the least.

Turning back on myself, I head toward the kitchen, telling myself that the promise of food and coffee is the reason I go there first. But really, it's where I expect them both to be.

The scent of rich, dark coffee permeates the air. They've been here fairly recently so I can't imagine they've gone too far.

But when I step into the vast room, I don't find anyone waiting for me.

My brows pinch as I look around, assuming my eyes must be playing tricks on me. But they're not on the couches, at the island, or in the kitchen.

Spinning around, I look back out into the hallway.

"Hello?" I call but get nothing but my echoed voice back.

Slowly, a slow smile curls at my lips.

Am I alone?

Truly alone in the king's castle.

A weird kind of excitement explodes in my belly at the thought of the freedom I might have.

I wiggle my fingers and toes as a whole host of ideas about what I could do with this newfound freedom fills my mind. Obviously, breaking into the basement is the most pressing issue, but there are so many more opportunities here.

But first, I need carbs and caffeine.

Walking back into the kitchen, I begin opening cupboards and searching each one until I find the mugs.

"Could you be any more boring," I mutter to myself when every single mug is black and the same style.

I mean, I know the owner of this castle has a stick shoved so far up his ass that I'm not sure it's possible to pull out, but still, I thought everyone had at least one novelty mug. Clearly, Reid Harris is too good for that.

Plucking one of the mugs out, I place it under his beloved coffee machine and press a couple of buttons until it starts whirring to life. The sound of beans grinding fills my ears before the liquid gold begins to flow, flooding my nostrils with its rich scent.

My stomach growls in excitement, my lethargic muscles already getting excited about the hit that will give them a whole new lease on life.

But while the coffee is much needed, it's not going to be enough.

Spinning around, I pull open both doors of the refrigerator and scan the shelves.

I'm unsurprised to find it fully stocked with ingredients to make a whole host of meals.

I pull the creamer from the door before focusing on the freezer.

"Bingo," I sing when a packet of partly baked pain au chocolat catches my eye.

It might be long past breakfast now but who gives a crap. Time stopped meaning anything to me the second I was dragged into this house.

Scanning the kitchen again, I find a top-of-the-range air

fryer sitting on the counter. Reid might not be into novelty mugs, but it seems the Devil of Harrow Creek didn't escape the air fryer epidemic of twenty-twenty.

Laughing to myself at how even the biggest of gangsters can be peer pressured by the right product, I pull one of the fryer drawers open and drop four pastries inside.

Greedy of me? Hell, yeah.

Do I care? Fuck, no.

I set the timer and reach for my coffee.

With a new sense of freedom—no matter how false—I cup the warmth in my palms and walk over to the floor-to-ceiling windows that I remember looking out before eating that fateful curry.

The sky is clear and the sun is shining bright. The need to feel that warmth on my skin is all-consuming and before I know what I'm doing, I have my fingers wrapped around the handle and I'm attempting to pull it open.

I shouldn't be disappointed, I was expecting it but still, my shoulders drop and a frustrated puff of air rushes past my lips.

I wouldn't even run...

Everything I want and need is in this house. I might have longer-term plans to run as far away from this place and the men who reside under this roof, but it won't be without the man currently locked in the basement. He's saved me time and time again, there isn't a chance that I won't do the same for him.

I remain in the same place, looking out over the town that has ruined so many promising lives over the years as I sip my coffee.

Each mouthful tastes like heaven, and the fact I'm able to drink it without having eyes on me or being forced to remember I only have it because they've allowed it makes it taste better than any other I've had here.

My stomach growls again right on cue and I rush over to the air fryer as it signals my pastries are done.

Sucking in a deep breath of buttery, sweet goodness as I pull the tray open, I quickly transfer them to a boring black plate and take them over to the huge, swivel chair that allows me to continue staring out at freedom.

"Oh my God." I moan the second I take my first bite.

Thank God I'm alone because the speed in which I devour every single one of them is nothing short of embarrassing. And the second I'm done, I force the chair around to gaze at the kitchen again, trying to remember what else I saw in the fridge that I could inhale.

Trying not to be a total pig, I talk myself down from eating my body weight in food. I haven't been locked up for days. I've no reason to believe that I won't have this opportunity again. I don't need to act like a crazy woman.

Instead, I abandon my plate and mug next to the sink. I don't bother washing it up because I suspect the mess will piss Reid off when he returns, and making his eye twitch in annoyance is totally worth it. After that I set about exploring my surroundings.

With my eyes locked on the wall of the hallway, looking for the elusive hidden door, I make my way to the next room.

If only I could remember more about the night I was brought up here. If I weren't so distracted by JD then I might be able to pinpoint exactly where the fucking door is.

"Oh wow," I gasp, stepping into what must be Reid's office.

It's... well... exactly as I would have predicted.

It's just like him. Every single thing in this room is bigger than life. Scary, overpowering. Intimidating.

From his colossal black desk to the ridiculous wing-backed chair that sits behind it and the floor-to-ceiling bookcases filled with row after row of books.

Stepping up to the seemingly endless shelves, I reach out, tracing the spines with my fingertips.

Shakespeare. Dickens. Austen. Hardy. Brontë.

A laugh of disbelief punches from my lips as I take in what I can only imagine to be special editions.

I never in a million years would have thought that Reid Harris and classic literature would ever be said in the same sentence. But then again, that man is turning out to be full of surprises.

Eventually, I make it to the other side of the room, and drop into what can only be described as his throne.

I laugh again at the pure insanity of all this. Maybe it's the sugar high and rush of caffeine, but once I start, I can't stop.

Although that all comes to a crashing halt when a door slams somewhere in the distance and a deep voice booms, "Bro, where you at?"

I swear my heart stops dead in my chest. It didn't occur to me before stepping in here that I might not be welcome.

He left the door open and me alone in the house, apparently. He must have known that I'd go snooping. He should have locked it if—

"Reid?" the voice bellows. "You trying to hide from us?"

My eyes dart from the door to the desk before me as I question whether I should be attempting to hide beneath it or if the man heading my way isn't about to blow my head off for being somewhere I shouldn't. But I can't. My body is frozen with fear for who's about to walk through that door.

The footsteps get louder and only a second later, shadows fall over the doorway.

My heart thunders, threatening to beat right out of my chest. My body is still immobile.

If this is Victor or one of his henchmen coming to collect me then—

"Well, well, well, lookie what we have here."

"Alana Murray, what a fucking surprise. Big bro didn't mention that you'd earned some privileges."

15

ALANA

The second I lock eyes on two of Reid's little brothers, Devin and Ezra, I relax. Although, not completely.

They might not be as infamous as their big brother but both of them could pull a gun on me without much thought.

"I guess you don't know all his secrets either then," I muse, keeping my shoulders wide and my head high.

If I don't cower to Reid then there is no fucking way I'm cowering to these two idiots.

"Fuck that. I've no interest in the twisted shit that goes on in his head," Ezra explains. "Could make use of his coffee machine though. Dev, you in?"

"You know it? Rapunzel?" Devin asks, his eyes holding mine as if he's waiting for me to be intimidated.

I might be sitting here in Reid's domain, wearing only one of his shirts, but Dev's going to need to try harder than that.

"Coffee would be great, thanks."

With a nod, Ezra ducks out of the room, leaving me under the piercing, curious stare of Devin Harris.

"So..." he starts, moving toward me ominously.

Pulling his gun from his waist, he lays it on the table before rapping his knuckles on the top, making me startle, much to his amusement, before he drops into one of the chairs opposite me.

He spreads his legs wide, his inked arms draped casually considering there is what I can only assume is a loaded weapon between us.

"Finally got on your knees and blew Reid well enough to be granted freedom then?"

"And that just goes to prove how well you don't know your big brother," I point out, crossing my legs and folding my arms beneath my breasts.

Like the predictable male that he is, his eyes drop.

"You might be weak enough to be bought by a sloppy blow job, but your brother isn't."

"So how'd you do it then?" he asks.

"He invited me to join him and JD for dinner one night. Haven't been back down since."

Devin considers this for a moment before nodding as if he actually understands.

"Where are they?"

He smirks before dragging his thumb along his bottom lip.

Devin is hot, don't get me wrong. But his pretty boy image doesn't do it for me like it does most other women in Harrow Creek. I like my men to be a little rougher with harder lines and fiercer eyes.

"And here I was thinking you had them wrapped around your little finger, Rapunzel."

"Can you stop calling me that? Rapunzel was locked up in a tower, not a basement. Maybe you should pick up a book or two every now and then," I say, gesturing to those surrounding us.

"Nah, I'm more of a 'get out there and experience the world' kind of guy."

"Long-winded way of saying you can't read, but whatever," I taunt.

His eyes narrow dangerously, but I don't show an ounce of fear.

If I can survive Reid Harris and his torture chamber, then Devin's anger will be a walk in the park.

"I'm a student at MKU, if you weren't aware."

Pressing my palms to the desk, I stand, holding his eyes as I tower over him.

"I wonder how much Daddy had to pay to make that happen. Between you and Ez, it must have cost him a small fortune."

Devin scoffs.

"Oh, come off it. We all know Ellis is the only one that should be gracing the campus of Maddison Kings U."

Devin's lips press into a thin line.

"Are you always this much of a bitch?" he asks. "No wonder Kane couldn't stand spending time with you."

I stumble back, hating that I show any kind of weakness. But damn it. His words fucking hurt.

I knew Kane was a job. That the only reason he was spending time with me was because Victor told him he had to. But being with him was the closest I got to spending time with a friend than I have in a very long time —Mav aside. I actually looked forward to our nights together.

Yes, it was all an act. The person I was when we were together was a fake. Designed to lure him in and do my job.

But still. Out of all the men, he didn't look at me like I was nothing. And we had a laugh. Or at least, I did.

Seems I might have been the only one who got anything good out of our time together.

"Oh, did that hurt, Rapunzel? You didn't actually think he liked you, did you?"

I shake my head hating that my eyes burn with tears.

"Aw, you did."

"There's only one man I want, Devin. And I can assure you, that isn't Kane Legend. He's all Letty's."

His lips pull into the briefest of scowls at the mention of Letty, but he quickly recovers.

I know all about the situation between them thanks to gossip from both Kane and Mav over the years. I might not have been involved in Harrow Creek personally much over the years, but that doesn't mean I don't know what happens out on those dark and corrupted streets.

"So," I try again. "Where are they?"

He watches me walk around the desk, his eyes dropping to my bare legs as I move.

"Meeting with Victor."

My steps falter and he notices. Of course he does.

"Why?" I blurt, my heart speeding up again. I sat and watched the entire time that Reid was in Mav's cell last night, desperately trying to lip-read their conversation. While I picked up on a few bits and the general tone of the discussion, no matter what I did to the TV, I couldn't get the audio to work.

Mav could have told him anything. Or everything.

Reid and JD could know it all. And they—

I reach for the wall to catch myself. Sucking in deep lungfuls of air, I try to keep my shit together.

I shouldn't care if they're going to have it out with

Victor. I shouldn't be worried about how he'd react. If he'd pull a gun and put them down there and then.

But I fucking do.

"Alana?" Devin asks, his voice softer than it has been since he found me here.

The warmth of his hand lands on my shoulder and I flinch away.

"Don't," I snap. I might not have an issue with Reid or JD's hands on me, but for some reason, Devin's feels wrong. It burns. And not in a good way.

"Uh..." he starts, instantly tugging his arm back. "Sorry?" The fact it comes out like a question, like he might be even a little bit uncomfortable with this situation right now makes me feel better. "How about that coffee, huh?"

"Sounds good," I mumble, finally getting my legs to move as my head spins and my shoulder continues to burn from his touch.

"What did you do?" Ezra barks, his eyes locked over my head as Devin trails me back to the kitchen.

"Me?" he asks innocently. "I didn't do anything."

Ezra ducks down, giving me little choice but to look at him. "You good?"

Sucking in a deep breath, I focus on his eyes as I fight to calm the riot in my head. They're kinder than his brothers, softer, although only slightly.

"Wonderful. Best day of my life," I deadpan.

"That's what we like to hear," Ezra says, playfully slugging me in the arm. "Here." He passes me a mug and gives me a small smile. "Ignore him. He can be an asshole when he wants to be."

"Takes one to know one," Devin mutters as he falls onto Reid's couch, spilling coffee on the cushion as he goes. I guess that half explains why everything is black.

I stand awkwardly as Ezra follows suit and sips on his steaming black coffee with the ease Reid does.

"We don't bite," he says when he notices me hovering.

"Not all the time," Devin adds.

I look between the two of them, trying to get my head around all of this.

"You knew he wasn't here," I state. "So why did you call out when you first got here like you were expecting him to pop up?"

"It was hours ago he called to say he was heading to the club," Devin says innocently. "Thought he might have been back by now."

"You're lying," I accuse. "He sent you to babysit me, didn't he?"

Devin chuckles. "Thinking pretty highly of yourself there, Goldilocks."

My teeth grind at the new nickname. Maybe Rapunzel wasn't so bad.

"He asked us to stop in once we were back from our job," Ezra confesses.

"What job?" I ask, already knowing they won't give me anything.

"Not much. Just hiding your husband."

"What?" I blurt. "He's downstairs, isn't he? I saw him. Him and Reid were— Oh my God. Tell me Reid didn't—"

"Whoa," Ezra says, standing in front of me, gripping my upper arms in his hands as I start to lose control of my lungs. "It's okay. He didn't mean literally."

He says the words, but I don't hear them. The only thing I can focus on is the blind panic the thought of either of them hurting Mav brings on.

My heart races and my lungs fight for air. I suck in heaving breaths but nothing happens.

"Shit. She's having a panic attack, you idiot."

"Me?"

"Yes, you. Why did you have to say it like that?" Ezra snaps.

"Because it's funny. I didn't think she'd actually take it seriously."

"Fucking moron," Ezra mutters as he pushes me back onto the couch beside Devin and drops to his haunches in front of me. "Look at me, Alana."

His voice and words float around me as I fight to catch my breath. I hear them, but I also don't at the same time.

"Alana?" he snaps, shaking my knees, giving me little choice but to look up. "Breathe with me, yeah?" He nods as if it'll help me agree before he begins breathing deep and slow. "In. Out. In. Out. That's it," he encourages before shooting over his shoulder, "if he comes back and there is a single thing wrong with her, he'll—"

"Honey, we're home," a familiar voice calls before the front door slams and two heavy sets of feet pound this way.

"What have you done?" Reid demands the second he marches into the room and surveys the scene.

"Dove." JD gasps before his shadow falls over me and Ezra is physically shoved aside. "What's wrong?" he asks, his voice rough and tormented as his palms slide up the outside of my thighs.

"Panic attack," Ezra says as I'm engulfed by Reid's darkness.

"Why?" he barks.

Ezra sighs. "Because of this idiot, obviously."

"The fuck did you say?"

"Jeez, it was just a fucking joke. Why does everyone have to take everything so seriously?"

The brothers continue to bicker around us, but my

focus is on JD and the warmth of his hands on my legs. I quickly find myself lost in his electric blue eyes. They're lighter than I remember from yesterday, less haunted.

"Breathe with me, Dove. In." He does as he says, pinching his lips together before releasing the breath. "Out."

I follow his instruction, allowing deep gulps of air to fill my lungs.

"I'm okay," I whisper after a minute or two, feeling stronger.

"Shit, Dove. You gotta stop scaring me like that," he murmurs, as if speaking any louder will scare me. Lifting his hand, he gently cups my cheek before leaning forward and resting his brow against mine.

I'm so lost to him that I don't realize everyone else has stopped arguing. Or at least until Reid's intrigued stare makes one side of my face burn up.

"I'm okay," I say louder, sensing that Reid needs to hear it too.

Glancing over, I find exactly what I'm expecting, his dark, concerned stare trained right on me.

"Why don't you take her upstairs," he suggests. "Show her what you got."

Now that gets my interest.

16

JD

Alana stares up at me with big glistening eyes. The shadows still linger from her panic attack, but they're clearing.

The thought of me being the one to be able to do that for her makes a lump crawl up my throat. For once, could I be enough?

I squash that thought as fast as it arrives. It's pointless thinking such things. I already know the answer. The only one who is enough for her in this house right now is residing under our feet.

With a sigh, I try to forget about reality and reach for her hand.

"Come on, I've got something for you."

Her eyes light up and her smile grows. My heart swells at the sight.

Yeah, that's better.

Without another word from the guys, I tug her out of the room before gathering up the bags I dropped in the doorway when I saw her sitting there with Ezra.

"I thought you went to see Victor?" she asks, her voice

cracking on his name, letting me know exactly how she feels about the cunt.

Feeling's mutual there, little dove.

Going to the clubhouse after being summoned by Victor was not my idea of a fun way to spend the morning, especially after the lack of sleep from the last few days.

Hell, I can't tell which way is up let alone be expected to hold my own with that prick.

Turns out, there are now not only issues with drug supply, but they're having problems with their weapons dealer too.

Fuck knows why we got called into that little discussion. I guess they had to make up numbers, seeing as Mav is MIA.

They didn't say much about him. Honestly, I'm not sure they really cared.

I couldn't help but wonder if they'd have the same concern over Reid vanishing. Victor likes to make out that we're all such important parts of the Harrow Creek Hawks machine, but the second a wheel falls off, he seems to just steamroll his way right through it.

First Gray, then Alana, and now Mav. Who else is going to vanish off the face of the Earth?

Hopefully him.

I let my imagination run away with itself for a moment, picturing a scene where Reid, his brothers, and I stand over Victor. All of us with our guns raised and him finally realizing it's over.

Fuck, it's been such a long time coming.

"Julian?" The soft voice drags me from my daydream and anchors me back to reality and I turn to look at her as I grab the last bag. "Where did you go?"

"Nowhere, Dove. I'm right here with you," I promise,

gathering all the bags in one hand and taking hers with the other.

"We did go to see Victor," I confirm, remembering that she asked a question as we climbed the stairs. Deep rumbling voices filter up from the kitchen, but I don't bother trying to listen. It'll just be Reid giving Devin and Ez a dressing down, I'm sure.

"Neither of you are covered in blood so I'm assuming he's still alive," she mutters.

"You'd assume correctly," I say regretfully as I take the final few steps and pull to a stop outside my bedroom door.

"What are you doing?" she asks, bumping into my back, as she continues to head for Reid's room.

"I think it's time I got you in my bed, little dove."

"Oh, not that's not hap—"

"You've spent hours in his room, making it smell all sweet. It's my turn," I say, tightening my grip on her hand and tugging her into the room before she has a chance to argue.

I slam the door behind us and stand in front of it, in case she has any crazy ideas about trying to escape.

She stands before me, her shoulders rising and falling with her rapid breathing as she takes in my room.

It's different to Reid's. I get that. But I can't imagine she's shocked by the state of it. She knows me well enough to know that I'm a bit of a hot mess.

"Is there room for me?" she teases.

"I know I'm not a neat freak like Reid, but it's not that bad, Dove," I say, pushing from the door and pressing my front to her back.

"JD," she half warns, half moans.

"Go sit on the bed, little dove. You've got something to unwrap."

Shamelessly, I grind my semi against her ass.

"I didn't come up here to play with your dick," she insists before stepping forward and finally doing what she's told.

"Why were you freaking out downstairs?" I ask, unable to forget the panic on her expression when I stepped into the room.

"Devin," she says with a sigh.

"Don't listen to anything that moron says," I tease.

"He said they'd been out hiding Mav," she confesses quietly.

I can't help but laugh, although there is no amusement in it. Only pain.

It doesn't matter that she's here, that she's sitting on my bed, in my room.

Her heart is still in the basement. And I'm not sure anything I ever do will be good enough to change that.

I pause, my need for her and my fears colliding into a maelstrom of confusion inside me.

But in the end, her sweet scent and her warmth is too much to deny and I drop onto the bed beside her.

"Mav is fine, Dove. He's still in your cell doing his time. You've been watching him," I guess. "So you knew that already."

"I know," she whispers, embarrassed by her reaction. "But Reid—"

"Reid won't touch him, Dove. You don't need to worry about that."

She swallows nervously but decides against arguing and nods instead.

"What's in the bags?"

"I'm glad you asked," I say with a wide smile splitting

my face. "After we saw Victor, I took Reid on a little shopping trip. Which, I might add, he loved."

"I'm sure he did," she mutters. "He seems like the average shopaholic."

I chuckle as I slide back, placing the bags between us.

"Go on," I say encouragingly.

Hesitantly, Alana pulls open the first bag and reaches inside.

I can't keep the smile off my face because I know she's gone for the best one first.

"You bought me lingerie?" she balks, holding a black lace bra and panty set in front of her.

"Hell yeah, I did. What do you think?"

She studies it, her head slowly shaking from side to side in disbelief.

"I— I think..." Her words trail off as she looks at the label. "I think you're way too familiar with my tits to have selected the right size."

"Dove, I'm nowhere near familiar enough with them," I confess, my eyes dropping to where her nipples are pressing against the fabric of Reid's shirt. "How about you try that on for me so I can see just how good a fit it is."

"Yeah... maybe not," she says, shoving the underwear back into the bag and reaching for another.

We got her everything we could think that she might need while living in a house with men.

Clothes, shoes, toiletries, hair stuff. I even went all out and bought her a new notebook with a matching pen that has a massive pom-pom on the top. Girly as shit. And unsurprisingly, it's the sight of the notebook that makes her eyes really light up.

"Figured a new start up here needed a new book," I explain.

She looks at me, her eyes once again glassy with tears.

"Thank you," she says, her voice quiet and broken.

Reaching out, I cover her hand that's resting on her thigh with mine. "Anything," I promise. "If we missed something, just tell me and I'll send Reid back out for it."

"You'll send Reid for it?" she asks, quirking a brow at me.

"Hell yeah. I've got a girl in my room. There's no fucking way I'm leaving."

"JD." She laughs, making me realize how long it's been since I heard it.

"I'm sorry," I blurt, my eyes holding hers in the hope she can see the honesty in those two words.

She stills, her eyes narrowing as tension pops around us.

She might be angry with me but that doesn't mean the chemistry that's always been between us isn't crackling away, waiting for the explosion.

"For what, exactly?" she finally whispers.

Reaching out, I tuck a lock of her short blonde hair behind her ear, making her shudder before I cup her jaw, ensuring she can't turn away from me.

"For everything I've done, and for all the things I can't."

Her eyes shutter as she absorbs my words.

"Yes, I made a stupid bet with Reid, but only because I wanted to prove to him that his fear tactics wouldn't work on you. And it might not surprise you to hear that he hates being proved wrong," I explain with a smirk. "I felt what we had, and it was a stupid thing to suggest. But I can assure you that this, us, it isn't because of that."

"There isn't an us, Julian. I'm married to the man you're currently holding hostage in your basement."

"Yeah, I know. I just..."

"You can't keep him down there just because you want me to yourself."

"He's down there because he broke in and held a gun to Reid's head."

"And Reid shot him. Isn't that enough?"

I shrug one shoulder.

"I need to see him, JD," she begs, her voice cracking on my name.

"I know, baby," I assure her, stroking her jaw with my thumb.

She leans into my touch and it makes tingles race down my arm and spread through my body.

"I meant it, Dove," I whisper. "I am so—"

Her fingers press across my lips, stopping my words.

She shakes her head, sadness filling her eyes.

"It doesn't matter. No amount of apologies will change either the past or the future."

"You need to talk to Reid. Really talk to him."

"I know."

"Everything he said yesterday, the things he alluded to..."

"They're true. All of them and more," she confesses, pain filling her eyes before she looks down at her lap.

"Hey," I say, wrapping my hands around her waist and effortlessly lifting her from the bed in favor of my lap.

She fights me, but not hard enough to think she doesn't want it.

Her legs fall on either side of my hips. I press one hand to the small of her back and slide the other up to wrap it around the side of her neck.

"You've got nothing to be ashamed of."

A self-deprecating laugh erupts from her.

"Easy for you to say. You don't know the half of it."

"It doesn't matter what I do or don't know," I force out, desperately trying to keep a lid on the anger bubbling inside me as I think about anyone touching her without permission. "You survived. You're here. And you're incredible, Dove. So fucking incredible."

"Anyone would think you just want to get laid," she muses, refusing to hear what I'm saying.

"Stop deflecting," I demand, twisting my fingers in her hair and dragging her head back so she can't hide from me. "We all have pasts, Dove. Things we'd rather forget, darkness that lingers just under the surface, waiting to suck us down and swallow us whole. Having them doesn't make us weak, Dove. They make us stronger. They make us survivors."

My chest aches and I have to fight to stop my hands from trembling as I rip myself open and show her a little bit of the real man who hides beneath the lazy smiles and stupid jokes.

Her eyes search mine, desperately trying to find a hint of that darkness I'm talking about. But while she's sitting on my lap, the warmth of her skin seeping into mine, I doubt she'll find any.

Her presence is better than any medication I've been forced to try over the years. Better than any pain I can inflict. One look in her eyes and it all ebbs away. My only focus is her and the way she makes my heart race, even when she's doing the simplest of things.

Straightening my spine, I close the inches separating us. She gasps as my chest brushes her nipples and my cock continues to swell beneath her.

I lean forward and she licks her lips, getting ready for

the kiss she thinks is coming. Only, at the last minute, I change direction and go for her neck instead, sucking on her sweet, soft skin until she moans, her body going lax in my arms.

Fuck, this woman. I can't get enough of her.

17

ALANA

My body erupts with sensation as JD's lips move against the sensitive skin just beneath my ear.

I thought he was going in for a kiss, but he knew that I could possibly stand strong and stop that.

This though?

I stand no fucking chance as desire shoots off around my body, making my core ache and my fingers and toes tingle.

It shouldn't be this good with him.

He should be off-limits.

No. I'm the one who should be off-limits.

I'm the married one.

But at some point, all the lines have been blurred. And while I know I should be stopping it, I can't.

I'm strong in so many ways. But not right now.

"Mav," I cry when his teeth sink into my skin, making my body burn for him.

"Dove." He growls. "I know you're aware of who's doing this right now."

"Y-yeah, I am," I stutter. "I need to see him, JD. Please."

"What if I need you more?" he counters, refusing to take his lips off me.

His hands slip under Reid's shirt. The heat of his palm makes my temperature soar.

"Julian," I cry when he grips my ass, dragging my pussy against his already hard length.

"Fuck. That's better."

"I'm not yours," I force out, knowing it's going to hurt him. He stills. His lips against my collarbone. "I can't be yours."

"Maybe not. But I'm willing to pretend right now."

A shriek rips from my lips as he flips us. I land on my back in the middle of his bed.

Dragging Reid's boxers from my legs, he spreads my thighs. Letting his eyes linger on my pussy as he reaches behind him and drags his shirt off.

My own mouth waters as he exposes his ink and muscles, but before I really get a chance to take him in, he falls on top of me, planting his hands on either side of my head.

"My dove," he whispers before finally dipping lower and stealing my lips in a filthy kiss.

I want to fight him, hold onto the frustration. But I can't. Once again, he's shattered through my walls and left them as nothing but a ruined pile of bricks.

"Fucking hell, Dove." He moans into our kiss. "I fucking missed you."

"Julian." I gasp when his hands slide under Reid's shirt, dragging it up my body, exposing me to him.

He only pulls away from my lips when the fabric forces us to.

"Look at you," he muses.

I don't follow his gaze. I don't need to see how skinny

and weak I am. It's a reminder I don't need of why I shouldn't be doing this right now.

"If I could, I'd give you the fucking world, little dove," he confesses before dipping his head and giving my nipple a teasing lick.

It's the first time he's touched them, other than cleaning them up after Reid pierced them.

"Oh shit," I gasp when the light touch alone sends a bolt of lust straight to my clit. They're sore still, but the hurt is so freaking good.

He smirks at me, loving how responsive I am.

"These are going to be so much fun."

But despite my wanting him to do it again, he lifts back up to claim my lips again.

He drops to one elbow, hooks my opposite leg around his waist and just kisses me.

We make out like teenagers for the longest time. He wants more. His hardness continually grinds against my pussy as if it can't wait. But at no point does he free his dick and slip inside me.

He could easily. I don't think it's a secret to either of us that I'm slick and more than ready. But he seems to be content just being close, having our limbs entwined and his lips on mine.

"Can't get enough of you." He groans in my ear before nipping the soft skin and making my hips roll. "Up you go," he says, before seamlessly flipping us and settling me across his waist.

Placing my hands on his chest, I grind myself against him, letting him know that I'm getting a little impatient to move this along.

"I love it when you're desperate for me. I can feel how hot and wet you are through my pants."

"Could feel it against your dick if you took them off," I counter, looking through my lashes at him.

"Whore," he whispers with a teasing smile.

Taking matters into my own hand, I shimmy down a little, giving me access to the buttons on his pants. I have them open in only a few seconds, and with his help, we have them over his hips, letting his pierced dick spring free.

"Fucking knew you'd love it," he croaks as I stare down at the ladder that climbs up the underside of his shaft.

My core clenches as I think about how it feels inside me, how all those extra notches hit every single nerve, leaving me flying higher than I think I've ever been before.

As much as I want to stare at the beauty of it, I need to feel it move against me so I climb back over him, grinding my sensitive skin against the bars.

"Fucking hell, Dove. Your pussy is fucking soaked for me."

With his deep voice filling my ears, I grind harder, letting my head fall back as I focus on the sensation.

"Julian," I cry, getting close to the release I'm so desperate for from this alone.

"Put me inside you, Dove. I want to feel your pussy strangling me."

"Oh God." I moan as his dirty words perfectly hit the mark.

Wrapping my fingers around him, I lift up and position him at my entrance.

I take his tip inside me and watch in delight as his eyes roll back.

I've always known that what I have between my legs holds more power over men than anything else in the world. It's why I made use of it when the opportunity arose, although I really wish I didn't have to.

Am I doing this now to get ahead? Am I hoping that by letting him fucking me again, I'll be more likely to convince him to let me downstairs to the man I really want? I'd probably be lying if I said no.

I might be a whore, but if it gets me what I want. If it gets me back in the protective arms of my husband, I'll cope. Plus, there's a guaranteed happy ending for me here. All seems pretty positive from my point of view.

"You're a tease, Dove." JD groans. "Sink down on my dick, baby. Let me feel you."

I bounce a little, taking a few more centimeters, but I hold off, intentionally driving him to the brink.

"Baby," he grits out as if he's in pain before finally taking over.

His fingers dig into my hips before he drags me down, forcing me to take all of him in one go.

"JULIAN," I scream as my body quickly adjusts to take his size.

"Fuck, yeah. Take it all, Dove. Every. Fucking. Inch," he spits as his hips punch up, ensuring he's as deep as he possibly can be.

"Oh my God," I pant as he takes me.

He's everywhere. Everything.

His hands burn into my skin, his cock stretches me open, his scent fills my nose and his eyes are locked on mine.

It might not be our first time, but something feels different.

There's something new crackling between us, something intense and unignorable. Something that wraps around my heart and squeezes until I can barely suck in the breath I need.

"Never been this good." He groans as I roll my hips in time with his thrusts. "Never."

"Please," I whimper, needing more. Needing everything.

Sitting up straighter, I lift my hands to my tits.

"Oh, sweet baby Jesus." He groans as I take their weight, pinching my nipples between my fingers. "Fuck, you just gushed over my dick, Dove."

"Yes. Harder," I beg, upping my speed as he does the same.

The sound of our heated skin slapping fills the room, leaving no doubt about what we're doing. Not that either of us gives a fuck.

"You think he knows?" JD asks as if he can read my mind. "It would almost be a shame for him not to be watching, or at least listening, don't you think?"

"Oh God." I moan, the thought of Reid on the other side of the door, hard, listening to us, is almost enough to push me over the edge. "You like being watched, don't you, Dove? You reckon Mav would be into it."

"Shit." I gasp as another man is thrust into my little fantasy.

"I bet they'd fucking love watching you bouncing around on my dick. They'll be so fucking jealous that I'm experiencing how hot and tight your pussy is and they have no idea. They'd be so fucking hard for you, Dove. Three of this town's most dangerous men totally at your mercy."

"Yes, yes, yes," I cry.

"They could touch you too. I might be willing to share. What do you think?" he continues, feeding my wicked fantasy. "One of them could take your ass, stretch you even tighter, while the other pushes past your swollen lips."

"Julian."

I'm so fucking hot. So fucking close that I can't even be embarrassed about the fact I'm so wet, I'm probably soaking the bed despite being on top.

But that image. Having them all at my mercy. All of them wanting me. Needing me. Taking from me.

It's—

JD's fingers find my clit and I crash.

One of the most powerful orgasms I've ever experienced rips through me. For long intense moments, my body doesn't feel like my own, my limbs don't feel attached to my body. I'm floating. No, soaring.

I'm nothing but a feather floating through the air without any cares in the world.

"Fucking hell, Dove. What are you doing to me?" JD groans, dragging me back to Earth as my muscles continue to tremble and my nerves tingle. "I was right though," he says cryptically before shouting. "It's only a fucking door. You can just open it, you know." And then his cock jerks inside me and his entire body locks up, his release rocking through him as he floods my pussy with his cum.

I collapse onto his chest, our sweaty bodies instantly sticking together as we fight for breath.

There is no noise around us, leaving me to believe he was joking about Reid being there. But then again, my skin continues to tingle like he might not be.

"Dude's a fucking pussy." JD laughs, his voice all light and blissed out.

"Was he really—"

"Of course he was. Saw the shadows of his feet under the door. Can't wait for him to cave."

"He doesn't want me," I argue. I've no idea why the words spill from my lips, but they do. It wasn't so long ago I had his dick in my hand while being beneath him on the couch. I'm fully aware of how much his body wants mine. I guess it's a shame that his head isn't on board.

Not that mine is either. He's the asshole who's done all this.

He should think himself lucky that I touched him, let alone expect anything else from me. I should have cut it off, not stroked it after everything he's done to me.

18

JD

For the second time in only a few days, I wake up sweaty with a hot woman wrapped around me.

It's fucking heaven.

Her legs are intertwined with mine. My dried cum sticking us together. Her arm is wrapped tightly around my waist while her head is resting on my chest. Each of her shallow breaths tickles over my skin, making goose bumps a permanent feature.

Lifting my hand from her waist, I begin tracing the bumps of her spine with my fingertips.

Her skin is so soft, so addictive. So sweet...

My mouth waters as I think about tasting her, spreading her thighs and licking—

"I can feel you getting hard beneath my thigh. What are you thinking about?" she whispers, letting me know that she's awake.

"Licking your pussy," I confess, my voice thick with sleep and desire.

"You like doing that, huh?"

A smile pulls at my lips.

"Sure do. Love having your taste on my lips."

"You're filthy, Julian Dempsey."

"So are you, Alana Murray."

The second I say her married name, her entire body tenses.

"Bit late to feel guilty now, Dove."

"I know. I just... He's here. He's right beneath us. I just need—"

She twists and shoves her face into the crook of my neck, cutting off her words.

"We should shower," I suggest, hating that she's struggling and needing to do something to make it better. "Then eat. Are you hungry?"

"Depends if you're going to try and cook or not," she mutters.

"I want to try and make things better not worse, Dove," I confess.

"Okay then. But only because I'm starving."

"Of course you are. I fucked you good."

"Yeah," she murmurs, rolling away from me, making me miss the heat of her skin.

I watch as she sits on the edge of my bed and stretches her back, lifting her arms above her head.

"I need to do some exercise or something," she says, pushing to her feet, letting me watch her ass sway as she heads toward my bathroom.

"You're looking pretty fine to me," I confess, rushing to follow her, not wanting to miss a second of looking at her skin.

"I feel weak and I hate it," she says, stopping in front of my sink to stare at herself in my mirror. "I'm skinny and—"

"Hot?" I suggest, stepping up behind her and holding her hips in my hands.

She mumbles under her breath as she looks at herself.

"Clearly, you can't see what I can. But if you want to work out, Reid's got a fully kitted-out gym."

"Of course he does."

"And I'm more than happy to be your workout buddy. I love getting all sweaty and out of breath with you."

"You're a nightmare."

"You love it."

Her eyes meet mine in the mirror, but she doesn't reply. Instead, she lowers her gaze and rips herself from my hold, darting toward the shower.

"Last one in is a loser," she calls behind her, attempting to lighten the mood.

Of course I wasn't hoping that she'd tell me she loved me. Only a crazy person would expect that after the short amount of time we've had together and everything I've forced her to endure.

You are a crazy person...

"Oh no. What's my punishment?" I counter, happy to play along.

She turns the water on and the second it's warm, she backs into it, letting me watch as the water runs over her body.

"Get on your knees," she demands, a wicked glint in her eyes.

"Now that I can get on board with," I say, immediately dropping down. "What next?"

"Surprise me," she teases, although the way she spreads her feet lets me know exactly what she's expecting. And I am more than happy to oblige.

"Dirty, dirty, Dove."

"I think you love it," she counters, stealing my line from earlier.

"I don't think, Dove. I fucking know."

Without waiting for a response, I crawl to her, staring up into her dark eyes as I give her what she needs.

With her taste still coating my tongue, I stare into the fridge as if I have a single clue as to what I'm looking for.

"Need some help?" Alana asks, stepping up behind me and ducking under my arm. "You really can't cook, can you?"

"I wasn't lying."

"So stop staring like an idiot and step aside." Pressing her hands against my chest, she forces me to back away before pulling packets from the fridge and laying them out on the counter.

"What are you doing?" I ask, studying her wearing clothes that fit her for the first time since I stole hers and replaced them with mine.

She looks hot in her tank and booty shorts. But there's a part of me that's missing her walking around in my clothes with nothing underneath.

Sure, the lingerie I chose for her is sinful. I almost ripped it right back off her when she put it on, but it's not the same as easy access.

"Making sandwiches."

"Okay, sandwiches I can do."

"Really?" she deadpans, turning around to search for the drawer that contains the cutlery.

"What the—" she starts before mumbling nonsense as she rummages around in the drawer for what she needs.

"What's wrong?"

"I need a knife. Reid must have some, he's practically a chef."

Guilt knots up in my stomach as more than a little self-hatred rushes through my veins.

"H-he keeps them somewhere safe," I confess through the lump in my throat.

"Why? Doesn't he trust you with them?" she asks with a laugh, giving up on her search and pulling out a butter knife instead.

I swallow nervously. "Something like that," I mutter, hoping like hell that she'll let it go.

Silence stretches out between us as she works.

After getting her off in the shower, she demanded that I take her down to see Mav. It wasn't a surprise. The second she allowed me to tug her into my room, I couldn't help but wonder if she had an ulterior motive.

Let me take what I needed, make my head spin with a knee-weakening orgasm or two and then make her demands when she has me wrapped around her little finger.

I'm not stupid. I knew she was playing me. But also, I wasn't strong enough to care. I'm still not.

If she gave up on that sandwich and offered herself up for another round, I'd take it and then probably lead her downstairs to her husband, without needing too much convincing.

But when we were done and she turned to me, the words out of her mouth weren't what I was expecting.

"I'm going to tell Reid everything," she blurted.

Even now, her total one-eighty makes my head spin. But I figure that I'm in no position to question her.

If she's decided for whatever reason that it's time. Then I am all over it.

There are too many secrets under this roof right now

and I hate it. Especially when those secrets are stopping us from moving forward.

I got it in the beginning. Reid has spent a long time working behind the scenes to infiltrate everything his father is involved in to find a way to bring him down. But fucking up the supply chains and making friends with some of his worst enemies was never going to be enough.

But what Alana has brought to the table, even the basic bits that I've figured out, it brings a whole new side to the plan that Reid wasn't aware of.

We've always known the Hawks have been in the sex trade; there is no secret there. We have strip clubs and brothels almost on every street corner. Even the girls who run the streets give a cut of their takings to Victor. But as far as we've ever known, that's as deep as it runs.

But child abuse... that opens up so many questions, so many other potential avenues. And as much as I know talking is going to rip her in two, we need the intel. If what she knows can help us, then ultimately, we're all going to get what we want. Reid can take control of this town like he craves, and Alana can get justice for her past.

I just really hope it's that fucking easy.

She works carefully and meticulously as she puts together two identical-looking sandwiches before sliding a plate toward me. It doesn't matter that she was forced to cut the tomato with the bluntest knife in this house, it still looks perfect. A million times better than I could achieve with every tool available to me.

"With you and Reid in this house, I'm gonna get fat."

She pauses with half of her sandwich almost at her mouth.

I know what she's thinking. I can see the words clear as day swimming in her eyes.

You're assuming I'm staying.

Picking up my own sandwich, I take a bite and instantly groan as the mix of flavors hits my tongue. But as incredible as it is, I have to fight to swallow it. The lump of fear clogging my throat from the thought of her leaving the second she's told her story is just too large.

I cough, trying to deal with the situation, and when the front door slams and heavy footsteps thump closer, I'm still practically choking.

"What the hell are you doing?" he barks, his eyes jumping between the two of us.

"Dying," I choke out.

"You're going to ruin your dinner," he chastises.

At that, I finally manage to swallow, stopping me from spraying the room with half-chewed sandwich.

"Jeez, calm down, Dad," I tease the second I can talk while Alana just stares at him like he just sprouted an extra head.

"You really are a barrel of laughs to live with, huh?" she deadpans, making Reid's lips press into a thin line.

"Pet." He nods. "Nice to see you wearing your own clothes for a change," he says, marching into the room with grocery bags in his arms. Fuck knows why, the kitchen is already fully stocked.

"Nice for someone to supply me with them."

"Good to see he didn't fuck the sass out of you."

"Good to know you were listening," she counters, leaving me chuckling under my breath while Reid's shoulders lock up tight.

She falls silent, leaving him to fume as he puts the food away.

It's not until he's pulled out a beer, uncapped it, and downed half that she finally speaks.

"I think it's time we talked."

Reid freezes, his body turning to stone as he stares at her in disbelief.

He recovers fast, his face hardening as he readies himself for her to laugh, to tell him that she's joking.

But she's not.

I'm not sure what got her here. Mav being downstairs with a gunshot wound, or the way Reid started bleeding her truth yesterday, letting her know what he knew, hinting at what he wanted in the long run. But at the end of the day, it doesn't matter. Everyone is about to get what they want. Reid is going to get the truth he craves, and then hopefully, he'll let Alana downstairs to see her husband.

Something wraps around my chest as I think about her leaving me behind and jumping into his arms. I fight to drag in the air I need as the pair in front of me continue their stare off.

The tension in the room ramps up, but it's not in a good way. There are none of the 'I must have you now' tingles. Instead, it's dread.

What is about to happen is going to be painful. Talking about it is going to wreck Alana, and it's going to make Reid blow.

I'm terrified.

She's already been through enough. She doesn't deserve to be forced to talk about all of this. And Reid... well, he's spent so long searching for this extra thing that's going to help take his dad down that he should be relieved, but something tells me that it's going to take a while for that feeling to override everything else that he's about to experience.

He might not want to admit it, but he cares about my little dove. More than he can even admit to himself. He

162

might want her to suffer, to cry, to submit. But he wants those things on his terms and under his control. Whatever she has to tell him, he has no control over. She had no control over it. It's going to make him lose his shit. I can already see it in the way his jaw tics.

"Grab some more beer," Alana finally says, breaking the silence. "Or maybe something stronger. We're probably going to need it."

19

ALANA

I startle when a bottle of vodka and three glasses land on the counter in front of me.

Reid pours three shots for us, but while they both reach for theirs and throw them back, I keep my hands knotted in my lap.

I don't want to do this.

I really don't want to fucking do this.

But there is no other option.

I've fought against them. Against Reid's demands for the truth. I've suffered the pain of refusing. But really, it was always going to end here.

I was never going to win against these men.

These Hawks.

That's not how my life goes.

I'm ruled by men. Held captive by men. Had and continue to have my body played by men.

The two standing in front of me now might be different from those of my past, but not in every way.

"What you said upstairs yesterday," I start, forcing myself to look up and meet Reid's cold, hard eyes head on. I want to be strong. To show them that I can fight just as well as they can, but I fear this is about to break me. "You were right. Your father was the first person my dad gave me to. He'd been abusing me for years, but I didn't know any different. Until the night I was told to be a good girl for Victor, like I was for Daddy."

Silence.

Acid swirls in my stomach as two horrified faces stare back at me in disbelief.

They both knew what I was hiding. Reid spelled it out pretty well yesterday, but saying words out loud. Hearing them in my own voice in a way I've never said them before is akin to taking a knife to my own chest.

My heart races, pounding so hard, thundering inside my chest that I'm sure it's trying to escape. And despite how tightly knitted my fingers are, my hands tremble uncontrollably as I await a response.

But it doesn't come. Well, not until there is a squeak of the stool JD is sitting on and he moves around behind me.

The second his arms wrap around my waist, and he tucks his face into my neck, breathing me in, holding me together, I nearly break.

I've come so fucking close to letting *them* win.

I've confessed to the very minimum; yet, they still want to take control. They want me so weak and disgusted that I'll keep their twisted secrets.

His warmth surrounds me, his strength immediately holding me up.

I swallow down the lump that crawled up my throat and blink back the tears.

He holds me tighter than he has before, and when I find Reid's tormented eyes, I can't help but wonder if JD is hugging me tight enough for both of them.

Reid's chest lifts and falls steadily. Too steadily. It's as if he's having to focus on every breath to keep himself under control.

I swallow thickly, before continuing. There's no point leaving it there. What I just confessed wasn't news to them, just confirmation.

"That was just the beginning, though. There were more, so many more."

"Dove," JD whispers, sending goose bumps racing down my neck.

"I'm okay," I lie, finally untangling my fingers and laying my hands over his.

"How many? Who?" Reid demands, his voice deeper than I've ever heard it.

He really is holding on by a thread.

It's a weird thing to witness—the unshakeable enigma of a man right on the edge.

Because of me.

"Honestly, I don't know. I never kept a tally. Razor, obviously. Jonno, although I don't think I was ever told his name." I name a few others, making Reid's fists tighten on the tabletop until his knuckles are white and threatening to crack.

"Your medical records?" Reid forces out.

"Because of them. But again, I don't know who. At some point, they all just became the same nameless, faceless monsters."

"What medical records?" JD asks, letting me know that Reid hasn't spilled all my secrets.

"Not now," I beg.

I expect him to argue, to force me to tell him everything, but to my surprise, he just whispers, "Okay," and presses a kiss to the skin beneath my ear, making me shudder.

It's such a welcome relief from the pain. My heart flutters as I squeeze his hands, needing him to know how much his support means.

"But that's only the tip of the iceberg," I confess, my voice already weak just knowing what I need to say aloud next.

"Jesus Christ." Reid groans, scrubbing his hand down his face.

"K-Kristie," I choke out, my heart in pieces just thinking about what might have happened to her. She never went to live with our mom." My words are quiet, barely a whisper. But both Reid and JD hear them loud and clear. Both of them turn to stone as they wait for more. Fear more. "That was a lie, just like I'm sure have been told for the other girls and young women who have gone missing from this town over the years."

I fall silent, unable to keep going as a lump of emotion the size of a basketball crawls up my throat and sticks.

Tears burn my eyes, my chest aches as I think about my little sister's sweet smile and kind eyes. It's like someone has wrapped barbed wire around my chest and refuses to let up.

"Pet?" Reid prompts when I continue to remain speechless.

Hanging my head, squeeze my eyes closed and ring my hands together in my lap. But nothing helps. Nothing ever does. The pain and devastation are always there. Like a living thing inside me. "She was sold, Reid," I blurt, my voice raw with emotion. But it quickly turns to bitter hatred when I say my next words. "My father, yours, Mav's. They're running—or at least involved in—some kind of human trafficking ring."

There is a beat of nothing before an inhumane roar rips from Reid's throat. Pushing to his feet, he reaches for one of the glasses on the table and smashes it against the counter before storming from the room like an angry beast.

"Shit," I hiss, watching him disappear through tear-filled eyes, leaving nothing but his thumping footsteps in his wake.

The pain that was already slicing up my heart only gets worse.

I startle when a door slams somewhere deep in the house. JD's grip on my body gets tighter before he lets out a heavy sigh that tickles over my skin.

"It's okay," I whisper, sensing that he needs to hear it. "I'm okay."

His entire body trembles with pent-up rage. While I hate it, I'm also more grateful than he could know that he hasn't succumbed to it like Reid and stormed off.

"They hurt you, Dove."

"It's in the past," I murmur, wishing like hell that was true. The pain now is just as raw and unbearable as it was back then.

"We're going to kill them," he promises. "We're going to gut every single motherfucker who ever touched you. Hell, anyone who's ever dared to look at you."

"Julian," I whisper.

"I fucking mean it, Dove. I'll fucking slaughter them all and let you bathe in their blood."

My stomach rolls.

"That probably won't be necessary," I mutter. "And if anyone is killing them, it'll be me."

He stills at my confession.

"What?" I ask.

"Nothing."

I whimper when he releases his arms, leaving me cold without his embrace, but not a second later, his hands grip my waist and he lifts me from the stool in favor of perching me on the counter.

Predicting his next move, I spread my thighs, allowing him to step between them.

His hands cup my face as he stares into my tear-filled eyes.

"You're so fucking incredible," he admits before slamming his lips down on mine.

I'm so shocked by his confession after discovering the truth about my past that it takes me a second to react. But the second his tongue pushes past my lips, filling my mouth with his taste, I cave.

He kisses me like he wants to devour me. It's hot and heavy and completely consumes me. After the pain of the last few minutes, it's everything I need.

Sliding one hand down my body, he grabs my ass and drags me to the edge of the counter, allowing me to feel how hard he is.

"Julian." I moan, my head falling back as he kisses down my neck.

My breasts swell with the need to be touched, the confines of my bra beyond restrictive after days of not wearing one.

"Please," I whimper, desperately needing more of him to rid myself of the memories of the past and the vicious touch of those monsters that haunt me every night.

"Fuck. I'd give you everything if I could," he confesses before diving for my lips again.

Our kiss gets dirtier and messier as our need for each other increases. Slipping my hands under his tank, I drag it up his body, desperate to feel the heat of his skin against mine.

He ducks down, allowing me to free him of the fabric before I discard it on the counter beside us.

"Can't get enough of you." He moans, his hands everywhere, teasing me, tempting me, building me higher and higher.

His fingers grip the bottom of my shirt, his knuckles grazing my stomach, but there's a loud crash from down the hall just before he drags it up.

"What was that?" I ask breathlessly as he pulls back to look over his shoulder as if that'll answer my question.

JD lets out a pained sigh before stepping back, removing his touch from my body.

"What are you—"

"Go to him," he says, his voice rough with desire.

"W-what?"

"Reid. He's in the gym. He needs..." He swallows thickly as he shoves his fingers into his hair and tugs at the roots harshly. "He needs you."

A rush of air passes my lips.

"No, he doesn't," I argue. "He doesn't want anything to do with me. I disgust him."

JD laughs. "Little dove," he murmurs. "That is far from the truth."

Moving closer again, he lifts me from the counter, setting me on my bare feet.

"Where's the gym?" I ask with a frown, wondering why the hell I'm even considering this.

"Right at the end, last door on the right."

I nod, taking a step back.

"He's angry..." I say nervously. "W-what if he—"

"He won't hurt you, Dove."

"Because it would be so out of character for him?" I deadpan.

"I'm trying to do the right thing here. Keep arguing, and I will forget all about it and take what I need instead."

As tempting as that is, I continue to move away from a tormented-looking JD. Something dark swirls in his usually bright eyes, making my stomach knot painfully.

"Will you be o—"

He forces a smile onto his lips. It's fake, and I hate it.

"I'm fine, Dove."

He holds my eyes, trying to prove his words are true. But I know they're not.

With a nod, I turn away from him and walk to the door. At the very last minute, I turn around and look at him.

He's no longer looking at me. Instead, he's staring at a shard of glass he must have picked up from the other end of the counter.

My stomach tightens and my heart aches, but still, I do as I'm told and walk down the hall toward the angry beast that awaits.

My hand trembles almost as violently as it did before I told them the truth as I reach for the handle.

Get it together, Alana.

You've endured worse than an angry Reid Harris.

Slowly, I twist it, allowing the door to open and reveal exactly what I expected. A state-of-the-art, fully functioning gym. It's a far cry from the makeshift one Mav has set up in our guest room.

One wall is covered in floor-to-ceiling mirrors, while another looks out into the woodland lining the back of the manor. But everything in the room blurs to nothing when my eyes land on the man with his back to me, his bloody palms resting on a wall with an upturned bike beside him.

His head hangs between his shoulders, his back rising and falling with his labored breathing. There's a dangerous aura surrounding him that should be warning enough to stay away.

But for some reason, JD thinks I should be here right now, and as much as I want to say he's crazy, that the last thing Reid wants is me encroaching on his moment, I can't help but move closer. Drawn to him like two ends of a magnet.

As I get closer, his heaving breaths hit my ears, and my skin prickles.

This could be one of the stupidest things I've ever done.

"Reid?" I whisper, my quiet voice sounding like a gunshot through the silent room.

But despite it sounding loud to me, he doesn't so much as startle.

His scent fills my nostrils as I step up beside him.

"Big Man?" I whisper again.

This time his breathing falters, although he doesn't move.

Without thinking about my actions, I press my trembling hand against his back.

He moves faster than I thought possible, and in a split second, I find myself pinned back against the wall with his hand wrapped around my throat.

His eyes are wild. His usually rich brown orbs are as dark as the night as he glares at me. His chest continues to heave, and much to my surprise, his hand trembles as much as mine.

I've yet to witness this side of Reid Harris. And I'm unsure if it's more or less terrifying than any of his other sides.

He's about to snap. And I have no idea which way it's going to go.

20

REID

There aren't many times in my life that I haven't felt completely in control.

Most of those times have been at the hands of my father.

He always knows how to disarm me. He's the only one who can see beneath my armor and really hit me where it hurts. It's one of the reasons why I hate him so much.

He trained me into the soldier I am now. He molded me how he wanted me. Which means he knows exactly how to pull my strings when he wants to.

But I'm quickly learning that he might not be the only one with that magic power. The girl with the blonde hair and haunted blue eyes seems to be able to reach inside me and find the one untainted, soft part of me, squeezing it until I completely lose grip on everything around me.

And that is exactly what happens when her warm hand gently presses against my back.

I act on instinct, my body jumps into action, and before I know what I've done, I'm staring into her terrified eyes as my fingers tremble around her throat.

Blood trickles from my palm, dropping onto her chest and running toward her white tank.

She swallows roughly, making her tendons tighten beneath my hold.

My head spins as the words she said in the kitchen continue repeating.

"She was sold, Reid. My father, yours, Muv's. They're running—or at least involved in—some kind of human trafficking ring."

Blind fury grips me in its hold as I fight to grasp control.

If I can't. If it continues to linger just out of reach, then I don't know what I might do.

"Reid?" she whispers, her face red with lack of air, her eyes wide.

Up until now, she's barely shown an ounce of fear. It hasn't mattered what I've done, what I've said. She's held my eyes and kept her head high.

But right now, I can see it all.

I just don't know if it's the memories from her past that are putting it there. Or me.

I should release her, find out the answer to that question.

But I can't.

No matter how much I tell myself to back up, my body doesn't listen.

If anything, it inches closer.

The lure of her sweetness, the heat of her body. It's all too much.

My head is too fucked-up with everything she said, with the knowledge that all this time, I've been searching for something more. It's been right under my nose.

Human trafficking. Child abuse.

How could that be happening right under my nose, yet I have no idea?

I should know. I'm so deep in Victor's dealings that it shouldn't be possible to keep it a secret.

But then, Victor Harris is the epitome of a secret.

If he doesn't want someone to know something, then they won't.

He holds enough power and wealth that everyone has no choice but to do his bidding. That or they can kiss goodbye to their lives, their families, and those they love.

You should have known...

"I'm not lying," she whispers, her eyes searching mine, trying to gauge my reaction to all this.

But I'm not angry because I think she's lying.

I know she's not.

I may not have any evidence other than her word. But I believe right to the depths of my fucked-up soul that she's telling the truth.

"I know," I choke, my eyes dropping to her mouth.

Her lips are parted, swollen from JD's kiss. They're so pink and full and—

"Reid?"

Ripping my gaze away, I find her eyes again, my hold on her throat releasing a little. While it might allow her to breathe a little easier, it does nothing for the tremble I can't seem to get a hold on.

"Say something. Do something," she begs.

The air around us crackles as she stares up at me.

Memories from being with her on the couch, her hand wrapped around my dick, come back to me, and my pants grow tight.

But still, I just stand here.

Staring.

Waiting.

Hoping.

"Reid? Talk to me. Please, I need—"

The fear of being forced to hear more of what she has to say right now is enough to get me moving. Although it's not in the direction I should be.

The length of my hard body aligns perfectly with hers as I pin her against the wall a beat before my lips descend on hers.

That's all it is at first, just the press of our mouths.

Innocent.

But then she whimpers.

Fucking whimpers, and I forget all about finding my control and let it fly right out of the fucking window.

Uncaring as to whether she's into it, I plunge my tongue past her lips and slide my hand to the back of her head, twisting my fingers in her hair so I can position her exactly where I need her.

The moment her tongue joins the party, something explodes inside me. Something hot, unstoppable, and so fucking addicting, I'm not sure I'll ever be able to stop.

Reaching out with my free hand, I slide it up the soft skin of her leg, my need for her only growing. Hitching her thigh up, I wrap it around my waist, opening her up for me and stepping deeper into her body.

The heat of her pussy burns through my pants, making my dick as hard as fucking steel.

Her sweet taste coats my tongue as her addictive scent fills my nose. Both make my head spin, but it's nothing compared to when she lifts her hands to my hair and rakes her nails over my scalp.

The groan I emit is nothing like I've ever heard from myself before, but I don't dwell on that thought. I can't. The only thing I can think about right now is more, I need fucking more.

Everyone's obsession with this woman is starting to make more sense.

She's fucking kryptonite.

Our kiss is filthy and messy. All teeth and tongues. But she's giving as good as she gets, so I forget about my sloppy performance and let myself drown in her.

My hips roll, grinding my cock against her. Her entire body trembles with need as my grip tightens on her thigh. Something hot surges through me as I think about adding to the marks that JD has already littered her body with.

Tugging on her hair, I drag her head back, exposing her reddened throat. My lips descend and she moans like the whore I accused her of being as I trace the marks my bloody fingers left behind with my tongue.

"Oh fuck," she whimpers as I suck on her skin. With her arms over my shoulders, she lifts herself, wrapping her other leg around my waist, climbing me like a fucking tree. And I am here for it.

Pressing my hips harder against her, I hold her in place as I find her mouth again.

My hands slide down her thighs until my fingers slip beneath the fabric of her shorts, gripping her ass tightly and making her cry out into our kiss.

"Feel how hard I am?" I groan into her mouth. "You do this to me. You."

"Please," she begs, her hips moving in time with mine in an attempt to get off.

Almost frantically, her hands drop to my shirt and she begins tugging, desperately trying to free me of the fabric.

"Desperate whore." I groan. But unlike all the other

times I've said it, I don't mean it as an insult. I fucking love it.

She drags my shirt up as high as she can, but seeing as I refuse to let go of her ass, she doesn't exactly achieve what she was hoping.

Instead, she goes for my pants.

Dropping her lower, helping her out, giving her the access she needs.

My cock jerks, precum already leaking from the tip with my need for her.

Pressing her hand against my abs, every muscle in my body tenses before she shoves it down, pushing inside my boxers.

"Fuuuuck." I groan the second her soft fingers brush my length.

As much as I want to enjoy it, the second we collide, reality slams into me.

Releasing her ass, I take a huge step back, giving her little choice but to pull her hand from my underwear and release my dick.

"Reid," she pants, her eyes wide and her lips swollen as she leans back against the wall as if she'll collapse without it.

"Fuck," I grunt, combing my fingers into my hair and tugging until it hurts. "That didn't happen. That didn't—" My words vanish, my mouth running dry the second she drops to her knees and begins crawling to me.

It might not be what I asked for, but fuck me, it's certainly a sight that I'll never forget.

Her eyes remain locked on mine as her ass sways from side to side.

"What the fuck are you doing?" I ask like a moron. I guess all my blood has rushed to my dick.

I glance down, finding it exactly as I was expecting, desperately trying to punch its way out of my pants.

Alana doesn't answer, instead she bites down on her bottom lip, dragging it through her teeth.

Jesus.

I swallow thickly, trying to remember exactly what it was that made me stop a few seconds ago.

My body jerks when she gets to me and wraps her hand around my waistband, her knuckles brushing the sensitive skin above my boxers.

"Let her suck you off, bro," a deep, raspy voice comes from behind me.

My teeth grind and my fists curl.

"It'll help chill you out, that's for sure. And she's so fucking good at it. I promise you won't regret it."

Tipping my head back, I squeeze my eyes closed.

Alana tugs at my pants and I just manage to catch her before she frees my dick.

"No," I bark, ripping her hands from me and taking another step back.

"What?" She gasps, sitting back on her heels, staring up at me in disbelief.

"I don't need anything from you. I got your secrets."

Her chin drops and her eyes immediately flood with tears. I'm pretty sure she'd have taken it better if I'd reached out and slapped her.

"Dude," JD chastises, his footsteps getting closer before he reaches for Alana.

The second she's on her feet, she plants her face into his chest, hiding.

"The fuck?" he asks, glaring at me.

'What?' I mouth.

He shakes his head in disbelief.

179

"It's okay, little dove. You can suck mine later to make up for it," he offers like an asshole.

Only the sound of her heavy breathing fills the room. I stare at her, the weight of what I just did pressing down on my shoulders.

Yeah, I'm an asshole. That isn't news to anyone. But maybe that was a bit below the belt.

But I can't... I can't let her touch any more than she has. I can't. Because if I do...

"Are we going downstairs or what?" I ask, desperate to shove my hand into my pants to rearrange my dick.

Alana squares her shoulders.

"You mean—" she starts, pulling her face away from JD to look at me. "You mean, I can see Mav?"

I hold her eyes for a beat, hating the pain I see within them.

I might not have caused it all, but at least a little bit is because of me.

If it were anyone else, I wouldn't care. But I'm quickly learning that Alana is not like anyone else.

"Yeah, Pet. You can see him."

She sniffles, even more tears filling her eyes, and fuck if it doesn't make my chest tighten.

"Now?" JD asks.

"Yes," I confirm through gritted teeth.

If we don't do it right the fuck now then there is every chance I'll change my mind.

My eyes hold JD's for a second, and I know he's thinking the same as me.

She's going to want him, not us.

But what the fuck am I meant to do? Keep him locked up down there for the foreseeable future in the hope she forgets about him?

Ripping my eyes away from them, I stride past them, only slowing to give JD's shoulder a squeeze.

My palm stings the second we make contact, reminding me that there's probably still glass embedded in it from the glass I shattered against the counter.

It's not until I'm at the door that I cave and look back. And fuck am I glad I do.

While Alana might look two seconds away from either bursting into tears or exploding with excitement, what I notice the most is the fact she looks like she's been mauled by a bear. Or more so... two Hawks.

I can't help but smirk as I make my way down the hall and I finally get to sort out my junk.

"You coming or what?" I shout when I get to the basement door.

If we're going to do this then it has to be right fucking now.

21

ALANA

"**W**hat are you waiting for?" I cry as I practically run out of the room the second Reid's deep voice rumbles through the air.

I'm pissed at him. Beyond fucking pissed for whatever that was back there. But if I'm honest, I'm more pissed at myself than him.

What the fuck was I even thinking getting down on my knees like I was desperate for his dick?

You were desperate for his dick...

No. It wasn't that. It wasn't him I was desperate for; it was a distraction, anything that would rid the images from my head that talking about the past dragged up. That and my need to finish off what JD started in the kitchen.

It's JD's fault. All of it.

"Yeah, Dove. I'm coming," he says reluctantly before his footsteps sound out behind me.

I tell myself that the second I walk out of that room, I'll forget about everything that happened inside.

He's taking me to Mav. That's what matters right now.

Butterflies take flight in my stomach and the tremble

returns to my hands as I step into the hallway and see Reid push the door open that I failed to find the other night.

He doesn't look back, and I'm grateful for that. I might be able to throw my shoulders back and hold my head high after that epic embarrassment back there, but I'd rather not have to.

I don't realize I've slowed to an almost stop until JD's warm palm presses to the small of my back, gently moving me forward.

"I thought you wanted this," he whispers.

"I do. More than anything. It's just..." My words trail off as my fears get the better of me.

I've no idea what he knows and what he thinks of me now.

It's hard to believe that Reid wouldn't have ensured Mav knows everything. He probably delighted in telling him what a whore his wife is.

For all I know, Mav might not want anything to do with me now.

Something—my past—always held him back from going all in with me. But how is he going to react to my present being just as twisted?

I blow out a slow, calming breath.

"He loves you, Dove," JD forces out, able to read my mind.

"It was never enough though, was it?" I spit coldly before I step over the threshold to the basement and begin descending the stairs.

The air instantly chills, making goose bumps erupt on my bare arms. Wrapping them around myself, I keep my eyes focused ahead as I continue down.

The scent of pain and death makes my stomach knot. I

didn't realize it smelled of anything while I was down here. I guess I just got used to it.

When I get to the bottom and turn the corner, I find Reid waiting for us at my old cell door. But as much as I want to step through it, I can't stop my eyes from drifting to the room that's over his shoulder. The one with the chair in the middle and the rings embedded in the floor and ceiling.

I squeeze my eyes closed for a beat as JD's words from all those days ago come back to me.

"Can you imagine what it might be like being tied up and totally at our mercy?"

Reid clears his throat, forcing me to focus on him.

I've no idea if JD painted the same picture for him, but even if he didn't, something tells me that he's conjured up a similar image all by himself.

"Ready?" JD asks, his hands clamping down on my hips as if he's concerned I'm about to bolt.

If you'd asked me an hour ago how I'd feel in this moment, I wouldn't have said so terrified that I was about to be rejected for the second time in ten minutes. Rejected by the one man I love more than anything else in the world.

I suck in another deep breath and nod.

It's now or never.

But the second the locks disengage, I make the stupid mistake of looking down.

I'm covered in blood. Reid's blood.

The memory of having his giant hand wrapped around my throat not so long ago, his fingers twisted in my hair, his lips on mine slam into me and I panic.

"No, wait," I cry, but it's too late.

"Alana?" a deep, very familiar voice asks and my heart jumps into my throat, all my previous concerns vanish as

Reid pushes the door wider and I get my first look at my husband in two weeks.

My legs take on a life of their own as I run into my old cell, my feet leave the concrete floor as I launch myself at his body, hoping like hell that he catches me.

Warm, strong, protective arms wrap around my body as my legs lock around his waist.

The familiar scent of his skin floods my nose a second before a sob erupts.

A deep groan rumbles in his chest. I feel the vibration all the way down to my toes before he says one sentence that makes me completely lose it.

"Everything's okay, Doll. I've got you."

We stand there in the middle of the cell, him holding me up as I soak his neck and shirt with tears and snot.

Tucking his own face into my hair, he inhales deeply, as if he's forgotten what I smell like.

"Fuck, I've missed you," he whispers so that only I can hear it.

As much as I might like to think we've been left to have this moment in private, I know we haven't.

Reid and JD's stares are like lasers burning into my back. They don't understand mine and Mav's relationship. Hell, I don't even think me and Mav totally understand it. All I know is that right now, I feel safer and more loved than I have in two weeks. I might be back in the basement, in this cell, but with his arms wrapped around me, I am home.

"I'm sorry, Mav." I sniffle, my voice rough with emotion. "I'm so fucking sorry."

His entire body tenses, letting me know that he's more than aware of all the things I have to be sorry about.

"I know, babe. Not now though, yeah?"

"Okay," I whisper, grateful for the reprieve. Although, I

know it's coming. He might be allowing me to keep the Band-Aid on for now, but I'm only going to get so far before I have to rip it off, no matter how much it hurts.

Finally, my uncontrollable sobs begin to fade and I unwrap my legs from around Mav's waist, aware that he's been holding me up for a very long time.

I might have lost some weight since he saw me last but that doesn't mean he can hold me up forever.

Wish he could though.

Balancing on my tiptoes, I press a kiss to his neck, right above his thundering pulse. I want to do so much more, but now isn't the time to go there, especially with our audience. So I allow myself to just indulge in the racing beat of his heart, reminding myself that he's here, that he's okay, and that we're together again.

"Doll," he breathes before swallowing thickly.

"I love you, Mav. Nothing has changed," I promise him, before reluctantly releasing him and taking a step back.

The air in the cell is charged with tension and testosterone. It's suffocating.

If I thought having Reid and JD inside this small space with me was intense then having all three of them watching me as if I'm about to turn to dust is seriously overwhelming.

As much as I'd love to know what they're thinking right now, I don't turn to look back at Reid and JD. My eyes are too focused on Mav. His skin has a grayness to it that I know all too well from my time down here. His cheekbones are a little more prominent than usual and he's got dark rings around his eyes. His hair is a mess, the scruff on his jaw is longer than he likes, and his clothes are rumpled. This is not the version of my husband that I'm used to. And it's all my fault.

Something tight and unforgiving wraps around my chest, making it almost impossible to breathe.

"I'm sorry. All of this is—"

"You motherfucker." Mav growls and it echoes around me.

I was too focused on not meeting his gaze as my guilt swallowed me whole to remember what I looked like and the image the state of me paints.

One moment I'm standing there with my heart in my throat as my husband glares pure death over my head, and next, I'm being shoved out of the way as he flies forward.

"Mav, no," I cry, managing to catch myself on the wall.

I watch in horror, everything happening in slow motion, as he cocks his fist back ready to plow it into Reid's face.

There's no hiding who's been touching me; Reid's hand is still dripping blood.

Thankfully, JD jumps between them, catching Mav off guard and halting the punch he was about to throw.

"I really don't think that's a good idea, man," JD says as calmly as possible as he presses his palms against Mav's chest and forces him to back up.

Despite the anger that's coming off Mav in waves, he's too weak to really fight.

"Like you're any better," Mav spits. Proving my previous thought totally wrong, Mav takes JD completely by surprise and throws his fist into his jaw.

"Ow, fuck." JD moans as his head snaps to the side.

"Mav," I cry, rushing forward and standing in front of him before he can make this situation any worse. "You need to stop," I beg.

"Me?" he asks incredulously. "I need to stop?" A dark, bitter laugh spills from his mouth as he looks from me to the two men standing behind me. "So this is how it is now, huh?" he asks, making my brows pinch in confusion. "You've been here two weeks and now you're siding with them?" he sneers, any relief he first had at seeing me seems to have vanished as if it never existed.

"What?" I shriek in disbelief. "Them?" I ask, pointing over my shoulder. "I'm not with them."

No one says anything as the tension continues to grow, crackling around us like a wildfire. I swear to God they're the longest few seconds of my life.

"I'm not with them," I whisper, needing him to know that all this time, the one person I've thought about more than any other is him.

But then JD scoffs, refuting my words.

"That's not what I've heard." Mav growls darkly. I've heard this tone many, many times before, but it's never been directed at me.

I stare into his eyes, begging him to believe me as my heart fractures in my chest.

"I love you, Mav," I confess, taking a step forward, pressing my palms against his chest and sliding them up. But before I can loop my arms around his neck, he grabs my wrist.

"Did you forget that while you were letting JD fuck you against the wall or when Reid painted you with his blood?" His voice is rough, cracked with emotion, and it cuts me down to my soul.

"Mav," I whisper, not knowing what to say.

He studies me. His eyes bounce all over my face, down to my neck, which I'm sure is littered with JD's hickeys and stained with Reid's bloody handprint.

"I'm starting to wonder if I even know who you are."

There are so many awful things he could say to me in this moment, so many things he could accuse me of being.

But hearing those words spill from his lips, I realize that none other would have hurt half as bad.

Wrapping my arms around my waist, I squeeze tight in an attempt to keep myself together.

Call me a liar, tell me that I'm a whore. I can take those harsh words.

But having him think he's never had the truest version of who I am... no. Just no.

His eyes stay on me, begging me to say something. But I can't. I can barely breathe let alone say anything.

Silence stretches out, as my heart continues to race and my guilt threatens to swallow me whole.

"We've got a guest room upstairs if you'd prefer that over this." To my surprise, Reid is the one to break the silence and if Mav's reaction is anything to go by, he's as shocked as I am. His eyes widen and his chin drops.

"Uh..." Mav hesitates, clearly thinking this is a joke.

"I told them," I force out. "They're on our side, Mav."

He shakes his head, scrubbing his hand over his face.

"Of course you did," he mutters in disbelief.

"She did the right thing in doing so," Reid assures him. "I had no idea."

A rush of air escapes Mav's lips as if he's just been punched in the back.

"You really expect me to believe that?"

"I guess that all depends on whether you want to extend your stay down here, huh?"

Reid turns, ready to leave Mav in his cell.

"No, he's coming up," I argue, reaching for Mav's hand and attempting to drag him toward the door before Reid locks it again.

22

MAVERICK

lana tugs on my arm, trying to force me to move as Reid walks out of the cell, quickly followed by JD.

"Mav, come on," she begs.

Her eyes are filled with tears, her distress over all this clear, but I'm struggling to get past everything else.

The swollen lips, the love bites, the blood stain around her throat.

For a few seconds, I thought it was her blood. But one glance at Reid and I knew exactly who it belonged to. And it quickly became clear what they'd been doing.

I've hated him all my life. But I have never hated him as much as I did in that moment, realizing that while I was locked down here, he was upstairs with his hands all over my wife.

Has every motherfucker in this shithole town had a taste of my wife aside from me?

I shake my head, refusing to focus on that question. I don't need to. I already know the answer.

"He'll lock you back up in here," she continues.

"Surprised you don't want that," I mutter, hating the level of self-loathing I've been reduced to.

"W-what?" she stutters, twisting around to look at me, her brows pinched together.

"You seem to be having plenty of fun without me." I sound like a little bitch. But I can't help it. I'm starving, I fucking stink and my mind is spinning at a million miles an hour.

I want answers, but as desperate as I am to hear them, I'm equally as terrified.

What if she's found a better life here with these two assholes than she's had with me over the past five years? They sure seem to be giving her something I haven't.

"No, Mav." She lowers her head in shame and runs her fingers through her hair. "Please." She tries to get me moving again. "Just come up and we can talk."

Unable to ignore the lure of a shower and a real bed, I find my legs moving, and before I know it, I'm out of the cell, my muscles screaming from lack of use as I climb the stairs.

"What room?" Alana asks once we emerge from the basement to find Dumb and Dumber waiting for us in the hallway.

Reid's hand is still dripping blood. It should give me some kind of satisfaction that he's hurting. But knowing that hand has been around my wife's throat wipes that out quite effectively.

"Door opposite mine, little dove," JD says.

Little dove?

The fuck is that?

"Do you need anything?" he asks, attempting to look like he cares.

Alana's blue eyes meet mine. I assume she's waiting for

me to say something, but she's going to be waiting a while. Only one of us needs to do any talking, and it's not me.

"Food?" she finally says after discovering I'm not going to respond.

"Reid will sort us out a nice family meal," JD says with a smirk that makes me grunt. "A prawn-free one," he adds like an asshole.

Alana rolls her eyes at his lame attempt at a joke before tugging on my arm. "Come on."

With a sigh, I follow her up the stairs, my eyes darting left and right, taking in every inch of the enemy's house as I can.

Honestly, it's pretty boring. It looks like... well, a house.

I'm not entirely sure what I was expecting, but this wasn't it.

When we get to the top of the stairs, hallways spread out to both our left and right, ensuring I don't miss just how colossal the devil's home is compared to ours. Or is it just mine now since she's got herself settled here?

My eyes linger on the door opposite the one she leads me to. Is that where she's been sleeping? In JD's bed. Or has she been jumping between the two of them?

Anger and disgust stir in my gut. I try to pull my hand from hers, her warm touch too much to take right now, but she continues to hold me with a death grip. It's as if she's scared that if she releases me, I'll run and never look back.

To be fair, she probably should be worried.

For two weeks, all I've wanted is to find her, to pull her into my arms and never let go. But the reality has been nothing like I hoped. I wasn't expecting to come face-to-face with the evidence that she's been with them. That she's been with everyone but me.

I'm more than aware it's my own fault. She's offered

herself up to me more than enough times over the past five years. I know that. But it doesn't stop the hurt.

We come to a stop in the middle of the room and she finally releases my hand.

Stepping away, she pushes a door open and pokes her head inside.

"It has a tub," she says simply, before returning and standing in front of me. "I know how this looks," she confesses, glancing down at herself.

"Do you?" I ask roughly.

"Mav," she sighs, shaking her head, "none of this was meant to happen."

"So you weren't meant to be Victor's whore?" I spit, hating how much venom is in my tone, but unable to do anything about it.

My words hit her like a bullet, but she doesn't crumble; instead, she squares her shoulders, ready for battle.

"No, I wasn't."

"How many?" I ask, needing to understand exactly what I'm dealing with here.

"Too many. But that doesn't matter. It's not exactly like I was an innocent virgin."

I can't help but scoff.

"I did it for you," she cries. "Everything I have done since that night in the woods has been for you." My teeth grind and my fists curl at her audacity.

"Oh, well, if that's the case, I really should be thanking you. Thank you for bouncing on every other motherfucker's dick but mine. You've really out-fucking-done yourself."

She moves faster than I give her credit for and before I get a chance to move, her palm cracks across my cheek.

My head snaps to the side, much like JD's did when I punched him downstairs.

I react on instinct, my arm darting out and my hand wrapping around her throat.

I force her back until she collides with the wall with such force, all the air in her lungs comes rushing out.

She stares up at me with huge, shocked, tear-filled eyes as my fingers tighten, cutting off her air supply.

It's been so fucking long since I've done this. Since I've forgotten about everything and taken exactly what I need from a woman.

But then she whimpers and I remember exactly who I'm manhandling. Reality is like a bucket of ice water thrown over my head.

"Is this what you want? You want to be treated like a whore. Thrown around? Strangled? Forced to take any dick pointed in your direction."

Her tears finally spill over, her body trembling in my hold.

"Mav," she whimpers. "Please, don't do this."

My chest heaves as I stare at her, the image that was so clear in my mind when I was forced to listen to her and JD together is more vivid than ever now that I'm staring into her eyes.

"I didn't do any of this," I confess, my anger starting to ebb the longer I watch tears freely fall from her eyes. "All I've ever done is what I've thought was best for you."

She swallows, her throat rippling under my fingers.

"I know, and I appreciate everything you've done more than I could ever express. But—"

Releasing her throat, I press my fingers to her lips, stopping whatever was about to fall from them.

I can't hear her say what I think she's going to say. I just can't. Not right now.

Letting the breath I was holding escape, I cringe at how

rank it must smell rushing over her face. But she doesn't cower. All she does is stare into my eyes, silently begging me to understand.

"Fuck, Doll. Don't do that to me," I whisper, letting my hand fall from her throat as my brow gently rests against hers.

With one forearm resting against the wall beside her head, I grip her waist with the other. I know at first look that she's lost weight, but feeling how much her waist dips in is more evidence I didn't need that she hasn't been treated right.

"They hurt you," I state. There's no question. It's not needed.

"Yes and no. The important thing is what happens next," she says, sounding almost hopeful.

I close my eyes for a beat, sucking in a deep breath full of her scent and try to tell myself that she's right.

But what if she's not? What if she's wrong and we're not suddenly all on the same team here?

"You sent JD to check on me, didn't you?" I ask, latching onto something that doesn't make me want to vomit or punch someone.

She nods, her head bobbing against mine.

"Reid showed me a video of your fight," she confesses, making my stomach knot.

"Not my finest moment," I mutter, ashamed that I even got in the ring that night, let alone my shitty performance. "I was so fucking lost without you."

"Same."

The emotion in her voice makes my eyes crack open.

"Babe."

Her hands slide up my chest before she cups my shaggy jaw, her thumb running over my bottom lip.

"I was so worried. He cut the video as you went down and I d-didn't k-know—"

"I'm glad you sent him."

Her eyes widen. "You are?"

"Well, I wasn't at the time. He turned up, invited himself in, and tried to convince me to let him be my replacement nurse. I should have known there and then that he had you. But it wasn't until later that realization hit."

"If you didn't then I might never have figured it out."

"You broke into Reid's house to get me." One of her hands drops to the bandage on my shoulder. "You got shot because of me."

I shrug the other shoulder. "Worth it."

Her eyes narrow, searching mine. I know what she's thinking.

"My head is fucked-up right now, Doll. I'm sorry."

"Trust me, I get it. I'll tell you everything, I promise. It's not all bad. I killed someone."

I rear back, shocked by her words. Or more so the proud smile playing on her lips.

"You what?"

"Reid had one of them locked up downstairs. I stabbed the fuck out of him."

A laugh punches from my chest. "I'm... uh... proud of you?"

"Thanks. I'm pretty proud of me too. And we're one step closer to wiping them all out now," she says with a massive smile.

My lips part to ask more about Reid being on our side when there's a knock on the door.

"Hold that thought," she says, before ducking under my arms to answer it.

"I brought you some snacks and coffee. Didn't know

how he took it so I guessed at black and strong like the other motherfucker in this house."

"Don't you ever fucking compare me to that twisted cunt," I bark at the half-closed door.

Alana and JD share a laugh at my expense, which makes me want to rip the door open and plow my fist into his face again. But before I even think about putting it into action, Alana is stepping back from the door with a tray in her hands and kicking it closed behind her.

The scent of coffee makes my mouth water and I reach for it without thought.

"Oh my God." I moan as the richness floods my mouth.

Alana watches me with heated eyes and a smirk on her face.

"What?" I ask.

"Nothing," she says, her smile growing as she places the tray on the bed. "I'm going to run you a bath."

She's gone before I can say anything, and as I throw a cookie into my mouth, the sound of running water hits my ears, making my skin itch to be clean.

I'd learned to ignore it, but now it's within reaching distance, my need to scrub my skin until it's raw and rid of the scent of the basement is too much to deny.

Downing the coffee, I stuff the remaining cookies into my mouth and shove my pants from my hips, leaving me in only my boxers, and I walk toward the scent of bubble bath and the temptation of my wife.

23

ALANA

The second Mav steps into the doorway, my temperature increases and my skin tingles with awareness.

"They haven't been feeding you properly," he states, announcing his presence.

"It's been a stressful couple of weeks," I confess.

"You're telling me."

"Tell me they've been feeding you more than their cocks."

Sucking in a sharp breath, I spin around and pin him with a glare.

He holds his hands up in surrender, his expression wrought with guilt.

"Sorry. I'm sorry. I just—" He shakes his head and rips his eyes from me. "Thank you. You've no idea how much I need this."

"Yeah, I do," I confess. It wasn't so long ago that I was desperate for exactly the same thing.

"I know I smell bad but you don't need to make me feel worse about it," he jokes.

"No, that wasn't—"

"I know, Doll."

Once he's standing in front of the bath, he turns his back on me and tucks his thumbs into his boxers and shoves them down.

"Shit. I'm gonna go and—"

"Stay," he says as water sloshes behind me. "Oh fuck, that's good." He groans, sounding entirely too erotic for something as simple as a bath.

"You sure you don't want me to leave you alone with the tub?" I tease.

"How long have I been down there?" he asks.

"It's Friday afternoon," I confess, still keeping my back to him.

"Doll," he whispers.

Tipping my face to the ceiling for a beat, I turn around, finding him surrounded by white fluffy bubbles.

His addiction to having a bath isn't news to me. The first time he told me he was going for one, I was convinced he was joking until I walked past the master bathroom at the house he first took me to and found it almost overflowing with bubbles, waiting for him.

Since that day, I've tried to imagine what the dangerous, inked-up gangster might look like submerged in the softness of the bubbles. Well, five years later, it seems I get my wish. And fuck, it's even more mind-blowing than I thought it would be.

"I-I need to go shower," I blurt, still standing in the middle of the room like a spare part.

His eyes drop to my white shirt, which is covered in Reid's blood, before he tracks the hand marks that cover my upper arms and throat.

He swallows, his Adam's apple bobbing. "Not yet. I'm not ready to share you again."

"Sh-share me?" I stutter.

"I know you're fucking them, Doll."

I stumble back until my ass collides with the vanity.

From what he's already said, it's obvious that he thinks I'm fucking both of the men under this roof on the regular, but hearing him say it so casually, well, it shocks me.

"I haven't fucked Reid," I say confidently, as if that's going to make this any better.

His hand emerges from the bubbles, so he can scrub at his jaw. It shouldn't be so damn cute when he leaves himself with a white beard, but damn it, it is. I'm not going to tell him that though. Something tells me that he wouldn't approve.

"Right."

"JD—"

"Don't even think about lying to me," he warns.

"I-I wasn't," I admit, holding his eyes. "We've been—"

"I know. I heard."

"He told you," I mutter. Of fucking course JD would go bragging to my husband about how good my pussy is. Asshole.

"Not in so many words," Mav confesses.

"What are you—"

"I heard."

My brows pinch at his simple, repeated statement.

"What are you—"

"He streamed the audio into my cell."

For a couple of seconds, disbelief floods me. But then, it settles.

I don't even know why I'm surprised. It's such a JD thing to do.

"Sorry."

"Why? Sounded like you enjoyed it."

"I... I... shit. Mav. That isn't fair."

Lifting both hands, he covers his face, cutting off our connection.

His pain and frustration is palpable, hanging heavy in the room between us.

"I'm gonna go and..." My words trail off because, honestly, I've no idea what I'm doing. Running away?

Never in the past five years have I ever wanted to run away from Mav. But despite hiding his face from me, I can see his wrecked expression as clear as day in my mind.

He's held back for five years, for whatever reason he's convinced himself of. I can only imagine what kind of hell it was to listen to another man taking me. A man he can't stand.

Knowing I've been out fucking others is one thing, but listening to it, experiencing it, is another.

"Alana," he says before I get to the door, making my steps slow. "I'll always love you, I need you to know that."

I hang my head feeling like the shittiest person in the world.

"It's not always enough though, is it?"

Without another word from either of us, I leave him to his bath.

I swear, I don't breathe until I get out into the hallway. But the second my eyes land on JD's door, the tension in my shoulders returns.

Before finding out that he live streamed our little fuck fest in the hallway straight into Mav's cell, I probably would have made a beeline to JD's room, especially after the dark look that was lingering in his eyes when he handed me that tray not so long ago. But now, I drop my eyes to the carpet and continue down to Reid's room.

Swinging the door open, I pad past the bed. I don't see or hear anything, my head is still in the guest bathroom with Mav.

I shouldn't have left him.

Pushing the bathroom door open, I step inside, arguing with myself about turning around and going back. The fact the room is full of steam doesn't register. Nothing does until movement in front of me catches my eye.

"Oh fuck." I gasp so loudly that my voice is clearly heard over the torrent of water.

Any images I had in my head about how Reid Harris looks standing behind that glass shower screen with water rushing over his muscles are shot to shit the second my eyes land on reality.

And ho-ly fucking shit.

"The fuck are you doing?" he barks, quickly cupping his junk.

But it's too late. I've already seen it all.

"I-I—" I stutter like a schoolgirl who's just had her first look at a semi-hard pierced dick.

My apology sits heavy on my tongue. It almost sneaks out before I remember what happened downstairs. And the second I do, my back straightens and my shoulders widen.

Our eyes hold in a battle of wills as my temperature surges and my heart rate increases.

Your husband is in the bathroom down the hallway, you whore.

Something at his feet drags my attention away and I balk at the sight.

"You're still bleeding."

"And you're still here," he counters. "Don't you have someone else to fuss over?"

"You're an asshole," I hiss.

"Original," he mutters, before reaching out with his free hand and turning the water off.

"Pass me a towel," he demands, making my brows shoot up.

Much to his irritation, I don't move. Instead, I cross my arms under my breasts, pushing them up, making his eyes drop to my cleavage.

Men are so fucking predictable.

"Pass me a fucking towel or get the fuck out."

I should do the latter, but then I never have been very good at doing the right thing.

Thoughtlessly, I reach out and snag a towel, not realizing it's the smallest one on the rack.

"Seriously?" he seethes.

"Take it or leave it, asshole."

He curses under his breath as he snatches it from me and attempts to cover himself up.

"Sit down," I demand, pointing at the toilet.

"Excuse me?"

"Sit your ass down," I repeat.

Turning my back on him, I open the cupboard beneath the sink and pull out the first aid kit I found when I was snooping a few days ago.

Slamming it on the counter, I rummage around inside for what I need.

"Why are you still standing?" I bark, sensing him looming over me. You'd think he'd be less terrifying when his armor has been stripped away. But actually, it's the opposite.

He's even more intimidating when all his toned muscles and ink are on display.

You should have walked straight back out...

"I'm more than capable of cleaning myself up."

"Is that why you're still bleeding?" I counter, placing a hand on my waist and jutting a hip out.

"Fucking hell," he mutters, finally sitting his ass on the closed toilet seat, leaving the towel resting over his lap.

"Hand," I demand, lowering myself to my knees beside him.

I wish the memory of being in this position with him not so long ago would vanish into infinity and never return. But sadly, that's not the case, and instead of forgetting it, my cheeks burn with shame.

Forcing the image of crawling to him, basically begging for his dick, to the back of my mind, I turn his hand over and inspect the damage.

Usually, I'd let him walk around with shards of glass in his hand, leaving it to get infected. But I'm very aware that the reason he smashed that glass in the first place was because of me.

And if we are going to be on the same team to bring Victor and his band of fucked-up cunts down, then I need him fully functioning. Not with a dodgy shooting hand.

Grabbing a pair of tweezers, I push the points gently into one of the cuts, where I can see a shard of glass glistening in the bright lights above us.

The second I make contact, he flinches.

"You don't need to do this."

"I do. But I don't need you to be a pussy about it. It's just a bit of glass."

I glance up to see his teeth grind and his jaw pop.

"Aw, does it hurt?"

"It's just a bit of glass," he sneers, copying my words.

"Right. Well, I'll make this as quick as possible for the baby who can't cope with a little pain. Maybe I should shove a needle through your nipples while we're here, see how you like it."

His eyes blaze with heat, making me wonder how much he likes the idea of that. Twisted fuck.

"Maybe just focus on the hand for now," he mutters.

This time when I dig for the glass, I'm less gentle.

"Ow, fuck," he hisses, failing to pull his hand away when I hold his wrist tight.

"Baby," I mutter, keeping my eyes down and focused.

I just wish that meant I could miss the way his dick begins to harden. And it only gets worse the more pain I inflict.

As I work, finally confident I've removed all the glass, the tension between us grows, as does the tent in the towel.

Just before I reach for a bandage to wrap around his hand, I risk looking up.

I know he's not looking at me. The second he shut his eyes, the tingles down the side of my face he was staring at lessens. But what I'm not expecting is to find his face taut with restraint. His eyes are squeezed closed; there's a deep crease between his brows and his lips are pressed into a thin line.

"If you're done, you can leave." He growls, clearly able to sense my attention, despite having his eyes closed.

"I-I'm not. I just need to—"

Reaching for the roll, I begin wrapping his hand. I've covered the deeper cuts with skin closures. I've no idea if it's enough or not, but the thought of actually stitching him up makes my stomach roll.

The warmth of his skin burns up my arm but I don't let that or the crackling intensity between us stop me.

Just do the job and get out.

Easy.

The second I'm done, I throw everything back into the first aid kit and get ready to run. Only, the second I lift the box from his lap, the towel comes with it, leaving his very hard, and very pretty—I'm never ever telling him that—cock exposed.

Jesus Christ. Is that a magic cross?

Asshole.

Time stops. Literally freezes with my eyes locked on his dick. It's long and thick with what I can only assume is the perfectly designed curve because I know for a fact that when that's inside a woman it's to hit—

My thighs clench as I try to imagine what it might be like to have him stretching me wide.

JD's size is more than generous, but I think Reid might have him on girth.

My mouth waters, my panties utterly ruined as precum beads at the swollen head of his cock, the metal balls on each side glinting in the light.

I lick my lips, unable to stop myself as the need to drop back to my knees to taste him, to figuratively bring this enigma of a man to his own fucking knees almost gets the better of me.

But then his words from earlier when I was in that exact position slam into me. *"No. I don't need anything from you. I got your secrets."*

It's lies. His dick is the only part of his body telling the truth right now and it wants everything I have to offer. It's just a shame I'm not willing to give it.

Suddenly, time starts again and I stumble back, as if he just said those words to me.

I pause at the door and look up, finding his dark eyes glaring daggers at me. It's almost enough to hide the desire. But not quite.

"Go back to your husband, Alana." He growls darkly.

I'm about to run when I remember why I'm here in the first place.

"No."

"No?" he asks, his brows jumping impossibly high at my defiance.

"You heard me. No."

24

REID

I stare dumbfounded as she blatantly defies me.

Who the hell does she think she is?

The woman who makes your cock harder than any other and the one who's standing in your bathroom like she owns it.

"I came in here to shower."

Her hands land on her hips as she glances into the stall that's got her girly shit in it.

I don't even remember allowing that to happen, but it seems to be there all the same.

"Fine." I huff, sounding like a petulant child as I push to my feet and reach for another towel to cover up. Not that I need to bother now. She's seen it all. Every tempting, hard inch of me.

She wants it. I can see it in her eyes. She's desperate to part those sexy full lips and suck my—

Lock it down, asshole.

Wrapping the towel around my waist, I stand tall before moving toward her. Most others would cower, but not Alana.

She knows the power she holds over me, and she's not likely to forget it any time soon. Neither am I, but that's another issue entirely and one I'm going to have to figure out how to deal with.

Somehow, the sanctuary I used to share with my best friend is turning into a goddamn hotel.

They're going to help you...

And now not only do I have a woman who oozes sex appeal fucking JD any chance they get, but I've got her cunt of a fucking husband here too. I guess the only good thing about that is that he's getting about as much action as I am.

Fuck me, I'm trying to find common ground with Maverick Murray.

Alana stands in the middle of the bathroom with her hands on her hips, glaring at me.

"Can't say I'm surprised," I murmur as I get closer. Her eyes shutter as she prepares for the pain I'm about to inflict in return. "If I'd just learned my wife had been up to the kind of shit you have, I wouldn't want you either."

Holding her head high, she refuses to take the bait.

"He's relaxing in the bath."

I can't help but snort. "The bath?"

"Nothing wrong with that," she says confidently before finally moving out of my way and dragging her bloodstained tank over her head.

"I think the main problem is that any other wife would be naked in it with him, using every tool at her disposal to help him relax."

"You can leave now," she shoots over her shoulder, before undoing her shorts and shoving them over her hips. "Or did you want to watch?"

More than you could believe.

The sheer amount of willpower it takes to turn my back

on her when she reaches for the clasp on her bra is almost more than I possess, but I do it, and I slam the door behind me for good measure.

My cock still tents the towel, but despite my need to rip it from my body and wrap my hand around my length, I resist. Usually, I'd hit the gym to shift the tension that's locking my muscles tight. But as selfish as I want to be, I've got a house full of people expecting dinner.

Angrily, I tug a pair of boxers up my legs, followed by some pants and a shirt.

I scrub the towel over my hair, leaving it however it falls and abandoning the damp fabric on the floor, a surefire way to piss her off when she walks out. Doing it makes my eye twitch, but I stand firm and leave the room.

"Why are you loitering?" I snap, unsurprisingly finding JD pacing back and forth down the hallway.

"What happened?" he asks, his eyes holding mine, begging for information.

"You need to find a way to get past this obsession, J. It's going to drag you down."

"I'm not ob—" He cuts himself off, shaking his head. "I'm just worried."

"Trust me, she's fine," I murmur, thinking of the way she defied me only minutes ago.

"B-but—"

"I'm going to make dinner. You joining me or are you going to continue pacing out here like an impatient puppy?"

"You're an asshole," he seethes.

"So I've heard," I mutter, marching past the door that hides Mav in his fucking bubble bath and jogging down the stairs in the hope it help rid me of the irritation and my raging hard-on.

"So, what's the plan then, Big Man?" JD asks, once he's

sitting at his spot at the island and I have my head in the refrigerator, ready to grab everything I bought for dinner.

"Don't call me that," I snarl.

"Why not? When Alana does, it makes your eyes go all weird."

My shoulders tense. "They do not."

"Bro, they so do. It's cute."

Standing back, I glare at him. "Cute?"

"I know," he says with a smirk. "I didn't think you were capable of it either, but I was proved wrong."

"And I'm the asshole," I mutter, returning to the job at hand.

"Seriously though, what's the plan?"

Lowering everything to the counter, I rest my palms on the cool surface and hang my head.

"I need to speak to my uncle. Let him know the latest. And get Ellis digging."

"Everything else is in place, though, yeah?" he asks.

"I hope so." Fuck me, do I hope so.

If this goes wrong...

I've already dug deeper than I should, got myself in the middle of Victor and his contacts. If I start looking into the human trafficking ring Alana talked about and I get caught...

Well, safe to say that none of us will be around to bring anyone down.

"I trust you, man. And when this is all over, you're gonna be the best boss this place has ever seen."

"Let's not get carried away. You want a job?" I ask, already knowing his answer.

"Do I have a choice?"

"Nope. This lettuce needs washing and you're just the man for the job."

Picking it up, I throw it across the room like a football. "Go long," I shout, giving him little choice but to jump from the stool and race after it.

"I hate you," he bellows as I stalk out of the room to go and find my hidden knives.

I like to think hiding them is overkill. But that look in his eye after Alana kicked him out of my room was fucking terrifying.

Hiding them might have made it worse, might have made him think that I don't trust him. But I am too fucking scared to test the theory. Plus, he hasn't mentioned it, so I've no idea if he's even noticed. It's not like he'd ever attempt to make anything more exciting than a slice of toast in my kitchen.

But the second I walk back into the room with the box in my hand, I know he's aware.

He glances at it briefly from his spot at the sink being my sous-chef, but he doesn't comment.

Maybe I did do the right thing.

We work in silence, him washing the lettuce like his life depends on it while I chop everything I need.

JD and I are more than comfortable without saying anything, but there's an edge of tension I don't like between us.

We don't have secrets, or at least, I don't think we do. He's the only one other than my uncle who is fully invested in my plan to take down Victor.

He might have made some less than stellar life choices in the past, but I trust him with everything I am. The future, should we succeed in my plan, will include him being my right-hand man, always.

But right now, there's a distance between us that makes my shoulders knot and my eyes shoot over to his equally as tense back more often than not.

And I know why. I know exactly why.

She's currently standing naked in my shower.

"You think Mav's gonna pull the stick from his ass now and fuck his wife?" he blurts when he finally finishes washing the last of the lettuce and turns to watch me.

"Fuck knows. Don't care," I mutter.

"Of course you don't," he teases.

"We both know you only do because if she starts bouncing on his, she'll want yours less."

"Sure, it could go that way. I was thinking that either he'd have forgotten how to use it and she'd prefer mine, or she might want both."

"Jesus, is this really what you sit up at night thinking about?"

"Little bit of that, little bit of world domination. Don't even try convincing me that you're any different. I saw that tent you were rocking in your pants when you left your bedroom earlier."

"Not the point," I argue.

"Exactly the fucking point. When are you going to admit that you want her?"

Gritting my teeth, I throw a handful of chopped onion into the pan beside me, letting the crack and pop of the oil fill the silence I'm not willing to do with words.

"I saw the way you kissed her before," he continues. "It was like you thought you might die without it."

"Moment of weakness after the intel she gave us."

"Oh sure, you wanted her wrapped around you like a snake because of the intel."

"Things got intense," I mutter, waving my bandaged hand at him.

"I guess she did that for you," he correctly assumes.

"Maybe I did it myself."

He laughs, his eyes glinting with amusement. If I weren't so happy to see it, I'd want to throw a knife at him to shut him up.

"I bet you gave yourself that boner while you were at it too, huh?"

"You're a prick."

Turning my back on him, I focus on the pan before me as he grabs us beers and knocks the tops off.

"Yep, you love me, though."

"Debatable."

"Can you at least tell me you're regretting it," he says, jumping up onto the counter, watching me as I add spices to my pan, letting the scent flood my nostrils.

"Regret what?" I ask absently.

"Not letting her wrap her lips around your dick and suck you dr—"

A throat clearing in the doorway cuts off JD's words. But while he might falter at our visitor, my movements don't. I refuse to let that asshole see even an inch of weakness.

"Hey, man. How are you feeling?" JD, the fucking traitor, asks, his voice a little higher than a few seconds ago. "You want a beer? Dinner won't be long. Reid's an epic cook, did you know that?"

Silence.

Well, this is just fucking great.

25

MAVERICK

The bath should be relaxing. I've been fucking dying for one for days. Desperate for the warmth, the lightness that comes with floating in the massive tub we have in the master bathroom at home.

But nothing about this bath is what I was hoping for.

With my head resting back against the side, I keep my eyes closed as all the awful things I said to Alana cycle through my mind. Each one dripping poison through my veins.

I shouldn't have said them. But I couldn't stop myself.

Seeing her with them. Knowing what she's been doing. Seeing the evidence of *his* touch on her body. All of that mixed with days of solitude in that freezing cell has fucked with my head.

But having her in my arms again, her scent in my nose, even if it was laced with them. Fuck. It was so fucking good.

I lie there with the water cooling around me, aware that I need to get out, but also not wanting to. When I thought about leaving that cell, at no point did I consider that I

215

wouldn't be allowed out of the house above. That I'd be lying here in a bathtub in Reid Harris's guest room.

Fuck my life.

Noise comes from the other side of the door, and my eyes spring open at the possibility of seeing her.

Shadows move, but for a few minutes, she doesn't appear.

The anticipation is so raw that when she does gently knock on the door, I startle.

"Yeah," I croak, my heart picking up speed as she pushes the door open and steps inside fresh from her shower.

Her shorter hair is hanging limply around her shoulders, and thankfully, she's scrubbed that cunt's blood from her body. But the relief that comes with that knowledge only lasts so long because I soon realize that she's wearing one of his shirts.

Motherfucker.

"Hey," she says almost shyly.

I hate it. Hate that I've given her reason to question me.

Lifting my hand from the water, I hold it out for her.

Her eyes drop to it, and when she doesn't move immediately, I almost tug it back.

Instead, I push myself up so I'm sitting.

"I'm sorry, Doll," I whisper.

My voice drags her from wherever she'd gone and she immediately rushes over, sliding her small hand into mine and perching her ass on the edge of the tub.

"Me too, Mav. Everything has been... it's been so crazy. I've hurt you, I know I have. But trust me when I say that I never—"

Reaching out with my other hand, I press two fingers against her lips.

"We've both done things we're not proud of, babe," I assure her.

"Maybe. But you haven't been fu—"

"Stop, please," I beg, taking both of her hands in mine. "There's time to talk about it all. But that's not right now."

"Okay," she agrees quietly, her eyes searching mine. "You don't hate me, though, right?"

"Doll," I breathe. "I meant what I said before you walked out of here. And," I add before she can say anything, "I want it to be enough."

"Me too." Her voice is barely audible as her eyes fill with tears. "What do you need?" she asks, studying me closely as if I'm about to break.

"Food and sleep."

"You got it." Tugging her hand from mine, she walks toward the towel rail, pulls one free and holds it out for me.

I can't help but chuckle when she averts her eyes so I can climb out.

"Thanks," I mutter, letting her know that it's safe to look.

I've no idea what she's scared of. She might look hot as shit with her side boob showing in that wide-armed tank, but I'm way too fucking exhausted for it to stir much. Tomorrow might be a different story.

Her eyes find mine before she loses her fight and drops them down my body.

"He attacked us with different types of guns then," she mutters almost absently as she stares at my chest.

"He shot you?" I balk.

She sucks in a sharp breath, her gaze darting back up to mine.

"Uh... no. He did leave me with a memento of my time down there, though. Just a different kind of hole to yours."

"Alana." I growl, taking a step closer, ready to force the truth from her lips.

If he hurt her, really fucking hurt her, I'll end him. Same fucking team or not, no one hurts my wife.

I have to do a double take when she reaches for the bottom of the shirt she's wearing and shamelessly lifts it, giving me an unobscured view of her tits.

Her... pierced tits.

"H-holy fuck." I grunt as my body happily proves me wrong. It seems I'm not too tired for my dick to work.

"They're still healing. But... I think I like them."

Thankfully, she must decide I've looked enough, and she drops the fabric, letting it hang back in place. But now I know what she's hiding under there, all I can see is the press of her nipples against the thin cotton.

"Y-yeah, they're... something."

"He tied me to the chair in his torture chamber, blindfolded me and went to town."

My fists curl, but fuck if the image she paints doesn't make my blood run hot.

"H-he—"

"It's okay. Nothing I couldn't handle. My hair was worse." Something like pain flashes in her eyes and it makes my stomach knot.

"He did that too?" I ask, horrified, reaching for a damp lock.

I mean, it looks good. Although, I'm pretty sure anything would look good on her. But I know what her hair meant to her, and I understand how painful it must have been when he hacked it off.

"Whatever," she lies, waving it off as if it's nothing. "What matters is where we go from here. He wants Victor as dead as we do. He's already got some kind of plan and he had no idea about any of this," she says, gesturing to herself. "With his help, Mav. We could end it all."

Fire lights up her eyes. It's infectious, making something akin to excitement flutter in my belly.

There's just one issue.

"We're going to have to work with him, Doll," I blurt.

"I know. And I know it isn't ideal, but I figure we can give them everything we know, help him finalize his plan to bring them down and then we fuck off."

"Fuck off?" I ask, a little more intrigued.

"That's what we always said we'd do, right? Justice then paradise. Just me and you?"

Taking a step forward, I cup her jaw, leaning in to press my brow against hers.

"Just me and you?"

Her eyes flutter closed, and she blindly reaches for me.

The second her palm connects with my waist, an electric current rushes through me, ending right at my dick.

"Fuck that sounds—" My words are cut off when my stomach growls loudly, successfully ending our little moment.

She laughs, her hand sliding from my waist to my stomach. Goose bumps erupt in its wake. There's no way she doesn't feel them, but for whatever reason, she also doesn't stop. And for once, I don't make her. "I know all this isn't ideal. But there is one positive, and that's the food. We're almost there, Mav. Everything we've planned. It's right in touching distance."

Stretching up on her toes, she presses a simple kiss to the corner of my mouth. It would be so easy to turn and make it more. To cave and take from her what everyone else seems to already have had.

But that's not what this is about. It never has been.

We want it to be though.

Paradise.

What we've always planned.

That's when we'll get to have the kind of relationship she's always deserved. When we're away from here and the pain of the past. Just the two of us against the world.

"I'm going to dry my hair. I'll meet you downstairs, yeah?"

"Really?" I grunt as she takes a step back, her eyes dropping down my body, lingering on the towel a little too long to be polite.

"Really. And do you know what else?" she asks, her playful eyes meeting mine.

"No, but I suspect you're about to tell me."

Her smile starts slow, but it spreads wide. The sight of it makes my heart sing. I want to believe it's the prospect of our future that gives her that hopeful look in her eyes, and not the two assholes downstairs. But while she might be saying the right words, I can't help but wonder if they've had more of an impact on her than she'd like to believe.

I guess only time will tell.

"You're going to play nice."

"Doll," I complain.

"Trust me," she says with a playful wink. "It'll be worth it."

Before I manage to think up an answer to that, she's gone, leaving nothing but her addictive floral scent in her wake.

Play nice with Reid Harris. Yeah, when hell freezes over...

I t's a nice thought, but the second I emerge from the bathroom, after making use of the brand-new toothbrush that had been left on the side, I find a neat pile of men's clothes waiting for me.

I don't need to ask who they belong to. I know the second my eyes land on them.

My teeth grind, my irritation growing. But what the hell am I meant to do? Refuse to make the best of this situation and starve?

If Alana is right, and this is the chance we've been waiting for it, then wearing his clothes, eating his food, laughing at his shitty jokes—assuming he knows how to crack one—should be easy enough. After all, I'll have her by my side. It'll be worth it. I have to believe that.

With my borrowed clothes on my weak as fuck body, I prepare to navigate enemy territory in search of the scent of food that's made its way up here.

The hallway is quiet when I poke my head out. It would be easy to snoop, but that'll have to come another day when I have more energy.

With my hand locked around the rail, I make my way down. I'm slow, pathetically slow. It's just more evidence that Alana is right. I need to do this, build my strength back up and then throw myself into whatever Reid is planning. I just have to hope it's enough, because if it isn't then we're all fucking dead and our fathers will be dancing on our graves.

A shudder rips through me.

Among the three of them, they've already taken enough from us. It's time the tide turned.

The rumble of deep voices float up to me as I continue on my painstaking mission of getting down the fucking stairs.

My stomach knots as I think about walking into a room to find Reid Harris watching me like, well... a hawk.

Shaking my head, I finally hit the ground floor, their voices getting louder.

It's not until I get to the doorway that leads to a seriously impressive kitchen that I register what—or who—they're talking about.

"Can you at least tell me you're regretting it," JD says from somewhere deeper in the room.

"Regret what?" Reid asks, almost sounding bored as I round the corner and find him standing at the stove. Not a place I ever pictured the prince of Harrow Creek, if I'm being honest.

"Not letting her wrap her lips around your dick and suck you dr—"

My entire world falls from beneath me as I picture Alana on her knees for that sick fuck. Before I know what I'm doing, I've marched deeper into the room, my eyes fixed on them as I clear my throat, announcing my presence.

Reid doesn't so much as flinch. It's almost as if he knew I was there.

JD, on the other hand, his eyes widen and his spine straightens in shock.

"Hey, man. How are you feeling?" JD rambles in panic. "You want a beer? Dinner won't be long. Reid's an epic cook, did you know that?"

"No." I growl. "I wasn't aware he had any redeeming qualities," I confess. "Water will be fine."

"Oh, you've got so many things to learn about the goings on under this roof."

"So it seems," I muse, taking a cold bottle of water from JD as Reid continues with what he's doing. He hasn't even bothered to turn around and greet me. Jerk.

"Good bath?" JD asks, trying to make conversation. "I'm more of a shower guy myself. I like to be in and out, not just sit there festering in my own stench."

"You don't like to do it alone though, do you, J? Why don't you tell Mav about how you prefer company and just how loud you make them scream."

Thankfully, light footsteps thunder down the stairs before Alana barrels into the room red-faced and wide-eyed.

"Can you stop," she begs.

"What?" Reid says, if he's trying to sound innocent, he falls about a mile from the mark.

She lets out a pained sigh before looking up at me, silently begging me to ignore them.

If only it was that easy.

"What's on the menu tonight, Big Man?" Alana asks, but the second her nickname for Reid rolls off her tongue, she stills.

All the air rushes from my lungs as I'm faced with the truth of just how close she's become to these men.

Sensing my horror, Reid finally turns around. His eyes almost immediately lock with mine as a smug as fuck grin pulls at his lips.

He might not have let her suck his cock for whatever reason, but he's in her head, and the motherfucker knows it.

"Mexican, Pet," he says, finally shifting his gaze to her. He holds her eyes for a beat before letting them drop down her body. "Look at that, buy a girl her own clothes and she still chooses to wear mine. I'll start thinking you miss smelling like me, Pet."

"Ignore him," Alana says, lacing her fingers through mine and attempting to drag me toward the couches that look out over the valley of Harrow Creek beyond. "If we're having Mexican, I assume someone is making me margaritas," she shoots over her shoulder.

"You got it, Dove. And if you're lucky, I'll let you lick the salt from my abs."

A deep growl rumbles in my throat.

They're baiting me, I know they are. And it's fucking working.

The second I'm in front of the couch, Alana plants her hands on my chest and shoves until I've no choice but to fall back. Almost as quickly, she drops beside me and snuggles into my side.

"They're only doing it because you're reacting. Lock it down, yeah?"

"Easier said than done. You're mine, Doll. I don't think they understand that."

Her lips part as if she's going to argue, but at the last minute, she thinks better of it.

She stares up at me, her big blue eyes wide and hopeful.

"Maybe you should show them," she suggests, leaning closer.

26

ALANA

I stare up at him, my heart racing, my fingers tightening their grip on his thigh.

I want him.

No. I *need* him.

For five years I've dealt with him holding back, with his rejection. But it seems that my time here without him might have been the final straw because my patience has run out.

Days of imagining what our life together could be like, hours telling myself what I would do the moment I saw him again, they've all come down to this.

There's movement behind me, but I ignore it. I don't care what they're doing, if they're watching. My only focus is the man in front of me.

My husband.

The man who rescued me.

The only man who's ever protected me.

"Please," I whimper, leaning so close the heat of his lips warm mine.

He's right here. Right fucking here, but still, he holds back.

"Mav," I cry.

"Fucking pussy," JD scoffs behind us, making Mav's chest catch.

He wants it. I can see his desire burning bright in his eyes. It's been there since I shamelessly lifted my top and showed him my new jewelry. Was it a low blow? Yeah, most definitely. But I figured he deserved a little treat after being locked up, and I'm not exactly opposed to forcing his hand. I've tried it many, many times before. One time it's going to break him, I know it is.

Finally, he moves. It's slight. So fucking slight, but it's there, and it makes my breath catch.

Time stops. I don't breathe. I don't do anything.

And the second his soft lips press against the corner of my mouth, all the air rushes from my lungs.

My eyes shutter as I make the most of the moment. It's innocent and nowhere near what I really need. But still, it's everything.

My hand moves of its own accord, sliding up his thigh, but the second I get within dangerous territory, his clamps down on top of it, stopping my progress.

Separating our lips, he rests his head against mine instead.

His eyes remain closed as he sucks in deep breaths through his nose.

Other than the sizzling of Reid's cooking, the room is blanketed in silence. The way my skin tingles tells me why. They're watching with almost as much anticipation as I feel.

After long, agonizing seconds, Mav's eyelids flutter open, and his tired, dark eyes find mine.

There's an apology in them that makes my stomach knot uncomfortably.

"Is that it?" JD barks. "She's been gagging for it for years. Be a man and take it, bro. Ow," JD complains, and I look back just in time to see him rubbing his shoulder, where Reid must have hit him.

I frown, watching the man in question turn his attention back to the pan as if he didn't just... what? Stick up for the enemy?

"Ignore him," I whisper, although I think I'm too late because when I look back at Mav, he's staring out the window at the view of the Creek below. "Looks better from up here, huh?" I mutter, remembering how I felt the first time I saw our hometown from this angle. It's easy to forget about the corruption, the pain, and the nightmares that haunt this place when you're no longer in the middle of it.

"Yeah," he muses, wrapping his arm tighter around my waist and holding me close.

It might not be exactly what I want. But I'll take it. I'll take any little scrap of him he's willing to give me.

Movement continues behind us, the scent of Reid's cooking making both our stomachs growl, but we let it all pass us by as we soak up each other's company.

There was a time not so long ago when I wasn't sure if I'd ever get this again. Now that I have it, I want to embrace every second of it.

He might still be unwilling to cross the invisible line he drew between us five years ago, but that's not the be-all and end-all. The relationship we've built, the connection. That is everything, and I never want to lose it.

"Dinner's ready," Reid says as the sun begins to sink behind the hill in the distance, casting everything in a burnt orange hue.

Twisting my fingers through Mav's, I lead him to the table for admittedly the most awkward, dysfunctional family meal of my life. And considering the state of my family, that really is saying something.

But despite the tension surrounding us, the second Mav's ass hits the chair, he begins shoveling food into his mouth, and he doesn't stop until long after I've had my fill.

I'm pretty sure he has to hit some kind of world record of taco-eating because it is borderline obscene.

"Anyone would think you hadn't been fed all week," JD teases when Mav finally looks like he's going to come up for air.

Mav looks up at the man opposite him, his expression is blank, but if looks could kill, I'm pretty sure the daggers shooting from his eyes would put JD six feet under.

"You were right, Doll. Reid does have one redeeming feature. Asshole can cook," Mav says, finally turning to me. A shudder rips down my spine when he pulls a lock of my hair away from my cheek and tucks it behind my ear.

"Is there dessert?" I ask, trying not to get so lost in Mav's eyes that I risk embarrassing myself by climbing into his lap.

"I have something in mind," JD says, his voice giving away his lust-filled thoughts. "Once Reid has cleared the table, we can lay you out and—"

"The fuck did your last slave die of?" Reid barks, correctly assuming where JD was going with that little image he was painting, and thankfully, cuts him off. "There's ice cream in the freezer if you want it," he offers, collecting up some plates despite his previous words.

"Pfft, not exactly what I had in mind."

"I'm going to bed," Mav says, refusing to look at anyone as he releases my hand. He shoves his chair back and walks away from the table. "Enjoy your evening," he mutters over his shoulder.

"Mav, wait," I cry, jumping up and racing after him.

Wrapping my hand around his upper arm, I draw him to a stop.

"I'm coming with you," I say quietly.

He sighs, his eyes locked on the wall ahead as he battles with whatever is going on in his head.

Exhaustion? Confusion? Anger?

It's not until his eyes finally meet mine that I get my answer.

Jealousy. It's so potent, I'm surprised his eyes aren't glowing green.

"You mean, you don't want to stay and offer yourself up as dessert?" he seethes through clenched teeth.

I know it's his exhaustion, but still, the suggestion that I might want that more than I want to be with him after being apart for so long stings.

JD's tongue is good, I can't lie. But there's no way I'd choose it over Mav right now. Not in a million years.

"No, I don't," I assure him, moving toward the stairs.

He's silent as we make our way up, and the moment he disappears into the bathroom, my stomach knots with anxiety.

What if he doesn't want me here? What if his taunt about staying downstairs and allowing Reid and JD to do wicked things to me is what he wants?

What if—

The second he emerges, my eyes lock on his tired ones. Every ounce of fight has drained out of him. Without bothering to strip down, he stumbles toward the bed, drags the sheets back, and collapses into it.

But he doesn't immediately pass out like I'm expecting. Instead, he cracks one eye open and slides his hand toward me.

"You getting in or just watching, Doll?" His voice is so deep and raspy that it sends a rush of tingles through my body.

What would it be like to hear him groan in my ear as he thrusts—

Shaking my head, I try to rid myself of that image as I move closer.

I can count on one hand the number of times we've slept in the same bed. My nightmares and reaction to them had to be really bad to convince him to do so.

But as much as I loved feeling his warmth beside me, or his soothing hand resting on my arm, it was never enough.

The second I lie down and shuffle closer, I discover that something has changed because when he reaches out, it's not just to hold me.

His fingers tighten on my hip and he drags me across the mattress until there is barely an inch between our bodies.

His dark eyes bounce between mine as he tries to search for all the information he doesn't know yet.

"I'm sorry," he whispers, making me swallow thickly. "You said you did this for me. I'm sorry."

"Mav," I breathe, reaching up to cup his jaw.

"I'm sorry I was never able to give you what you needed."

My eyes flood with tears, and despite doing my best to blink them back, the torrent is too strong.

"You're everything," I whisper, my heart shattering for this incredible man before me. All he's done for five years is protect me, try and give me everything he thought I deserved, and treat me like a princess. It's not his fault that every now and then I need to be treated like the whore I was molded into.

He shakes his head, his hand skimming up my side until he mimics my pose, swiping my stray tear away with his thumb.

"I might hate it, but I know they've given you something you needed. I can see it in your eyes. I heard it in the way you screamed his name."

"I'm sorry," I whisper. It's so quiet that there's no chance he would hear me if he weren't so close. We're so close that it doesn't take much movement for him to brush his lips against mine.

A sob threatens to erupt as he gives me what I was craving downstairs. A realization flickers in my mind that he wanted to do it, just not in front of an audience.

I close my eyes, absorbing the sensation of having his lips on mine as he tugs me closer, removing the lingering space between us and tightly pinning our bodies together. So tightly I can feel everything. This kiss might not be the kind that leads to more, but he's certainly thinking about it.

Butterflies flutter in my belly. I feel like a teenage girl who's just discovered her crush likes her back.

It's ridiculous. He's my husband, and it's not like it's the first time I've experienced him getting aroused around me. But this time is different. His hardness pressing against my stomach is the sign I needed that everything might just be okay. That he doesn't totally hate me for everything I've done, for what I've been forced to do. Maybe once all of this is over, there really is something salvageable between us.

But as happy as that makes me, part of the excitement fades as I think about JD. About walking away from something else I've discovered here.

A tormented sigh passes my lips as Mav pulls away. But while my eyes open to take him in, his stay closed, and only a few seconds later, his breathing evens out and his lips part in slumber.

I study him. His hair that's longer than he likes as it falls over his brow, his thick eyelashes resting down on his cheekbones. Tracing my fingertip over the long stubble that's covering his jaw, I make my way to his lips, relearning the lines of his face.

Releasing his jaw, I trace Mav's lips with my fingertip, wishing they were pressed against my skin again.

Unable to stop myself, I lean forward and steal a kiss.

"Sweet dreams," I whisper, falling still beside him and closing my eyes as I wait for sleep to claim me too.

All I can hope is that with him back by my side, it keeps the monsters at bay.

27

ALANA

My scream rips through the air, but it doesn't help. The hands gripping me, the darkness that consumes me, neither leave.

"No, please. No. I'm sorry. I'm sorry," I chant as if it'll do any good.

"Too late. You had the chance to do as you were told and you chose wrong."

I can't see a thing, but that doesn't mean I don't know exactly where I am. If the cool air whipping around my almost bare body wasn't enough, the scent as we close in on the old, abandoned shed at the end of the garden tells me everything I need to know. It's moldy and dank, and it makes my stomach turn over the second it hits my nose.

I hate this place, even more than I hate the house. And I fucking hate that place with a fiery passion.

The rotten old door creaks loudly in the night as he rips it open, and my blood runs cold as he steps inside. Despite already being blindfolded, my surroundings get darker as we lose the brightness of the moon sitting high in the sky.

I tell myself not to react, I've already given him too

much, but the second I'm released from his hold, a scream rips from my throat a beat before I collide with the wall.

The old wooden planks this place is made of rip into my skin, and my shoulder instantly burns in pain.

"I'm sorry. I'm sorry," I try again.

It's pointless.

He doesn't care. He's proved that time and time again over the years. But there's still a very small part of me that hopes he'll remember one day that I'm his daughter. His little girl that he brought into the world and promised to protect. Well, I assume that he did at some point. I like to think that Mom wouldn't have stuck with him long enough to have me, let alone Kristie too, if he was always a sick fuck. But then, maybe that's nothing more than an illusion.

Kurt Winson gets exactly what he wants every single time.

It's a fantasy to think that Mom was here by her own free will. The likelihood is that she was here against her will like I am.

She was probably trying to protect me, just like I am Kristie. The only difference is that she failed, paying the ultimate price for her dedication to her kids.

I haven't met that fate yet, leaving Kristie at the hands of a monster, but I'm under no illusion that it could happen at any time.

A sob rips from my throat as I think about leaving Kristie with him.

So far, he lets her live her life like an almost normal little girl. She gets to go to school. She has friends. A life.

But just like my existence, that could all change very very fast.

A pained cry spills from my lips as my bound hands are

yanked back before being secured to the hook he installed in the floor not so long ago.

Apparently, merely locking me in here wasn't enough. I had to be bound and unable to protect myself if a wild animal, or worse, one of his friends, came searching.

He grunts and groans as if this is a hardship on him as he secures me.

Once he's done, his boots smack against the unforgiving concrete floor as he steps back to admire his handiwork.

My skin prickles with disgust as he runs his eyes over me.

Before they blindfolded me, I was wearing leggings and a hoodie, but since then, I've been stripped to my panties and tank. A shiver rips through me as the realization that I'm going to be spending the rest of the night out here freezing settles in my brain.

I continue to sob, but I don't try begging or pleading again. I knew it was pointless before and I know it would be now. The words spill out anyway in a lame attempt.

A lame attempt to help myself. It's pointless. There is no one out there who can help me. This is my life. My reality. My hell.

The footsteps move farther back, toward the door. There's a part of me that dreads him leaving. He might be a monster, but to a point, he's predictable. But there's another part that is desperate for him to leave, so I can break down properly alone.

I never, ever want him knowing how much any of this really hurts me.

I'll punch, kick, scratch, refuse to be the good little compliant girl they want. But I will not let him watch me break. Not really.

The second the door creaks closed, a sob grows at the

back of my throat, but I fight it, keep it trapped down until his footsteps finally fade. And then I let it free. Loud, angry, body-wracking sobs rip through me as my tears soak through the fabric covering my eyes and snot streams from my nose. My body aches, my muscles screaming in pain at the way I've been treated. They might not have gotten to rip my panties free and spread my legs, but they've abused me in every other way.

Thrashing against my bindings, I fight to free myself. But it's pointless, they're too tight.

Collapsing onto the ground, I curl up in a ball in an attempt to save some body heat. I've no idea how I manage it, pure exhaustion and my body shutting down I guess, but eventually, I cry myself to sleep.

Shivers still wrack my body, but my need to shut down is stronger.

I just wish the slumber brought some relief.

By the time the loud creak of the rickety old door echoes through the silence, my body is covered in sticky cold sweat from my nightmares, and that doesn't get any better when the footsteps approach.

A whimper of relief threatens to escape, but I swallow it down, pretending I haven't heard him.

He crouches, his whiskey-laced breath washing over me, making my stomach roll in disgust.

"I'm going to count to three, and then you're going to do as you're told," he says.

I've no idea if he thinks I'm faking being asleep, or if he's hoping I can't hear him and will defy him again.

Something tells me that it's probably the latter. Sick bastard.

The bindings holding my wrists hostage are suddenly cut free before his deep voice rocks through the air.

"One." My heart rate picks up.

"Two." I squeeze my eyes tighter, trying to predict where this is going to go. "Three." Pure fucking terror washes over me, freezing me to the spot.

But then he says one more word that makes me move faster than I ever have before.

"Run."

Lifting my hands, I rip the blindfold from my face. Ignoring the searing pain in my shoulders, I blink against the darkness and take off.

Shadows linger in the darkness surrounding me, but I ignore them and force my feet to pound faster, harder against the ground. I don't even feel the sticks and stones against my bare skin. The only thought floating through my head is my determination to outrun them.

It's pointless. Hopeless. But still, I hold onto a little nonetheless.

One day I'll win.

One day I'll—

A scream cuts off my thoughts as hands grab at me from behind. Hot, unforgiving fingertips dig into my skin, but I'm soaked with sweat and I easily slip out of their hold, continuing through the trees, praying that the cover from the moonlight will work in my favor.

Pain shoots from my bare feet, but my fear still overrides the pain as I run until my lungs feel like they're going to collapse.

But just like I knew would happen, shadows appear all around me, trapping me.

Tree. Monster. Tree. Monster.

I have nowhere to go. Nowhere to run to.

Looking up, I consider climbing, but what's the point? I'm never going to win this game.

They'll keep going until they kill me.

Collectively, they all step forward.

But as outnumbered as I might be, I still fight. I still scream. I still let every one of them know what I really think of them.

28

JD

I wake up sitting in the middle of my bed and not a second later, I discover why.

The screams.

Her screams.

Instantly, I'm wide awake as I launch myself across the room and rip the door open.

Lifting my foot to step out, my heart jumps into my throat when she runs past me, almost taking me out.

"Dove?" I call as she runs full speed toward Reid's end of the hallway.

But she doesn't stop, I'm pretty sure she doesn't hear me.

"No, no, no," she chants when she gets to the end and finds herself trapped by walls.

The second she spins around, reality hits.

Her eyes might be open, but they're glazed over.

She's asleep.

Asleep and living out one of her night terrors.

"Dove," I say a little harsher. "I need you to wake up for me," I demand as I approach.

She sees me coming. Well, not me exactly. A person. A man.

Fear like I've never seen from her before rips through her, making her wobble on unsteady legs.

Her chest heaves with exertion and her arms lift, ready to defend herself.

"It's okay, little dove. It's me. It's JD," I offer softly.

But she doesn't hear me.

Instead of focusing on me, seeing that I'm no threat, her eyes jump around, searching for a way out. But she's trapped herself at the end of the hall.

The only door is to a closet. I've already passed Reid's and the guest bedroom, not that they would have offered much of an escape.

"No, please. No," she begs, the words seeming to fall from her lips without instruction from her brain.

"Baby, it's me. I'm not going to hurt you." I hold my hands up, pain ripping through my own chest as I watch her suffer.

Fuck I hate this. No wonder Mav has spent five years trying to protect her.

If this is the lingering effect of everything she's suffered half a decade later, I can't even begin to imagine what it was like immediately after.

I step closer, and the screams start up again. Her arms flailing, her legs kicking out in an attempt to stop me.

Not gonna lie, each hit hurts. Girl's got some force behind her. But it'll take a hell of a lot more than that to make me give in.

"Alana, you're asleep. Wake up for me. Please, just wake the fuck up for me," I bark, staring into her eyes in the hope I'll crack through something while she continues to rain blows down on me. "I'm not going to hurt you, Dove. I'm going to take care of you."

She swings her arm out, but I'm too busy trying to wrestle the other one, so I don't see the hit coming. But I sure as fuck feel it the second her small balled-up fist connects with my temple.

"Ow, fuck, baby," I complain, my head spinning.

But if she felt any kind of pain from the punch then she doesn't show it and it sure as shit doesn't wake her up.

"Okay, I think that's enough now," I say, once my vision has cleared.

"NOOOOO," she screams when I finally manage to restrain one wrist, pinning it back against the wall.

I'm hardly surprised when a door opens behind me and a gruff, "The fuck is going on?" fills the hallway.

"Night terror," I explain, without looking back as I fight to grab her other arm.

"She's sleeping?" he asks in disbelief.

"Yes, asshole. She's fucking sleeping. You gonna help or what?"

"Christ," he mutters, slipping unnoticed behind her.

In a flash, he has her other arm in his grasp and has them both pinned at her sides.

Cautiously, I step forward, very aware that her next weapon of choice is going to be her knees, and I'm a little too fond of my dick to allow that to happen.

"Alana," I say firmly as I cup her cheeks, "can you wake up for me, little dove?"

Nothing.

"It's just me, baby," I say, my touch getting a little firmer. "Come back to us. You're okay. You're safe and—"

Her entire body tenses.

"Dove? It's just me, baby."

My heart thunders, my concern for her all-consuming as she fights to grasp what's real and what's not.

"You're safe. No one is chasing you." Reid shifts behind her and our eyes meet. "We're going to look after you. I just need you to look at me."

Finally, her eyelids flicker and hope blooms inside me.

Her dark and haunted blue eyes appear. They're swimming in unshed tears.

"Hey, Dove," I say softly, brushing my thumb over the soft skin of her jaw, the pad grazing the tempting swell of her bottom lip.

She blinks at me, but she doesn't do or say anything. She might be awake, but it's more than obvious that she's still lost to the images of her nightmare.

"We're not going to let anything happen to you here. You're safe. I promise."

Reid makes a weird noise in the back of his throat, and I glance up.

'What?' I mouth.

I might not make many promises in life, but that is one I know we can keep.

The only men she has to fear here are us, and something tells me that she's already seen the worst that we can deliver.

He shakes his head as Alana begins to tremble violently in his hold.

It rips me in two that I don't know how to help, how to take her fear away, how to make the night terrors stop.

I fear that even killing every single cunt who hurt her won't be enough. I'm willing to give it a good fucking go, though.

"Dove, what do you need?" I ask helplessly.

But she still says nothing.

"Kiss her," Reid demands.

"W-what?" I stutter, sure I misheard him.

"Kiss her. Distract her. Give her something else to focus on."

Ripping my eyes from hers, I stare up at my best friend.

"You know it'll work. You've already proved it."

I want to feel smug that I was right, that it was desire, not fear, that helped peel back her layers, but right now, all I feel is concern.

"Fuck. Yeah, yeah," I mutter, stepping closer to her.

Her body is burning up and it instantly makes my temperature soar and my dick twitch.

"You okay with that, little dove?" I whisper, brushing my thumb more purposely over her lip this time.

Her eyes lock on mine, but she doesn't say anything; she doesn't move. But there's something in her gaze, a desperate plea for me to do exactly what Reid suggested. To drag her out of this horror and replace it with pleasure.

Tilting my head to the side, I gently brush my lips against her.

It's simple, innocent, but fuck if it doesn't instantly make me want more.

Never in my life have I craved a woman like I do Alana. I swear, it's almost a sickness in itself. And I really don't need another one of those.

She doesn't react, but I know she wants to. My body recognizes it in hers.

I do it again, only this time, I let my tongue slip out, teasing her bottom lip, giving her a taste of what I have to offer.

It's quiet, so fucking quiet, that if there were any other sounds than our heaving breaths, we wouldn't notice, but she whimpers.

"There's my girl," I praise, before deepening the kiss and letting my tongue slip past her lips in search of hers.

And this time, she moves, kissing me back.

"That's it, Pet," Reid encourages gently.

She startles at the deep growl of his voice and I panic that she's about to pull away. But much to my relief, she does the very opposite and glides her tongue against mine.

"Fuck." I groan, my dick growing to full mast against her belly.

Dropping one hand to her waist, I hold her close, ensuring she can feel it.

"You drive me crazy, Dove," I confess before diving deeper into the kiss.

With every swipe of our tongues, she comes back to me. And before long, our kiss has turned filthy.

"Oh God," she whimpers when I suck on her bottom lip. "More."

"Yeah?" I ask excitedly, looking into her eyes for confirmation before glancing at Reid.

He's still holding her arms, and as much as I crave her touch, having him restrain her is hot as fuck.

He nods discreetly as she begs me in her sexy, raspy voice.

"I don't need telling twice, little dove."

Sliding my hand from her hip, I dip it under Reid's tank she's wearing before plunging it inside her panties.

"Fuck, she's soaked." I groan, unsure if I'm talking to myself or letting Reid in on the secret.

Parting her, my fingertips graze her sensitive nub. She cries out in pleasure as her head falls back against Reid's shoulder.

I've no idea if she knows he's there or not, but I'm not

about to point it out, not when I've got her juices coating my fingers.

"Julian," she cries when I spear two digits deep inside her.

"Christ." Reid grunts as she sags in his hold.

"That's it, little dove," I praise, my eyes focused on her face as the pleasure begins to force the fear aside. "You're going to be a good girl and come all over my fingers."

Out of the corner of my eye, Reid's jaw ticks.

Oh yeah, I bet I'm not the only one who's hard as fuck for her right now.

"Yes, yes," she chants as I start fucking her hard, circling her clit with the pad of my thumb, building her higher and higher.

Suddenly, she gasps and a rush of her juices runs down my fingers.

"Oh God." She moans and when I look down, I find that Reid's no longer restraining her arms and instead has slipped his hands into the wide armholes of his tank and has her tits in his grasp.

"That feel good, baby? You've got both our hands on you."

She doesn't reply. She doesn't need to.

She's fucking loving it.

No more words are said between us as we work her in sync to an intense release. She screams out as her body convulses, ridding her of the haunting memories and giving her something a hell of a lot more satisfying to think about when she wakes in the morning.

I don't stop until she's spent, her head resting back against Reid, her eyes closed and her lips parted as she tries to catch her breath.

She looks stunning. What I wouldn't give to pick her up

and carry her to bed to continue what we've started out here.

But I can't. I know I can't.

Pulling my hand from her panties, I take her jaw in between my clean fingers and force her to watch as I suck her juices from my skin.

Her pupils dilate as I groan in delight.

"So fucking sweet. Maybe next time I'll let Reid get a taste," I offer, although I'm not sure I mean it. Letting her lean against him is one thing but letting him get in on the action more than a grope of her incredible tits...

What the fuck am I talking about? Hell yes, I want to watch him make her come.

She whimpers as if she's thinking about it right now. But while her head might be on board, it seems her body isn't.

"Shit," Reid grunts when her knees give out. Before he can pull his hands from her tits to help, I have her in my arms.

"Come on, little dove. Back to bed for you," I muse, shifting her closer as my boner tries to force its way out of my boxers.

One glance at Reid and I quickly discover he's having a similar problem.

The second she rests her head against me, I'm pretty sure she falls asleep.

"You gonna admit that you want her yet?" I ask with a know-all smirk playing on my lips.

"Fuck off. I was just trying to help."

"How generous of you," I mutter, turning my back on him and walking down the hallway toward my room.

I'm just about to turn toward it when I pause.

"What's wrong?" he asks, proving he's watching.

"Nothing," I mutter, doing a one-eighty and returning her to the room she ran from.

Something tells me that despite running, the place she wants to be right now is beside her husband.

With a sigh, I step inside the room with her still in my arms before lowering her into the middle of the bed.

A light still on in the adjoining bathroom allows me to see her clearly with Reid's tank ruched up around her waist, exposing her tiny panties.

Reaching down, I squeeze my dick.

Sensing her presence, a still passed-out Mav reaches for her. His fingers find hers and they twist together as if they were made for each other.

The sight hits like a baseball bat across the chest.

They're meant to be together. They're married. Mav has been the one trying to put her back together all this time. She's right with everything she's said about him. He's done everything he can think of to try and make her life better; he just doesn't realize that in trying to be a better man than those she's known, he's been denying her a part of life she craves in a way he could never understand. At least, not until he experiences and sees the way she responds.

I stand there for the longest time watching them sleep. I should probably feel like a creep, but I don't. And when I finally move, it's not toward the door. Instead, I crawl onto the bit of space left on the edge of the bed and tuck myself against Alana's hot little body, ensuring her ass is tucked right against my dick.

29

MAVERICK

"Oh God," Alana whimpers, making my heart jump into my throat.

I'm about to reach for her when reality slams into me, or more so her ass grinds back against my morning wood.

"Yes, right there."

"Fuck, you're squeezing my fingers so tight, little dove."

The second the deep voice hits my ears, my eyes fly open. And the moment my surroundings become clear, I discover that I'm staring into a mischievous dark pair as he peppers kisses along my wife's shoulder.

Anger surges through me, mixing with the desire that's already turning my blood to lava just from hearing her cry out.

My lips part to say something, but he shakes his head, his eyes urging me to go with it.

I shouldn't. It's wrong.

But fuck... do I want to.

Still trapped in his warning stare, I gently roll my hips.

I have to bite back a moan at how good her ass feels against me.

'Enjoy it. She wants it,' JD mouths, before kissing back up her shoulder until he's nuzzling her neck.

She moans in a way I've never heard before, but hell if it doesn't make my dick jerk in excitement. It might be him making her feel good, but it doesn't matter. I'm here too.

All three of us...

I squeeze my eyes closed, unable to process that thought and instead, I focus on feeling. It seems like the easiest of the many options facing me right now.

JD finds her lips and I'm forced to listen as they make out.

Unable to just lie here grinding against her like a horny teenager, my hand jerks out, my fingers wrapping around her hip, holding her back against me. The warmth of her skin burns my palm, letting me know the tank and her panties are gone, leaving her exposed.

The moan that rumbles in her throat when we connect is the best fucking sound I've ever heard.

Her body stills as she realizes what's happening, but before she can turn to look at me, JD captures her chin and forces her to look at him instead.

"Be a good girl, Dove," he murmurs, making her entire body sink into the mattress.

She loved that.

No. She *needed* that.

The realization that there's so much I don't know about my wife hurts like a bitch. But I know I've only got myself to blame.

"Fuck, that feels good." He groans.

My eyes pop open again, but this time, all I'm greeted with is Alana's messy blonde hair.

Tightening my grip on her hip, I grind into her harder, leaving her under no illusion that I'm awake.

"Oh fuck." She groans. "Yes. Mav, fuck."

Sweet fucking Jesus. I nearly come then and there, just hearing her moan my name.

Best fucking sound ever.

"Christ, baby. You just gushed all over my fingers. You like that, huh? My dick in your hand, my fingers inside your cunt and Mav grinding against you from behind."

I swallow thickly as my mind conjures up a very vivid image of what we must look like.

"Yes, yes."

"I bet you'd look so beautiful taking both our dicks."

"Oh God." She gasps, spreading her thighs and hooking one leg over mine, giving JD better access.

My fingers itch to feel what he's feeling, to understand how wet she is and how badly she needs this.

But I don't.

Instead, I do exactly what I probably shouldn't. I grip onto her hip tight and use her in a way I said I never would.

For pleasure.

As if she can sense where my head is at, the warmth of her palm lands on the back of my hands and she squeezes encouragingly.

"I want you," she half moans, half begs. "Stop thinking."

Her grip tightens and she tugs, leaving me no choice but to let her guide my hand up the soft skin of her stomach and all the way to her breast.

Oh shit.

I'm so fucking close to embarrassing myself it's ridiculous.

"Oh, you like that, don't you, baby?" JD groans.

Her body rocks with the movement of her other arm

and I lean forward, pressing my brow against her shoulder as I squeeze her, making her moan as our hips rock in time.

"They're perfect, huh? And the piercings... pretty sure they're the best decision Reid's ever made. So fucking pretty, don't you think?"

"Perfect," I confess, letting him know that I've seen them.

I can't imagine what he must think of me. Probably that I'm some sex-starved head case who doesn't know how to please a woman.

I shouldn't care.

But I do.

I want to be Alana's everything, and I want everyone around us to think I am.

But they know the truth.

They know that all this time, I've been too much of a pussy to let go of my fears and give her what she needed. JD shifts, the bed dipping under his weight. Risking a glance up, I find him on his knees with her delicate fingers wrapped around his shaft.

Jesus. That shouldn't be so hot.

"Can you take another, Dove?" he asks, making my brows pinch.

I swear to fuck if he's about to invite Reid in here to join, then I'm out... I think.

Fucking hell, a few days in captivity and they've turned me into a fucking head case. I can't seriously be considering a fucking gang bang with my wife, my enemy, and his wannabe joker of a best friend.

My thoughts are shattered when Alana suddenly howls in delight, letting me know the 'another' JD was referencing was apparently another finger inside her.

Fucking cunt.

Dragging my eyes down his outstretched arm, I focus on where he's fucking her with his fingers.

My grip on her breast tightens as I grind harder against her ass.

"You like that, Doll?" I ask, the words falling from my lips without conscious thought. I'm too lost. Too fucking gone to the ache in my balls and the heat of her body burning up against mine.

"Yes. Yes."

"Help me out a little, yeah?" JD asks, making my entire body freeze momentarily. "Do her clit, bro. Let's get her there together."

"Oh my God." Alana gasps.

"I-I don't—" I stutter like a fucking moron who doesn't know what a fucking clit is.

I do. I had more than enough experience in my younger years. But I can't lie, it's been a while.

Unwilling to wait for me to have my internal freak out, Alana does what she does best and forces my hand.

My palm slides back down her smooth belly until my fingers graze her mound.

Oh God.

I swallow as I attempt to keep the tremble out of my hand.

I'm not nervous. I'm fucking terrified.

For years I've told myself that I can't have this. That if I do, I'll be no different from the men of her past, using her because of what's between her legs.

If she were to ever look at me and see a monster, I don't think I'd survive.

But then, my fingertips collide with her soft, wet, hot—pierced—flesh and she lets out this filthy moan.

I've barely touched her, and she sounds like she's right on the edge.

"Oh fuck, look at you, little dove."

She spreads her legs wider, fully opening herself up for us, leaving me rutting into her hip instead of her ass, but I really don't care.

This isn't about me or my pleasure. It's all about her. Just like it should be.

"Don't be too gentle, our girl likes it rough, don't you, baby?"

Our girl...

"Yes. Yes. Please. Oh God," she cries when I apply more pressure and circle her clit. "Mav, fuck. Yes. Right there."

Pushing myself up onto my elbow, I run my eyes down her body, obsessed with the sight of my fingers on her. She's so wet, they're glistening with her arousal already.

"That's it, Dove. Give it to us. Let us watch you fall. You're so fucking beautiful when you do," JD encourages.

"Yes. Oh fuck. Fuck. Fuck. Fuck," she chants before her body locks up. JD groans as she clamps down on his fingers and then she screams as her back arches off the bed and her entire body convulses.

My eyes jump to her face, and my chin drops at what I find.

She's staring right at me with wide, pleasure-filled eyes.

'I love you,' she mouths, making my own movements falter.

"Fucking perfect," JD mutters, finally pulling his fingers free from her body as he shuffles closer and covers her hand on his dick with his, stroking himself faster.

The fingers he just had inside her slip past his lips, and he sucks them before his release crests and he throws his head back as he comes all over her tits.

Everything goes silent other than the sound of our heaving breaths before reality hits me so fucking hard, it makes my head spin.

"I'm sorry," I mutter, before releasing Alana as if she burned me and rolling off the bed.

The second my feet hit the carpet, I all but run toward the bathroom.

"Mav, wait. Please," she begs from behind me, making me feel like the world's biggest asshole.

My head hangs, my eyes dropping to my feet. Only it's not those I really see.

Fucking hell. I'm the world's biggest asshole with a massive fucking boner.

Can life get any more mortifying?

"Bro?" JD murmurs, reminding me that, yes, life can get fucking worse.

I wasn't just grinding up against my wife like a horny teenager, but I did it in front of Julian fucking Dempsy, who no doubt is going to run straight to Reid to tell him what a fucking loser I am.

With my hand on the doorframe, I risk looking back at the woman laid out on the middle of the bed like an offering.

The tank that had been pushed up to expose her tits has fallen back around her waist now that she's sitting, but her thighs are still spread, showing me just a hint of what all the men of Harrow Creek seem to want.

"Mav, please don't run. I want you." Her eyes drop lower. She might not be able to see the rather large issue I'm rocking from this angle, but she's felt enough in the last few minutes to know it's there. "Let me make you feel good."

My eyes shutter as regret drowns me.

"I'm not them, Alana. I don't expect anything from you."

"That isn't the reason I want to do it," she argues.

"You need to get out of your fucking head, man. You've got a woman here who's dripping wet and desperate. For. You."

Emotion crawls up my throat.

"If you don't give her what she needs, you'll end up losing her to someone who will."

His words ignite a fire inside me. "Someone like you? Like Reid?" I sneer. "Over my dead fucking body."

"Exactly. Then start doing something about it," he warns before diving for my wife, making her shriek. I've no idea if it's in delight or horror; I don't stick around long enough to find out. Instead, I march into the bathroom and slam the door closed behind me as self-hatred slowly poisons me from the inside out.

30

ALANA

"Fuck," I whisper, curling onto my side and burying my face into JD's chest.

The first thing I saw when I woke this morning was his electric blue eyes staring down at me, as if he was waiting for my eyelids to open so he could search for my soul. It was as overwhelming as it was comforting.

The second thing was the nightmare. Although the dark shadows that were still clinging to the edges of my psyche were soon pushed aside as I remembered what happened when I woke.

Fuck knows how I ended up in the hallway pinned between two gangsters, but I have a good idea.

Mav's told me before that I've slept-walked, although something tells me that I might have slept-ran last night.

I tried running from the motherfuckers who haunt me, straight into two that...

Heat flows through me like a wave as I remember two sets of burning hands on me.

Reid cupping and squeezing my breasts; JD with his fingers deep inside me, his thumb against my clit.

They knew exactly what I needed, and then gave it to me without question.

It's fucked up needing that to break free of the nightmare, when it was exactly what the men who were chasing me wanted—well, not exactly—but it works. My fear morphed into pleasure and the only thing I could focus on was them and their touch.

Suddenly, I felt brave, strong enough to face any demons who came to me while I had them working my body.

I was so lost in the memory, I barely noticed JD reach and drag my panties down my legs. I sure as hell noticed when he brought them to his nose and inhaled my scent.

"Addicted, Dove," he murmured before diving for my lips and teasing me with his touch until I had no choice but to part my thighs, giving him access to the part of me that was throbbing in need.

My husband was behind me sleeping. It was wrong. It was also hot as hell. And even if I wanted to, I couldn't stop.

As I laid there, I fantasized about Mav waking up and joining in. It was only a fantasy, though, I never thought that—

I swallow thickly, remembering when he wrapped his hand around my hip and dragged me back. Fuck, I could have screamed in delight as he ground against me, using me for his pleasure.

It's all I've wanted for so long. To drive him so crazy with need that he forgets all the shit that's going on up in his head and just takes me exactly as he wants me.

I've heard the rumors about his past exploits that rumble around the club. I know he's not a vanilla, missionary position in the dark kind of man. As far as I'm concerned, that only makes him more appealing. Who wants a man with a stick shoved up his ass when you can have a dark and dirty gangster? I know I fucking don't.

A shudder rips through me as I remember their hands on me, the way they work me to perfection, totally in sync.

God, it was heaven.

Heat floods my pussy and my nipples pucker just thinking about it.

If only it didn't have to end...

Where could we have been right now...

My mouth wrapped around one while the other filled me so perfectly.

A sob rips from my throat, the sense of loss too much to take, despite the fact that JD is right here.

He is right fucking here, wrapping me up in his strong arms and holding me together.

But it's not enough. I need the man who just ran as well.

"He's scared, little dove."

"Why?" I whimper. "It's just me, and I want him."

"I know, baby. It's gonna take time."

"He's disgusted by me. By everything I've been through. You should be too."

His entire body goes still, his muscles tense as I talk about myself like that.

"That's bullshit and you know it," he spits, barely able to contain his anger.

"Is it though? It's been five years. I've done everything I can think to do to tempt him. He doesn't want me. Not the way I need him."

JD's chuckle is so at odds with the tension locking up his muscles.

"Why are you laughing?" I demand, pulling my face from his chest and glaring at him.

"Little dove, did you not feel how hard he was for you? He was about three seconds from jizzing in his pants because of you."

I shake my head.

"His face when he touched your clit and you moaned like a whore. Thought he was going to explode. He fucking loved it."

"Then why did he run?"

"I don't know him well enough to give you a real answer, but I think he's scared."

I lean forward, pressing my brow against his sternum and sucking in a deep breath.

"Go to him, Dove. Talk to him, show him what he's missing. Go make his day and blow his mind."

When I glance back up again, there's a conflicted expression on JD's face that makes my stomach knot.

"J—"

"It's okay," he lies. "He's your husband. Go give him what he needs. I'll be downstairs when you're done."

He presses a kiss to my brow and then rolls away. He pauses at the door and looks back, his eyes running up the length of me.

"Thanks for a great morning." He winks, and then he's gone, leaving me in the middle of the bed with a heavy heart and a knot of dread in my stomach.

JD might be smiling, but it's only skin deep. Mav might be scared, but JD is hurting, and I'm not sure I have the power to fix them both.

With a loud sigh, I slide my ass across the bed before getting to my feet. For just a moment, I stand and stare down at the messy sheets, trying to picture just how we looked together. Tangled limbs, sweating skin and heaving breaths.

Fuck. I bet it was so hot.

Fleetingly, I wonder what Reid would have thought if he'd have walked in on it. His best friend and his enemy bringing the girl he locked up in his basement to ruin.

With one more lingering look, I turn on my heels and hesitantly walk toward the bathroom.

Whenever he's drawn the line between us before, I've backed away. Maybe it was the wrong thing to do, but it felt right.

But this time, I'm going to heed JD's advice and take the bull by the horns... I'm not sure if I mean that literally or metaphorically, only time will tell.

Cracking the door open, I get hit in the face with a cloud of steam. My heart jumps into my throat and flutters erupt in my belly at the thought of him being naked in the shower.

Stepping into the room, I instantly find him standing in the stall with his palms on the tiles and his head hanging defeated between his shoulders as the water rains down on him. His chest rises and falls rapidly with his heaving breaths.

As I stand there watching him suffer, his pain becomes my own.

The last thing I've ever wanted to do is cause this incredible man to suffer. All he's ever done is protect me, put me first, and above all else.

As much as I appreciate everything he's done for me, it's time for that to change. Someone needs to make him a priority for once. And I know exactly what he needs. Even if he thinks he doesn't.

Dragging Reid's tank from my body, I abandon it on the floor next to Mav's clothes and step toward the shower.

My fists curl as my nerves begin to get the better of me. But I refuse to let them stop me.

He still has no idea I've joined him as I step into the shower and get sprayed with the water bouncing off his strong, inked back.

"Mav," I whisper, needing to give him some kind of clue that I'm here.

But there's no reaction. He's too lost in his own head to hear or register anything.

Sucking in a calming breath, I step closer then place my hands on his sides and slide them around to his stomach.

He stills the second we collide, his muscles pulling taut.

"It's just me," I murmur as my hands begin to descend lower, but it's too late.

I'm thrown against the wall with his unforgiving forearm pinning me in place.

"It's me," I gasp, my cheek burning from its collision with the tiles as my body fights to accept the coldness.

"Oh fuck," he pants, instantly releasing me, allowing me to spin around.

He stares down at me, confusion and self-hatred swirling in his dark eyes, but I don't focus on them, instead, I let my gaze drop.

Holy shit.

He's big. Hard. So fucking hard it has to be painful. The head purple and desperate for—

"You shouldn't be in here." He growls.

"You're wrong. I think I'm exactly where I need to be. Where you need me to be," I correct.

His dick jerks at my words, as if it's in full agreement.

I reach out, more than ready to feel him beneath my

261

fingers, but before I make contact, he grabs my wrist, pinning it back against the tiles.

"Don't." He growls before ripping his eyes from mine in favor of the floor.

"Or what?" I taunt, more than prepared to fight for what I want. What he needs.

"Or..." He pauses, the tendons in his throat pulling as he swallows.

Reaching up, I grip his jaw and drag his face back to mine.

"You're scared," I state, zero hesitation in my words.

A bitter laugh spills from his lips. "Scared? Doll, I'm fucking terrified."

"Of me?" I ask with a frown.

"Yes. No. No, not of you. Of... of your reaction."

"To what, Mav? I love you; I want you. I promise you, there is nothing that could happen here that would change that." Sliding my hand up to his face, I tap his temple. "Whatever is going on in here needs to stop." He closes his eyes for a beat, but before I get to demand it, he opens them again and he does so freely.

"I'm here, Mav," I say, holding my free arm out to the side. "I'm offering you everything. Begging you for everything. You want it rough? I'm more than happy. Kinky? I'm down. Want to watch me do some unusual fetish stuff? Sure. For you, Mav, I'd do it all. Whatever you need. Willingly," I add, assuming that that is the crux of the problem here.

His grip on my wrist loosens and my hand slips free from his wet grasp.

I gasp when his hand sweeps across my chest. It's not a tender movement or a teasing one and it makes me frown.

"His cum is still on your tits," he explains flatly.

"Oh," I breathe, cringing hard.

Not exactly the way to seduce your husband.

"Forget about him. This is about us," I confess, raising my chin confidently. "About you."

"No," he argues.

"Yes," I shoot back, placing my hands on his pecs and slowly sliding them down. "If I didn't want this, I wouldn't be here right now," I tell him, his abs jumping as I move over them.

I'm desperate to watch his dick jerk in excitement, but I don't move my eyes from his, needing him to see the truth behind every word.

"All you've ever done is look after me. Now let me return that favor, yeah?"

His eyes shutter as my fingers trace the V that will take me to where I want to be.

When his lips twitch to speak, I'm expecting an argument, so I'm floored by the words that follow. "You're so fucking incredible. I don't deserve you."

"Mav," I breathe, "you're the incredible one here, don't you ever forget that."

Before he can register my words or say anything else, I wrap my hand around his dick and squeeze.

"Holy fuck," he barks as he jerks so violently, I'm half-expecting to find him coming already.

Leaning forward, his forearm lands just above my head as he stares down at me.

"Okay?" I whisper, barely moving for fear he'll freak out.

"Your hand. Fuck, that looks good."

I can't help but beam at his praise. Something he notices as he searches my face.

"If you're looking for any sign of hesitation, you won't

find any." Reaching up on my tiptoes, I let my lips brush over his ear before I whisper, "I want your dick, Mav. Now stop thinking and let me work my magic."

"Oh fuck." He breathes as I drop to my haunches, his cock right in front of my face.

I stroke him slowly, root to tip, making the most incredible groan rumble deep in his chest.

"That's it, babe," I encourage. "Just enjoy. Just watch my hand stroking your dick. Looks good, doesn't it?"

He groans again before nodding just once.

"You've thought about this, haven't you?"

I glance up again just in time to see his teeth clench and his jaw pop.

"You don't need to imagine it anymore. Anything you want, I can give you. Anything," I emphasize as his cock swells larger in my hand.

My pussy throbs, and I squeeze my thighs together to try to stop it.

This isn't about me. It's about him, but hell, if it doesn't get me as needy as he is right now.

"I'm so wet for you right now," I whisper, needing him to know just how hot he gets me.

"Doll." He groans through clenched teeth.

"It hasn't been just you fantasizing about this," I confess. "Used to lie back in my bed and spread my legs to the thought of you in your room jerking off."

"Christ." He grunts, his hips punching forward in desperation.

Upping both my pressure and speed, I work him harder, my eyes locked on his length as precum leaks from the tip.

"Come for me, Mav. Show me how much you want this because I know you do."

"Alana, fuck. Fuck." His fist slams against the tiles

above me before a roar rips from his throat, his cock jerks in my hand, and ropes of cum spurt over my chest.

His eyes burn with heat as he watches himself mark me, just like JD did not so long ago.

He leans forward, resting his brow on his forearm as he fights to catch his breath.

"I love you," he pants, his cheeks flushed with pleasure and his pupils blown.

It's a really good look on him—certainly, one I want to see over and over again.

31

MAVERICK

"JD and Reid have gone out," I say over my shoulder after finding a note on the kitchen counter.

"Oh," Alana breathes behind me, sounding annoyingly disappointed by that news.

"Miss them already, Doll?"

"No, it's not that," she says, walking around me to the coffee machine. "It's just weird knowing they're not here and we are."

"Anyone would think they trust us."

She laughs, echoing my own feelings. "I'm not sure Reid trusts anyone," she says, reaching for two mugs.

"Before all of this, I might have agreed, but you've been living in his inner sanctum for a while now. He has to trust you on some level."

"So are you," she points out, looking at me over her shoulder with a smirk.

"True," I mutter, lowering my ass to the stool at the counter, my eyes locked on her.

Everything feels lighter after our shower. I feel lighter. The tension in my shoulders has relaxed, but it's nothing compared to my balls. They no longer ache like they're about to explode. It's not something I've experienced in a very, very long time. And it's all because of her.

"You okay?" she asks, studying me closely as the beans grind. Twisting around, she rests her ass against the counter and temptingly crosses her arms under her breasts.

Unable to stop myself, my eyes drop and my tongue comes out to lick my lips.

She notices, of course she does. I'm pretty sure it's the reason she stole the shirt she's wearing.

Once upon a time, I think it was a t-shirt, but now the arms and neck have been ripped out and the skull printed across the front of the white fabric has cracked and faded. It's not something I would ever look at twice if a guy—JD, I assume—was wearing it. But on Alana, it's fucking sinful. The neck falls over one shoulder, exposing the swell of her tit and the arm holes are so big, every time she turns around, I get more than a flash of side boob. And that's not mentioning how thin the fabric is; it's practically translucent, allowing me to see the pink of her nipples beneath.

She's doing it on purpose, I'm more than aware of it. And fuck me if it's not working.

After she made me come in the shower, I tucked my hands under her arms and lifted her to her feet. The need to throw caution to the wind and throw everything I've told myself over the past five years out the window was almost too much. But I held strong, even if my dick was hard again. That sucker barely even got soft with her standing naked before me.

She wanted it. Not only did she tell me in not so many words, it was clear in her eyes.

But fucking her against the wall in the shower wasn't going to happen.

She might have cracked my resolve, evidenced by the fact that my cum was still glistening on her chest, but I wasn't succumbing.

Years of telling yourself you can't have something doesn't get shattered in a few minutes or after one incredibly intense orgasm.

So instead of giving her more, I reached for the sponge, loaded it up with shower gel, and cleaned her up.

It was nice. Really fucking nice. Especially when she turned that sponge on me and worked her way over every single inch of my body.

Shifting on the stool, I tug at my borrowed sweatpants, much to her amusement.

"You good there?"

"Perfect." I grunt. "The coffee is done," I point out when she continues to stand there watching me. Something tells me that her head is back in that shower with mine.

It takes a second for her to register my words and when she does, her eyes widen and she spins around, giving me another shot of her boob.

She works in silence, setting up the next mug and grabbing the creamer for her coffee before walking toward me with both mugs in her hands.

"Here," she says, passing mine over, our fingers brushing as I take it, sending a bolt of electricity shooting up my arm.

"We need to talk," I say, ensuring her eyes jump to mine.

She swallows nervously.

"Yeah," she admits quietly. "I guess we do."

She takes off toward the couches and I'm powerless but to follow.

After folding her legs beneath her, she turns to where I drop onto the other end of the couch, my eyes locked on her.

"You don't have to tell me everything right now," I tell her, letting her off on some of the details that I need but really don't want to hear. "But I need to understand how you ended up here and what the hell is happening next."

She nods, lifting her mug to her lips and blowing across the top.

"Victor blackmailed me into working for him. He knew my weakness and he used it against me to ensure I'd agree."

"You're weak—"

"You, Mav. He threatened you."

My stomach drops like a rock. "What?" I gasp.

"He knows, Mav," she whispers, making my stomach knot and my heart sink like a rock.

"Shit."

"And he also knew that I'd do anything to protect you, just like you have me so..."

"Here we are," I mutter. "Fuck, I hate that cunt."

"You're not the only one," Alana muses with a heavy sigh.

"So?" I prompt.

"Right, yeah. So he tasked me to go after Kane and try to stop him from leaving."

"Jesus, talk about setting you up to fail. Kane's had one foot out the door for a long time."

I shrug. "We all knew that. But Victor wants what he wants. And he decided that I had what it took to convince him otherwise."

My teeth grind. I've no experience, but is her pussy really good enough to keep men that in line?

I guess the fact that Kane is now gone and embarking on a new life might prove it's not.

Fuck.

My fists clench. The nails of my free hand dig painfully into my palm while the other trembles as I grip the mug so hard, it's at risk of shattering and covering me in boiling coffee.

Tipping my head back, I stare up at the ceiling and take a calming breath.

"Are you sure you want to hear this?" Alana asks hesitantly.

No, absolutely fucking not.

"Yeah," I force out, lifting my head again and looking her dead in the eyes.

She nods and continues, "It wasn't working, and it only got worse when Letty returned. He was—is—so in love with her, it was painful to watch. I was going to fuck everything up for them, but I didn't have a choice. Victor was breathing down my neck, desperate for results. But I couldn't get them for him. So he made a suggestion that he thought would work."

She sips her coffee, averting her eyes from mine.

"He told me to tell Kane I was pregnant, but that I needed to go through Letty first. Make it believable. Make her break his heart and be the one to pick up his pieces."

"Fucking hell, Doll."

"I know. I know," I agree. "But what else was I meant to do? Let him come after you?"

"He could have tried."

"Mav, if he wanted to take you down, he could. Razor's

son or not. You're not Reid," she says, making my eyes narrow.

But as much as I might hate her words, I can't deny that they're true.

As the future boss, Reid has a certain level of protection. Especially as the next in line is Devin, and I'm not sure that fuck could run a marathon, let alone a gang.

"I know," I mutter bitterly.

"You know, you two really are alike."

"Excuse me?"

"You and Reid, you're—"

"Please stop," I beg.

"Just saying. I think if you can find common ground then—" I glare at her and she thankfully stops talking. "Anyway, I told Kane, showed him the bullshit scan photo I had doctored to look like mine and well... all hell broke loose. Turns out, it was the worst possible thing I could have done to Letty, and as punishment, I ended up in Reid's custody."

"Kane knows the truth now though, right?"

"Yeah. Reid got Ellis to pull my medical records. Shared them with Kane. I've since told Letty everything too."

"You've spoken to her?"

"Yeah, she came to visit me in the basement. It was... weird. But kinda good in a strange way."

"Right. So where do we go from here? Do you really trust them?"

She falls silent for a few seconds, but I already know her answer, I can see it swirling in her light blue eyes.

"Yes. I think I do."

"Fuck's sake."

"I know how you feel about this. Trust me, I do. But I truly believe that we want the same outcome here."

"Reid just wants power." I scoff.

"No," she argues. "He wants what's right for this town and the people in it. And that isn't Victor."

"Says the drug dealer?" I quip.

"If you're going to try and take the moral high ground like you're better than him then you're barking up the wrong tree here, babe."

With a sigh, I agree. We've all done plenty of bad shit over the years for a whole host of reasons. I'm not in a place to judge anyone.

"So we're all going to become friends, make an army and take them down one corrupt fuck at a time?"

"I don't know the details, but according to JD, Reid has been working on a plan for a long time."

Lifting my hand, I scrub it across my face as I try and process all this.

I came here to free her, to bring her home, to remove her from Reid's clutches. And yet, here I am being sucked right in alongside her.

"Can't we just walk out the front door and go home?" I ask, hopefully.

"We probably could. I haven't tested the doors, but something tells me that I'm not locked up anymore. If they are locked, I'd be inclined to say that it's to keep others out, not us in."

"They really have left an impression on you, haven't they?"

"Other than the obvious?" she asks, flicking her drying hair from her face and thrusting her tits out to signify her new piercings.

"Yeah," I mutter, swallowing thickly as I think about those pretty little gems in her nipples. I've never been a massive fan of piercings or ink on girls. Call me old-fashioned, but I like my women feminine. Probably because I spend most of my time with foul-mouth gangsters. Coming home to someone a little softer, prettier, and who smells a hell of a lot better than those sweaty motherfuckers has been heaven. But fuck if those little pink gems didn't do it for me.

"You're thinking about them, aren't you?" she teases, her eyes darting to my quickly swelling dick because, yes, I'm very much thinking about them. "I didn't think I'd like them either. Seems that Reid might know me better than I know myself."

"He's an asshole for forcing them on you."

She shrugs one shoulder. "Would you judge me if I said the whole thing was pretty hot?"

I still. "I never judge you, Doll."

She raises a brow. "No?"

"No." I hold her stare.

"So all this time you haven't held back because you've judged me for the past?"

"What? No. You think that?"

She shrugs again. "I don't know, Mav. We've never talked about it. Not really. Whenever I've tried, you've passed it off with 'I'm trying to do right by you' and then found a way to change the subject or leave the room."

"Jesus, Doll. Is that what you really think?"

"What am I meant to think? You want me, I've seen— felt—the evidence. I have for years, but you won't touch me. It's like I'm pretty enough to look at but too fucked-up to touch."

"That's not—" I cough, needing to clear my throat as regret bubbles up, stopping me from talking. "Shit, Doll. That's not it at all."

"So," she says, reaching over to place her empty mug on

the coffee table. The tank falls away from her body, giving me a perfect side view of her tits that does little for my semi, and when she looks back, she finds me tugging at my pants. "Case in point," she mutters, before crossing her legs beneath her and resting her hands in her lap. "So... go on. We have nothing else to do. You wanted to talk. Let's talk. Openly. Honestly."

I stare at her, the truth balancing right on the tip of my tongue.

"I've always wanted you. Even when you were too young to do anything about it," I confess.

Her lips part to respond, but I continue before she can say anything.

"But that made me as bad as them. You were sixteen when I caught you in those woods trying to escape. You were sixteen. A child. I was twenty. A man. I had no right looking at you in any way other than as a child."

"I wasn't a child, Mav. I don't even remember ever being one," she manages to squeeze in.

"But that's not the point."

"So what is?"

"You deserved to be a kid. You deserved to eat ice cream for breakfast and cereal for dinner. You should have been able to run around the backyard in a swimsuit, without having someone perving at you, wondering how you looked without it. You should have been spending time with friends, talking about boys, having first kisses and movie dates, doing homework and pulling all-nighters to get assignments done. You should have been trying out for the cheer team and going to football games and parties and—"

Her fingers press against my lips, cutting off my tirade of all the shit she never got to experience.

"I know, Mav. Trust me, I know all that shit. Do I wish I

274

had it? Yeah, honestly, I do wish I got to experience most of it. I've never had a friend oth—" My eyes widen as hurt slams into me. "Let me finish. I've never had a friend other than Kristie, and then you. I don't know what it's like to go to class, to skip, to hide behind the bleachers, or to experience my first kiss. I'll never know what an awkward first time is like, or watch the football player I'm crushing on kill it on the field. But it's okay."

"No, Doll, it's not. They fucked up your entire life, and I want you to have it, everything you missed I—"

"Mav," she says, taking both of my hands in hers. "You have given me so much more than all those bullshit teenage experiences."

Her glassy eyes search mine, begging me to hear her words and accept them.

Her bottom lip wobbles, but she continues nonetheless. "You've shown me how a man should love a woman. You've shown me what true friendship is about. You've given me laughter and happiness, and memories that don't keep me up at night screaming. You gave me a home where I feel safe and a pair of arms that I know will hold me up and keep all my broken and shattered pieces together when all I want to do is fall apart." She loses her fight with her tears and they finally break free from her lashes, landing on her cheeks with a splash. "You've made me feel worthy, beautiful, sexy, wanted—even if you won't do anything about it," she adds with a sad laugh. "You gave me my life, my body back, Mav. Never ever underestimate how much that means to me."

I act on instinct, something I have never allowed myself to do with her before. My hand wraps around the back of her neck, tilting her where I want her before my lips land on hers.

Neither of us moves for long, painful seconds, but then

she mimics my movement and wraps her hot hand around the side of my neck, and I snap.

My lips part, and hers instantly follow, and our tongues dart out, gently brushing together. We're both hesitant, but then she shifts and throws her leg over my waist, settling herself on my lap, and my restraint shatters.

With one hand on her neck, the other drops to her waist, dragging her closer as my tongue plunges into her mouth and I kiss her like I've been imagining doing for years.

And it turns out that my imagination is shit because the reality is so much better than anything I've ever pictured.

32

JD

I sit beside Reid as Richie, the Ravens leader, and his two little bitches, stare at us like we're furniture that doesn't quite suit. Fitting, really, seeing as we're in a warehouse with nothing but a desk and three chairs.

"You're playing a very dangerous game here, little Harris. But you already know that, don't you?" he asks, his forearms resting on the desk, his gun right there and already pointed right at my best friend. Not that Reid gives a shit. He hasn't once glanced at it.

He's all business, just like he always is in these kinds of situations.

"I know what I'm doing," Reid states, his voice firm and his face determined. "What I need to know is if you're with me or not."

Reid's been working his way around the local gangs. Hell, and a few that are very much not local, but who hold enough power and sway to be able to support him on his mission.

It's risky, Richie isn't wrong.

Sabotaging Victor's business dealings is one thing, but

going behind his back to collude with his allies is fucking dangerous.

But Reid always knew this was going to be perilous. But he's been at it too long to get scared off now.

Richie regards him, finally sitting back, and crosses his arms over his chest.

But while he might appear to relax, his two little bitches stand taller, both their hands poised to reach for the guns holstered at their hips.

He nods once, and I release the breath I didn't know I was holding. There isn't any love lost between the Hawks and the Ravens, but like most businesses, money speaks louder than that pride, although, only a little louder.

"Yes, I'm with you."

"Fantastic," Reid states simply before pushing from the shitty plastic chairs we were offered to sit in and standing tall, putting Richie at a major disadvantage, not that the pretentious prick cares. "I'll be in touch when the time comes."

"I look forward to doing business with you, little Harris." Reid's shoulders tense at his stupid nickname, but he bites back a response.

I stand, and with a jerk of my chin, I march around my chair and step up to Reid's side.

Not a word is said between us until we're safely inside his car, the engine running, his shoulders back and his neck cracked.

"So, are we going to talk about last night or just ignore it like it never happened?" I ask as Reid, taking his mind off the meeting we just had, floors his Charger racing out of Ravens' territory.

"There's nothing to talk about." He practically growls as he white-knuckles the wheel.

"Oh, sure there isn't," I tease. "I must have imagined you slipping your hands inside Alana's tank and helping me to get her off so that she could get out of her own head and forget her nightmare."

I didn't think it was possible, but his knuckles get even whiter. If the cuts across them were fresher, they'd have split right open.

I study the hard set of his face as he stares out the windshield and his jaw ticks in irritation.

"You two are as fucking bad as each other."

"Don't compare me to him," he spits.

"Sorry," I mutter, looking ahead again. "My bad, you're nothing like each other. Pig-headed motherfuckers. You've no idea when you've got a good thing right under your hands."

Now that gets a reaction.

"He's touched her?"

I try to fight my smirk of accomplishment, but it's too hard, and it spreads across my lips.

"Yep, he couldn't resist her allure either. We both got her off this morning."

He tries not to look interested, but he fails fucking miserably.

"Both?"

"Yep," I state proudly. "I was knuckles deep in her pussy, and he took her clit. You should have seen the way she came for us. Fucking beautiful, bro." Just to be a prick, I do a little chef's kiss to really drive the point home. "But then again, you didn't see how she came for us either, did you? Too much hiding behind her like a pussy."

"I was restraining her to stop her from hitting you."

I chuckle. "She wasn't about to slap me with her tits," I tease.

"Fuck you."

"We've been over this. Not interested in what you have to offer. Alana's pussy is all I need. But like I said, I'm willing to take that and offer up her ass for you."

"How selfless of you."

"You know me, I'm all about sharing the love."

He scoffs, shaking his head.

"Just... don't get attached," he warns. Although when he glances over, I catch the knowing look in his eyes, and I think he's already aware that it's too late. "Fuck, J," he says, scrubbing his hand down his face and rubbing his jaw.

"You'd get it if you manned up to what you wanted and fucked her."

"Or maybe that's exactly the reason I haven't," he counters.

"What are you talking about? You're holding back because you're a masochist. How are those balls holding up, anyway."

"You're an asshole. I'm just trying to—"

"Warn me I'm about to get my heart broken?" I offer. "Trust me, I'm more than aware of that."

"I need you focused, J. All this shit, it's about to—"

"I know. And I'm right here, bro. I got you."

He wrings the wheel again; although, he's noticeably relaxed since first dropping into the car.

"Let's just hope they're all as easy as Richie, yeah?"

"Something tells me that won't be the case." He grunts before his phone starts ringing through the car and Victor's name pops up on the screen. "Shit."

"You checked for trackers, right?" I ask, dread sitting heavy on my chest.

"Of course I fucking did. I'm not an amateur. If that

fuck has sold us down the river already though, he's going to find his family dead by sunlight," Reid warns darkly.

"I'm sure it's fine," I say, although I sound unconvincing as fuck as he hits the accept button on the wheel and lets the call connect.

"Victor." He grunts, letting his father know with just one word how excited he is to talk to him.

"What the fuck is going on with shipments? Devin said—"

"Fucking Devin," Reid mutters under his breath. "It's fine. I've spoken to our supplier, it'll be here before sundown."

"Fucking better be or we'll be missing another weekend of revenue."

"When have we missed a weekend?" Reid asks, knowing full well that we haven't. Yes, he's fucking about, making things as awkward as hell to show his father up, but the money is still rolling in.

"Just get it sorted. I handed you solid suppliers that I've worked with for years. I never had this kind of fucking problem."

"Good for you, Victor," Reid praises, his voice dripping with sarcasm. "Can I get on with my job now?"

Victor mutters something intelligible down the line and Reid's thumb hovers over the end call button, but pauses in cutting him off when Victor speaks again.

"You heard anything from Mav?"

"Why the fuck would I have spoken to that asshole?"

Victor sighs. "Razor can't—"

"Not my problem." Finally, he cuts the call, plunging us into silence.

Reid takes a left off the freeway and sends me crashing into the door with the speed he takes the turn.

"Dude," I mutter.

"Focus, J," he spits impatiently. "If this blows up in our faces, we're not going to get a warning shot."

"Well, you sound confident."

"I am confident," he states. "There will be shots fired before all this is over, and something tells me Victor will be the first to pull his gun."

"Then we'd better hope the old man's shot is off target."

Reid mutters something in response, but I can't make it out, although I can guess.

As we cross the border into Harrow Creek, the tension in his shoulders returns, and I decide the best course of action is to keep my mouth shut and let him ruminate on whatever is spinning through his head. I've been told a time or two before that he can't think when I'm rambling shit, so I lock it down and let him do his thing.

It's not until we're almost back that a thought flickers through my mind.

"You managed to speak to Knox about any of this Raven shit?" If I thought my question was going to help, then I'm immediately mistaken.

"No. Fucker still won't take my calls," he barks, just as pissed off as the last time we spoke about him.

It hasn't always been just the two of us. Before I came along, Reid already had a BFF in the form of Knox Bowman. I'm pretty sure neither of them was in the market for a stray, but for some reason, I was lucky enough to be taken in by them.

Despite Reid and Knox being friends since they were in diapers, Reid and I immediately connected, or at least I did with him. I then gave him very little choice in being my friend when I started following him around like a puppy. He was just so... solid. Everything about me and my life was

RELENTLESS

not. From as early as I can remember, everything had been crumbling around me. I was pushed from family to family, to group home to group home. My friendship with Reid was the first real, tangible thing I had, and I grabbed onto it with both hands. And to this day, I won't fucking let go.

If it weren't for him, I'd be dead now. I know that for a fact. I owe him everything. What little of my sanity I have, and my entire life. I just wish he understood how fucking amazing he is.

Knox was fucking awesome too. The shit the three of us got up to growing up was fucking epic. But a few years ago, some shit went down with his family, his dad—a Hawk—started fucking around on Victor, and Knox was the one who ended up paying the price. He's now doing a stretch in Iron Marsh and refuses to talk to anyone.

It's no secret that that place is flooded with Hawks, Ravens, Devils and a handful of other gangs from the state. If anyone's going to get us intel on the Ravens and whether we should be trusting Richie right now, then it would be Knox.

"Maybe you should try again," I suggest.

"You think I haven't been?" he snaps.

"Sorry," I mutter as he pulls off the road in favor of the track that will lead toward the hidden entrance to his lair. "You reckon he's fucked her yet?" I muse as the manor looms above.

"You're a little too concerned with Mav's underused dick for my liking. You wanna lick it or something."

"Hell no," I bark. "I know you won't admit it, but we need him. And he's no fucking good to us if he dies of exploding balls."

Reid turns to me as he waits for the gate to open, his eyes wide and his brows high.

"Seriously?"

"Yep. Google it. The fear is real."

"Not for you with the number of times a day you jerk off."

"Nothing wrong with that. At least I'm not an uptight asshole like someone I know."

"I'm trying to overthrow my father and take over this fucking town. I'm allowed to be a little stressed," he argues.

"Sure, but sinking balls deep in Alana's pussy—"

"Isn't happening." He grunts.

"I give it a week," I tease.

"You willing to put money on that?" he asks.

Making a wager over her again would be a really fucking stupid thing to do. But then, I never pretended to be smart.

"Hell, yeah. Hundred bucks say you tap her by this time next week."

"You really have no faith in my self-restraint."

"Sure, I do. I just happen to know that Alana's pussy is just that good. One taste and you're gonna be as obsessed as I am. Best fuck I've had... well, maybe ever."

He glances over at my confession, quite clearly not believing a word of it.

"And you've sure had plenty of experience for that to be a valid conclusion."

"Exactly," I state proudly, which I don't think was the result he was hoping for. "I'll await your opinion by this time next week, and I'd like my hundred in crisp twenties please."

"Arrogant motherfucker."

By the time the gate is securely locked behind us and we pull up out front of the house, Reid has noticeably relaxed a little.

"Come on then, let's go and find out what the love birds are up to."

"Can hardly wait," he mutters, trailing behind me as I let us in and march down the hallway.

The second I turn into the kitchen doorway, my eyes widen and my lips curl in delight at what I find.

Reid—clearly paying zero attention to his surroundings —slams straight into my back.

"What the—"

"Shush," I hiss, not wanting to distract the horny couple on his couch.

"Oh, for the love of God," he complains.

"What?" I gasp. "It's hot."

Alana is sitting astride Mav's lap, one of his hands is on her ass and the other is resting on her waist, hitching her tank up, giving us a little view of her body.

She's rocking back and forth over what is obviously his erection as they practically devour each other. They're so lost to it; they don't even realize they've got an audience. Either that, or they do, and they're more than happy to have us watching the show. I'm sure as fuck here for it.

"You're a fucking creep, bro," Reid mutters, although it doesn't escape my attention that his eyes never leave them.

"Takes one to know one."

"Whatever, I've got calls to make," he says before taking off toward his office to go and do dull shit while I get to enjoy the live porno happening right before my eyes.

It's so hot, I can't even be pissed that he's winning our bet by walking away.

33

ALANA

I'm flying. Soaring through the sky on a Maverick Murray-shaped cloud. Every single nerve ending in my body tingles, my skin burns and my core aches in the most delicious ways as our tongues tangle together.

I've no idea how long we've been kissing for. It doesn't matter. It could be a week and it wouldn't be enough.

It's like five years' worth of kisses have been bottled, and together, we've knocked the top off and dove in to make up for lost time, refusing to surface for air.

My lungs burn with my need to take a deep breath, but I can't. I can't take my lips from his.

They're so soft, so warm, so... perfect.

His kisses are everything I always knew they would be and more. So much fucking more.

I'm drunk. Utterly and completely wasted on his kisses. It's the best feeling in the world, and I never want it to end.

We could take it further, both of us are desperate for it. His solid length is like a steel rod between us. I can only imagine how painful it must be. But this is just too perfect to stop or to even make the effort to move the thin layers separating us.

It'll come. I know it will.

Finally, fucking finally, I've managed to push through the barriers he put up all those years ago and I'm able to give him everything I've always wanted to. Well, not quite everything. But I figure, we've waited this long, so what's a little longer when, together, we're so perfect.

His hand that is resting on my waist twitches and begins to slide up.

Oh God, yes.

A whimper spills from my lips as his thumb brushes the underside of my heavy breast, making me gasp, finally ripping our lips apart.

"Oh God." I moan when he takes me in his hand.

My head falls back and heat shoots to my core.

I'm so close already just from his kisses and grinding down on him, that one pinch of my nipples and I'm sure he's going to push me right over the edge.

"Mav, yes," I cry when his other hand slips under my shirt, joining the party.

Cool air rushes over my heated skin as he hooks the fabric over his wrists, exposing me to him.

"Fucking hell, you're perfect, Doll."

He leans forward, his full, swollen lips parted and glistening in the low sunlight spilling through the huge windows beside us.

But just before his lips make contact with my needy skin, he pauses.

"It's okay. They'll be okay," I whisper, assuming he's stopping because of my fresh piercings.

His breath rushes over me, making my nipples harden

even more, desperate to feel his heat, but he doesn't do anything.

Dropping my chin, I stare down at him through glassy, lust-filled eyes to find his lips barely an inch from my skin, but his eyes locked on the other side of the room.

Instantly, a shiver rips down my spine as reality dawns.

We have an audience.

"Don't stop on my account," a teasing voice says.

"Julian." It's meant to be a warning, but my voice is nothing more than a breathy moan.

"Look at you, little dove," he says, pushing from the doorframe, his eyes locked on mine before they drop down my body.

Mav's hands twitch, as if he wants to cover me up, but he holds steady.

"Do you mind?" Mav growls. "My wife and I are—"

"In the middle of the kitchen looking hot as fuck. Have you made your husband nice and hard down there, Dove?"

Mav groans as I agree.

"And he's not inside you?" JD asks, shooting a teasing look at Mav.

"You're seriously not going to leave, are you?"

"Communal area, dude. You wanted privacy, you should have taken this to the bedroom."

"Because that worked so well last night."

"Bro, not my fault that you weren't there when she needed you and I was."

Mav goes rigid beneath me. "What?"

My breath catches when JD slides his fingers into my hair and drags my head back, forcing me to look at him.

"Your little doll had a nightmare that sent her running out of your room screaming. At first, I thought maybe you'd shown her your little cock," he teases, making my lips purse in anger.

"JD," I hiss.

"Sorry, low blow," he apologizes. "She needed me, and I was there while you were KO'd. Reid was there too, wasn't he, little dove?"

"Is this necessary?" I ask, turning to look at Mav's reaction to his taunting, but JD's grip stops me.

"Of course it is," he agrees with a smirk. "Mav did a pretty good job of making it up to you this morning. And it seems to me that he's trying to continue with it now, but you need more, don't you, Dove?"

My refusal sits right on the tip of my tongue. What Mav is giving me right now is everything, but the naughty glint in JD's eyes stops me from saying the words.

My chest heaves as I stare up at him, his grip on my hair sending the most perfect bite of pain down my neck.

I don't say a word, but he knows. He always knows.

"Suck on her nipples, Mav. And don't feel the need to be gentle. Our girl likes a little bit of pain, don't you, baby?"

Nothing happens. The only sensation I get is Mav's continued rapid breaths rushing over my sensitive skin.

"Mav," I beg. "Please."

"You hear that, man? She's begging you."

"I'm not fucking deaf," Mav snaps. Something tells me that if I weren't pinning him to the couch right now that he'd already be long out the door.

Sure, he could easily cast me aside, but the fact he hasn't gives me hope.

"Then do as you're told. Her body is screaming for you. Can't you smell her? So fucking sweet."

The house is so quiet, I actually hear Mav swallow.

"He's right," I confess. "I want your mouth on me. Everywhere."

JD releases his grip on me and I'm finally allowed to meet Mav's eyes.

Whatever he sees in them helps him make a decision because not a second later, his hand cups my breasts again and the heat of his mouth surrounds my nipple.

"Yes," I cry out when he sucks on me, his tongue teasing the bars, driving me crazy.

"I knew they'd be sensitive. You think you could come like that, little dove?"

"Maybe." I gasp.

"You want to see if Mav can make it happen, or do you need his lips elsewhere as well?"

Liquid lust pools between my legs at JD's suggestion.

If Mav hears it, then he doesn't react as he switches to my other breast and gives that the same attention as the first as I continue to grind down on his length.

With one hand resting on the side of Mav's neck, loving the way his pulse thunders beneath my fingers, I reach back for JD, slipping my hand under his shirt and pressing my palm to his abs.

"That all you got, little dove?"

I blink back at him before my eyes drop to the more than obvious bulge in his pants.

My fingers itch to reach for him, but then Mav's teeth graze against me and I cry out, forgetting everything but the growing desperation inside me.

I panic when JD's fingers leave my hair, but it doesn't last long because his knuckles soon brush the sides of my breasts as he relieves me of Reid's tank I've been teasing Mav with all afternoon. I don't want to be smug or anything, but it worked like a charm and has helped me continue working on those walls of his that JD began knocking down this morning.

"Oh fuck, more," I beg when JD steps right up behind me, his hardness against my shoulder and his hand around my throat.

Mav's eyes dart up, taking in our position as JD's grip tightens, teasing me with his fingers and the promise of oblivion.

"She likes being choked out," JD muses, filling Mav in on my preferences. "Makes her come so hard."

The memory of the first time I was with him and I came so hard, I ended up as a snotty, crying mess slams into me and my eyes snap shut.

"More," I beg, needing to forget about that weird moment between us.

"Fuck, yeah. You can have whatever you want, little dove. Isn't that right, bro?"

JD tucks his hands under my arms and lifts me out of Mav's lap, forcing him to release me with a pop.

Mav makes this weird noise in the back of his throat and he looks up at me with disappointment etched in his features. He looks like a child who's just had his favorite toy taken away. Although, he makes no move to fix it despite the fact that I'm right here.

"Take her panties off," JD demands, taking charge when he sees Mav's hesitation.

Sliding to the edge of the couch, my eyes drop to the tent in Mav's sweats as he reaches for me.

My mouth waters to get up close and personal with him again. But something tells me that isn't on the cards right now. JD seems to be focusing on me, and I am not going to complain.

"Prettiest cunt in Harrow Creek right there," JD muses

as Mav drags the soaked lace down my legs. "We're lucky fucking bastards. Lift your feet, baby. Let him have those panties as his prize."

I lift my foot, allowing Mav to snatch them up. Curling his fingers around the scrap of lace, he looks up at me. His eyes are darker than I've ever seen them.

"Go on," JD encourages, sensing what Mav's so desperate to do.

He hesitates, his hand visibly trembling as he holds himself back.

"Do it. You won't regret it," JD adds.

Mav's nostrils flare.

Slowly, he moves. His hand lifts toward his face and he holds my panties in front of his nose. The second he inhales, my cheeks burn red hot, the flush quickly spreading down my neck and onto my chest.

His eyelids lower as he breathes me in until they're practically closed.

"You want the real thing?" JD asks, his voice so deep that it startles me.

It must surprise Mav too because his eyes fly open, searching for JD, but he's already moving.

I shriek when my feet leave the floor and I'm falling onto my back, only when I land it's not on the hard and cold coffee table like I'm expecting but a warm wall of muscle.

"Spread your legs, little dove. Show your husband what he's been missing."

Resting back on JD's chest, I do as I'm told and part my thighs.

Mav's eyes instantly drop and I get even wetter with his attention.

JD's hands wrap around my thighs and he spreads me

impossibly wide, hooking my feet over his legs and spreading them, showing Mav every inch of me.

"She's soaked, isn't she?"

Mav swallows roughly before nodding.

"And that gem is so pretty, huh?"

"D-did R-Reid—" he stutters.

"Nah, she already had that little beauty. She been hiding it from you, bro?"

He swallows again before reaching up to wipe his lips.

"You want a taste?" JD asks. His chest vibrates with every word, making me writhe on top of him with the need for some friction on my heated skin.

Silence.

"It's all yours if you want it," JD offers. "You put a ring on it, remember? She walks around wearing it and using your last name. This is yours. Isn't that right, little dove?"

"Yes, please," I cry. "It's yours. Mav. Take it. Please." My head falls back against JD's shoulder, my neck unable to hold it up any longer.

There's a rustle of clothing and then the dull thud that I pray is Mav's knees hitting the floor.

"Oh fuck, yes," I cry when a stream of air rushes across my flesh. My hips jerk up, my need for more almost unbearable. "Mav, please. I need your tongue."

"Taste her, Mav. Lean forward and take everything you've been dreaming about for five long, painful, *hard* years."

There's a beat of silence and I squeeze my eyes closed because I'm convinced I'm about to hear his footsteps walking away before the pain of his rejection wraps around my chest until I can barely breathe.

But then, the most incredible fucking thing happens.

The heat of his mouth singes my burning flesh, and the softness of his tongue sweeps up the length of me.

My thighs threaten to close around his head, the sensations almost too much to bear, but then his hands press against my thighs, keeping me wide open and he really goes to town.

"Tell me that you've found something," I demand the second Ellis answers the phone.

"Hey, bro. Nice to hear from you. I'm great, thanks for asking."

"Great. I'm glad. What have you dug up."

"You're in a great mood right now. I guess what I've heard Dev and Ez talking about is true then."

"Ellis," I bark. "Focus. This shit is more important than those two gossiping pricks."

"Can't really argue with you there. But I hate to disappoint you. The reason you don't know about this is because they've got it all locked down pretty tight."

"Fuck," I mutter, scrubbing my hand down my face.

I knew it was a long shot, but I was really hoping my little tech nerd of a brother was going to be able to hack into this human trafficking ring easily and give me all their dirty secrets.

"I've spoken to Griff," he says, mentioning our uncle in Seattle. "He's got his guys on it too. Sounded pretty confident they'd get something."

"How long?" I ask, my impatience over this already getting the better of me.

"Honestly, I dunno. This kind of shit isn't buried just under the surface, Bro. It's top-level dark web shit. If they've set it up with the intention of having no one find it, then that's almost how it'll be unless we can find a weak link."

"Don't you think I'm fucking trying?"

"I know you are. We all are. Someone has to know something."

"Obviously. But I can hardly go running around town asking questions. No one can know we're aware of this."

"I know, Bro. We've got this. It's going to happen. We've planted all the seeds, all we gotta do is press go and his world is going to start crumbling around him."

Ellis might not be aware of everything I've been doing, but other than JD and our uncle, he's next in line. Something that I'm sure will piss Devin and Ezra off in time. But fuck it. Their skills lie more in the heavy lifting. There isn't much their spot-on marksmanship or muscle can do right now. Their time is coming though. When we go running head first into this war, it's them I'm going to have standing beside me. The rest of my army right behind.

Ellis continues talking, filling the line with technical dark web jargon I don't stand a chance at understanding.

With a sigh, I lean forward and turn my monitor on. The second it comes to life, I'm assaulted with footage of what's happening in my kitchen right this very second.

Oh fuck.

All the air leaves my lungs as I get an eyeful of Alana as her husband drags her panties down her legs before lifting them to his nose and inhaling.

For a man who's withheld for five years, he sure looks excited by the current situation.

Shifting my position, I tug at my jeans. The sight of her perfect body and the diamonds I put in her nipples glinting in the sinking sun already has my cock swelling.

"Oh fuck." I grunt as JD lies back on the coffee table, taking her with him and spreading her wide open.

There's a part of me that is sure it's a coincidence he's done that right in shot of my camera in the corner. They're just there because it's where Mav and Alana were when he joined them.

But there is another part that wonders if he's doing it on purpose. He knows full well that this entire house is hooked up with cameras. There is too much bad shit that could go down here not to have them running twenty-four-seven. It never occurred to me that they'd end up filming live porn.

Other than Letty, Alana is the only other woman who's been here. We've certainly never brought any of the club whores here. We made a pact long before we moved into this place that it was going to be ours only. Any time we felt the need to indulge in pussy, it had to happen elsewhere.

"You listening, Bro?"

"Y-yeah, of course," I croak out as I rub myself through the thickness of the denim covering me.

This was not part of the plan, I think, as JD spreads her legs wide, letting me see just how wet she is for both of them.

My mouth waters as I watch JD taunt Mav with Alana.

Okay, so maybe he's not completely sure of this situation.

Watching him like a fish out of water makes me smirk. I always thought he was so sure of himself.

Maybe Alana is right. Maybe I have got him wrong.

Time seems to stop. I certainly don't hear a word Ellis is saying in my ear as I wait for something to happen.

Alana squirms on JD, probably driving him to the brink because there's no way he's not on the edge right now.

I know I am, and she's not even close to touching me.

Suddenly, it's like someone flips a switch on Mav and he drops to his knees. He looks like a man at the altar, who's about to drink his wine and make his pledge of allegiance to God, or whatever the fuck goes down in a church. It's not like I've ever dared go inside one. Pretty sure someone would strike me dead the second I dared touch the door let alone step over the threshold.

The moment he drops to his knees and leans forward, licking her from ass to clit, I lose the fragile grasp I have on my restraint.

"I appreciate what you're saying, Bro. But I gotta go," I bark impatiently into my cell, before throwing it onto my desk and ripping my fly open.

I knew it was a mistake not jerking off after letting JD walk off with her last night.

But I wasn't fucking expecting this live-action show.

Leaning forward, I hit the volume button on my keyboard. Instantly, my office is filled with Alana's needy cries.

You did this, I chastise myself. *You let her up here. Fuuuck.* I groan, wrapping my hand around myself, stroking with a pressure that I know will have me blowing in only a few minutes.

It's her fault I'm this on edge.

JD is right... you need to fuck her.

Slamming that thought down in the lockbox it deserves to be in, I watch them.

Mav holds her thighs wide, allowing him full access to her cunt while JD makes the most of her incredible tits.

He teases, pinches and tugs on her nipples, making her cry out and her back arch for more.

It's fucking beautiful.

She is beautiful.

Her cheeks are glowing and the blush spreads right down to her tits. Her lips are swollen and parted. And with her head tilted the way it is, it would be so easy to slide right past them and into the heat of her mouth.

I groan, precum leaking from my slit as I imagine doing just that, unable to forget JD telling me how good she is at it.

She's a whore, she should be good at it.

"FUCK," I bark, my hips jumping from the chair as my own thoughts about her piss me off.

Yeah, she's a fucking whore all right. Look at her.

But she's not Victor's whore.

Or Harrow Creeks' whore.

She's ours.

All fucking ours.

With Mav's fingertips digging into her thighs, he eats her until she's screaming and coming all over his face.

Lucky fucking bastard.

"That's it, little dove. Let him have it. Fuck, you're beautiful. Can you feel how hard I am for you?"

She nods, her eyes heavy and her body limp after her intense release.

It's not until Mav gets to his feet that she comes back to herself and her eyes widen.

There's a moment of hesitation between all of them and my movements on my own aching dick slow as I wait to see what's going to happen next.

Is he going to freak out and bolt, or is he—

JD pushes her to her feet and quickly jumps up behind her, holding her steady when her legs refuse to.

Mav's shoulders tense but then she throws herself at him, kissing him as if his face isn't still covered in her release and his tongue isn't coated in her taste.

Their kiss is wild and dirty and everything it should be after years of holding out.

Behind them, JD rips open his pants and pulls his metal-loaded dick out.

If Mav hasn't been scared off this far, then one look at that thing should do it.

I might have two bars through mine, but fuck if I was subjecting myself to the kind of torture JD did.

With his dick in his hand, JD leans forward and whispers something in her ear.

I can't hear, but it doesn't take a genius to guess what it was. And it becomes pretty fucking clear when she sinks like a stone to her knees, dragging Mav's borrowed sweats down with her.

His dick springs free, but she doesn't miss a beat, instantly wrapping her hand around it.

"Fucking asshole," I mutter, noticing that her fingers barely meet. Of course he's fucking packing in the junk department. Pussy doesn't seem to have any piercings, though. Not that I'm looking that closely.

His head falls back in pleasure, but it doesn't last long because she leans forward and licks up the length of his shaft before sucking on the head.

His eyes dart down to watch her as she swallows him down and his fingers sink into her hair, controlling her movements.

Meanwhile, JD is still wanting behind her, jerking his own dick. I'm amazed he doesn't try sneaking in on the action to get a little head of his own. He is all about sharing the love after all.

Smug fucking asshole.

But he seems content just watching her and playing with himself.

I would call him pathetic, but at least he's a known participant in this little gang bang.

In an embarrassingly short amount of time, Mav's previously smooth hip movement becomes jerky and erratic and he throws his head back, roaring out his release so loud, I don't need the speakers to hear it.

Alana, the good little whore she is, swallows him down before he collapses back onto my fucking couch in a sweaty heap of limbs.

"Dove." JD growls, reaching for her hair and dragging her around like a rag doll.

In seconds, she's parted her lips for him, but my eyes don't linger on them, instead, they find Mav who's watching them with a heated, yet slightly horrified expression on his face.

He's probably spent years imagining what it might be like to get sucked off by his wife. I bet in none of those fantasies there was another man waiting to fill the hole he just vacated.

I continue stroking myself, my own release tingling at the base of my spine as I turn my attention back to Alana as she hollows her cheeks and takes as much of JD as she can.

His teeth clench, his jaw pops, and every muscle in his body pulls tight before he also spills down her throat.

I shake my head as jealousy floods through my veins.

What I wouldn't fucking give to walk out there now and take my turn.

I won't, though.

She's already a big enough distraction from what's really important here. The second I cave to temptation, I know that I'll be fully pulled in by her magical voodoo pussy and I'll lose sense of what I should be doing.

My hard-on wanes as I think about Victor and the end game I've been working toward for far too long now.

My eyes are still focused on the screen, but I don't see what's going on, my vision is blurred as I fist myself harder, desperate for the release the others have already found.

I've no idea how much time passes but movement at the door makes my heart jump into my throat. The second I discover who it is, though, my erection returns full force because she's standing there naked with my tank hanging from her fingers.

"You really are a perv, aren't you, Harris?" she sneers, her voice rough from her screaming orgasm not so long ago. Her eyes move from mine to the computer screen that clearly shows Mav and JD lying out on the couches like they've had their souls sucked from their bodies to my aching dick.

Her tongue sneaks out, wetting her lips as I keep stroking myself.

"You want me to taste you too?" she asks, pushing from the doorframe and stalking closer.

Her hips sway, and her tits bounce. The pink diamonds glinting under the spotlights pointed at her.

Lifting her free hand, she traces her lips with her fingertip. "You want me to get on my knees for you and suck you deep into my mouth like you just watched me do for your best friend and my husband?" she taunts before letting her hand drop lower, playing with her tits, teasing those bars I pierced her with.

"Or was it a taste of me you're yearning for?" she asks,

walking her fingers down her stomach toward the apex of her thighs.

"Pet." I growl, my body burning, my cock swelling.

"Beg me," she demands.

My teeth grind.

"You won't get anything if you don't beg," she teases, sitting her ass in JD's chair on the other side of my desk and spreading her legs.

"Fuck. Fuck. Fuck," I mutter, seeing how wet and open she is. It would be so fucking easy to—

She presses two fingers to her clit, and my mouth runs dry.

"Oh yeah." She moans. "Reid, yeah, just like that. Deeper, harder."

Hearing my name roll off her tongue like that is my undoing, and I bark a curse as I come into my hand like a pussy.

The second the first rope of cum spills free, she snaps her legs closed and stands.

Pressing her palms to my desk, she leans close, staring at me with her top lip curled in disgust.

"I hope you filmed that too because it's the only time you're going to hear me moaning your name. Now clean up, Big Man. You've made one hell of a mess."

Spinning on her heels, she saunters away, putting as much sass into her movements as possible.

And as if that wasn't mortifying enough, there's a round of clapping and cheering when she emerges into the hallway.

"I fucking hate you, Julian Dempsey," I roar, which only makes him laugh harder.

35

MAVERICK

JD is still laughing when Alana rushes past us—still naked—and runs up the stairs.

I take a step forward but a large hand clamps down on my shoulder, making me wince.

Considering Reid shot me, it hasn't been all that painful. Sure, it helps that his shot was a little off. I'm not sure he intended to graze me, instead of putting that bullet right through my heart. But here we are. Something else he's going to have to live with.

"Give her space," JD commands, making my brows shoot up.

"Who the fuck made you the expert on my wife?" I growl.

"No one." He grunts. "You want a drink?" he offers, releasing me and walking off. His swagger is even more prominent than usual. Can't say I'm surprised after what just went down.

Alana did. Alana went down... on both of us.

I hang my head and close my eyes for a beat, but the

second darkness comes, all I see is her on her knees, her lips stretched around my dick as she swallowed me down.

My cock jerks in my sweats, desperate for a repeat.

Fucking hell.

"She's good, right?" JD mutters, clearly able to read my mind.

"Uh..."

"Dude, it's too late to be a fucking prude."

"I'm not." I scoff, walking over as he holds out a bottle of beer for me.

"You totally are. So I watched your wife suck your dick? It was hot."

He drops his hand and rearranges himself to drive his point home.

"I'm more than happy to share."

He chuckles when a possessive growl rumbles in my throat.

"You should be thanking me. I hope you know that," he says after gulping down over half his beer.

"Whatever."

"I mean it. If it weren't for me, you'd still be a blue-balled motherfucker like that miserable fuck out there."

I don't want to think about what went down a few minutes ago while my wife was naked with Reid Harris.

"You two are as bad as each other. You listen, though."

"Is that meant to be a compliment?" I ask after swallowing a mouthful.

"You just had your cock sucked because of me, take it however you like, man," he says before turning around and reaching into a cupboard.

"There's something wrong with you."

"Wanna tell me something I don't know," he says, running the faucet until the water turns warm and filling a bowl that he then pours salt into. "Be good, yeah. I won't be long."

"What are you doing?" I bark as he marches across the room, on a mission.

"Alana's nipples aren't healed, and you've had them in your mouth. Need to make sure they don't—"

"I'll do it," I shout, jumping from the stool I'd settled onto.

"You want to go play with your wife's tits, Mav?"

My jaw ticks at his teasing.

Yes. "I want to take care of her. It's my job."

He studies me for a beat, and just when I think he's going to make me fight for it, he hands the bowl over.

"Thank you."

"Don't do anything I wouldn't do," he calls after me.

"Asshole," I mutter under my breath.

"I heard that."

Shaking my head, I try to keep the smile off my face, but it's a fight I can't win. Despite everything surrounding us, I'm feeling better than I have in a very long time.

And it only gets better the closer I get to my wife.

I come to a stop at the top of the stairs and stare down the hallway. I know that JD's room is opposite the one they put me in, and that Reid's is right at the end. But which has she chosen to slip into?

Yesterday, she escaped to Reid's bathroom. But after what just went down, something tells me that his space will be the last place she wants to be.

I move closer, and the second I notice that my room is the only one with the door cracked open, I get my answer.

With the bowl of salt water in my hand, I make my way through the bedroom and toward the bathroom door, which is also open in invitation.

I knock because it's polite, not because I want to. I don't want to give her any chance to turn me away to tell me that she regrets what happened downstairs. JD's presence aside, it was the best thing that's happened to me in years.

Fuck. The sight of her wide, glassy eyes staring up at me as she took my dick...

"Doll?" I rasp, pushing the door wider.

I find her with a towel wrapped around her body, another twisting up her hair as she stands at the mirror.

The second she sees me in the reflection, her entire face lights up.

"Hey," she says, spinning around to look at me. Her eyes drop down the length of my body, lingering on my crotch long enough to acknowledge just how much she affects me before she finally finds my eyes again. "You okay?"

Stepping closer, I abandon the bowl on the counter and wrap my hand around the side of her neck instead.

"Yeah, Doll. I'm really fucking good." I hold still, letting her search my eyes so that she can see how sincere I'm being.

She lets out a long breath of relief, her shoulders relaxing.

My thumb traces her jaw, and she shudders.

"You're incredible. Do you know that?" I murmur, pressing my head to hers.

"Uh... you did just watch me suck JD off, right?" she asks with a humorless laugh.

"It was a bit blurry," I confess. "This mouth." My thumb traces across the fullness of her bottom lip, before dragging it down. "For years I've been thinking about this, about how you'd feel."

"Yeah?" she asks, her eyes darkening with every word that rolls off my tongue.

"It's better than I ever could have imagined. Fucking perfect."

She swallows roughly, her tendons pulling taut beneath my palm.

"I thought you were going to freak out."

"Still might," I confess. "This... none of this was what I was expecting, Doll. You've taken me completely off guard. But that downstairs... fuck, babe."

"I know," she agrees, her small hand wrapping around my forearm as she leans closer.

Her fresh from the shower scent wraps around me, luring me in.

"I'm going to give you everything you deserve, Doll, and more," I promise, my eyes closing as the heat of her lips burn mine.

Our kiss isn't like the ones we shared downstairs. It isn't frantic and desperate but gentle, loving, and it holds just as much promise.

"I'm an idiot," I confess when we finally break apart, our chests heaving.

She giggles. The sound is so light and free, it makes something flutter in my chest. "I've always known that, Mav." She takes a step back from me, severing our connection. "You could have had this the whole time."

She tugs the towel from her body, letting it float to the floor and pool at her feet—not that I spare it a second glance. How could I when she's standing before me looking like that?

"Go on then," she encourages, looking down at herself.

"Uh..." I stutter like a preteen boy staring at his first pair of real tits. My tongue sneaks out, wetting my lips as I prepare to do... something.

She laughs again, the sound wraps around me like a warm blanket.

"I'm assuming that's a bowl of salt water that JD sent you up with," she teases.

"Uh... yeah. He was going to... and I..."

"Well, go on then," she says, thrusting her tits toward me.

"Jesus, Doll," I mutter.

"Cotton is under the sink."

"Y-yeah, great. Thanks."

After soaking a ball in the warm liquid, I step closer, my eyes locked on my prize, my dick aching in my pants once again.

"Do they hurt?" I ask, gently dabbing her tender skin.

"Not really," she murmurs, watching my every move. "Really sensitive though. But I guess you already know that."

I don't respond, I just keep working. Probably for a lot longer than necessary, but JD is right, we don't want them getting infected. That would be really, really bad on many levels.

"Do you want to talk about it?" she asks, after a long silence where I do nothing but shamelessly stare at her rack.

I know I should probably say yes. What happened downstairs was huge. But right now, I'm happy to ignore the heavy shit in favor of just being with her again, even if the dynamic has totally changed.

A slamming door downstairs stops me from answering and instead, I drop the ball of cotton into the bowl and stand to full height again.

"You must be hungry." I need to find some level footing.

Her eyes drop down my body, lingering at the tent I'm rocking.

She sucks her bottom lip into her mouth and drags it through her teeth.

"Yeah, I guess I am."

"Get dressed and I'll see what I can find."

"Or you could get un—"

"Damn," JD curses when he shamelessly storms in. "I was hoping to walk in on something a little more exciting than this."

"Well done for knocking, asshole," I mutter.

He waves me off as Alana reaches for the towel and wraps it around herself again.

"Boo," JD complains with a pout.

"What have I told you about trying to be cute?" she teases.

"You love it."

His words make my heart beat faster.

Does she?

"Anyway," he continues when all she does is raise a brow in question. "Reid's thrown a tantrum and stormed out."

"Why?" Alana asks.

JD chuckles. "I think we all know why, Dove. Our fearless leader is feeling a bit left out."

"He got to come," she states flatly.

"Not sure he had quite the same experience we did," JD says, his eyes tracing Alana's curves as if she's still standing there naked.

"Good, he doesn't deserve to. He should be relieved he got to come at all after what he did to me."

JD's eyes flash with understanding.

"What did he do?"

"You know," JD muses. "I could tell you. It was hot. I'm sure you'd appreciate it."

"JD," Alana snaps.

"Or one day, maybe I should show you. Give you the full experience."

"Julian," she tries again.

"What, Dove? I think it would drive your husband here crazy. And we all know you want that, don't you?"

"You're a nightmare," she states.

"Maybe so, but you wouldn't have me any other way. Now, let me see those nipples up close. I want to make sure your man has done a proper job."

"Nice try," she says, holding the towel tighter.

"There's always later."

"What's the plan?" I ask.

JD shrugs. "Don't have one. But with Reid gone, it looks like we're going to have to fend for ourselves."

"He means we're going to have to cook because JD can burn air," Alana explains.

"Shouldn't be too challenging, there's enough food in the fridge to feed an army."

"Let's just hope he's out building us one as well. Something tells me that we're going to need it."

A ripple of unease goes around the room as the weight of the situation we're in the middle of presses down on us.

"He's got this all under control, right? He knows what he's doing?" Alana asks, looking unsure of herself for the first time since she walked into my cell yesterday.

"Uh... yeah, sure. Totally got it all wrapped up."

"Gee, could you sound any less convincing?" I mutter. "What exactly is his plan here?"

"You good, little dove?"

When she nods, JD walks toward me and throws his arm around my shoulder.

"You serious?" I bark, trying to throw him off.

"Dude, we practically shared a blowy. We're BFFs for life now," he muses, dragging me out of the bathroom as Alana laughs behind us.

"Play nice."

"Only if you promise to join," JD counters.

"Do you ever stop?" I mutter.

"Nope. Now do you want the details or what?" he asks.

36

REID

Ringing fills my ears as I sit in my car a little down the street from Devin, Ezra, and Ellis's place in Maddison County.

Just like most weekends, the party is raging.

It's hardly a surprise. Everyone who is anyone knows that where the Harrises are, the decent product is.

There might be others trying to earn a living in this town, but just like Daddy Dearest planned, we stormed in here when Dev started at MKU and we've practically taken over.

It would have been even easier for them as well if I weren't in the background messing around, making Victor more enemies and making myself allies.

Not that I expected anything different. Devin and Ezra have fucking killed it. They've got themselves involved in every part of life here and made friends in all the right places to ensure they sell out every weekend. And with Ellis in the background, keeping tabs on everything, they're an unstoppable team.

We're an unstoppable team. Or at least we will be soon.

Guilt niggles at me as I watch a girl stumble across the road, clearly off her head on something my brothers have given her. But it only lasts so long.

If it weren't us, it would be others. And the one thing I can say proudly about all of this is that I know exactly where our product comes from. And I know it's pure. Decent. As it fucking should be.

Others are probably peddling shit laced with rat poison through the halls of MKU. Something I will never do.

These students are looking for a high, an escape, a way to let go. And if selling them our product means they're not taking other shit, then so be it. I'll be the bad guy more than happily.

"Sorry, I'm here," a familiar voice floods through my speaker when the call finally connects.

"About time. Do you know who I am?" I tease.

"Oh, pipe down, young one."

"What's the deal then? You got any intel yet?" I ask, anticipation soaring as I wait for our uncle on our maternal side, Griff, to give me something.

"Not as much as I'd like, but we've made some progress. I've got a contact for you."

My grip on my cell tightens as relief floods through me.

"Who?" I ask impatiently.

"Luciana Rivera," he says quietly, as if he's scared of being overheard.

"Rivera?" I parrot, my eyes wide in shock.

"Yeah, I know. I didn't see that one coming either," he confesses.

"What the fuck are the cartel doing getting their fingers in human trafficking?"

"I don't know. And honestly, I'm not sure how much Luciana knows, but I came across her doing her own

314

digging. I get the impression we're looking for very similar things."

"You trust her?" I ask, my brows pinching together in confusion.

I'm pretty sure on any other occasion, his answer would be fuck no. But something tells me this is different.

"Luciana isn't..." he trails off.

"She isn't what?"

"She's... different."

"You've had dealings with her before?" I ask, aware that their reach is almost countrywide.

"Her husband and his father, yes. She was in the background and kept on a leash."

"Seems like someone might have let her off it if she's digging through the dark web."

"I wouldn't be surprised to discover that she severed her own leash."

"What?"

"Her husband is dead," he says, not telling me anything I don't already know.

"And you're saying what exactly? That she killed him?"

"I'm not suggesting anything," he says coyly.

"Sure you're not," I mutter. "You spoken to her?"

"Briefly. I thought you might want to do it yourself. Told her to expect your call."

"Anything else?"

"Not of any importance. How's things on your end?"

I breathe a sigh of relief. Mostly because he's probably the only person in my life right now who isn't secretly asking if I've fucked Alana yet.

"Tense," I confess.

"I want to say it's going to improve, but I'm afraid that it's probably going to get worse before it gets better."

"Don't I fucking know it."

"It's going to happen, though. With this new intel, we're finally going to take him down."

"I fucking hope so. She deserves justice." They all deserve justice. Every poor fucker who's ever had their lives touched by Victor Harris.

Griff sighs, even all these years on, his grief is palpable.

"Yeah," he agrees sadly. "How's my boy doing?" he asks after a beat of silence.

"He's great. Keeping his head down, doing his job."

"Fantastic. Let's hope it continues. Listen, I gotta go, but let me know what Luciana says, yeah?"

"You got it, old man."

"Hey now, enough of that, kid."

"Whatever," I tease, unable to keep the smile off my face.

For years, I had no idea that our family extended past the border of Harrow Creek. Dad—probably wisely—kept a lid on the fact that Mom wasn't a Creeker born and bred like we were always led to believe. It wasn't until Ellis discovered his love of computers, or more specifically, hacking, that he started looking into our background.

Turned out Mom was originally from Seattle. And she certainly didn't come from a nice little conservative family with two-point-five kids and a picket fence. Instead, she seemed to have stumbled out of one gang and tripped straight into another.

It's only recently the truth of how all that came about has come to life, thanks to Griff. I knew it was going to be bad. Anything that involves Victor fucking Harris is bad. But I was not expecting what I discovered.

The second Griff says goodbye, the call cuts, leaving me in silence with my head spinning.

Not two seconds later, my cell buzzes with a contact.

I don't need to open it to know who it belongs to.

Luciana Rivera.

Griff is right. The only time I've met her, she was standing behind her husband and father-in-law, towing the line and looking beautiful while doing it.

I knew her husband had died, that wasn't a secret. But Griff's suspicions sure make me wonder.

That meek and mild redheaded woman didn't look like she'd be capable of such a thing. But then, I guess appearances can be deceiving. Just look at Alana. No one would believe she'd endured the kind of abuse she has. She's so strong and determined. Unshakable.

I shake my head when I realize that my thoughts have pinged straight back to her.

Running away from the house was a pussy move. I'm more than aware of that. But after the way she left me with cum dribbling down my fingers, I could hardly have then joined them for dinner.

She's messing with my head.

No one has ever made me question my decisions or my life before.

I don't fucking like it.

Before I drive myself insane, I kill the engine, pocket my cell and step out of my car.

There are even more students loitering around, coming and going from the house in all kinds of inebriated states than when I first pulled up.

I'm almost at the driveway when some girl trips over her own feet and collides with me.

"I'm gonna puke," she wails, giving me an excuse I really didn't need to shove her away.

"Sorry, man. She's wast— Oh fuck." He grunts when his

eyes lock on mine and he realizes who his girlfriend just nearly threw up all over.

With a scowl in his direction, I continue toward the house, ignoring all eyes that are slowly turning on me.

We might not have had much to do with Maddison Country before Victor set his sights here, but it hasn't taken long for word to spread about who's behind the entire college having the best product in the state.

No one else dares to say a word to me as I make my way inside the house. The music booms and the stench of cigarette smoke and weed makes my eyes water.

"Aw, look who decided to pay us a visit," a clearly wasted Devin slurs as he rushes over and bear-hugs me like a douchebag.

"So much for working sober," I mutter.

"Bro, we've had an epic weekend. Just enjoying living the high life. Something you should really try every now and then."

"Sure. Whatever you say," I mutter, shoving him off me. "Tell me Ez is still able to have a conversation."

"Doubt it." He scoffs. "Last time I saw him, he had his head up some chick's skirt."

"Fuck's sake."

"Ellis is somewhere playing with his computer, though. I'm sure you can have a grown-up conversation with him while we party."

Devin gives me a shove in the direction of the kitchen and I take off. Although, I don't quite get there.

"Well, well, well, if it isn't Reid Harris," a female voice says before a familiar, tall brunette steps in front of me and leans forward to kiss both of my cheeks.

"Long time no see," I say, a genuine smile pulling at my lips at the sight of an old friend.

"You could say that," she purrs, making a show of checking me out. "You've sure... grown."

"Could say the same about you," I mutter. I can't help but notice the increase in her chest since I last saw her.

"You like?" she says, thrusting them together. She's not trying to tempt me. Aubrey knows I won't be going there. But it doesn't stop her from being a shameless flirt.

Our paths crossed a few years ago when I was out of town meeting a supplier. She turned up in the bar I was drinking in with her sights set on a mark. I got the pleasure of watching him fall hook, line, and sinker for every single one of her moves.

It was impressive. Really fucking impressive.

They disappeared for her to finish the job, and I assumed that would be the last I ever saw of her. But to my surprise, an hour or so later, she stalked back through the bar, looking as calm and collected as she had previously. But this time, she was practically glowing with accomplishment.

I've no idea what she did with or to the guy that night. Even after introducing myself and buying her a drink, she never gave me the details. I didn't need those though to understand it was all a honeytrap. And color me intrigued. We spent almost all night in that bar chatting.

We've spoken a couple of times since, and we met up once when her work landed her close to Harrow Creek.

"They're... certainly distracting."

"They work like a charm," she says with a wink.

"Those losers really don't know how unlucky they are," I tease.

"So," she purrs, threading her arm through mine and continuing in the direction I was heading, "I assume my first-class ticket to Harrow Creek for more than a social visit."

"You would assume correctly."

"OUT," I bark the second we step into the kitchen.

Ellis looks up, unconcerned about my demand, while everyone else practically piss their pants, rushing to follow orders.

Glancing from me to Aubrey, Ellis stands from his computer and lowers the lid, intrigue clear in his eyes.

"Thought you were having too much fun at home to grace us with your presence," he teases.

I grunt, remembering what I was distracted by when we spoke before.

"Ellis, this is Aubrey," I say, introducing them instead of continuing with his topic of conversation. "Aubrey, this is my little brother and IT geek, Ellis."

They smile at each other, although Ellis eyes her warily.

"I need you to grab some intel for her. She's going to help us out."

Ellis's eyes find mine and narrow.

"Are you sure that's a good idea?" he asks, correctly guessing what I'm going to ask her to do.

Irritated by his lack of confidence in her, Aubrey crosses her arms under her ample tits, pushing them up.

His gaze drops, but only briefly. He's about as distracted by them as I am.

"I'm a professional, Ellis," she states coldly. "And I can assure you that I've got intel out of more powerful and dangerous men than you've ever had the pleasure of meeting."

"Right," he mutters, irritated by her assessment.

"I'll need times, dates, and details about what you want

out of the mark. I promise you that I'll get exactly what you need."

Ellis chews on his bottom lips for a beat before focusing on me.

"Are you sure this is a good idea?" he urges.

"Do you have a fucking better one?"

His lips part to argue, but no words spill out. And after a couple of seconds, he looks down at his computer, lifting the lid once more to get Aubrey what she needs.

37

ALANA

When I rejoin Mav and JD downstairs, things are tense.

They're each sitting on a couch, both resting their elbows on their knees, their heads dipped low, looking as serious as they do hot.

Something flutters inside me as I study their profiles.

My life might be a clusterfuck of epic proportions, but it sure has been worse than it is right now.

Two men who look like that and who can make my spine arch and toes curl. And I've barely touched on what Mav can do...

"I know you're watching us, Doll," Mav murmurs, cutting off whatever JD was saying before he slowly turns toward where I'm resting against the doorframe.

His eyes blaze with heat so intense, it makes my muscles clench. For a few seconds, they hold mine before he lets them drop.

"You'd look better in my clothes," he points out, after finding me in another of JD's shirts.

"Nah, she's perfect as she is."

"I could also do with some of my own clothes," he points out.

"Victor and your dad think you're having a vacation in the asscrack of nowhere. But if you want to blow that cover and head home, be my guest," JD offers, holding his arm out to gesture toward the door.

"You don't mean that," I say, stepping deeper into the room.

"And get you all to myself again?" he teases. "I think I do."

I shake my head, coming to a stop between them at the coffee table.

My body burns and my skin tingles with their attention. Both of them try to silently lure me in, to pull me to them, to make me choose one over the other.

But how am I meant to do that?

Sure. Mav would be the obvious choice. He's my husband.

But JD...

There is something about him. The playfulness mixed with the tortured soul that hides beneath the surface that I don't think he's aware I see. His boyish smile and the shadows in his eyes. Both sides of him are as addicting as each other.

"Julian," I warn, staying put, unable to make a decision between them. "Have you filled Mav in?"

"Yep. And he thinks he's got an in with the Devils?"

"Oh?" I ask, turning to my husband.

"Razor sent me to sort out an issue with a shipment a few weeks ago. I had no idea I was about to walk into a shitshow that Reid had created with all this. But I might have won them over enough to get them on our side."

"If that's true, Reid might just worship at your feet. They've been the hardest to crack."

Mav laughs. "That'll be the fucking day."

"You give him a way in with Sidney Hyde and he'll be putty in your hands," JD confirms.

"This is good, right? Progress?"

"Oh hell, yeah. I reckon they could be BFFs by the end of next week. In fact, I'd put mon—"

"No more bets," I beg, interrupting where JD was going.

His lips part before something I don't like dances in his eyes.

"What?" I ask on a groan, making Mav sit forward curiously.

"Nothing, nothing. I was just yanking Reid's chain about you. Bet him that he'd be between your thighs by the end of next week. If Mav is true to his word, Reid might just be sucking his dick too."

"Julian," I snap. "That jerk isn't getting between my legs by the end of the year, let alone the end of next week."

JD pushes to his feet, letting me take in the inches upon inches of taut, muscular, inked-up skin he's left on show.

He's done it for my benefit, there is no doubt about that.

I want to say I'm ungrateful, but I'm really, really not.

There's got to be perks to living with gangsters, right?

"Sure, he's not," he taunts, stepping closer.

"JD," Mav warns, but there isn't much heat to it.

"He's in your head, Dove. Just like you're in his. As much as I love watching him squirm after everything he put you through, we all know that it's inevitable."

He reaches out to grab a lock of my hair and I slap his hand away.

"You and Mav," he muses. "You and me. You and Reid. It all makes perfect sense."

"I'm sorry," I say, shaking my head in confusion. "Are you proposing something here?"

He smirks, his hand coming back to my face. His large warm palm engulfs my jaw before his thumb teases my bottom lip.

"As far as I see it, little dove, we're well past proposals. This might be fucked up, but that's the only kind of family I've ever known. And this one trumps every other I've ever experienced."

My eyes bounce between his, searching for the joke. But there isn't one.

He's serious.

He—

"You want this?" I blurt. "This... I don't even know what this is."

"Sure. Why not? You can't tell me that it doesn't work."

"You locked us in your basement. You shot—"

"You're both still here."

"Because we don't have a choice. We—"

"Don't you? You've been up here for days, and yet you're still standing in front of me, wearing my clothes. By choice," he adds. "And I haven't seen Mav running for the door either."

"We can't, they're locked—"

"Are they?" he asks, his eyes lighting up with amusement. "When was the last time you tried the doors, little dove?" he asks, tucking a stray lock of hair behind my ear before leaning in closer. "Because something tells me that you haven't. You want to be here. You like being here. You like fucking me. You like tempting Mav. Hell, you even like fighting with Reid.

"You could have run, but you're still here. Both of you are still here."

I stare up at him, my heart pounding and my hands trembling.

He's right. I know he is.

My eyes dart to the huge doors that lead outside and I remember trying them the day I found myself here alone.

It was locked then.

But I haven't tried since.

Before I think better of it, I dart around JD and rush toward it.

The second my fingers wrap around the handle, I suck in a deep breath.

What if this is open?

What if JD is right and we're not trapped here?

What do I do then?

Justice or freedom?

Or is there a way to have both...

My muscles tense as I tug the handle.

"Oh my God." I gasp when the door opens easily, allowing the cool evening air to rush over my skin.

I act on autopilot, stepping out onto the deck, letting the last of the day's rays warm my skin.

Closing my eyes, I turn my face to the sun and just absorb the feeling I didn't realize I missed so badly.

It's been two weeks since I've breathed in fresh air, and it's... incredible.

I don't realize I've moved until the rail presses against my stomach.

The sound of water drags my eyes down, and I gasp when the sight of Reid's state of the art pool and hot tub clears before me.

My skin itches with the need to dive in, to feel myself

cutting through the water, to be utterly weightless while we've got all this bullshit weighing me down.

Wrapping my hands around the railing, I have to physically stop myself from jumping over the edge.

I startle when a warm hand curls around my waist and a solid wall of muscle presses against my back.

I know who it is long before he speaks. Words have never really been necessary between us.

Leaning back, I rest my head against his shoulder as his arms wrap around me, holding me tight.

"Never thought I'd say it, but it looks beautiful from up here," he whispers. It's almost as if he's scared talking too loudly will ruin it.

"Yeah. Shame it's not the truth," I muse, my eyes locked on the down and out town in the distance.

"Where's your head at, Doll?"

"I—" I cut myself off, quickly swallowing whatever I was about to say.

"JD's right. You, we, could have run." I nod, knowing he's right. There's just something about this place, or maybe it's the men within it that stop me from wanting to do so.

Sure, the need to run to the other side of the world and leave all this behind lessened when Mav gave me a home. But the thought was never far from my mind. But here... the last few days. It's barely been a whisper. Swallowed by the promise of justice, revenge and... pleasure.

"I think... I feel like I've been found but yet, I'm still lost." He stills at my confession. "I know that doesn't make any sense but—"

"It does," he assures me. "Things are different up here. Perspectives and opinions aren't the same as when you're down there."

Silence falls between us as the final bird song of the day

fills the air around us and the breeze trickles through my hair.

I wish I had an answer for him. Something solid.

But JD is right. It's not just Reid who's up in my head. It's all of them.

I do enjoy JD's brand of punishment, and this new development with Mav. And bickering with Reid, yeah, it's frustrating as hell, but also, kinda... fun.

But it's crazy to think this could be something. The only reason we're here is because we want the same men dead.

It would be stupid to think that there's anything more.

When—if—we achieve our goal, the reality is that Reid will step into Victor's shoes. He and Mav will go back to hating each other, and JD... well...

My chest constricts just thinking about where that might leave him.

It's not until the sun finally dips behind the hill in the distance, bathing Harrow Creek in the darkness it thrives in, that I spin around.

My breath catches the second our eyes connect.

Mav's are so dark, so full of longing and want. Full of promises and hopes for the future.

Sliding my hands up, I cup his unshaven jaw in my palms.

"I know that I want you," I whisper. "What we've found here, it means everything to me."

He drags his bottom lip between his teeth, his throat rippling and his Adam's apple bobbing on a swallow.

"But what about them?"

I shake my head.

"It's about us," I argue. "All of this, it's for our future."

He licks his lips.

"It doesn't look the same as it used to though, does it?"

His words give me pause. I think about us walking down the beach again, but unlike back then, there are two more figures with us.

But is that just a fantasy? Some stupid, fickle version of Stockholm syndrome from being stuck here with them.

All my life, I've craved connection, stability. The brand they've given me has been fucked up. But it's there nonetheless.

"I don't know anymore," I confess honestly.

He stares down at me, conflict and concern darkening his eyes.

"I love you, Maverick Murray," I whisper, pressing my body harder against his, loving that I can feel what our closeness does to him against my belly. "That will never change." His breath rushes over my face as he dips his brow to rest against mine. "Kiss me," I demand, needing more. Needing everything.

38

MAVERICK

For the past five years, I've truly believed that the most terrifying thing I faced was to have Alana look at me like I'm nothing more than a man from her past. I was so fucking scared of ever doing anything to make her think for even a second that I could be like that, that I've held back on everything.

Do I regret it?

No. Not for a second. I could never regret anything that has involved spending time with my wife.

But do I think I possibly could have handled it better? Sure. One hundred percent.

I guess looking back, the biggest problem is that I couldn't tell anyone.

In those first few years, she was my dirty little secret.

Kurt was pissed off for a while. Someone had taken away his favorite toy; I guess he had a right to be irritated. But honestly, he must have seen it coming. He couldn't have ever truly believed that she wanted to be subjected to the hell he was putting her through. Surely he was aware that she spent her days dreaming about freedom while her

330

nights were left haunted by everything he'd allowed to happen.

But eventually, everyone just kinda forgot about her. It was a relief, albeit a sad one.

It was such an insult to what an incredible person she is that she could be forgotten like she never existed.

It sure helped make life easier for me though.

With no one searching for her, I could do my job. I could protect her and help to build a life for her that she deserved.

But as I stand here now, staring down into her hungry eyes with her body pressed up against mine, I realize there was always a threat out there much bigger, much scarier than her looking at me like a monster.

And I've just witnessed it.

The way she looked up at JD as he laid out her truths about staying here.

That was way more terrifying than her looking at me like a monster.

Looking at him with the same fire and passion in her eyes she's always giving me was fucking heartbreaking.

And he's given her everything...

"Mav?" she whispers, her brows pinching when I don't move. Too lost in my own head, my own fears, to even really hear her demand.

Her hands slide down my back, making my muscles jump before they find my ass. She squeezes hard, forcing our bodies impossibly tighter. There's no mistaking how her closeness affects me, and if the way her eyes sparkle tells me anything, it's that she loves it.

Just another reminder of how much I fucked up.

"M-Mav, please, I need yo—"

The crack in her voice, the desperation... I can no longer

deny it. I opened the floodgates this morning by caving to the endless tension between us and now I've no chance of stopping what we started.

"Anything." I groan. "Any-fucking-thing."

My fingers twist in the hair at the nape of her neck, tugging her head back exactly as I want, before our lips collide.

And the second they do, I swear something explodes. Cliché, I know, but it's fucking fireworks.

I always knew we'd be electric. From the few tastes I've had, the teasing touches and the taunts she's tried so hard to break me with, I knew our collision would be beyond anything I'd ever experienced. It's why I waited. I knew it would be worth it when the time came. I just never could have imagined that time looking like this.

As our tongues slide together, the knowledge that we're being watched prickles my skin.

I don't need to turn around to know that JD is right there, standing at the window.

He was the first to move when Alana discovered she had freedom, but to my surprise, he didn't follow her out.

I've no idea if he was allowing me to do so, or just giving her some space. I really don't give a shit because right now, the only person I care about is in my arms, giving me everything I've spent years dreaming about.

"Fucking hell, Doll," I groan into our kiss, "I can't get enough."

Releasing me, she grips the rail behind her and stretches. Helping her out, I wrap my hands around her waist and lift her. My shoulder pulls, but it's nowhere near enough to stop me. The moment her ass is perched on the thin strip of wood, her legs part in invitation.

Not needing anything more, I step between them and

immediately wrap them around my waist.

Dipping my head, my lips brush her neck, making her shudder.

"Never going to get enough."

"You don't have to." She groans, threading her fingers through my hair before scratching my scalp. "I need more, not less."

"Jesus." I hiss, kissing her jaw to find her lips again. "Soon," I promise.

"I'm right here, Mav. I'm ready," she begs, grinding the scorching heat of her pussy against my hard-on.

"I know. Fuck. Trust me, I know."

"So what are you waiting for? I don't need soft and gentle. This isn't my first time."

"Maybe not, but it's our first time," I say, sounding like a fucking pussy. "And it's not happening with you perched on the railing of Reid Harris's deck."

"God," she moans, her head falling back as I hit the right spot, "but it would be so hot."

"One day," I promise. "But not today."

"Mav." She moans.

"Trust me, Doll."

Her eyes find mine. They're dilated and full of emotion.

"Always," she promises, before wrapping her hand around the back of my neck and dragging my lips back to hers.

I kiss her almost hard enough to drown out the little voice in my head that says I'm a fucking idiot to turn down a chance of sliding inside her.

But I know I'm right.

What we have... it's more than a quickie against the railing. It deserves more than that.

Time ceases to exist as we continue making out, the skies turning dark around us, the wind picking up and rushing over our heated skin.

But I can't stop. My addiction to her knows no bounds, and it seems she might just feel the same. Fuck, I hope so. We're all lips, teeth, tongues, hands. Dirty, wet kisses and teasing caresses. It's everything. Every-fucking-thing.

Until there is a loud crash from somewhere behind us.

"What was that?" Alana asks, startled, effectively ripping our lips apart.

"I don't know," I whisper, unwilling to put much thought into it when I have her in my arms.

"MOTHERFUCKER," echoes loudly from the house before another crash.

"Shit, we should—"

Before I can argue, Alana is on her feet and pushing me back.

She rushes into the house, and my overwhelming need to protect her—even if it only is from JD's frustrations—ensures I follow right behind.

"What the fuck have you—"

"JD wait," Alana calls as the man who's caused the destruction flees from the room. "JD," she cries when he fails to stop.

"Leave it, Dove," he barks, a warning clear in his voice. "I'm not worth it."

"What? Shit. Julian, stop please," she begs as he takes off, his footsteps pounding up the stairs.

The floor beneath us vibrates with the power he puts into slamming his door.

"Fuck," Alana curses, dropping her head into her

hands.

"Just give him a minute," I say, understanding his need for a breather.

Reaching for her hand, I tug her back into the kitchen. Also known as the disaster zone.

"What the hell was he doing?"

There is some kind of white sticky mixture everywhere, a dirty yet empty upturned bowl on the floor and—

Picking up the cheese and pepperoni, I hold it out for Alana to see.

"Making pizzas?"

"Christ. I know he said he can't cook but this is—"

"A fucking war zone?" I offer, watching as a glop of very badly made dough drips onto the floor.

"He tried."

"He's certainly trying," I mutter.

"Mav," she warns. "Don't be mean. It wasn't so long ago that you ordered takeout every night."

"I guess we haven't all had a hot teacher," I mutter, reaching down to pick up the bowl.

"Exactly. I'll whip him into shape in no time."

That fear from before returns, knotting up my stomach.

She wants to stay here.

"You're assuming Reid hasn't tried. I hate to admit it, but he can cook. Surely he's attempted to teach him."

"Control freak Reid Harris?" she asks with a laugh, although when I glance back, her expression is wrought with concern.

"Fair point," I mutter, reaching for the paper towel, ready to scoop up the dough explosion.

"I should go and make sure he's okay," Alana says, glancing at the doorway.

"He's a big boy, Doll. Give him some space."

"But— Yeah, you're right. Fancy making pizzas for dinner?" she says, ripping off her own bit of towel to help me.

"With you, I'll make anything."

"Smooth, Mav. So fucking smooth."

We keep the conversation light as we work, she asks me about Sheila and Daisy and what they've been up to, but at no point do we broach the current situation. It's as much of a relief as it is frustrating.

I want to know exactly what she's thinking, what she wants. But something tells me that, really, she doesn't know. She's as confused as everyone else under this roof.

"Do you think it's going to work?" she asks, finally breaking our unspoken agreement not to talk about the serious shit as she begins putting toppings onto the four pizza bases laid out before us.

"Do I think Reid can outsmart Victor and take control?" I ask, confirming that we're on the same topic here.

"Yeah," she muses, laying out circles of pepperoni in perfect formations.

"Yeah, I think he can," I say honestly. "Reid is a lot of things." A lot of things I didn't even realize. "But his determination to win is definitely one of them."

I should be relieved he's not making a play for my girl because, if he were, something tells me he'd win that race too.

He wants her. That much was obvious before what happened between them earlier. I mean, of course he wants her. My wife is fucking stunning, and smart, and everything most men could possibly want. But what happens when he realizes it?

"Yeah, you're right. This is big though. Really fucking big," she continues, unaware of my internal freak out.

"Yeah. Something tells me that he can handle it though."

"We're pretty fucked if he can't."

"And we can't hide out here forever. Victor might be a corrupt bastard, but he's not fucking stupid. One sniff of what Reid's doing and he'll have his own army mobilized ready to take all of us down."

Alana stills as the weight of my words hit her.

It takes a few seconds, but eventually, she looks over, our eyes connecting.

"I can't lose you, Mav. Promise me you won't do anything stupid."

I swallow, unable to force the words past my lips.

"You deserve justice, Doll. And I promised you that you'd get it."

"I deserve a life with my husband more," she counters. "If it comes down to it, I'll choose you over ruining them any day."

"Fuck, Doll," I breathe.

"Promise me, Mav. If it comes down to it being us or them, you need to choose us. Me.

"Reid has his own reasons for this fight. He can take them down. I can live with the knowledge that we helped out with intel but stepped back from pulling the triggers."

My teeth grind and my jaw pops as I stare back at her.

'Please,' she mouths.

"Fuck, babe. Yeah. Yes," I say, closing the space between us. "I can't have a future with you if we're both dead."

Our kiss isn't like the one outside. It's short. Just a brush of our lips and a glide of our tongues, but that doesn't mean it isn't full of promise or longing.

I might fucking hate the promise I just made, but I'll do everything in my power to keep it. To keep her.

39

ALANA

My concern for JD only grows as the minutes pass. But I don't go after him.

Despite those dark shadows that linger in his eyes, and the fact that the words that he said to me right in this very room not so long ago are completely true, he isn't the man who gave his life to protect me, who planned his future with me.

As much as it hurts to think it, JD is just the man that was here. He was the man who made this whole fucked-up situation better. He's the man who showed me pleasure instead of pain and makes me laugh instead of cry —mostly.

He isn't the man that changed his entire life to make mine better. He just... made a bad situation bearable.

"You okay?" Mav asks when a pained sigh falls from my lips. "Here, this should cheer you up," he says, sliding a glass toward me.

My eyes light up at the sight.

"Oh my God, is that a raspberry margarita?" I ask, hope blossoming within me.

He smirks at me, and it makes my stomach flip excitedly. "Almost. Reid's missing a couple of things."

Eagerly, I reach out and slide it closer before taking a sip.

"Oh my God." I moan when the fruitiness hits my tongue, mixing with the salt of the rim of the glass and the strong alcohol. "This is going to go straight to my head," I confess, after just one sip.

It's been a while since anything but beer passed my lips. This is going to take me down fast.

"We'd better get the party started then. Any idea how to play some music in this place?"

I shake my head before kicking the smart speaker into action like I've heard JD do a couple of times.

"Really?" he asks when the song starts playing.

"Really," I confirm, lifting my drink to my lips for another sip. "So good." I moan.

My skin burns with his attention, my cheeks heating when I realize he's staring right at my lips.

Pulling the glass away, I make a show of licking the salt away.

"You good?" I ask, my voice rough and sexy.

"H-huh, yeah." He grunts, his hand shifting beneath the counter giving away what's going on beneath.

"Come here," I demand, spinning around on the stool and opening my legs for him to step between, while the music fills our ears and the scent of our pizzas cooking floods the air.

He takes my face in his hands and dips down low. "I knew that once I started, I'd never stop," he confesses.

"Who's asking you to?" I groan, wrapping my legs around his body and dragging him closer.

And that's exactly how JD finds us a few minutes later.

I'm not sure if it's the promise of the meal he attempted or if he's just calmed himself down from his freak out, but I can't deny that a rush of excitement shoots through my veins at having them both with me again.

"Is this a private party or can anyone join?"

Mav groans into my neck at the interruption.

"Well, not just anyone," I half say, half moan when Mav sucks on the skin beneath my ear, marking his territory. "But we might make an exception for you. Hungry?" I ask, risking a look over Mav's shoulder.

My breath catches at the darkness I find in JD's eyes.

There is so much more to this playful man than meets the eye. And despite my earlier thoughts, I can't help but want to dig all his secrets out to discover what makes him really tick.

There's just something about him, something that calls to me.

My lips part to say something, but the buzzer goes off on the oven, calling time on our little make-out session.

"Can we eat them outside?" I ask.

Yeah, the sun has gone down, and I've no doubt it'll be cold, but the thought of the fresh air rushing over my skin is too much to ignore.

"Reid has heaters," JD says. "They're—"

"I'll find them," Mav states, pulling the pizzas from the oven and leaving them on the side for me to deal with. Turning to me, his eyes track down my body before he marches over and whispers, "You good?" in my ear, making a shudder run down my spine. His hand grips my waist, squeezing possessively, and I burn even hotter.

"Yeah. We'll be right out."

After dropping a kiss on my temple, he takes my drink along with two bottles of beer for them and heads out.

No words are said as Mav's footsteps float away but that doesn't stop JD from focusing on where he disappeared.

"Julian?" I whisper, lowering myself to my feet and walking over.

He keeps his eyes locked on the open door, but I don't miss the way his chest deflates.

His muscles jump when I press my hand against his abs and his breath catches.

"Hey," I whisper. "You okay?"

He lowers his head, his eyes closing as he takes a moment to figure out how to answer that question. I've no idea what he tells himself, but when he opens them again and looks at me, the darkness has all but disappeared and the Julian I know is back.

His electric blue eyes sparkle with life and excitement and his lips pull into his signature smirk.

"Of course," he lies, his smile widening. "Just had to shower all that crap off me. Told you, Dove. I can't cook for shit."

My eyes bounce between his, searching for the darkness, desperate to grab hold of it and force him to talk about it, but it's gone, swallowed whole by vibrant blue that's full of life and excitement.

"Dove?" he questions, his brows pulling together when I don't say anything.

"Whatever it is, you can tell me," I whisper, reaching for his hand and twisting our fingers together.

He steps closer, the tension between us charged before he reaches for me, dragging his thumb across my bottom lip.

"Can't stop thinking about these," he murmurs. "Kissing me, sucking me—"

"JD," I warn. "That wasn't what I meant."

"Nothing else to talk about, little dove."

He releases me so fast, it gives me whiplash before turning around and gazing at the pizzas almost as longingly as he was me.

"These look amazing. Grab some plates. Let's go eat."

"Should..." I pause, and he glances back from finding the pizza cutter in a drawer. "Should we save some for Reid?"

His eyes twinkle and his smirk grows.

"He's a big boy, he can look after himself. But he'll love to know that you're thinking of his well-being."

"I'm not," I argue. "I was just thinking that it's his food."

"Sure you were. Come on," he says, somehow managing to balance all the trays in his hands.

I follow him out with a deep frown marring my brow and concern swirling in my stomach.

I shouldn't care what's going on with him. Mav and I are only staying here for one reason: to get our revenge and then embark on the rest of our lives.

But with every minute that passes, I'm finding it harder and harder to convince myself that's all I want.

"**H**oly shit that's strong." JD gasps after taking a sip of my second cocktail of the night. "Bro, you trying to get your wife drunk or something?" he asks, looking up at Mav.

His usual naughty twinkle is back in his eyes, and I'd be lying if I said it didn't excite me. If having both of these men around me while I sit at the head of the table doesn't exhilarate me.

Mav shrugs innocently. "Just making it how she likes it."

"Sure," JD teases before shifting in his chair and

sinking his hand into his pocket. "You really want her easy though, you need this," he says holding up a pre-rolled joint.

It's been a long time since I got high. A really fucking long time. But my mouth waters for it.

But while I might be all for it, Mav's entire body stiffens with the suggestion.

"No, that's not what I—"

"Chill, man. I'm only teasing. Jeez," JD mutters, also digging out a lighter. "M'lady, would you like the first taste," he offers, holding it out to me.

Playing it cool, I cross my arms, pushing my tits up. "What's in it for me?"

"Whatever you fucking want, little dove," he says with a smirk. "It's yours."

Mav shifts uncomfortably in his seat.

"That's a big promise, Julian. I'm not sure you've got the tools for the job," I tease, the alcohol already loosening my tongue.

Deep down, I know that getting wasted is a bad idea. But right now, I do not care.

I want to let my hair down, have fun, and forget all the serious shit we're stuck in the middle of.

For just one night, I want to be carefree, let the world float away, and enjoy the company of these two incredibly sexy men.

JD chuckles. "I think we all know that I've more than got the tools, little dove. If you need a reminder..." He pushes to his feet and tucks his thumb into his waistband.

"No, no," Mav barks. "We're all good."

"You're just jealous," JD decides, falling back into his chair and finally handing the joint over. Pinching it between my lips, he lights it up, and I suck in a hit just as he says, "You know your naked dick can't pleasure her as well as mine can."

The hit gets stuck in my throat and a cough erupts.

"Oh shit." Mav gasps, jumping up to help me.

"I'm okay," I splutter, tears falling from my eyes. "I'm okay."

"Fucking moron," Mav mutters, shooting JD a dark look.

"What? Not my fault she prefers my dick to yours."

"How the fuck would you know that?" he hisses.

"Oh, I know. And one day, when you're man enough to take her for a proper ride, you'll find out too. Let me give you a little tip though, when you do it, make sure you grind a little to the le— Ow, you—"

"Fucking asshole," Mav grumbles as the empty beer bottle he threw at JD crashes to the deck.

"That hurt," JD complains, rubbing the side of his head.

"Not as much as it could have," Mav warns before turning his eyes on me. Instantly, his expression softens. "You good?"

"Yeah," I say, a lazy smile spreading across my face as the weed begins to take effect. "This is some good shit," I confess. "Here, try it." Turning the joint around, I hold it up for Mav.

"Hey now, I said I wanted you easy, not him," JD teases.

"Don't worry. It doesn't matter how high I get, I will never see your metal-riddled dick in any way appealing."

JD scoffs, looking way more offended by Mav's words than he probably should.

"Dude, you've no idea what you're missing out on."

"He's right," I blurt before I can catch the words. "It's really good. Those little balls hit all the right spots."

Mav's eyes harden, his jaw ticking as jealousy surrounds him like a storm cloud.

"You should really consider it. Now she's had a ride on this, a bare one is going to be so... meh."

"Take a hit," I encourage, practically shoving the joint into his mouth. "And ignore him. Your dick is beautiful."

Mav preens at my praise.

"Oh yeah?" he asks, shooting JD a smug look.

"Oh please, until it's found her G-spot and had her screaming, there is no comparison."

JD's words float around us like the smoke that Mav exhales.

"Ignore him, he's baiting you."

"I know. Doesn't make his words untrue though, does it," he whispers, his eyes searching mine.

Sliding my hand up his chest, I wrap it around the back of his neck and drag his face lower.

"Kiss me then dance with me," I demand.

"As if I could say no to that," he mutters, before stealing my lips in a wet and filthy kiss, letting JD see exactly how good he can be.

Yes, JD's piercings are outstanding, but something tells me that Mav is going to be just as good. In fact, after five years of foreplay, it'll probably be even better.

40

REID

I sit out front of my house for the longest time with the rain lashing against the windshield.

Everything is in motion, people are putting my plans into place around me, but there isn't anything I can do.

Not yet anyway.

All I can do is hope that all the players stand by their word and that when the time comes, they'll step forward and prove their loyalty.

If they don't. If everything they've told me, the promises they've made, have been bullshit... Well, I'm dead. And so are those I love.

I think of my brothers, of JD, of the few people I can just about call friends. I think of the woman inside my house right now. The one who despite all odds seems to have wrapped all of us around her little finger.

No wonder Victor wanted her on his side.

Maybe he was onto something sending her after Kane. Maybe her allure really is that powerful.

It's sure worked on us. Not that I'm going to admit that to anyone other than myself.

All of us deserve a shot at a better life.

And I have the chance of making it happen.

Sucking in a deep breath, I prepare to face the downpour and to discover what's waiting for me inside.

JD's car is here, so at least they haven't put themselves at risk by doing something stupid like leave.

The second I open the front door, I hear the music. It might not be as loud as the party I left not so long ago, but something tells me that the people under this roof are going to be having just as much fun.

The image of the three of them on the coffee table, not so long ago, comes back to me, fueling my frustration, and I storm down the hallway.

I've no idea what to expect when I march into the kitchen, where the music is booming, but it's certainly not what I find.

The room is deserted with the lingering scent of something I assume Alana has cooked. My brows pinch in confusion, but then movement outside the doors catches my eye and I move closer.

"What the hell are you doing?" I bark, the second I find Alana standing on top of my outside table. She's wearing one of JD's shirts, but there's not much point because it's soaked through and clinging to every curve on her body.

Her hair is plastered to her face and neck as she sways her hips in time with the music. And unsurprisingly, the two assholes out here with her are staring up at her as if she's just hung the moon.

"Aw, honey, you're home," Alana shouts before launching herself off the table in my direction.

"Holy fuck." I grunt, managing to catch her before she

stumbles to the deck. "Seriously?" I bark, steadying her on her feet with my hands around her slim waist.

She looks up at me, her sopping, see-through shirt soaking me when she presses the length of her body against mine.

I should shove her away, but I can't bring myself to do it when she's looking up at me with huge, wide—

"You're wasted and stoned," I blurt, suddenly understanding why she's willing to get this close without trying to castrate me.

"Mav makes the best cocktails," she slurs. "And JD has the best weed."

"So he should. It's Hawks weed." I grunt.

I stare down at her as her eyes search every inch of my face as if she's looking for something specific. I know the moment she finds something because her entire body tenses and her lips press into a thin line.

Reaching out, she traces something on my cheek before she leans in and… sniffs me.

"You've been with a woman," she states, her voice hard and cold as she harshly shoves me away from her.

"What?" I snap. "I haven't been—"

"You're right, little dove. There's definitely lipstick on his collar," JD teases, looking equally as stoned as Alana.

"I haven't been with a woman. I went to the guys' party and… wait, are you jealous?" I ask, looking at the fuming woman standing before me with her arms crossed under her tits.

Her chin drops at my accusation, her full pink lips forming a perfect O.

"Jealous?" she spits. "Puh-lease. I'm feeling sorry for the woman, is all."

My lips curl into a smirk.

"Oh yeah, that's totally the issue."

"Any woman outside this house is welcome to you. Now," she says, turning her back on me so fast that I only just miss getting slapped by the wet strands. If I hadn't hacked it off last week then it definitely would have. "I'm not letting you ruin our party. JD," she demands, grabbing his hand and dragging him toward her tabletop dance floor. "You and me, let's move."

His eyes find mine a beat before he's pulled up and what I find lingering makes my chest tighten. Something happened here tonight. Something bad.

But as he grabs her hips in his hands and drags her ass back against his dick, I can't find it in me to rip him away from enjoying himself.

Mav stares up at them from his seat. His grip on the beer bottle in his hand so tight the whiteness of his knuckles are visible from here.

With one more look at the gyrating couple, I head back inside. Just from the few minutes standing out there, my shirt is soaked through. But it feels weirdly good. And like fuck am I running away like a little bitch again.

So instead, I grab a bottle of whiskey and three glasses before heading back out.

The song has changed, leaving Alana and JD dirty dancing to a popular Rihanna song.

I don't want to be fascinated by them and the way they move together, but it's harder than I expect to rip my eyes away when I kick the chair out next to Mav's and drop my ass into it. Sensibly, he's sitting under the canopy, although his clothes tell me that he's not always been sitting here. It makes me wonder if he's had his fair share of time up there molesting his wife.

When I finally manage to rip my gaze away and look at

him, I find him glaring right at them, his jaw ticking in irritation.

Sloshing a generous amount of whiskey into two of the glasses, I pass one over.

"What's this?" He grunts, staring at the drink as if I'm handing him poison.

"You look like you need something harder than beer," I explain. "It's good shit," I say, pushing it closer to him.

He hesitates, his eyes bouncing between me and the glass.

"Fair enough," he says eventually, abandoning his bottle and taking the whiskey.

Turning his attention back to the show, he lifts the glass to his lips and takes a small sip.

He nods when he discovers that I'm not lying to him and quickly swallows a bigger mouthful.

"I can probably get you a meeting with Sidney Hyde, or at least one of his right-hand men," he offers, as if we're talking about something as simple as the weather.

Unfortunately, I'd just taken a mouthful of whiskey, and I almost spray the deck with it as I cough in shock.

"You serious?" I ask once I've recovered enough to speak.

"Yeah. JD said you've been struggling with them and—"

"Yeah, I want it. Set it up."

"Would it kill you to say please?" he mutters like an asshole.

I glare at him. Really fucking glare, but he doesn't give a shit.

Reaching for the small table on his other side, he lifts one of JD's joints and lights it up.

"I got all the time in the world, man. Apparently, we're not going anywhere."

He takes a hit before letting his head fall back against the chair and blowing it out. All the while, his eyes never leave his wife. In fact, they track every single one of her moves. It's almost like he's categorizing them.

"Thank you." I eventually grunt.

"See, wasn't so hard, was it?"

In celebration, or what the fuck ever, he passes the joint over, offering up a hit.

I hesitate. It's been a long time since I kicked back and enjoyed what we have to offer.

His eyes hold mine, allowing me to see more of him than I have in years.

"Thanks," I say, reaching out to take it.

I take a hit, letting the smoke fill my lungs and the weed do its work. It hits almost instantly, and I relax back.

"See, you don't need to be an uptight asshole all your life," Mav mocks.

My lips purse to bite back a snide remark but then Alana cries out and his eyes shoot to her instead.

"This must be killing you," I muse, also turning to watch the show.

JD's hands are everywhere as they continue to dance, her back to his front.

Her head is resting against his shoulder as the rain continues to soak them.

His hands lift from her hips, sliding up her waist until he takes the weight of her tits, squeezing them until she moans again.

"She's happy," he says, his voice deep and raspy.

"Pretty sure he is too," I quip. "Five years without touching her and now you're sitting here and watching this. Man, you've got the self-control of a fucking rock."

He laughs, but there's no humor behind it.

"It's just her," he says as if it's meant to make sense. "She's—" He cuts himself off, unable to find the right word to finish that sentence.

When I look back, JD has spun Alana around as they're locked in a heated and filthy kiss. He's hooked her shirt up to palm her ass, giving us a great view in the process.

Mav grunts, and I catch him tugging at his pants out of the corner of my eye.

"Fuck knows why, but she fucking loves you, man. All of this. Everything she's done. It's because of you."

"Fucking hell." He groans. It's almost as if those words cause him physical pain.

"I doubt there are many men out there who can say their woman has done something so fucking fierce for them."

"She's one of a kind."

JD hooks her leg up around his waist, grinding into her and making her cry out again. Her voice echoes into the night as they continue as if no one is watching.

"That she is."

I don't think he's going to say anymore, so I'm surprised when he speaks again, although his voice is so low, I have to strain to hear it over the loud music and torrential rain.

"And all I've done is let her down."

I stare at him, really fucking stare. Forcing myself to see beyond the man who's irritated me most of my life to the man who's clearly hopelessly in love with a woman he doesn't believe he's worthy of.

If my soul wasn't completely black and fucking ruined, I might even feel sorry for the poor fuck.

I sigh, unable to believe I'm having this kind of heart to heart with a man I can't stand.

"Then you're a fucking idiot because that is the very opposite of what she thinks."

"She wants that," he hisses, pointing at Alana and JD.

My breath catches when I find that she's facing us again with her shirt hooked around JD's wrists as he plays with her tits, blatantly teasing us—Mav—with what he can have if he man's up and takes it.

"Jesus." I grunt, barely able to resist also adjusting my pants as I watch them.

"And I haven't given her that. I've run at every opportunity." He drags his hand down his face, scrubbing at his rough jaw. "She begged, pleaded with me for it. But I just... fuck. I don't—"

"You were trying to do the right thing. That's... admirable, I guess."

"Is it. Or am I just a fucking loser?"

I can't help but bark out a laugh.

"Bro, you have always fucking been that," I tell him happily as I reach for the bottle and fill both our glasses. "But if you're looking for advice from someone who doesn't have a fucking clue how relationships work, then maybe he'd say that it's not too late."

"She's practically fucking JD up there," he complains, pain etched into every inch of his face.

"Didn't stop you from getting involved earlier," I quip.

"You're a sick fuck for watching." He grunts, tugging at his pants again.

I shrug despite the fact his attention clearly isn't trained on me. "Been called worse. You know she wouldn't turn you away if you went over there right now and dragged her from him. There's a good chance that all of that," I say, waving my hand in their direction, "is all for your benefit anyway. She wants you. Fuck knows why, but she does."

Finally, he rips his eyes away and stares right at me.

"That hurts, doesn't it?"

"What does?"

"That she wants me over you."

"I don't give a fuck who she wants," I say, praying he doesn't hear the lie.

"That's bullshit and we both know it. I remember that summer in her backyard. You were watching her like she was the only girl on the planet."

"We were kids."

"So? Not everything changes. You want her, and I was the one who got her." He laughs bitterly. "I guess that explains a lot."

"The fuck are you talking about?"

"It doesn't matter," he says, throwing his whiskey back and swallowing thickly, his eyes back on them. "At some point, I was going to win something. And I am more than okay with it being Alana. You claim your town, take control and do what you want. That woman up there," he says, nodding at her, "she's mine."

"Doesn't look like it right now," I tease.

"We're all allowed a bit of fun. But at the end of the day, it's my ring she's wearing and my name she uses. The rest is white noise."

"If you say so," I mutter, crossing my arms over my chest and spreading my thighs as I focus on them kissing again.

Alana has completely lost her shirt now, dancing in only her tiny panties as if she doesn't have a care in the world.

It's a lie, we all know that. But watching her right now helps me to believe that maybe there is something good to come out of all this.

"You think she's yours?" I taunt. "You need to prove it."

41

ALANA

"**C**an you feel their eyes on you, little dove?" JD groans in my ear as he grinds his aching dick against my ass.

The rain continues to pound down on our bodies. My skin is cold, every raindrop like a razor cutting me, but inside I'm burning. My blood is racing through my veins like lava.

"Yeah," I whisper. I might not have my eyes open, but I know they're watching. My skin tingles with their attention.

I shouldn't have let JD drag his shirt from my body, but I was powerless to stop him. The cool air and the rain feel too good against me.

"They want to join," he muses.

"They're welcome to."

Reaching back, I thread my fingers through his short hair and tug until he hisses.

"You're bad, Dove."

"You love it."

"Yeah," he mutters. "I think I do."

Before my fuzzy brain gets a chance to register those words, he spins me around again, slides one hand down my back to grip my ass and the other into my hair to drag my head exactly where he wants me.

His lips descend on mine, and in a heartbeat, I'm lost to him again.

My hands are everywhere, tracing the lines and muscles that cover his torso. But after a few minutes, my need for more gets the better of me and I slide my hand under the waistband of his sweats.

"Oh fuck." He grunts when my fingers brush over the short hair there before wrapping around his length. "Dirty, dirty, Dove."

"Just as you like me," I say with a smirk, staring up into his blown eyes.

Something inside me relaxes when I discover those shadows from before have been swallowed by the effects of the weed, alcohol, and desire.

I'm not naïve enough to think they've been banished for good, but I'm happy to be able to give him some kind of relief from them.

"You wanna put on a real show for our spectators?" He growls, lips right by my ear as I slowly stroke him.

A whimper spills from my lips as I consider what filthy ideas are filling his mind right now.

He doesn't wait for me to respond, instead, his grip on my hair tightens and he growls. "Get on your fucking knees and suck my cock, little dove."

Unable to do anything but what he demands, I drop to my knees and begin tugging at his sweats.

They aren't the easy access I'm used to when they're soaking wet and JD ends up helping in my quest to free his dick.

The second he does, I lean forward, licking the precum that's beading at the tip.

"Holy motherfucker," he bellows over the loud music.

I've no doubt that Reid and Mav are watching, but if they turned away for any reason then that bellow of delight certainly will have regained their attention.

"Fuck, little dove," JD praises as I lick him like a popsicle. His taste mixes with the rain as I drag my tongue up the length of his shaft and then wrap my lips around the head.

He roars in delight, his fingers sinking into my hair as I take him right to the back of my throat.

"Fucking love having you here," he groans.

Crawling my gaze up his bare torso, I find his dark eyes staring down at me. The electric blue has been completely swallowed by black. And fuck if it doesn't draw me in.

Baring my teeth, I gently graze his shaft as I pull back off, and just as I'm expecting, it drives him fucking crazy.

With my ass in the air, I rub my thighs together, desperately trying to find some friction.

My pussy is soaked and aching, and the noises coming out of JD don't help in any sense.

"Oh fuck. Yeah, just like that. Take me, little dove. All of me."

His dick jerks deep in my mouth as a rush of salty precum floods my mouth.

"I bet your pussy is fucking dripping."

I groan around him in response, arching my back, shamelessly offering myself up.

"You want someone to eat your cunt, Dove?"

I groan again.

Reaching down, he cups my jaw, smoothing his thumb over the hollow in my cheek.

"Who do you want to taste you?" he asks, his eyes searching mine. But he clearly doesn't expect a response because he doesn't release me from his cock. "Your husband? You want him to have another taste?"

I nod willingly.

Please.

Fuck, I want it. No. I *need* it.

Ripping his eyes from mine, he looks over at where both Mav and Reid are sitting.

"What do you say, man? Fancy dragging her panties aside and eating her while she chokes on my cock."

A rush of heat soaks my already ruined panties as the image he paints appears clearly in my mind.

Finally, his grip loosens in my hair, allowing me to release him.

Glancing over my shoulder, I find Mav sitting forward in his chair, his eyes locked on my pussy.

"Please," I beg. I've no idea if it's loud enough to reach his ears. But not a second later, his gaze jumps to my face and he swallows thickly at what he finds staring back at him. "Mav, please. I need you."

His jaw ticks as he battles with his conscience. I get it. He's spent five years trying to treat me right. And this right here is the opposite of what he thought I needed. Unfortunately for him, it's exactly what I crave.

"If you're not man enough, I'm sure Reid would happily take your place."

My entire body tenses at the thought of Reid being the one to drag my panties aside and drag his tongue up the length of me.

I squeeze my eyes closed.

Fuck. That should not get me as hot as I am right now.

"Yeah, that's what I thought."

My eyes pop open at JD's words and I breathe a sigh of relief when I find Mav on his feet, his hand shoved down the front of his borrowed sweats as he deals with what's happening beneath.

The knowledge that watching me gets him hard does little for my desperation.

"That's it. Your wife needs you, Mav," JD praises.

I startle the moment his hot hand lands on my ass.

"Oh God, please." I moan, arching again for him.

"That's it," JD says, giving Mav a confidence boost. "Tuck a finger under that lace and tell me how wet her cunt is."

I whimper when a rush of cold air runs over my heated flesh.

Spreading my knees, I arch my back deeper, offering myself up.

"Fuck." Mav groans, making my temperate soar.

Unable to stop myself, I look back over my shoulder.

My mouth runs dry at the look of awe on Mav's face as he stares down at me.

"It's yours," I breathe. "Take it. Please."

His grip on my ass cheek tightens until it's almost too much. But the second he leans forward, his hot breath against my wet core, I forget all about the pain and focus on the pleasure.

"HOLY SHIT," I cry when his tongue laps at me. "Yes, yes, yes," I chant when his other hand lands on my ass cheek, opening me up for him.

"Don't be selfish, little dove." JD groans, fisting his own cock now that I've abandoned it.

I twist around to face him again as Mav eats me like a man possessed and immediately draw him back into my mouth.

He groans in pleasure as the deep rumbles of Mav's voice rushes through me, ensuring I flood his mouth with my juices.

We work in perfect sync and I fly higher than I ever have in my life.

I thought earlier on the coffee table was good. But this... this...

Fuck.

The only thing that would be better would be if someone else were to join. But I think JD has already managed to work a miracle where Mav is concerned. There's no chance in hell of Reid Harris's resolve cracking.

One of Mav's hands releases me, and I cry out at the loss, but only a second later, his tongue spears inside me. I lose all sense of reality as my release comes rushing forward.

Taking JD deeper, I breathe through my nose so I don't pass out. His length swells, letting me know that he's just as close.

"She nearly there?" JD grunts.

I've no idea what Mav replies with, but the vibration of his deep voice is everything.

Fucking me with his tongue, he reaches up and pinches my clit.

I scream, although the sound is muffled by JD's cock.

"That's it, little dove. Come for me. Let Mav drink you down. Is he eating you good, baby? Like you always wanted."

I nod as much as I'm able to.

"Such a good girl for us," he praises, holding my face so gently as his hips begin to thrust frantically. "You gonna swallow me down, Dove?"

I nod again.

"You want my cum, baby? I bet you want Mav's too, huh?"

I've no idea what Mav does, but the release that was in touching distance suddenly slams into me like a freight train.

"Oh shit. Fuck. Fuck, FUCK." JD roars, his cock thickening and then jerking in my mouth, his cum filling my throat.

But I barely feel any of it because I'm flying. Pleasure locking up every inch of my body as Mav continues to eat me through it.

The second JD is spent, he pulls his dick from my mouth and forces me to look up at him.

I probably look worse than I did after days down in the basement, but I don't care.

As I gaze up into his eyes, all I care about is being looked at like I'm something important, something special and precious.

For that look alone, I'm pretty sure I'd do anything.

Suddenly, he drops to his knees, and with very little effort, he flips me over.

I find Mav at the end of the table, his face glistening with my release and his eyes wild with desire.

Dropping them lower, I find his sweats have been shoved down and he's stroking his dick almost violently.

Leaning over me, JD twists his fingers in my panties and rips them from my body, leaving me exposed to all of them.

Briefly, my eyes shoot to where I last saw Reid. And to my surprise, he's still there. His expression is hard, every muscle in his body strung taut but it's what's happening below his waist that makes my breath catch.

He's also got his cock out, although his movements are much more restrained than Mav's.

"Spread your legs, little dove," JD instructs. "Let Mav see everything."

My knees fall to the sides and Mav's eyes drop.

"Take her, she's all yours."

The tendons in his muscles pull tight as he steps forward.

"You need to feel how fucking tight she is. You've never felt anything like it, I fucking promise you that."

But despite how close he is, Mav never closes the space to touch me, let alone push inside me.

"Mav, please. Just tak—"

His roar of pleasure swallows my words as his cock jerks and he unloads all over my pussy, covering me in cum, marking me.

Fuck. It's hot.

"Oh God," I whimper as the heat of his seed burns me from the outside in. "Fuck. That was—" My words vanish as the alcohol, weed, and exhaustion slam into me.

The world around me starts to spin as hands move over me.

"You got her?" JD asks.

"Yeah. I've always got her," Mav assures him.

And then we're moving. I've no idea where to. But while I'm in my husband's arms, I know I have nothing to worry about. He'd die before letting anything happen to me.

The chill from outside vanishes in favor of the warmth of running water. But my feet never hit the floor and the arm around me never leaves.

"I love you, Maverick Murray. I love you so fucking much."

"I love you too, Doll."

I'm surrounded by something soft and my body begins to drift.

"Sleep, Doll. I'll be right here when you wake up."

Unable to do anything but follow orders, I drift off, my body sinking into the mattress.

42

ALANA

I wake with a startling realization. I didn't have a nightmare.

I lie still, searching the depths of my brain for the lie.

They always come for me. Every single fucking night they come for me, reminding me of everything I spend my waking hours trying to forget.

But there is nothing. No lingering fear, no disgust. No... nothing.

It's only as that realization settles in my brain that the weight of the arm resting on my waist makes itself known.

A smile plays on my lips as I think about Mav but that quickly changes as the memory of what happened last night takes over.

My temperature quickly soars.

Holy shit.

We did that.

And in front of Reid.

Who was enjoying it...

'Oh my God,' I mouth, not wanting to wake up my bedmate as I cover my face with my hands.

Heat rushes through my body as the image of us on top of the table plays out in my mind in high definition.

You're such a whore, Alana Murray. And you love it.

I shake my head, unable to argue with my thoughts.

I did love it. Being at the mercy of Mav and JD is a fine place to be.

After a few seconds, I manage to get myself under control and lower my hands.

I blink against the darkness, but my eyes quickly adjust thanks to the sunlight peeking through the crack in the curtains.

But when I look down, all the air rushes out of my lungs.

I'm not pinned down by one arm. But two.

Holy shit.

I look between the two sleeping gangsters on either side of me with my heart in my throat.

When I passed out, I was in Mav's arms. I don't remember coming to bed, and I certainly don't remember them both joining me.

I lie there for the longest time watching them both sleep. They look so peaceful, so at ease. I wish it were the same when they were awake, but both men are battling with demons only they have the ability to banish.

As much as I want to stay wrapped in their strong arms, absorbing their warmth, my need for the bathroom gets the better of me.

As gently as I can, I move their arms from my body, watching each one, waiting for them to wake as I do so. But they're too far gone, their breathing barely even hitches.

Carefully, I slide down the bed until my feet hit the thick carpet.

Spinning around, I take in the sight of them, both shirtless and only in a pair of boxers. What a fucking sight.

Ripping my stare from them, I rush into the bathroom to take care of business.

I wince when I come to stand in front of the mirror. My hair is wild. I try running my fingers through it, but it's impossible. Rummaging through the bag of stuff JD got me that I abandoned in the drawer, I search for a hairband. Christ knows how he thought to get me hairbands, but right now, I'm too grateful to question it.

Tying up my short locks, I tuck a loose strand behind my ear and really look at myself.

Yes, I'm exhausted. I've no idea what time Mav put me to bed last night or what time it is now, but I've clearly not had anywhere near enough sleep. I could probably crawl back into bed with them and sleep away the rest of the day. It's a tempting thought being tucked between those two incredible men.

But there's more than just my tiredness staring back at me.

For the first time in a long time, there's a sparkle in my eyes. I look... well, alive, I guess.

I've found a lot of things under the roof of this manor, a lot of things I'll happily forget. But I've also found things that I'll treasure forever, no matter where all of this ends up.

Joy, happiness, laughter, pleasure.

With a smile playing on my lips, I shake my head as my thoughts return to the two men in the bed beyond the door.

Having Mav's hands on me, his lips on mine... and other places, is everything I've dreamed of for five-long frustrating years. And if all that comes out of this is that we've broken down that barrier then I'm okay with that. If we achieve a few other things along the way then even better.

After brushing my teeth and splashing my face with water, I step back into the bedroom.

Both men are in exactly the same position as when I left them and I stand there for the longest time just watching them, studying their ink, their expressions, and their bodies before I manage to convince myself that I need coffee more than I need to perv over them.

Okay, I'm not sure that could possibly be the case in any universe, but I'm happy to lie to myself in order to leave them in peace.

The house is silent as I make my way downstairs and into the kitchen. And for the first time ever, the scent of rich coffee doesn't permeate the air.

Could I have beaten Reid to the machine?

The morning sun streams in through the floor-to-ceiling windows, any evidence of the storm the night before long gone.

My eyes linger on the table as the image of dancing up there with JD comes back to me, my blood heating as I think about how it must have looked to Mav and Reid.

Shaking my head, I push those images aside and make a beeline for the coffee machine, getting it started. I might be awake and seemingly functioning, but that doesn't mean I'm not suffering from overindulging the night before.

I can't remember the last time I drank that much and my dehydrated body knows it.

Pulling a bottle of water from the refrigerator, I down the whole thing.

I repeat my actions from the other morning and pull a couple of frozen part-baked pastries from the freezer and throw them into the air fryer. And once everything is done, I decide to make the most of a different room in the house, seeing as I'm alone.

The living room is much cozier than the kitchen. The couches are huge, the soft cushions look like they'd swallow me whole.

Curling my legs beneath me, I settle into the deepest corner of the sectional and breathe a happy, sated sigh.

Ignoring my coffee for a bit—because I'm not as hardcore as Reid—I focus on my pain au chocolat. I devour the first one, hunger from my exertion the night before taking over, before I start on the second one.

Regretting not cooking more, I abandon my plate on the cushion beside me and reach for my coffee.

I enjoy it in a way I don't think I have since the morning before my fateful date with Kane over two weeks ago now.

It was a lovely late summer morning and I took my coffee and breakfast out to our deck after Mav left for the clubhouse to meet with his father.

Hell, what am I saying? It was way before that I sat and drank my morning coffee without the weight of the world pressing down on my shoulders. The morning of the day I found myself in the back of one of Victor Harris's goons' cars being driven out to a secret location so the man himself could steal my soul and sell it to whoever he felt corrupt enough to manhandle it for an hour or so.

Anger churns in my stomach as I think about that day. As he laid out every single reason why I couldn't argue. Being in the middle of nowhere with four armed assholes was the least of my worries.

I knew the second I was dragged into the back of that car that I was fucked. If Victor wanted me then I knew he'd have enough dirt to ensure I did exactly as he wanted.

Although I have to confess, I didn't ever expect to end up here.

A laugh bubbles up, spilling easily from my lips, and it doesn't stop.

It feels good, freeing to let it flow. And before long, I'm reaching up and wiping tears from my eyes.

Am I still drunk and stoned from last night? Yeah, there's a really good fucking chance.

Feeling on top of the world, despite everything that's happening around me, I climb across the couch to grab the remote for the massive TV Reid has strapped to the wall opposite me.

Turning it on, I find his apps and scan through what he's got.

"No fucking way." I gasp when I find one that steals my attention. "Who really are you, Reid Harris?" I mutter, opening the app and scrolling through to find what I want.

I've no idea how long I'm going to be alone, but I figure I may as well make the most of it. Mav might have humored me a time or two with my childhood movies, but I doubt the others will.

Hitting play on my number one guilty pleasure, I grab one of the dark gray cushions and hug it to my chest.

It doesn't matter how many times I watch this Aladdin, I might as well be seven again, sitting inside a blanket fort Kristie and I made, with a massive bowl of popcorn between us.

"What on Earth...?" Mav gasps from the other side of my blanket.

Embarrassment floods me and I drop my face into my hands.

He told me he was going to be late tonight. If I thought

for even a second that he'd come back and catch me then I never would have set this up.

It's mortifying.

Beyond mortifying.

I'm still hiding when the flashing from the TV is blocked by his big body.

"Alana?" he breathes, his voice softer than it was when he first found me.

"Can you just go out again and pretend this never happened? Give me ten minutes and I'll have everything back to normal."

"Doll," he warns, shuffling closer.

Tears burn my eyes as my mortification burns hotter. I'm seventeen. Almost an adult. I shouldn't be doing this. It's childish and embarrassing and—

"What the hell are you doing?" I gasp when he moves closer still, the heat of his big body burning down the length of mine.

I risk a glance over and watch as he plunges his fingers into the bowl sitting before me and stuffs a massive handful of popcorn into his mouth.

"I've never seen this one. How far in is it?" he asks around his mouthful.

"You're kidding?" I sniffle, trying to discreetly wipe the tears away that are clinging to my lashes, threatening to spill over.

"No. Rewind it, we'll watch it from the beginning."

I gape at him in total disbelief.

"B-but... it's a girl's movie. A little girl's movie."

"Says who? The chick is hot for a cartoon," he confesses, nodding to the screen.

I stare at his profile, not believing what I'm hearing.

Over the past year, Mav has blown me away time and

time again with his kindness and generosity. I hate that he spends money on me. No one ever has before and it makes me all kinds of uncomfortable every time he does it. But his time... I'm obsessed with monopolizing that. Every time he looks at me, talks to me, gives me any kind of attention, all I do is desire more. I'm like a junkie craving my next hit. And given the chance, I'd OD on him any freaking day.

"You gonna start it again, or what?" he asks, finally turning to look at me.

His breath catches when he finds the tears that are refusing to disappear.

"Doll," he says, reaching out to catch one when it finally falls. "What's wrong?"

I look up at the blanket that's covering us before gesturing to the pillows we're now both lying on like little kids.

"We're in a blanket fort, Mav. You're an adult and I'm —" A mess of a human being.

"So fucking what? We can all pretend to be a kid again every now and then."

"You did not make blanket forts when you were a kid."

"Well, it wasn't top of mine and Brody's to-do list when we used to hang out. We spent most of our time with a basketball or seeing who could give each other the darkest bruises.

"Sounds like fun," I deadpan.

"But you're forgetting that my best friend growing up was a girl, Doll. I've done plenty of things most guys haven't."

"Oh my God, tell me she made you do face masks and painted your nails." I laugh, almost able to picture a young stubble-free Mav with a gunky mess on his face and cucumbers on his eyes.

"Uh—"

"Oh my God, you did."

He shrugs one shoulder. "Watched Ten Things I Hate About You while we did it too."

"Oh my God," I cry, my tears of mortification now replaced my happy ones. "I'm so talking to Ivy about this," I blurt without thinking.

Mav's eyes drop from mine as he thinks about what his best friend is going through right now.

"I'm sorry," I whisper, hating that I put that look on his face.

Here he was trying to cheer me up and look at what I did.

"It's okay, Doll. Really," he assures me, spotting the remote hiding under one of the cushions and rewinding the movie back to the beginning.

"You know all the words to this, don't you?" he asks, a teasing lilt to his voice.

"Umm... maybe," I whisper as it starts over.

"Good. Don't hold back. Pretend I'm Kristie."

"Dude, you're a six-foot-four man. I have no chance of pretending you're a little four-year-old girl."

"Well, try. I want to give you the full experience of what you're trying to recreate here."

"Mav," I breathe, getting all emotional again.

"Shhh... It's starting."

He keeps his eyes on the screen as the movie starts to play. But I don't pay attention. I mean, I've seen it hundreds of times before, but right now, he's more captivating than any movie that could be playing.

"Doll, you're meant to be watching this."

"I know," I murmur. "Sorry."

He turns to me, his eyes hard and determined. "What have I said, you never ever have to be sorry about anything."

I swallow thickly, trying to force the lump from my throat, but it's pointless.

"Thank you," I whisper.

"Anything, Doll. Anything."

43

JD

I come to with my head pounding and memories from the night before playing on repeat, ensuring my semi goes full mast.

Without opening my eyes, I slide my hand across the bed, searching for my little dove.

Why isn't she right next to me with her hot little ass pressed against my dick?

It seems to take forever for my fingers to collide with hot, soft skin.

I groan, my need for her all-consuming.

I've never been with a woman before that I haven't been able to get enough of. Previously, once I've shot my load, I'm ready to bail. Does that make me an asshole? Yeah, probably. Do I care? Absolutely fucking not. The chicks we pick up at the clubhouse or on the streets of Harrow Creek are whores. Plain and simple. They want something from us, just as much as we want something from them. All's fair in love and war and all that.

But Alana. Fuck me. Every time I have her, it just gets better and better. And I don't even need to get inside her pussy. Just one touch and I yearn for more. It doesn't even need to be my dick she's touching. Just holding her hand like a pussy does it.

I need her on a level I've never experienced before. Which is why I know I'm royally fucked when this all blows up in my face.

It's going to. I have no doubt about that. There's only one man under this roof that she really wants, and no matter how much fun we have, no matter how many times I get her off, she's always going to turn to him.

If I were stronger, I might be able to take a step back, put some space between us and attempt to protect my heart. But I'm not strong. I'm fucking weak. Nothing but a slave to my cravings and my desires.

I've always been the same. To this point, I've been able to drag myself from the darkness—if not me then Reid's done it for me. But I'm already terrified of what's coming my way.

"Dove." I groan, unable to think about the what-ifs when I know she's here for the taking.

But when a voice fills the air around me, it's not her soft, light one but a much darker, much angrier one.

"The fuck are you doing?" Mav snaps, throwing my arm back to my side of the bed.

My eyes fly open just before my hand crashes to my chest.

"Jeez, dude."

"Why the fuck are you touching me?" he snaps, sitting up and dragging his hand down his face. "Fuck my head hurts."

"Reid's whiskey," I muse. "And I wasn't trying to touch you. I prefer someone less hairy and inky to snuggle with."

At the mention of his wife, his head snaps up.

"Doll?" he calls out as if she's about to pop up from under the bed. "I can't believe she left me in bed with you," he mumbles, throwing the covers back and pushing to his feet.

"Don't even pretend you didn't enjoy it," I tease, nodding to his obviously tented boxers.

"Fuck off." He grunts before slipping into the bathroom.

I wait for a beat, listening for voices, but when none fills the air, I roll on my back and throw my arm over my eyes, willing the pounding in my temples to lessen.

Water runs, the toilet flushes, and his feet shuffle against the floor.

At some point, I figure I must drift back off to sleep because I startle when something lands on my chest.

"Get dressed," Mav demands.

Pulling my arm away, I find him glaring down at me.

"Are you always this much fun in the morning?" I mutter, pushing up on my palms.

"Where is Alana?"

"Downstairs drinking coffee probably," I assure him, not feeling as concerned as he looks.

"And if she's not?" he barks.

"I don't know. But standing there snapping at me isn't going to help."

"Fucking asshole. It's all fun and games until shit gets serious."

"I can do fucking serious," I bark as he retreats toward the door. "I kept her fucking safe for you, didn't I?"

"Not sure I fully agree with your style of protection," he argues.

"You're just jealous," I point out as I finally climb out of bed. "I know how fucking epic it feels to have her pussy tightening down around my— whoa," I say, a playful smile spreading across my lips when he throws a really sloppy punch in my direction. "Come on, bro. We're friends now."

"Are we?" he mutters, finally pulling the door open and stepping out.

Not wanting to be left behind, I quickly take a piss, rinse my mouth out and then rush after him.

"What's going—"

"Shhh," Reid hisses when I descend the final few stairs and find him and Mav standing on each side of the doorway that leads into the living room.

My brows pinch in confusion, but it only lasts a few seconds before the sound of Alana's voice fills the air.

She's singing. And it's... really good.

She might have belted out a few lines last night, but she was wasted. Now though, she's putting her all into it and it makes the hairs on the back of my neck lift. And it seems that I'm not the only one enthralled by the sound because those two schmucks can't take their eyes off whatever she's doing inside the living room.

"What's going on?" I ask a little quieter, unable to stop myself as I move closer.

The song she's singing is familiar, but I can't quite pinpoint it.

No one answers; they don't need to. The second I step up to the doorway, I get my answer.

My little dove is once again up on a table, only it's the coffee table this time, and she's belting out a song from a Disney movie. I catch a glimpse of two characters flying around on a magic carpet, but other than that, my attention is firmly on Alana as she throws her arms out wide and sings at the top of her voice.

All three of us stand there silently, completely

enraptured by her. That is until she spins dramatically, whipping her head around so fast that the tie holding her hair up flies across the room like a tiny missile, barely missing Mav's head as it shoots past us. She misjudges a back step and her heel falls over the edge of the table. She screams, her body plummeting.

All three of us dart forward at the same time, but it's Reid—the asshole—who gets there first, sweeping her into his arms and cradling her against his chest.

Again. Fucking asshole.

She glances over his shoulder, shaking her wild hair from her face and finds me and Mav hot on Reid's tail.

"Oh my God, were you all watching me?" she guesses, her cheeks turning an adorable shade of pink that climbs all the way to the tips of her ears.

"You were putting on a show, little dove. Of course we were watching," I say happily.

"You good?" Reid asks, after dropping his ass to the couch, suspiciously keeping her on his lap.

Mav and I stand shoulder to shoulder, watching them, but while anger comes off Mav in waves as Reid touches his girl, I'm nothing but curious.

"Yes. Thank you," she sasses, attempting to scramble off his lap.

Reid grimaces, his jaw popping. "What's wrong, Big Man? She making it hard?" I tease.

"Shut up, Julian," Alana hisses, before finally getting to her feet and fleeing from the room as if her ass is on fire.

"Look what you did," I say pointing at her retreating back, glaring at my best friend. "You made her run away."

"Me?" He gasps, his brows hitting his hairline.

"Yeah, you. Couldn't have been nice and touched her up a bit. Get her engine revving."

I'm so busy teasing Reid about his obvious desire for the woman I can't get enough of that I don't notice Mav slip out of the room after her.

"You're just jealous you were left with your own right-hand last night." I laugh. "How's that working out for you?"

Suddenly, Reid surges to his feet and steps right in front of me.

His eyes bore into mine as his jaw continues to tick in frustration.

"Get your fucking head on straight." He growls. "She's not a fucking sex doll, and we've got other shit to be focusing on right now."

My mind shoots back to everything he explained to Mav and me after he put Alana to bed. About his friend Aubrey going to get some intel straight from the horse's mouth and what Griff said about Luciana Rivera. That little nugget of intel is still making my head spin. But I'm all for it if it helps us move on sooner rather than later.

Every day that passes, we're at risk of Victor finding out that Reid's been going behind his back. And the second he does, we're going to need one eye over our shoulders at all times.

That cunt won't spare any of us a chance to beg for our lives—not that we would, of course, that's not how Hawks roll—he doesn't care who's at the end of his gun.

"I'm focused, man. I'm fucking ready for it."

He searches my eyes. I know exactly what he's looking for, and I'm afraid that he might just find it.

"You should consider taking your meds," he says quietly. His words are like a knife through my chest, forcing all the air from my lungs.

I get it. I know why he thinks it would probably be a good idea right now.

But fuck that.

He isn't the one who has to take them. To have his entire life dulled to gray.

Yeah, cycling through my own misery and issues isn't fun when I embark on that dark road. But fuck having my entire life dulled because something might happen one day that sends me back there. When it happens, I'll deal. Just like I did last week when I had a slip.

"I've got this. I'm here and I'm ready.'

"J." He sighs.

"I know," I assure him. "I know how this is going to end, and I'm prepared."

One of his brows quirks in a silent, 'are you?'

"Trust me, yeah. No motherfucker out there is bringing us down. Not your cunt of a father and not that hot little blonde in your kitchen."

"Yeah," he says, reaching up to scratch the back of his neck before he turns toward the door, the scent of coffee luring him away. "But what if they do?" he says so quietly, I don't think I'm meant to hear, but I do.

Unease trickles through me at his lack of confidence, but I refuse to allow it to take hold.

We've got this. We're going to win.

We have to believe that or all of this, everything we've been working toward, has been for nothing.

When I finally join the three of them in the kitchen, Mav and Alana are cuddled up on the couch, Reid is resting his ass back against the counter, sipping his mug of lava, pretending he's not watching the happy couple, and there is a fourth mug waiting for me.

"So what delights does today hold, Boss?" I ask him, smirking when he realizes he's been caught perving.

"I'm going to see if I can make contact with Luciana," he states.

"Luciana?" Alana echoes, letting us know she's listening.

Mav turns to her and whispers something in her ear.

"Rivera?" She gasps. "They're like... the cartel. They're... dangerous."

"Baby, look around you," I say, holding my arms out from my sides. "We're all fucking dangerous." *But no one in the room wields her power like you do, little dove. You have no idea, but you're the most dangerous out of all of us.*

"Arrogant much." She scoffs before looking at Reid. "You really bringing the cartel into this?"

"The cartel? No. Just Luciana. It seems she might be on the same trail as us."

"Is that a good thing or—"

"Only time will tell," Reid says before abandoning his mug in the sink and disappearing from the room.

"And what about us?" Alana asks. "What do we do?"

"Wait?" I offer. "War is coming, baby. You've just got to be patient."

She stares up at me, swallowing nervously. There are so many things dancing on the tip of her tongue, but she swallows them all down and just nods.

"Wait," she repeats. "Sounds like fun."

44

ALANA

Thankfully, after my mortifying morning, things improve. Although I still cringe every time I look any of them in the eyes. Mav isn't so bad. He already knew my guilty pleasure after finding me in my blanket fort all those years ago. The other two, not so much. I might have failed a time or two during my stay here, but I've done my best to be strong, to appear like nothing can faze me, and there I was singing my heart out to a kid's movie. Doesn't exactly scream 'I am a strong, independent woman.'

No sooner had Reid finished his nuclear coffee, he set about making us all breakfast. But while the scent of bacon filled the air, making my stomach groan happily and my mouth water, the elephant in the room only grew.

I know this thing we're all embarking on is huge. No one just takes down gang royalty. There are protections and allies in place for a very good reason. But getting the cartel involved... unease races down my spine at just how fast this is growing.

Since the day Mav promised me that he'd do whatever

it took to ensure anyone who ever hurt me paid the ultimate price, I'm not sure I ever really believed it would happen.

It was a dream. The kind that helped to force my nightmares aside so that I could think of a future, where they might not torment me any longer. But I'm not sure I ever took it seriously.

We're just two people. Yes, Mav is next in line for Hawks royalty with his father being second-in-command. But he doesn't have an army. A handful of loyal friends sure. But that was never going to be enough.

But with Reid on our side, we stand a chance. I believe him when he says he's got a plan and that he has things in place.

Mav might be dubious, but I've seen the level of hatred in Reid's eyes when he's spoken about his father. I might not know all the reasons behind it, other than Victor being a controlling cunt who's run every second of Reid and his brothers' lives. Something tells me that there is much more to it than that—maybe even I've played a part, who knows— but whatever it is, his desire to end his father is as strong as mine. I more than recognize the need for vengeance that lingers in his dark and dangerous eyes.

I might have been nervous overhearing them discuss other local gangs. The Ravens. The Devils.

But the freaking cartel...

We're heading into seriously dangerous territory with them.

While Victor might be corrupt and untrustworthy, the cartel is fucking terrifying. All of them. They breed fucking psychopaths, and the last thing I want is any of us tangled up with them.

It wouldn't be the freedom I've always dreamed of. It

would be hell. Worse than I've already endured. Worse than I'm sure all of us have lived through.

If Victor has the right—or the wrong—connections with them and we fuck it up. Well... it isn't even worth thinking about.

A violet, uncontrollable shudder rips down my spine.

"You okay, Dove?" JD asks.

For the last hour or so, we've been lying out on a swing seat in the sun in Reid's garden.

Reid and Mav disappeared into his office not long after breakfast was cleaned up. There's a part of me that wants to go and check on them. Make sure they're playing nice with whatever they're doing, but there's another part of me that doesn't want to know.

"Yeah," I say, smiling at JD.

I can see his own curiosity staring back at me, maybe a little bit of rejection too.

Something tells me that on any other day, he'd be the one in the office discussing game plans and tactics. It's not that he wasn't invited when Reid jerked his head in Mav's direction to demand he follows, but JD's name wasn't specifically mentioned.

"You think they're both still breathing?" he asks, his voice is light enough, but it's a cover.

"You can go in there if you want. Contrary to popular belief, I don't actually need a babysitter."

Irritation flares in his eyes, making me regret my words instantly.

"Dove, I'm not here because I have to be," I say.

"No, I know. I just—"

"I want to spend time with you," he says, his eyes dropping from me as he nervously rubs the back of his neck.

"And trust me when I say, that isn't anything I've ever said to someone I'm fucking."

I rear back at his final words, although I'm not sure why. They're true. We are *just* fucking. There is nothing more to this relationship. We're not even captor and captive anymore. Just like last night, I walked out here freely, and I could have kept going if I wanted to. Yet, I'm still here.

"No, I know. I was just saying. If you want to go catch up on what's happening, I don't mind." I hold up the open notebook resting on my lap. "I have a friend to keep me company."

He studies me for a moment before his eyes drop to my neat scrawl on the first few lines of the page.

"Have you always written in a diary?" he asks curiously, his brows pulled as if he doesn't quite understand the concept of why I'm so obsessed with it.

"From as early as I can remember, yeah."

"Why?"

"It's... therapeutic."

"But don't you just write all your thoughts and shit?"

I can't help but laugh. "That's pretty much the long and the short of it way." Tearing my eyes from his, I stare out over the town beyond while he continues to rock us back and forth on the swing. I've no idea what the time is, but it's late afternoon already, the sun already sinking in the sky, the town we all know and hate ramping up for another night of debauchery and corruption. The dealers, pimps, the hookers... the Hawks. All of those nocturnal creatures that keep Harrow Creek... thriving are getting ready to start their days.

I shake my head. How can somewhere that looks so beautiful be so toxic?

"I've had a lot I've needed to process over the years. For

a long time, the only person I had to talk to was Kristie, but I couldn't poison her with the truth of what I was dealing with. She was too young, too innocent, too pure. And then." I sigh, pain coiling around my chest like barbed wire.

"How old was she when she... went?"

Tears immediately burn my eyes as I think of the last day I saw my little sister. "Her thirteenth birthday. I had no, I—"

"Thirteen?" JD spits angrily. "She was a child, she—"

One of the tears I'm fighting so hard to keep in finally drops, rolling down my cheek and landing on my page. I watch with my head bowed as the single drop of liquid spreads. My breath catches as it forms a wonky kind of heart shape.

"I know," I whisper, my voice cracking with emotion. "I'd made her a whole party. Our lives were pretty shitty despite how easy Dad had it. He spent the money on drugs and pussy from what I can figure. The house was a dump, falling down around us. I always wondered if he had a wife and a family in a decent house somewhere else. I could never figure out why he wanted to live in our shithole, so I figured it was all he deemed us worthy of."

"Dove," he whispers, and when I glance over, I find my own pain reflected in his eyes.

It's no secret that JD grew up in foster care, bouncing around group homes and foster homes all over town. It makes me wonder what kind of similarities lie in our childhoods.

None of us have grown up with loving parents around us, but I suspect that JD and I have more in common than we'd like to confess.

"I'd made her cupcakes—thirteen, obviously—decorated the house with handmade bunting because I had no way of getting her anything better. I did everything I could. I lived for seeing her smile, seeing her happy. It was about the only joy I got in life, so watching her face light up when she found it all made my entire year. If only I knew what was in store for us later that day."

"Jesus," he mutters. "And he told you that she was going to live with your mom?"

"Yeah, but I never believed him. Mom wasn't off somewhere living her best life without us. I knew it was all bullshit. She was gone, probably by his own hand, and so was Kristie. I had no one left to save me, to make me smile. Life from then on was just... hell."

"So you ran?"

"And Mav found me. The rest is history, I guess."

"You've been with him since you were sixteen?"

"Yep. He found me after Dad put a call out that I'd bolted, and—"

"I remember. Reid and I were at the clubhouse when the call came in. We were out looking for you too."

"And what would you have done if you'd have found me first?" I ask, although I'm not sure I actually want to hear the answer.

"I had no idea, Dove," he says sadly. "If I did, I never would have sent you back there. I would have tried to do what Mav did, although, I'm not sure I'd have done such a good job."

Reaching over, I take his hand in mine. "I think you'd have been perfect."

His smile is short and hollow, his lack of self-confidence shining through.

He shrugs. "At least I'd have fucked you."

Silence falls between us, the truth of that statement pressing heavily on my shoulders.

Yeah, JD would have fucked me if he'd found me all those years ago. If he knew the truth, he possibly would have protected me. But something tells me that he wouldn't have given me everything Mav has. The security, the safety, the confidence that even if the worst happened, that he'd be there for me.

"You should try it, you know," I say after long minutes.

"Try what?" he asks, turning to look at me. The side of my face burns with his attention, but I don't return his stare.

"Journaling. It might help with your..." I trail off, unsure how he'll feel about me addressing the darkness that lingers in his eyes sometimes. "Mental health," I add quietly.

I glance over, expecting to find a hard, closed-off expression on his face, so I'm surprised when I see his lips curl up and a laugh spill from his lips. Although, it doesn't hold any joy, just bitterness that makes my stomach knot.

"What's funny?" I ask, confused.

"Nothing. You're just not the first person to tell me that over the years."

"Oh," I breathe. "Have you tried it?"

"No," he says, ripping his eyes from mine and gazing out into the yard. "But then, no one has made it sound as tempting as you."

"How have I made it tempting?"

His smirk grows, and this time it's his signature one that I'm used to.

"You'd be naked while I did it, right?"

"Julian." I laugh, rolling my eyes at his playfulness.

"What? Seems like a good idea to me. You get naked and I'll go and find a notebook and pen."

He pushes to stand, letting the seat swing free.

"I'm not getting naked with you," I argue, despite the

fact I'm barely clothed as it is. I've once again forgone the clothes they brought me in favor of one of his tanks.

"Oh no?" he asks, taking a step closer, leaving me in his shadow.

"Nope," I state, popping the P for good measure.

"Wrong answer, little dove," he warns, kicking my legs wider, allowing him to stand between them.

I yelp when he suddenly leans forward, tilting the swing back to the point I almost slide out before lowering his face to mine.

"What are you doing?"

His smile grows, his eyes flashing with excitement.

"Proving you wrong."

In a split second, I'm in his arms and he's running across the deck toward the—

"No, JD. NO," I scream, as he closes in on the pool.

All I get in response is his deep chuckle.

"JD," I scream. "J—" But it's too late. He dives right off the side with me in his arms.

45

MAVERICK

"Your contact is Malakai Saint?" Reid snaps, his face hardening.

We might have talked at length last night about everything that he's been planning, but we never got around to how I could help with my own contacts. Although now we have, I'm regretting even mentioning it.

I should have known that I'd never impress the mighty Reid Harris with anything I've done in my life.

I could take Victor down single-handedly and he still wouldn't be impressed, or even grateful. Asshole.

"Yeah, and? He's about as close to Sidney Hyde as you're going to get. What more do you want?"

"His right-hand man would have been nice."

"Yeah, well. It would be nice if Santa Claus was real too, but we can't all get what we fucking want, can we?"

"All right, chill your fucking tits. I was just saying that Malakai wasn't who I was hoping for."

"He's Sidney's stepson. I'd say it's pretty fucking good."

"Yeah," he agrees, although it's forced as fuck. "It's great. I'm so glad you're here."

I raise a brow. "Sincere, thanks."

"What the fuck do you want?"

"Nothing. So do you want me to call him or what?"

He sits back in what can only be described as his throne and gestures for me to go ahead.

I shake my head, wondering what the hell Alana has seen in him in her time here that puts that look in her eyes when she watches him.

As much as I hate it, it's there every time they're in the same room.

They're an unexploded grenade waiting to go off.

Sliding my cell from my pocket, I find the number I have stored under a fake name and hit call, all the while being under the intense stare of the man on the other side of the desk.

It rings and rings and rings, and eventually cuts off without the option of leaving a message.

Reid's eyes never leave me, and despite the fact he could clearly hear my attempt at reaching out has been unsuccessful, I murmur, "No answer."

His brow lifts as if to say, 'No shit, asshole,' before I lower my cell.

"So what's next?" I ask.

"Try again later, just like I will with Luciana," he states. I'm not the only one who's had unsuccessful attempts at reaching out today. His call to Luciana also went unanswered.

"And what the fuck are we meant to do in the meantime?"

I sit there waiting like a little bitch as he makes some more calls, leaving them all on speaker so I'm party to every bit of information he is.

I can't help but feel like he's testing me. Testing my

loyalty. He doesn't need to though. Sure, there might have been plenty of times in the past I've thought about selling him out so that I could watch his epic fall from grace right alongside his father. But now, while he's working on giving Alana everything she's dreamed of, I can't find it in me to do it.

Sure, we might never see eye to eye enough to be friends, but he's offering me an olive branch right now, fuck knows why, but I'll take it.

I'm more than aware that JD should be the one sitting here right now, getting firsthand information from Griff, his uncle, and Ellis, Reid's little brother. But for some reason, he's not, and I am. Although, I'd be lying if I said I wasn't a little jealous about the fact that he's keeping my wife company while I'm sitting in here with this irritating asshole.

"What are we doing here?" I ask when he hangs up on his next call.

He studies me. "Planning to take over Harrow Creek one corrupt asshole at a time. What do you think we're doing?" His expressionless eyes hold mine.

"I meant me and you. Why am I sitting here right now listening to all of this?"

Pressing his palms to the top of his obnoxiously huge desk, he glares at me.

"Don't make me think too hard about it or I might remember all the reasons I don't trust you."

"Give me one solid reason why you don't."

He continues to glare at me, his nostrils flaring. But just like I suspect, he can't come up with anything. Because there is nothing. Just like my reasons for hating him, they're superficial, and over the past week, I think we've both discovered that our opinions and hatred of each other might have been nothing more than bullshit childhood rivalry.

"Didn't think so," I mutter, sitting back in my chair, refusing to cower.

His lips part, ready to growl something back at me, no doubt, when a high-pitched scream rips through the air. My blood instantly turns to ice and I'm on my feet and running to the door before my brain has caught up with my body.

"The fuck was that?" Reid asks darkly behind me as I rip the door open and race out.

Acting on instinct, I reach behind me for my gun but quickly remember the jerk behind me stole it not long before his own bullet collided with my shoulder.

"You got a gun?" I ask when Alana shrieks again.

"Fuck off, man." Reid grunts as he shoves me forward, forcing me to run faster.

But as we race through the living room and spill out into the yard, we soon discover there was no reason to panic.

"What the fuck are you doing?" Reid barks as Alana and JD splash around in his pool

"Swimming, what the fuck does it look like?" JD calls back, his eyes dropping to where Reid's gun is hanging loosely at his side. "We got trouble, man?" he asks.

"We heard screaming."

"Yeah, I threw Dove in the pool."

"So we see," I mutter, watching as she swims closer to the steps and emerges.

I swear to God, it happens in slow motion like some fucking James Bond film. Only, she's about a million times hotter.

The light gray tank she's wearing clings to every inch of her insane body, and as the light breeze rushes over her wet skin, goose bumps erupt, and her nipples harden.

"Jesus." Reid grunts beside me as he tucks his gun away.

"Are you perving over my wife?" I ask as she closes the space between us.

"Dove, where are you going? I haven't fucked you against the edge yet. I had this idea about laying you out and—"

"Can you blame me?" Reid asks, cutting JD off.

I want to argue with him, but shit. She looks fucking sinful.

She looks between us, her brows drawing together.

"You two good?"

"Yeah, Pet. No blood has been lost."

"Have you... made any progress?"

"Not really," he confesses. "But we will. I'm going to make lunch. Go take a shower. I'm not having you two dripping all over my food."

"Fucking party pooper," JD calls before diving under the water and kicking hard enough to ensure the splash reaches us.

"Stupid fucking asshole," Reid mutters before marching off toward the house, following Alana's wet footprints.

I do the same, hating that I look like his new little pet.

"You want a beer?" I ask when I get to the kitchen and find him pulling a pan out already.

"Yeah," he agrees before he continues getting everything out he's going to need. Then he abruptly abandons it all and marches out of the room.

But he's only gone for a few seconds, and when he returns, he's holding a set of knives.

"Any reason they don't live in the kitchen? Had a falling out with the frying pan or something?"

The glance is quick, so quick that if I weren't studying

him so closely that I would miss the ways his eyes dart to the window.

"Or something," he mutters a second before a dripping wet and naked JD stalks through into the room.

"Fucking seriously?" Reid snaps, watching as his best friend leaves a trail of water in his wake.

"What? I took my pants off to try and help. Not my fault you're offended by my dick."

"Jesus fucking Christ," Reid mutters, turning his back on his friend to get to work.

"Jealous, man?" JD questions when he realizes he doesn't lose my attention. I don't want to stare at his dick, although it's impossible not to notice, the prick is harder than fucking steel and standing there loud and proud. "I already told you," he says, pointing to his metal. "Drives her fucking crazy. You should really consider—"

"Shower, JD. And don't even think about finding Alana and—"

"You really are fucking boring," JD points out before finally leaving the room.

"You're worried about him." It's not a question. I've seen the way Reid has looked at his best friend a few times over the last couple of days.

"She's going to break his heart," he comments, focusing on slicing up what looks like ingredients for a salad.

"What makes you say that?" I ask, selfishly hoping for one single answer.

He stills, his shoulders widening. If I were facing him, I know I'd be seeing his jaw tic as he grits his teeth.

"Because no matter what happens, she'll choose you."

"Do you ever make anything that isn't restaurant standard?" Alana asks, sitting back in her seat and rubbing her belly.

At her request, we had our lunch outside. A fresh garden salad with avocado and pork chops, which were seasoned and cooked to perfection.

It's really quite annoying just how good at everything he is. It's a reminder of why I hated him when we were kids.

Jealousy.

It hurts to admit it, even all these years after, but that was the crux of it.

He had it all. A father with all the power, a stepmother that loved him and his brothers, and friends who'd stand by him through thick and thin.

I was... well, I was just there. From as early as I can remember, Dad was happier being anywhere but at home. He seemed to prefer his women and the other kids he spawned all over town. It wasn't until Ivy entered my life that I felt like I belonged, but there was still something missing. And I didn't discover what it was until the day I dragged Alana into my life, and everything changed. I finally found the point in my life, the place I was meant to be. And it was easy to forget that she didn't really have a choice but to stay.

"Oh my God, do you remember those burgers you made not long after we moved in here?" JD asks with a laugh before tipping his beer bottle to his lips.

Reid doesn't say anything or react in any way.

"Oh, don't give us that blank, *I've no idea what you're talking about face.* I know you do. You were so fucking mortified."

"Whatever." Reid scoffs, pushing his chair back. He

takes all our plates and abandons them on the kitchen counter.

JD's cell dings and he pulls it out, but before he can react to whatever it is, Reid barks out a loud curse.

"What is it?" Alana asks.

"Victor," Reid states, his voice hard and cold.

"Shit," Alana hisses, jumping to her feet. "Here? Now?"

"Yes," JD confirms.

"Fuck," Reid barks, storming from the room.

"Where the fuck is he going?" I ask, watching him depart.

"Fuck knows. But you two need to disappear," JD instructs before racing after Reid.

"This wasn't meant to happen," Alana says quietly.

"No, but it was inevitable. The cunt is Reid's father, after all."

"Fuck. Come on," she says, threading her fingers through mine and dragging me from the room.

Part of me expects her to lead me to the basement, so it comes as a bit of a surprise when she takes the stairs just as an ominous bell rings through the house, forcing us to pick up our speed.

46

ALANA

With my heart in my throat and dread flooding my veins, I drag Mav up the stairs.

My entire body trembles with fear.

If he knows we're here...

If he discovers we're here...

My stomach rolls and my mouth waters with the need to vomit.

"Where are you going?" Mav asks as I bypass the room that's been allocated as his in favor of one farther down the hallway, his voice deeper than usual, showing his own concern.

"If he's suspicious, the first place he'll go is the guest rooms," I explain. If I weren't panicking so much, I might be second-guessing walking Mav into Reid's inner sanctum, but what's the other option? Hiding in the basement? Yeah, that's not happening. I've done my time down there. We both have.

"I guess," Mav muses.

We spill into the room as a deep, familiar, blood-curdling voice pierces the air.

"Shit," I hiss, darting forward faster.

Mav closes the door behind us and follows me in.

If I were to look back, I suspect I'd find him studying the bare space curiously. I know I did the first time I came in here. It's luxurious and comfortable, sure. It looks like what I imagine a fancy hotel to look like. But there is nothing personal. If you didn't know the room belonged to Reid then there is nothing—literally nothing—that could indicate that. No photos or childhood achievements, no mementos of anything. Yeah, it's a nice room, but it's also kinda... sad, I guess. It has no heart, no life despite the very real man who resides in it.

"This is..." Mav trails off.

"Yeah, I know. I guess I should have expected it. Downstairs isn't much different."

He's right. There are also no happy family photos, but there are paintings and ornaments, other things that clearly mean enough to Reid to have them on display.

It's the total opposite of the home Mav and I have created. I might be a little biased, but that home is full of love and life. Photos of our five years together cover the walls and sideboards, and mementos from trips we've taken fill each room.

It's home. It's ours and it's one hundred percent us. I love it.

I miss it.

"You okay, Doll?" Mav asks, stepping up to me and placing his large hands on my hips, tugging me closer.

"I—" I start, but he cuts me off when he rests his brow against mine and holds my stare with his dark eyes.

"Breathe, Doll," he whispers in a calming voice he's had to use on me one too many times over the years. "He has no reason to believe we're here. No one outside these walls knows where you are, and—"

"What about you? What if he's been to where Devin and Ezra 'hid' you? What if he knows he's being played and—"

"I can't believe I'm going to say this but... You need to trust Reid."

I nod, but his words don't help relax me.

"Doll?" he urges, his eyes begging me to calm down.

"I'm okay," I eventually breathe, my voice barely audible.

But from the dark, concerned look in his eyes when I risk glancing up, I'm not sure he believes me.

"He's probably just coming for coffee with golden balls."

I shake my head, unable to find any humor in his attempt at a joke. Mav might think that Reid believes he's better than everyone else because of his surname, but it's just not true. He's proven that today already by allowing Mav in on the planning, by keeping us in his home, cooking for us.

"I'm not sure they have that kind of relationship," I confess before an idea hits me. "But I think we can probably find out."

"What are you doing?" Mav asks when I twist out of his hold and scan the room for the TV remote. I find it on Reid's bedside table. The thought of him lying out here watching me downstairs with that fucking vibrator inside makes my stomach burn with fury just as much as it heats my blood. It was frustratingly hot.

"This entire place has cameras," I say, pointing the remote at the giant screen and waiting until it comes to life.

"We just need to figure out how to find the room they're in."

"Motherfucker." Mav growls the second an image emerges on the screen.

Safe to say, Reid probably hasn't watched it for a few days. My old cell looks stark and cold. The cot in the corner is unused, with no evidence it's had two occupants recently.

"Probably the least of what you need to be worrying about," I mutter, pressing the menu to try and figure out a way to change the camera to one a little more useful.

It takes longer than I'd like, but eventually, I manage to find out how to change the camera. All the while, Mav mutters his irritation about the fact Reid was sitting up here watching me while I was suffering in the basement.

"It's over, Mav. Done. We need to look forward, not back."

"I know, but that doesn't mean it's right."

"Reid hasn't touched me," I say before risking a glance at him. I find his brow quirked. "He hasn't. Not really."

Mav's teeth grind and his jaw pops but he doesn't say anything.

I cycle through the other cells, making Mav move closer to the screen every time we find one that's occupied.

"Holy shit," he suddenly gasps. "Is that—"

"Not important," I say, barely sparing the prisoner a second glance. "We need to find them, not the assholes Reid has locked up like pets."

Mav doesn't disagree, but I can see his mind is turning at a mile a minute when I glance over again.

"Bingo," he says eventually when the kitchen, or more importantly, the men appear on the screen.

They're sitting on the couches with coffees on the table

between them. Reid and JD on one side and Victor on the other.

I wonder if he has any idea that the coffee table is like a battle line between them.

My eyes linger on Victor. He's sitting back, resting against the couch with his thighs spread wide and his arms laying across the back of the cushion as if he has no worries in the world.

How nice it must be to be so apathetic about what's happening around him.

Daily, people die in Harrow Creek because of him. The whores on the street, risk their lives with every John they agree to let inside their bodies just to scrape enough cash to pay Victor their dues and keep a roof over their heads and food in their bellies. The addicts who shoot up too much and put an end to their miserable lives that are only so shitty because of one man. The kids who've lost fathers because they believed that to be respected in this town, you had to become a Hawk and be one of Victor's little minions.

And yet he sits there like the fucking king of the world, not giving two shits about anyone but himself.

He doesn't even care about his kids, not really. All he wants are five boys who are willing to continue his legacy, no matter how much it breaks them in the process.

"You need to get the audio working, this is fucking pointless otherwise," Mav barks, his irritation about being left out of this getting the better of him. "Shit," he hisses before wrapping his arms around my waist and resting his chin on my shoulder. "I'm sorry. This is just—"

"I know. It's okay." Grabbing the other remote, I figure out how to get the volume up.

Both of us step closer as if we're equally as scared as

each other to put it high enough to alert those downstairs that there are people up here.

"Razor has business that needs attending to. Mav needs to sort himself out and get back to work. What fucking pussy runs away because his wife doesn't want him anymore?"

Mav's muscles lock up, his grip on me almost too tight as he listens to Victor talk about him.

"I'm sure it's nothing that Razor or one of his boys can't handle. Mav obviously needed a few days to get his head back in the game," Reid explains.

Victor's eyes widen suspiciously.

"Shit," Mav hisses. "He's being too nice. Victor will see right through him."

I want to argue, but I can't. I might never have seen the way Reid and Mav react to each other at work, but I can't imagine they offer each other too much compassion, even on a good day.

"If he's not interested in the life he was born into then we have plenty of others who can take his place. That's all I'm saying," Victor says, a dark warning in his tone.

Anger surges through my veins at the flippant way he's willing to cast one of his most loyal soldiers aside because he's got a broken heart.

Maybe it shouldn't be such a surprise, it's not like Victor has a heart. Just a dark, rotten soul.

They continue talking business. It's dull as shit, but while my mind wanders, Mav is focused, absorbing every single word as if Victor is talking in some kind of secret code that only he understands. All the while, I keep my eyes glued on him, watching every time he glances away from Reid in favor of looking around the room.

What is he looking for? Evidence?

Does he think we're going to suddenly jump out of hiding and scare him?

Whatever it is he's doing, my heart rate never slows and the trembling on my hands never abates.

Every second feels like it lasts an hour as we silently stare at the screen waiting for something to happen.

But it never does.

The mostly boring and uneventful visit eventually comes to an end.

My heart is in my throat as Victor claps his hands on his knees and pushes to stand.

Reid and JD follow, both looking noticeably tenser than Victor. I expect him to be the careless cunt that we know him to be, so when he picks up his mug and walks toward the kitchen with it, my breath catches.

Ice rushes through my veins as he closes in on the sink.

"Tell me they cleaned up from lunch?" I beg, my voice barely a whisper as my panic begins to get the better of me. The image of Reid abandoning four plates and walking out plays in my mind like it's happening before my eyes.

Mav doesn't respond and it does very little help to settle my anxiety at all.

"He'll probably think it was Devin or something," he eventually mutters, but it's unconvincing. "Change the camera, follow him out."

With dread sitting heavy in my stomach, I begin flicking through the channels once more with trembling hands until I find the hallway.

"Have you spoken to Richie?" Victor asks Reid as they walk toward the front door, JD lingering behind in the kitchen doorway.

He hasn't said much throughout the whole meeting, but

I assume that's standard. JD is Reid's right-hand man, and Victor treats him as such.

"Yes," Reid agrees. "He assures me everything is fine. He's aware his issue with supply is putting pressure on us but he's promised everything will get better. He knows the consequences otherwise."

Victor studies his son closely. It's as if he's searching for the evidence of the lie he just told.

I might not be privy to most of Reid's plans, but I've heard little bits here and there and I know he's fucking about with Victor's suppliers.

Unable to find what he's looking for—or at least I hope that's the case—Victor continues toward the front door. But just before he passes the dresser I stubbed my toe on the other night, he pauses, his gaze darting downward.

"What's he doing?" I whisper-hiss.

"I don't know," Mav replies just as quietly.

Giving a rare show of emotion, Victor's shoulders lock up. But instead of saying anything or giving anything away, he bends down, swiping something from beside the dresser.

My brows crease.

If I thought Mav was tense behind me, then I was wrong, because that one move has turned him to stone.

What the hell could he have found beneath a dresser in a hallway that's purely there to hold their keys as far as I can see?

I lean closer, squinting as if it'll help me see better. But it's not clear enough. And by the time Victor stands and turns back to Reid, his fingers are curled around whatever he picked up.

"What was that?" I ask nervously.

Victor uncurls his fingers very briefly glances at what's in his hand before passing it to Reid.

Reid was already strung as tight as a bow, but the second he registers what his father just passed him, his shoulders pull even tighter.

My stomach bottoms out.

All the air rushes from Mav's lungs tickling across the back of my neck as he does so. All the hairs on the rest of my body lift as the unease and dread racing through my system get stronger.

No words are spoken between father and son, but even through the screen, I can feel the tension. It presses down on my shoulders and wraps around my chest, making it hard to breathe.

Taking a step back from Reid, Victor's lips curl into a smirk, one that shoots poison through my veins.

"Oh God," I whimper.

My eyes are still glued to the screen when Victor finally spins around and continues walking toward the door. Finally, he pulls it open and disappears from our sight. The second it slams closed, Mav takes off like the devil is snapping at his ass. To be fair, it could be.

"Mav, wait," I call, hating being in the dark about all of this.

I race after him, but he's faster, his footsteps thundering down the stairs before me. By the time I get downstairs, he and Reid are talking in hushed voices in the living room. Both of their bodies are taut, their words short and sharp.

If I didn't know they'd come to some kind of truce over the past couple of days then I'd think they were arguing.

I want to interrupt, but the tension coming off both of them in waves stops me from even stepping over the threshold to the room.

It's easy to forget how formidable and dangerous these

men I'm living around really are. But standing in the doorway, watching Reid and Mav together—a sight I never thought I'd see—reality hits me hard.

There's a crash in the kitchen and after a quick look over my shoulder, I head in that direction.

I find JD loading the dishwasher and my stomach knots.

"What's going on?" I ask, startling him.

He doesn't turn around immediately; instead, he hangs his head for a beat, sucking in a deep breath. Once he's composed himself, he finally turns.

The smile on his face should be comforting, but it falls flat.

"Victor saw all of this, didn't he?" I ask, my voice cold and hard.

"It's fine, Dove. Reid's smarter than his old man," he reasons, but the shadows in his eyes and the doubt in his voice give him away.

I stare at him, my chin dropped.

"You can't be serious? All of this it's—" I shake my head, lifting my hands to my hair and pulling until it hurts. Something tells me that it's got nothing on what's heading our way.

I want to believe him. I do. I truly believe that Reid will overthrow Victor and take control of his town. But I also refuse to underestimate Victor.

He has trained Reid to be the future leader he wants, which means, he knows his moves and will recognize his tells. And that is very dangerous for us. One wrong move and he'll take us down before we've even realized something is wrong.

I'm about to respond when heavy footsteps move our way.

"What's—"

"I'm going out," Reid states. "Stay here, don't do anything stupid."

"Bro, you know we—"

"What's going on?" I ask, my eyes bouncing between Reid and Mav's. "What did Victor find? What happened before he left?"

"Nothing, Doll," Mav says, walking over and wrapping his arm around my waist, tugging me into his body and letting me drown in his scent. "Trust us, yeah?" he whispers before pressing a kiss on my temple.

Anger ripples through me. The need to shout and scream until they answer my questions and tell me what I need to know is almost too much to deny.

But in the end, all I do is whisper, "Yeah," because what else can I do?

47

ALANA

The rest of the night is tense. Reid never returns, and despite asking both JD and Mav multiple times, neither of them gives up where he went. Mav also refuses to discuss what the two of them were talking about immediately after Victor left.

Victor has sucked all the life and fun out of this house, leaving nothing but the heavy weight of dread in his wake.

It has been easy to push reality aside with these tempting men surrounding me, but one sight of the enemy has reality crashing down.

None of us even attempts to make any dinner in Reid's absence, not that I was hungry. My stomach has been churning with dread ever since Reid announced Victor's arrival.

Whatever happened down here during that short visit was bad. I knew that from watching the exchange alone. But the fact that Mav hasn't relaxed an inch since Victor left only confirms that I'm right to be on edge.

We spend the night in the living room. Me and JD on one couch, a brooding Mav on the other.

Every time they look at each other, a silent conversation passes between them, reminding me again that they are keeping me in the dark about something.

I meant what I said to Mav a few hours ago. I trust them. But that doesn't mean that I'm not having a hard time with all the secrets that are flying around right now.

When my next request to be told something falls on deaf ears, my irritation gets the better of me and I rip my legs from where JD's been absently massaging my feet and bring myself up to bed.

For the first time since Mav was released from the basement, I question which bedroom I want to slip into.

Reid's is tempting because he isn't here, and there is every chance he won't return until sunrise. But the thought of him finding me curled up in his bed stops me.

Mav is the obvious choice. I've slept in there with him—and JD—the last couple of nights. It makes me wonder if they'd both come and join me at some point, or if their guilt would stop them, or at least one of them.

But the second my eyes land on JD's door, I remember our conversation in the yard earlier in the day about my journaling and the shadows in his eyes, the way he confessed that he's had the suggestion of doing so before. My legs move before I'm aware my brain has made a decision.

I step into his room and I'm instantly hit by his masculine scent. It floods my nose and wraps around me like a warm blanket.

It's always been the same with JD. He might be the silly playboy to everyone else, but he's also a gentle protector who's helped me in my darkest moments under this roof.

His room is as messy as it was the first time I came in here. Clothes are strewn everywhere. Pens, notebooks and scraps of paper litter the small desk. There's a part of me that wants to dig through to see if he has tried his hand at journaling already. But I don't.

Instead, I make use of his bathroom before fixing his messy sheets and slipping beneath them.

His scent only gets stronger as I lie my head on his pillow. Shamelessly, I press my nose against it and breathe him in.

Despite the concern nagging at my brain, I manage to drift off to sleep surprisingly fast.

I'm alone in the house. It's the only time I don't totally hate living here. Just for a few minutes, a couple of hours, if I'm lucky.

I've cleaned the entire place, knowing that he'll be expecting it whenever he returns later. It never seems to matter how drunk or excited he is, he always notices if I haven't perfectly done the jobs he left for me. And finally, I tuck myself into the back corner of my bed, cross my legs, and open my diary.

It's about the only thing I have to myself under this roof.

I keep them hidden beneath my bed. I don't dare to allow Dad to know they exist. He'll use them against me.

I barely get the date written when the doorbell rings.

My heart jumps into my throat, dread seeping through my veins, my muscles suddenly heavy with the thought of my peace being ruined.

To start with, I don't move. Praying it's just some try-hard salesman or a druggie who's hoping Dad will take pity on him and give him a free hit.

But when the ringing starts up again a few seconds later, I finally close my notebook, hide it, and make my way to the front door.

If it's Dad who's forgotten his keys, or worse, one of his friends, he'll ensure I'm punished for it later. I'm not sure I've got that in me today.

The bell continues to ring as I descend the stairs, and the second I look through the peephole, my heart sinks.

There's a part of me that assumes he's here looking for Dad. But I know better. He's here for me. He knows I'm alone and he's trying his luck.

Swallowing down my fear, I wrap my fingers around the doorknob and pull it open.

"Good evening, Victor. What can I do for you?" I ask politely while my stomach churns with the need to vomit.

Something jolts me from my nightmare, and I fight to come back to myself. I'm more than happy not to continue down that road and relive another time in my life when that monster turned up unannounced.

The mattress dips a second before a large, hard, hot body slides next to mine.

"This is a nice surprise, little dove," JD murmurs, his arm snaking around my waist, pulling me flush against him. "Shit, you're shaking," he says, holding me tighter. "Nightmare?"

"It was just starting," I confess roughly.

"Well, I'm glad I could help."

My eyes burn with emotion, and I swallow thickly, trying to force the lump down.

"Everything is going to be okay, Dove. I promise."

I don't say anything. Even if I could force words out, I wouldn't even know where to start with that promise.

It's one he can't make. I'm pretty sure he's as aware as I am of that.

"I've missed having you in my bed," he whispers, sliding his hand to my ass, squeezing hard before hooking my leg over his, allowing me to feel how hard he is already.

But he doesn't make a move to do anything about it. Instead, he just rests his brow against mine, and stares down into my eyes.

"I know it's hard not knowing exactly what's going on, but you need to trust Reid. Trust us. All of us, we only want the best for you."

"Why?" The word is out before I get a chance to stop it.

"Little dove," he sighs. "You've no idea how incredible you are, do you?"

I shrug the shoulder I'm not lying on. "Haven't heard it much in my life, JD. Easier to remember all the shit."

"I get that more than you could know," he confesses.

I search his eyes in the dark, wishing I could see more.

"Do you want to talk about it?" I ask, sensing that he might be searching for a reason to get something off his chest.

He lets out a rush of air that's filled with nothing but pain. Pain I know all too well.

"About as much as you do," he finally whispers. "My childhood was... well, it wasn't as bad as yours but—"

"This isn't a competition, Julian. Pain and abuse don't sit on a scale of best to worst. It's all the fucking worst, no matter what form it comes in."

He doesn't respond to that, I guess because he wants to argue.

But no matter what I've been through, I'll stand by it. Abusing kids in any form is wrong. It fucks up their entire lives, no matter what.

The evidence of that is lying right here in this bed.

"I've been thinking about what you said," he whispers vulnerably.

"Which bit exactly?"

"The journaling. I found a notebook and... I'm going to

413

give it a try. Figure I've got enough thoughts swirling around up here." I just notice the darkness of his hand lift to tap his temple.

"It might help calm them. Make sense of them."

"Yeah, maybe," he mutters skeptically.

"Julian—" His fingers press against my lips stopping my words.

"Not tonight. We've already got enough to worry about."

My lips part, but he still doesn't allow me to say anything, only this time he distracts me with something better. His tongue finds mine, twisting and stroking in the most dizzying way. I know I shouldn't, but with his mouth on mine and his hands on my body, I forget about reality and drown in everything that is Julian Dempsey.

Eventually, making out isn't enough and he reaches down to push the head of his dick against my entrance.

He pushes inside so slowly, it makes a sob rip up my throat. Thankfully, he swallows it down without mentioning it.

He fucks me so gently, so slowly that it makes my eyes burn with tears.

I've never experienced anything like it.

It's almost like he's making love to me. But that can't be right. I'm just a broken girl everyone uses until they're bored and then discards. The only person who's ever given me anymore is Mav, but I assumed he was an anomaly in the man department.

"Can't get enough of you, little dove," he whispers, his fingers digging into my ass to get us closer, to get deeper.

"Julian." I moan as he grazes my G-spot.

"Fuck, I love that sound," he says before claiming my lips, his tongue mimicking the action of his dick until he brings us both to the edge, sending us crashing over simultaneously.

Once we're done, he doesn't pull out of me. Instead, he holds me closer, tighter, and with our heaving breaths mingling, we come down from our highs and fall asleep wrapped in each other's arms.

Thankfully, I drift off into a dreamless sleep. I don't know if it's JD's presence that keeps the monsters at bay, or if my body refuses to lose the lingering effects of my recent high with the horrors of my past. Whatever it is, I'm grateful for the peaceful rest.

That is until a large hand lands on my shoulder sometime later.

At first, I think I'm dreaming. I'm so deep in sleep, it's like swimming through mud to try to get back to reality to attempt to figure out what's going on.

"Alana," a deep, familiar voice whispers. "Doll, wake up. We need to go."

Now that wakes me up.

"Go?" I whisper-hiss back. "Go where?"

"Shhh, don't wake JD."

"What? Why?"

"Doll, please," he begs, letting me hear the desperation, the fear, in his voice. "I'll explain everything, I promise. But not right now."

Reluctantly, I release a sleeping JD, and as if I weigh nothing more than a feather, Mav lifts me from the bed, cradling me against his chest like a child.

With one last look at JD, blissfully unaware that I've just been ripped from his bed, Mav closes the door behind me and silently walks us down the stairs.

"Put this on," he says once we're in the hallway.

The house is completely dark, stopping me from seeing

his features clearly, but the tone of his voice says everything.

Do not argue and do as you're told.

I pull on the black leggings and long-sleeved shirt before turning to him.

"Are we going to rob a bank or something?"

Mav sighs, taking my face in his hands before leaning in close. Our noses brush before he rests his brow against mine.

"I made you a promise the other day, Doll. This is me keeping it."

"B-but—"

"There are no buts. You told me that you wanted us to have a future above all else."

My lips part to argue, but I quickly close them again. He's right, I did say those words. Forced him to make that promise.

I just didn't expect it to happen so fast. Or that the prospect of leaving this house would hurt so much.

I glance above us at where JD is sleeping. I've no idea where Reid is, but something tells me he's here too.

Do they know? Is that what the gentle lovemaking was about?

Was it a goodbye?

Need to know more? One-Click your copy of **Lawless**, book #3 in the Harrow Creek Hawks series.

THE REVENGE YOU SEEK
SNEAK PEEK

Chapter One

Letty

I sit on my bed, staring down at the fabric in my hands.

This wasn't how it was supposed to happen.

This wasn't part of my plan.

I let out a sigh, squeezing my eyes tight, willing the tears away.

I've cried enough. I thought I'd have run out by now.

A commotion on the other side of the door has me looking up in a panic, but just like yesterday, no one comes knocking.

I think I proved that I don't want to hang with my new roommates the first time someone knocked and asked if I wanted to go for breakfast with them.

I don't.

I don't even want to be here.

I just want to hide.

And that thought makes it all a million times worse.

I'm not a hider. I'm a fighter. I'm a fucking Hunter.

But this is what I've been reduced to.

This pathetic, weak mess.

And all because of *him*.

He shouldn't have this power over me. But even now, he does.

The dorm falls silent once again, and I pray that they've all headed off for their first class of the semester so I can slip out unnoticed.

I know it's ridiculous. I know I should just go out there with my head held high and dig up the confidence I know I do possess.

But I can't.

I figure that I'll just get through today—my first day— and everything will be alright.

I can somewhat pick up where I left off, almost as if the last eighteen months never happened.

Wishful thinking.

I glance down at the hoodie in my hands once more.

Mom bought them for Zayn, my younger brother, and me.

The navy fabric is soft between my fingers, but the text staring back at me doesn't feel right.

Maddison Kings University.

A knot twists my stomach and I swear my whole body sags with my new reality.

I was at my dream school. I beat the odds and I got into Columbia. And everything was good. No, everything was fucking fantastic.

Until it wasn't.

Now here I am. Sitting in a dorm at what was always my backup plan school having to start over.

Throwing the hoodie onto my bed, I angrily push to my feet.

I'm fed up with myself.

I should be better than this, stronger than this.

But I'm just... I'm broken.

And as much as I want to see the positives in this situation. I'm struggling.

Shoving my feet into my Vans, I swing my purse over my shoulder and scoop up the couple of books on my desk for the two classes I have today.

My heart drops when I step out into the communal kitchen and find a slim blonde-haired girl hunched over a mug and a textbook.

The scent of coffee fills my nose and my mouth waters.

My shoes squeak against the floor and she immediately looks up.

"Sorry, I didn't mean to disrupt you."

"Are you kidding?" she says excitedly, her southern accent making a smile twitch at my lips.

Her smile lights up her pretty face and for some reason, something settles inside me.

I knew hiding was wrong. It's just been my coping method for... quite a while.

"We wondered when our new roommate was going to show her face. The guys have been having bets on you being an alien or something."

A laugh falls from my lips. "No, no alien. Just..." I sigh, not really knowing what to say.

"You transferred in, right? From Columbia?"

"Ugh... yeah. How'd you know—"

"Girl, I know everything." She winks at me, but it

doesn't make me feel any better. "West and Brax are on the team, they spent the summer with your brother."

A rush of air passes my lips in relief. Although I'm not overly thrilled that my brother has been gossiping about me.

"So, what classes do you have today?" she asks when I stand there gaping at her.

"Umm... American lit and psychology."

"I've got psych later too. Professor Collins?"

"Uh..." I drag my schedule from my purse and stare down at it. "Y-yes."

"Awesome. We can sit together."

"S-sure," I stutter, sounding unsure, but the smile I give her is totally genuine. "I'm Letty, by the way." Although I'm pretty sure she already knows that.

"Ella."

"Okay, I'll... uh... see you later."

"Sure. Have a great morning."

She smiles at me and I wonder why I was so scared to come out and meet my new roommates.

I'd wanted Mom to organize an apartment for me so that I could be alone, but—probably wisely—she refused. She knew that I'd use it to hide in and the point of me restarting college is to try to put everything behind me and start fresh.

After swiping an apple from the bowl in the middle of the table, I hug my books tighter to my chest and head out, ready to embark on my new life.

The morning sun burns my eyes and the scent of freshly cut grass fills my nose as I step out of our building. The summer heat hits my skin, and it makes everything feel that little bit better.

So what if I'm starting over. I managed to transfer the

credits I earned from Columbia, and MKU is a good school. I'll still get a good degree and be able to make something of my life.

Things could be worse.

It could be this time last year...

I shake the thought from my head and force my feet to keep moving.

I pass students meeting up with their friends for the start of the new semester as they excitedly tell them all about their summers and the incredible things they did, or they compare schedules.

My lungs grow tight as I drag in the air I need. I think of the friends I left behind in Columbia. We didn't have all that much time together, but we'd bonded before my life imploded on me.

Glancing around, I find myself searching for familiar faces. I know there are plenty of people here who know me. A couple of my closest friends came here after high school.

Mom tried to convince me to reach out over the summer, but my anxiety kept me from doing so. I don't want anyone to look at me like I'm a failure. That I got into one of the best schools in the country, fucked it up and ended up crawling back to Rosewood. I'm not sure what's worse, them assuming I couldn't cope or the truth.

Focusing on where I'm going, I put my head down and ignore the excited chatter around me as I head for the coffee shop, desperately in need of my daily fix before I even consider walking into a lecture.

I find the Westerfield Building where my first class of the day is and thank the girl who holds the heavy door open for me before following her toward the elevator.

"Holy fucking shit," a voice booms as I turn the corner, following the signs to the room on my schedule.

Before I know what's happening, my coffee is falling from my hand and my feet are leaving the floor.

"What the—" The second I get a look at the guy standing behind the one who has me in his arms, I know exactly who I've just walked into.

Forgetting about the coffee that's now a puddle on the floor, I release my books and wrap my arms around my old friend.

His familiar woodsy scent flows through me, and suddenly, I feel like me again. Like the past two years haven't existed.

"What the hell are you doing here?" Luca asks, a huge smile on his face when he pulls back and studies me.

His brows draw together when he runs his eyes down my body, and I know why. I've been working on it over the summer, but I know I'm still way skinnier than I ever have been in my life.

"I transferred," I admit, forcing the words out past the lump in my throat.

His smile widens more before he pulls me into his body again.

"It's so good to see you."

I relax into his hold, squeezing him tight, absorbing his strength. And that's one thing that Luca Dunn has in spades. He's a rock, always has been and I didn't realize how much I needed that right now.

Mom was right. I should have reached out.

"You too," I whisper honestly, trying to keep the tears at bay that are threatening just from seeing him—them.

"Hey, it's good to see you," Leon says, slightly more subdued than his twin brother as he hands me my discarded books.

"Thank you."

I look between the two of them, noticing all the things that have changed since I last saw them in person. I keep up with them on Instagram and TikTok, sure, but nothing is quite like standing before the two of them.

Both of them are bigger than I ever remember, showing just how hard their coach is working them now they're both first string for the Panthers. And if it's possible, they're both hotter than they were in high school, which is really saying something because they'd turn even the most confident of girls into quivering wrecks with one look back then. I can only imagine the kind of rep they have around here.

The sound of a door opening behind us and the shuffling of feet cuts off our little reunion.

"You in Professor Whitman's American lit class?" Luca asks, his eyes dropping from mine to the book in my hands.

"Yeah. Are you?"

"We are. Walk you to class?" A smirk appears on his lips that I remember all too well. A flutter of the butterflies he used to give me threaten to take flight as he watches me intently.

Luca was one of my best friends in high school, and I spent almost all our time together with the biggest crush on him. It seems that maybe the teenage girl inside me still thinks that he could be it for me.

"I'd love you to."

"Come on then, Princess," Leon says and my entire body jolts at hearing that pet name for me. He's never called me that before and I really hope he's not about to start now.

Clearly not noticing my reaction, he once again takes my books from me and threads his arm through mine as the pair of them lead me into the lecture hall.

I glance at both of them, a smile pulling at my lips and hope building inside me.

Maybe this was where I was meant to be this whole time.

Maybe Columbia and I were never meant to be.

More than a few heads turn our way as we climb the stairs to find some free seats. Mostly it's the females in the huge space and I can't help but inwardly laugh at their reaction.

I get it.

The Dunn twins are two of the Kings around here and I'm currently sandwiched between them. It's a place that nearly every female in this college, hell, this state, would kill to be in.

"Dude, shift the fuck over," Luca barks at another guy when he pulls to a stop a few rows from the back.

The guy who's got dark hair and even darker eyes immediately picks up his bag, books, and pen and moves over a space.

"This is Colt," Luca explains, nodding to the guy who's studying me with interest.

"Hey," I squeak, feeling a little intimidated.

"Hey." His low, deep voice licks over me. "Ow, what the fuck, man?" he barks, rubbing at the back of his head where Luca just slapped him.

"Letty's off-limits. Get your fucking eyes off her."

"Dude, I was just saying hi."

"Yeah, and we all know what that usually leads to," Leon growls behind me.

The three of us take our seats and just about manage to pull our books out before our professor begins explaining the syllabus for the semester.

"Sorry about the coffee," Luca whispers after a few minutes. "Here." He places a bottle of water on my desk. "I know it's not exactly a replacement, but it's the best I can do."

The reminder of the mess I left out in the hallway hits me.

"I should go and—"

"Chill," he says, placing his hand on my thigh. His touch instantly relaxes me as much as it sends a shock through my body. "I'll get you a replacement after class. Might even treat you to a cupcake."

I smile up at him, swooning at the fact he remembers my favorite treat.

Why did I ever think coming here was a bad idea?

Chapter Two
Letty

My hand aches by the time Professor Whitman finishes talking. It feels like a lifetime ago that I spent this long taking notes.

"You okay?" Luca asks me with a laugh as I stretch out my fingers.

"Yeah, it's been a while."

"I'm sure these boys can assist you with that, beautiful," bursts from Colt's lips, earning him another slap to the head.

"Ignore him. He's been hit in the head with a ball one too many times," Leon says from beside me but I'm too enthralled with the way Luca is looking at me right now to reply.

Our friendship wasn't a conventional one back in high school. He was the star quarterback, and I wasn't a cheerleader or ever really that sporty. But we were paired up as lab partners during my first week at Rosewood High and we kinda never separated.

I watched as he took the team to new heights, as he met with college scouts, I even went to a few places with him so he didn't have to go alone.

He was the one who allowed me to cry on his shoulder as I struggled to come to terms with the loss of another who left a huge hole in my heart and he never, not once, overstepped the mark while I clung to him and soaked up his support.

I was also there while he hooked up with every member of the cheer squad along with any other girl who looked at him just so. Each one stung a little more than the last as my poor teenage heart was getting battered left, right, and center.

With each day, week, month that passed, I craved him more but he never, not once, looked at me that way.

I was even his prom date, yet he ended up spending the night with someone else.

It hurt, of course it did. But it wasn't his fault and I refuse to hold it against him.

Maybe I should have told him. Been honest with him about my feelings and what I wanted. But I was so terrified I'd lose my best friend that I never confessed, and I took that secret all the way to Columbia with me.

As I stare at him now, those familiar butterflies still set flight in my belly, but they're not as strong as I remember. I'm not sure if that's because my feelings for him have lessened over time, or if I'm just so numb and broken right now that I don't feel anything but pain.

It really could go either way.

I smile at him, so grateful to have run into him this morning.

He always knew when I needed him and even without knowing of my presence here, there he was like some guardian fucking angel.

If guardian angels had sexy dark bed hair, mesmerizing green eyes and a body built for sin then yeah, that's what he is.

I laugh to myself, yeah, maybe that irritating crush has gone nowhere.

"What have you got next?" Leon asks, dragging my attention away from his twin.

Leon has always been the quieter, broodier one of the duo. He's as devastatingly handsome and as popular with the female population but he doesn't wear his heart on his sleeve like Luca. Leon takes a little time to warm to people, to let them in. It was hard work getting there, but I soon realized that once he dropped his walls a little for me, it was hella worth it.

He's more serious, more contemplative, he's deeper. I always suspected that there was a reason they were so different. I know twins don't have to be the same and like the same things, but there was always something niggling at me that there was a very good reason that Leon closed himself down. From listening to their mom talk over the years, they were so identical in their mannerisms, likes, and dislikes when they were growing up, that it seems hard to believe they became so different.

"Psychology but not for an hour. I'm—"

"I'm taking her for coffee," Luca butts in. A flicker of anger passes through Leon's eyes but it's gone so fast that I begin to wonder if I imagined it.

"I could use another coffee before econ," Leon chips in.

"Great. Let's go," Luca forces out through clenched teeth.

He wanted me alone. Interesting.

The reason I never told him about my mega crush is the fact he friend-zoned me in our first few weeks of friendship by telling me how refreshing it was to have a girl wanting to be his friend and not using it as a ploy to get more.

We were only sophomores at the time but even then, Luca was up to all sorts and the girls around us were all more than willing to bend to his needs.

From that moment on, I couldn't tell him how I really felt. It was bad enough I even felt it when he thought our friendship was just that.

I smile at both of them, hoping to shatter the sudden tension between the twins.

"Be careful with these two," Colt announces from behind us as we make our way out of the lecture hall with all the others. "The stories I've heard."

"Colt," Luca warns, turning to face him and walking backward for a few steps.

"Don't worry," I shoot over my shoulder. "I know how to handle the Dunn twins." I wink at him as he howls with laughter.

"You two are in so much trouble," he muses as he turns left out of the room and we go right.

Leon takes my books from me once more and Luca threads his fingers through mine. I still for a beat. While the move isn't unusual, Luca has always been very affectionate. It only takes a second for his warmth to race up my arm and to settle the last bit of unease that's still knotting my stomach.

"Two Americanos and a skinny vanilla latte with an extra shot. Three cupcakes with the sprinkles on top."

I swoon at the fact Luca remembers my order. "How'd you—"

He turns to me, his wide smile and the sparkle in his eyes making my words trail off. The familiarity of his face, the feeling of comfort and safety he brings me causes a lump to form in my throat.

"I didn't forget anything about my best girl." He throws his arm around my shoulder and pulls me close.

Burying my nose in his hard chest, I breathe him in. His woodsy scent mixes with his laundry detergent and it settles me in a way I didn't know I needed.

Leon's stare burns into my back as I snuggle with his brother and I force myself to pull away so he doesn't feel like the third wheel.

"Dunn," the server calls, and Leon rushes ahead to grab our order while Luca leads me to a booth at the back of the coffee shop.

As we walk past each table, I become more and more aware of the attention on the twins. I know their reps, they've had their football god status since before I moved to Rosewood and met them in high school, but I had forgotten just how hero-worshiped they were, and this right now is off the charts.

Girls openly stare, their eyes shamelessly dropping down the guys' bodies as they mentally strip them naked. Guys jealousy shines through their expressions, especially those who are here with their girlfriends who are now paying them zero attention. Then there are the girls whose attention is firmly on me. I can almost read their thoughts— hell, I heard enough of them back in high school.

What do they see in her?

She's not even that pretty.

They're too good for her.

The only difference here from high school is that no one knows I'm just trailer park trash seeing as I moved from the hellhole that is Harrow Creek before meeting the boys.

Tipping my chin up, I straighten my spine and plaster on as much confidence as I can find.

They can all think what they like about me, they can come up with whatever bitchy comments they want. It's no skin off my back.

"Good to see you've lost your appeal," I mutter, dropping into the bench opposite both of them and wrapping my hands around my warm mug when Leon passes it over.

"We walk around practically unnoticed," Luca deadpans.

"You thought high school was bad," Leon mutters, he was always the one who hated the attention whereas Luca used it to his advantage to get whatever he wanted. "It was nothing."

"So I see. So, how's things? Catch me up on everything," I say, needing to dive into their celebrity status lifestyles rather than thinking about my train wreck of a life.

"Really?" Luca asks, raising a brow and causing my stomach to drop into my feet. "I think the bigger question is how come you're here and why we had no idea about it?"

Releasing my mug, I wrap my arms around myself and drop my eyes to the table.

"T-things just didn't work out at Columbia," I mutter, really not wanting to talk about it.

"The last time we talked, you said it was everything you expected it to be and more. What happened?"

Kane fucking Legend happened.

I shake that thought from my head like I do every time he pops up.

He's had his time ruining my life. It's over.

"I just..." I sigh. "I lost my way a bit, ended up dropping out and finally had to fess up and come clean to Mom."

Leon laughs sadly. "I bet that went down well."

The Dunn twins are well aware of what it's like to live with a pushy parent. One of the things that bonded the three of us over the years.

"Like a lead balloon. Even worse because I dropped out months before I finally showed my face."

"Why hide?" Leon's brows draw together as Luca stares at me with concern darkening his eyes.

"I had some health issues. It's nothing."

"Shit, are you okay?"

Fucking hell, Letty. Stop making this worse for yourself.

"Yeah, yeah. Everything is good. Honestly. I'm here and I'm ready to start over and make the best of it."

They both smile at me, and I reach for my coffee once more, bringing the mug to my lips and taking a sip.

"Enough about me, tell me all about the lives of two of the hottest Kings of Maddison."

"Okay... how'd you do that?" Ella whispers after both Luca and Leon walk me to my psych class after our coffee break.

"Do what?" I ask, following her into the room and finding ourselves seats about halfway back.

"It's your first day and the Dunn twins just walked you to class. You got a diamond-encrusted vag or something?"

I snort a laugh as a few others pause on their way to their seats at her words.

"Shush," I chastise.

"Girl, if it's true, you know all these guys need to know about it."

I pull out my books and a couple of pens as Professor Collins sets up at the front before turning to her.

"No, I don't have diamonds anywhere but my necklace. I've been friends with them for years."

"Girl, I knew there was a reason we should be friends." She winks at me. "I've been trying to get West and Brax to hook me up but they're useless."

"You want to be friends so I can set you up with one of the Dunns?"

"Or both." She shrugs, her face deadly serious before she leans in. "I've heard that they tag team sometimes. Can you imagine? Both of their undivided attention." She fans herself as she obviously pictures herself in the middle of a Dunn sandwich. "Oh and, I think you're pretty cool too."

"Of course you do." I laugh.

It's weird, I might have only met her very briefly this morning but that was enough.

"We're all going out for dinner tonight to welcome you to the dorm. The others are dying to meet you." She smiles at me, proving that there's no bitterness behind her words.

"I'm sorry for ignoring you all."

"Girl, don't sweat it. We got ya back, don't worry."

"Thank you," I mouth as the professor demands everyone's attention to begin the class.

The time flies as I scribble my notes down as fast as I can, my hand aching all over again and before I know it, he's finished explaining our first assignment and bringing his class to a close.

"Jesus, this semester is going to be hard," Ella muses as we both pack up.

"At least we've got each other."

"I like the way you think. You done for the day?"

"Yep, I'm gonna head to the store, grab some supplies then get started on this assignment, I think."

"I've got a couple of hours. You want company?"

After dumping our stuff in our rooms, Ella takes me to her favorite store, and I stock up on everything I'm going to need before we head back so she can go to class.

I make myself some lunch before being brave and setting up my laptop at the kitchen table to get started on my assignments. My time for hiding is over, it's time to get back to life and once again become a fully immersed college student.

"Holy shit, she is alive. I thought Zayn was lying about his beautiful older sister," a deep rumbling voice says, dragging me from my research a few hours later.

I spin and look at the two guys who have joined me.

"Zayn would never have called me beautiful," I say as a greeting.

"That's true. I think his actual words were: messy, pain in the ass, and my personal favorite, I'm glad I don't have to live with her again," he says, mimicking my brother's voice.

"Now that is more like it. Hey, I'm Letty. Sorry about—"

"You're all good. We're just glad you emerged. I'm West, this ugly motherfucker is Braxton—"

"Brax, please," he begs. "Only my mother calls me by my full name and you are way too hot to be her."

My cheeks heat as he runs his eyes over my curves.

"T-thanks, I think."

"Ignore him. He hasn't gotten laid for weeeeks."

"Okay, do we really need to go there right now?"

"Always, bro. Our girl here needs to know you get pissy when you don't get the pussy."

I laugh at their easy banter, closing down my laptop and

resting forward on my elbows as they move toward the fridge.

"Ella says we're going out," Brax says, pulling out two bottles of water and throwing one to West.

"Apparently so."

"She'll be here in a bit. Violet and Micah too. They were all in the same class."

"So," West says, sliding into the chair next to me. "What do we need to know that your brother hasn't already told us about you?"

My heart races at all the things that not even my brother would share about my life before I drag my thoughts away from my past.

"Uhhh..."

"How about the Dunns love her," Ella announces as she appears in the doorway flanked by two others. Violet and Micah, I assume.

"Um... how didn't we know this?" Brax asks.

"Because you're not cool enough to spend any time with them, asshole," Violet barks, walking around Ella. "Ignore these assholes, they think they're something special because they're on the team but what they don't tell you is that they have no chance of making first string or talking to the likes of the Dunns."

"Vi, girl. That stings," West says, holding his hand over his heart.

"Yeah, get over it. Truth hurts." She smiles up at him as he pulls her into his chest and kisses the top of her head.

"Whatever, Titch."

"Right, well. Are we ready to go? I need tacos like... yesterday."

"Yes. Let's go."

"You've never had tacos like these, Letty. You are in for a world of pleasure," Brax says excitedly.

"More than she would be if she were in your bed, that's for sure," West deadpans.

"Lies and we all know it."

"Whatever." Violet pushes him toward the door.

"Hey, I'm Micah," the third guy says when I catch up to him.

"Hey, Letty."

"You need a sensible conversation, I'm your boy."

"Good to know."

Micah and I trail behind the others and with each step I take, my smile gets wider.

Things really are going to be okay.

DOWNLOAD NOW TO KEEP READING

ABOUT THE AUTHOR

Tracy Lorraine is a *USA Today* and *Wall Street Journal* bestselling new adult and contemporary romance author. Tracy has recently turned thirty and lives in a cute Cotswold village in England with her husband, baby girl and lovable but slightly crazy dog. Having always been a bookaholic with her head stuck in her Kindle, Tracy decided to try her hand at a story idea she dreamt up and hasn't looked back since.

Be the first to find out about new releases and offers. Sign up to my newsletter here.

If you want to know what I'm up to and see teasers and snippets of what I'm working on, then you need to be in my Facebook group. Join Tracy's Angels here.

Keep up to date with Tracy's books at
www.tracylorraine.com

Knight's Ridge Destiny: Epilogue

Harrow Creek Hawks Series

Merciless #1

Relentless #2

Lawless #3

Ruined Series

Ruined Plans #1

Ruined by Lies #2

Ruined Promises #3

Never Forget Series

Never Forget Him #1

Never Forget Us #2

Everywhere & Nowhere #3

Chasing Series

Chasing Logan

The Cocktail Girls

His Manhattan

Her Kensington

Made in the USA
Middletown, DE
03 August 2024

58431385R00267